Summer of Hopes and Dreams

Sue McDonagh

Where heroes are like chocolate – irresistible!

Published 2022 by Choc Lit Limited
Penrose House, Crawley Drive, Camberley, Surrey GU15 2AB, UK
www.choc-lit.com

A CIP catalogue record for this book is available from the British Library

ISBN 978-1-78189-496-5

Printed and bound in Great Britain
by Clays Ltd, Elcograf S.p.A.

Pippa, for reading the same chapter written a different way a million times without complaint.

Acknowledgements

To Allan and my family and friends, who are patient when I seem to be talking about the same scene for the millionth time and when once again, my attention veers away from them and I scurry for a notebook to jot something down before I forget.

To fellow writer Jan Baynham for arranging regular Zoom meets for our Cariad Chapter writing group, and for always being the ear on the other end of the phone.

To my friend Annie and chocolate shop owner, Pippa, for being my honest and encouraging beta readers, as ever.

I am indebted to Pete Walker of Robert Walker (Haulage) Ltd, for chatting through my ideas and for the completely true giraffe story!

To my retired solicitor friend, Anthea Guthrie, for fact checking.

To my editor, who should win an award for her patience and dedication in helping me to realise the shape of my story, and to Choc Lit, who have believed in me throughout and continue to encourage and support and allow me to use my own paintings on my covers.

Thanks must also go to the Tasting Panel readers who said 'yes' to this manuscript and made publication possible. Special thanks to: Amy Nordon, Carolina Castro, Jenny Mitchell, Vanessa Wick, Shona Nicolson, Sharon Walsh, Jenny Kinsman, Jo Osborne, Fran Stevens, Alan Robertson, Barbara Wickham, Honor Gilbert and Ruth Nägele.

Chapter One

The printed notice on the door of the Art Café read: "Closed for Private Function". Inside, hearty laughter and reminiscences abounded in the age-old tradition of a "good send off".

'Only Lana could have such a stylish "No Black Clothes" funeral.'

'Remember that exhibition she put on?'

'Was that the one she streaked through? Naughty girl!'

'Indeed it was. Cheers.' Glasses clinked together in a toast to the dearly departed.

'She had the figure for it though.'

'Goodness me, yes. Ever the supermodel. That was Lana.'

'If you've got it, flaunt it.' There was a ripple of laughter.

Unless you have as much of it as I have. Rosie, Lana's only child, tried not to look down at the purple linen dress stretched across her thighs, riding up to reveal her dimpled, forty-seven-year-old knees. Purple had been the darkest colour she could think of in an attempt to look slimmer. Reflected in the polished hearse containing her mother, she'd looked like an overripe blueberry.

'Good old Lana. She never stopped flaunting it.'

'Bless her. So sad to go like this.'

The table rumbled with assent.

Rosie knew precisely none of these people. Her mother's "friends and collectors", they'd stayed away in their droves as her body was ravaged by the cruel fingers of Parkinson's disease.

She felt their curious glances and her stomach clenched.

'Lovely send off, um ...'

'... Rosie,' said Rosie, after a slight pause. Her fingers darted across the tablecloth to straighten, tidy, collecting empty envelopes for the sympathy cards that she'd barely begun to acknowledge and which would probably go straight into the bin.

'Yes. Well done.'

'Very nice.'

'Your mother was a force of nature, my dear.'

'She was indeed.' Rosie felt their eyes on her. A tendril of curly, auburn hair sprang free and stuck to her forehead. Perspiration trickled down her back.

'But we can't all be the star of the show, hmm?' The woman's gaze raked Rosie's crumpled dress. 'Some people are better in a supporting role.' The table rumbled again like the House of Lords as the speaker looked round at them for approbation.

Rosie's lips tightened. These people and their chalkboard psychologies. Support – dictionary-defined as "to keep from falling". How very noble. Talking about support, her spandex all-in-one was creeping upwards. She sucked her stomach in and gave a little wiggle to see if it would settle back to where it had been. Elderly eyes swivelled towards her bosom, transformed with the intake of breath into a magnificently swelling purple shelf.

'Indeed.' Crossing her arms over her chest, she hooked her thumbs into the optimistically named "body-shaper" and attempted to tug it downwards. It was currently shaping her into a salami. 'Lovely. Thank you for coming.'

'Wouldn't have missed it for the world, um ...'

'Rosie,' Rosie said, through gritted teeth. What was wrong with these people? She swallowed an urge to throw herself, howling like a toddler, onto the floor, screaming, 'I want my mummy back!'

It wasn't what grown-ups did though, was it? Besides, she'd never get back up in this purple dress without ripping it or showing her knickers. She hurried towards the ladies' loo with a wide-legged gait as her underwear drifted higher.

It was engaged. There were more loos but she couldn't walk another step without being garrotted by her gusset.

Nobody needed her out there. The star of this particular show had sunk theatrically into the bowels of the crematorium some hours ago, behind a crimson curtain.

Lana had loved the Art Café. Situated on one of the most beautiful beaches on the Gower Peninsula, they'd visited often, in all weathers. The staff would always find them a nice table by the window, even when, as time went on, the visits included a wheelchair.

When her mother had asked if they would host her wake, they were a bit taken aback, but agreed. Mother had enjoyed planning the party almost as if she was going to be there herself. She'd made a list of guests and sent them to her solicitor, a man who Rosie was sure had numbered amongst Lana's many unrequited suitors.

Rosie had found it macabre and also belittling. In the strange vacuum of time between someone dying and the funeral, it's received wisdom that some comfort is derived from the preparations for mourning. Lana had taken all that from her daughter. She'd organised her own funeral so tightly that Rosie had nothing to do but spectate and sing the chosen hymns. As if Rosie couldn't be trusted. Dozy Rosie, her mother had nicknamed her when she was little. It seemed that she'd never grown out of it, as far as Lana was concerned.

The quiet voice at her elbow startled her.

'How are you coping, Mrs Bunting? I was so very sorry to hear about your mother.' The café owner looked at her kindly. Rosie remembered her name. Lucy. She owned this place with her business partner, blond chap, what was it? Richard. That was it. Tall, didn't say much, but my goodness, he could make a cake. Even if each contained a thousand calories, as her mother used to say, nibbling her way round one and then leaving it, despite being rake thin.

'I'm fine, thank you. It's a wonderful spread, exactly what Mum would have wanted ...' Rosie began, and then blurted, 'But, do you know, I don't know anyone here and ...' She swallowed, shamed abruptly by her pity party for one. God. Whatever must this lovely, sensible girl think of her?

'Shall I bring you out a nice tray of tea and some food?' Lucy asked, ignoring the tears that balanced precariously on Rosie's eyelids. 'It's lovely and sunny on the veranda, even though there's a brisk wind. We have throws to put out there. Hard to believe it's nearly June, the weather is so changeable.'

'Oh, would you? That would be so lovely.' Rosie was touched by the woman's kindness. Hesitantly she added, 'Could I ask – I'm sorry to be a nuisance – would you mind serving my tea in a mug? The bigger the better. I don't need a teapot. Just the mug. My mother would have been scandalised.'

Lucy returned a wide smile. 'No problem at all. I like a mug myself. Stays hotter for longer.'

'Definitely.' The loo became free and Rosie excused herself to dive into the cubicle.

Readjusted, she blew her nose and, her mood improving at the thought of the tea, and yes, the food, she sashayed past the tables onto the veranda. Immediately, the salty tang in the air soothed her and she pulled it deeply into her lungs. As deeply as the compression suit underwear would let her. Blasted thing. She should have taken it off in the loo. Who on earth was she trying to impress? She was never ever going to live up to her mother's memory, and, she told herself, firmly, she didn't give a fig about the opinions of all those judgemental people in there, eating and drinking her mother's money.

A few neighbours had popped in briefly. More, Rosie felt, to sample the food in the famous Art Café than out of any sympathy for her mother. Lana had moved in with her daughter permanently around five years ago. It had been party central at first, but as her condition worsened, people stopped calling round.

Thinking about her mother led her thoughts to her grandparents. Just the one set, as she hadn't known her father. Her grandmother – tiny, neat as a sparrow and with *standards*. Antimacassars on the three piece suite, serviettes even with sandwiches, and those with the crusts trimmed off.

Grandfather though, big, bluff and hearty; an engineer and erstwhile inventor. His workshop had always produced the most wonderful things. The doll's house, in which he'd shown her how to wire up tiny bulbs to batteries to make working room lights, how to cut balsa wood to make furniture and fencing, and how to wire a plug. It was due to him that she'd tackled the renovations on her house. He would have loved to see it now. Wouldn't he have been proud of her? Her grandmother would have sniffed derisively, made cucumber sandwiches with the crusts cut off and told her that her hands and fingernails were a disaster.

A smile flitted across Rosie's face, recalling them. Her gran was so tiny that Grandad's hands encircled her waist, finger to thumb. Lana had inherited her mother's delicate features, the sharp cheekbones and retroussé nose. She, Rosie, followed her grandfather, she decided, with a self-deprecating snort.

Leaning on the balcony, she watched the families playing on the wide, sandy beach, recalling fondly the times she'd done the very same with Tom, now twenty-seven, and Keira, twenty-one. Tom, working on the other side of the world, wanted to get back but hadn't been able to. She knew he was thinking of her though.

Rosie wasn't at all sorry that her musician ex-husband Chester hadn't made an appearance at the funeral. She stared up into the cloudless blue sky. Not that she'd expected him to. He and her mother had not got on. Plus, she had no idea where he was. Five and a bit years ago he'd left muttering something about a huge opportunity in Spain and promised to let her know. He never did. Fighting down the irritation that rose inevitably with thoughts of Chester, Rosie took several deep, calming breaths and focussed her eyes on the white ribbons of surf, crystalline against the cobalt sea. Children jumped the waves at their lacy fringes, and she smiled. But those pesky memories shunted back into position, front and centre.

Keira, their beautiful daughter, who had been his undisguised favourite, had been devastated when it was clear he wasn't coming back. Rosie had the distinct impression that Keira blamed her for his absence.

Had Rosie secretly hoped he'd come back? Or had she been so relieved that he'd gone that she'd pushed him right out of her mind? They'd been on shaky territory for a good few years before, but stupidly she'd been hopeful that he'd grow out of the relentless womanising. When, last Christmas, her mother had prompted her yet again, Rosie had finally got her arse into gear and divorced him.

It had been sadly obvious that it was going to be Lana's last Christmas. Rosie made a huge effort with a tall, beautiful real tree that reached the high rafters in the open plan lounge, and had got the school choir in to sing carols. It had been magical and her mother, her tiny, birdlike figure bent up in the bed, smiled, even though she hadn't made it to the end before falling asleep from all the drugs.

Rosie's attention was caught by a familiar voice, and she gratefully allowed it to pull her away from her sad thoughts. Her eyes scanned the beach. Wasn't that Charlotte, one of Keira's mates? Keira had arrived at the funeral with a gaggle of pals. She at least had a boyfriend, even if Rosie didn't. He went by the – in Rosie's opinion – ridiculous nickname of

Peck and hadn't been able to get the day off, apparently, from the electrical warehouse where he worked.

Taking one look at the braying, tipsy crowd in the café, Keira and her friends had backed out, murmuring something about ice-cream and chips and Rosie really couldn't blame them.

Where were they? Rosie leaned over the balcony, and spotted them on the sand below, their backs against the struts of the old prom. Their long limbs were folded like whippets, lean and smooth.

'Yes, I really am going to miss Granny. She was *so* amazing. Such an inspiration.'

Rosie smiled sadly. It was lovely that her daughter and her mother had been so close. Lifting an arm to wave and call down to them, she froze as Keira's next words reached her.

'I know this sounds terrible, but – why couldn't my mother have died instead?' Keira's voice was loud with passion. 'She's so – God, you know – *boooorrring!*' She said it just like that. Dragging out the vowels like a caricature teenager. 'She's going to have to get a job now Granny's gone. The money won't last forever, and she has *no* skills. Who would *ever* employ *her?*'

Paralysed in horror, Rosie braced herself on the railing. Surely she hadn't heard that correctly? Her ears strained to listen.

'Even my dad left because she was so boring. It's true!'

Rosie yanked her hands off the balcony as if they burned. Her ears rang. Had Chester told her that was why he'd left? The utter, betraying, disloyal bastard.

Keira's hateful words spun in her brain. The bright beach shrank to a letterbox slit. She had to get away. Out of earshot, away. Anywhere to escape those vicious words. She stumbled backwards.

Bustling onto the veranda with the tea tray bearing

Rosie's big mug of tea and daintily arranged sandwiches and cakes, the waitress did her best to sidestep Rosie's retreat. Whirling, Rosie watched the mug empty its contents in slow motion before smashing on the tiled floor.

'Oh God, I'm so, so sorry!' She stood in the chaos, paralysed as the waitress bobbed down to gather the detritus. Tea dripped from Rosie's now sodden purple dress. Lucy was there in a flash, with two staff.

'Come with me, let's get some cold water onto you.'

Rosie allowed herself to be led into the quiet kitchen. She sat, like a child, as Lucy examined her and ran cold water over the bits of her that required it. The dress, being loose, had absorbed the tea without sticking to her. The unyielding underwear had saved her skin, it seemed. Rosie didn't care. Her daughter's words scorched, hot and bleeding, into her brain.

Lucy dabbed with blue catering roll and a dubious expression. 'I don't know whether this will come out of your lovely dress. I'm so sorry. How did it happen? Of course, we're insured, if you need to make a claim ...'

'I hate this dress,' Rosie confided. It didn't matter what she said any more. She was nobody. Nothing to anyone. 'It was my fault entirely. I'd ... had a bit of a shock, and I walked straight into your waitress. She couldn't have avoided me. I hope she's okay. And I'm so sorry, I broke your lovely big mug.' To her utter humiliation, tears poured without warning down her cheeks.

'Oh no! You mustn't worry about a mug!' Lucy handed her a tissue. Rosie mopped her face and felt Lucy's shrewd gaze resting on her. She couldn't look up. Distantly she thought, she must look a complete wreck. 'You sit there, and I'll make us both a nice cup of tea. In a mug.'

They sat companionably, sipping their tea. Lucy chatted easily about this and that, allowing Rosie time to compose herself.

Rosie heard Lucy's words but they slithered away, unheeded. She felt ridiculous sitting in this kind woman's café kitchen, in the soggy and crumpled purple dress and the stranglehold underwear. At least she wouldn't be bumping into Keira.

No knife in that kitchen was sharper than her daughter's tongue. Keira's words drowned out everything, whirling in her head, locked behind her lips. Did she deserve them? How could she ever admit that her own daughter had said them?

So nobody was more shocked than Rosie to hear her own voice. 'What would you do if someone you cared about, accused you of being boring? Behind your back?' *And wished you were dead.* She couldn't say that. She couldn't.

Lucy's eyebrows bounced upwards. She blinked. Rosie had read the articles about her. How, approaching forty, she'd learned to ride the powerful motorbike that she'd won and changed her life. Dumping her two-timing, bullying husband, she'd found true love with her handsome bike instructor, and – as a motorcycling artist – became the subject of a series of entertaining television programmes. Not for one single minute, could anyone in their right mind accuse Lucy of being boring.

'Erm ... I suppose it would depend on who said it.' Lucy spoke slowly, rotating her mug between her hands. 'If I didn't like that person then I'd ignore it. If it was somebody whose opinion I cared about, then I'd wonder what prompted them to say it. Maybe, I'd take an honest look at my life if I thought there was something in it.'

'What if I've, erm, *somebody* – had got themselves into a bit of a rut, looking after um, *people*, and sort of, er, lost themselves a bit – a lot – in the process?'

There was a pause as Lucy thought about it. Rosie liked that about her. 'Well, perhaps that person could get away from their environment for a little while to begin with.

Experience something different. Something that challenges them. Take their mind off things. A new skill. Maybe meet some new people. That sort of thing.' She stopped as if she'd thought of something, got up and plucked a leaflet from a small pile on the worktop. 'Maybe something like this. I don't know if it's your thing …' She shrugged. 'These were left here yesterday. There's been a couple of cancellations so …?' Her voice lifted at the end in an unfinished question. 'I didn't put them out on the counter. It seemed a bit disrespectful, somehow, for a …' Her voice faltered. She held the leaflet out.

Rosie took it and read the cover. A weekend in the Welsh mountains that promised to "Push your boundaries". Rock climbing, abseiling and white-water kayaking. Suitable for all abilities. An eternity ago she used to love the water, but, gulp, abseiling and rock climbing? A little voice in her head that had been battering at the Keira words with an axe told her, '*Go! Run away*'.

Chapter Two

'You didn't bring a sleeping bag?' Gareth Merwyn-Jones stared down at her, incredulously. He usually asked if people had their medication. Never *had they brought their sleeping bag*? 'What sort of weekend did you think this was?'

'One where I got something to sleep in, at least!' Rosie planted her small hands on her rounded hips and glared up at him. Auburn hair bounced on her shoulders.

'Didn't you read the emails?'

'Of course I read the emails. I'm not an idiot, Graham.' She yanked her phone out of a tiny, pointless waist bag. 'There was nothing that said to bring a sleeping bag. Don't you think I would have brought one if I'd been told to?' She thumbed to her emails with a shaking hand. 'Look. Show me the bit about needing a sleeping bag.' She thrust the phone at him.

'Gareth. My name's Gareth.' He blinked at the screen and then at her. 'Good Lord. I think the astronauts in the space station could read this.'

'What?' Rosie peered over his arm and he inhaled her subtle perfume. 'Oh, for goodness' sake. It's because of my mum. She couldn't see the small print.'

'Aren't you a bit old to have your mum checking your phone?' His gaze rested on her for a moment. She blinked rapidly and looked away. He smoothed his thumb upwards on the screen.

'Don't be ridiculous. My mum—' She clamped her pink lips together and he saw them, bloodless. She cleared her throat. 'I just haven't changed the—'

'Look. Here it is.' He turned the phone round to show her. 'Bedding …'

'See! Bedding!'

'... not included.' He passed the phone back. 'Scroll down.'

'What?' Her thumbs flew over the little screen, swiping up and up until, 'Oh ... poop.' She stared around her as if bedding might arrive courtesy of a flock of Disney bluebirds. He sighed, silently. Something told him she was going to be a challenge this weekend.

'I've got it. Curtains!' she announced, in a headmistressy way. 'Give me a hand to take them down, if you wouldn't mind, and I'm sorted.' She marched towards the windows, collecting a short stool on her way. Climbing onto it, she began to unhook the flowery material.

'Oi! Are you just going to let her do that?' The speaker was tall with muscular shoulders in a top-brand climbing vest. Gareth was familiar with her from previous courses.

'Unless you want her sharing your sleeping bag, Leanne, yes.'

'But we'll be woken up so early without any curtains. The sun will come straight in!'

'First of all, this is Wales, so there won't be any sun. And this room faces west, as you ought to know.' Gareth grinned at her. 'Secondly, you'll all be up early anyway, so now you won't need an alarm clock.' Leanne rolled her eyes but she returned a reluctant smile.

'*Okaaay*. Come on, I'll give you a hand.' Leanne strode to the window. 'You better tell those stinky boys no peeping in the girls' dorm!'

'Thank you, Leanne,' Rosie said. She stretched her neck that was clearly cramping from reaching up so high.

He couldn't help but think that if she struggled to take a pair of curtains down, how on earth was she going to manage an outdoor pursuits weekend? He reached up and unclipped them, handing the fabric down to Leanne, who made an attempt at folding it before handing the bundle over to Rosie.

She nodded a thank you with a prim smile. 'I think I'd better go and shake the dust out of these, or I'll be keeping everyone up sneezing all night.'

'Very resourceful.' He nodded, relieved that she seemed to have sorted that dilemma. He had an idea it wouldn't be the last. 'Don't forget, we're all meeting in the Common Room at five o'clock for a briefing, and then we're walking down to the pub for dinner.'

'Pub? Excellent. Things are looking up already!' Rosie grinned inanely at them both, and turned away from their perplexed expressions. She paused at the doorway.

'Right turn for the garden,' Gareth supplied.

'I totally knew that!' She bustled away. He wasn't sure whether to laugh or not. The hints of a cut-glass accent were at odds with what she actually said.

'Spare us from middle-aged mums looking for adventure.' Leanne sniggered quietly as they watched Rosie scurry into the corridor, trailing material. There was a heavy thump, and Gareth started towards the door.

Rosie's voice floated back to them. 'I'm okay! I just tripped on the ...' Her footsteps faded away.

'Give her a chance.' Gareth studied Leanne, covertly. Her physique showed that she was well beyond the scope of these weekends. He wondered what kept her attending his basic courses. 'You've been doing these weekends for a while. Try and remember what it was like when you were new. And to be fair, I didn't think of using the curtains.'

'Yeah. I take your point. She seems okay, I guess.' She eyed the other two women in the room, who were studiously avoiding each other. 'At least she was friendly,' she muttered.

'They just need a bit of direction,' he murmured as he bent forward. He straightened up and added, loudly, 'So, if you'd like to be Dorm Monitor, Leanne—' He grinned back at her murderous glare. 'See you all later, ladies.'

*

In the windy hillside garden, struggling beneath the unwieldy burden of dusty curtains, Rosie cringed with humiliation. This was what came of booking something in a knee-jerk reaction, she told herself, on a tiny phone, after half a bottle of Dutch courage Prosecco. Who was she kidding? The bottle was empty by the time the confirmation email had struggled along the agonisingly slow broadband that was the curse of living so rurally.

Since the funeral, Keira had stayed at her boyfriend's place, to Rosie's relief. Expecting her key in the door at any moment though, Rosie had become jumpy and nervous. She'd caught herself once, holding the empty Prosecco bottle by the neck, like a club. Surely that wasn't normal. She *had* to get away.

It was a relief to be finally waiting in the lane for the taxi to Swansea. Standing beside her mother's smart, wheeled suitcase – Rosie hadn't been anywhere for years and her own suitcase was almost vintage – she'd been hailed by the postman.

'Sorry to hear about your mother,' he'd said, eyeing the case. 'Going away then?'

Rosie rather enjoyed telling him she was going on an outdoor pursuits weekend. His eyebrows rose and his mouth dropped as if his face was made of chewing gum. So shocked, he'd almost forgotten to hand over her mail; an envelope postmarked from her mother's solicitor. She'd stuffed it hurriedly into her handbag as the taxi arrived.

She had a car, but years of criticism had robbed her of her confidence. The thought of finding the Bryn Mawr Lodge on tiny, unfamiliar mountain lanes amongst the deepest Welsh mountains, alone, was too awful to contemplate.

A big outdoor clothing store had met her key shopping requirements for the course. Or so she'd thought. In the large stationer next door, she'd browsed reading materials via the shelves of magazine racks that hectored her with promises of the perfect *house/garden/body/relationship* and family life. Luckily for Keira, there wasn't a publication called *How to Murder Your Daughter*. She'd bought none of them and couldn't concentrate on a novel.

Instead, her eye was caught by an embossed, deep pink notebook. Softbound in faux leather, it was wrapped with a cord on which was threaded a small copper leaf shape. There was something about it that spoke to Rosie of journeys. Journeys that she'd always planned to take and which had been shelved to nurture strong, growing legs and her husband's career. She'd bought the notebook.

At The Circle, a series of bereavement workshops she'd attended, there had been suggestions that she write her feelings down. Keep a journal. Rosie had smiled politely and ignored the idea. What on earth was the point? Surely it just prolonged the pain of loss, kept it alive to be brought out, inspected and wept over. A waste of time.

On the train though, as her thoughts whirled in endless loops, she unwound the soft tan lace, and smoothed her hand over the first page.

It felt bizarrely like her schooldays, this need to keep the first page perfect and neat. To ensure that what she wrote was weighty and worthy. Her pen hung over the faint lines. Should she title it? She stared out of the window. Nobody was going to read it but her. It didn't matter what she put on the first page, she told herself. Just start writing. The train tipped and jolted unexpectedly and her pen made its first marks all by itself. It looked like a pair of surprised eyebrows, so Rosie doodled a face beneath it, and then there was no holding her back. Her overnight in an economy hotel near the train station had left her lonely. Raw and emotionally scoured, she'd felt stripped bare of a protective layer she hadn't even known she wore.

Was she boring? Didn't every child think their mother was boring? Surely though, not every child wished their mother dead. Keira's words drilled into her brain, over and over. Boring was a word like "disappointing". A whole world of dreadfulness that meant nobody wanted to spend time with you. Not that Rosie had anybody in her life now, anyway.

Keira had been right about one thing though. Rosie needed a job. She was squandering her mother's money right now, doing this course. Except for full-time caring, she had few skills for the modern workplace. Retiring early wasn't an option. She needed money to finish the house. She remembered when she and Chester had bought the wreck that he'd said was their dream, forever home. There'd be a music studio, he'd said. They could have concerts in the grounds, and people could camp. Rosie's eyes had travelled over the tangled undergrowth and seen "Work". "Maintenance". "Money". She'd smoothed the writhing, jabbing belly that contained Keira, and smiled down at six-year-old Tom, already exploring for the insects and wildlife with which he'd long been fascinated. But she'd believed in her husband then and said yes.

It had been fun at first. A home of their own at last. And within energetic strolling distance of a crystal clear ultramarine and turquoise sea, and a beach in rainbow hues when lit by the sinking sun. A frequent visitor with young Tom, and later with baby Keira in her pram, she remembered the strength in her long tanned thighs as if that body had belonged to somebody else. It seemed then that she could do anything.

Her pen skittered across the paper as if it bypassed her brain. The neat, upright hand was an oblique scrawl by the time she'd turned the first page. She reached into her handbag for the tube of peppermints she always had stashed there, and her fingers found the corner of the envelope that the postman had passed her the previous morning.

She used her pen to slit the flap open, and read with increasing astonishment.

Chapter Three

Gareth strolled down the stone-flagged corridor, studying his folder of attendees. Eight adults, all ages and abilities, four men, four women, for a long weekend of abseiling, rock climbing and canoeing. Unusually, apart from Rosie, they were all around the same age, in their early thirties. He wondered how Rosie, that much older at forty-seven, would cope. But finding out what they were really capable of was the whole point of these weekends and he acknowledged with a self-deprecating grin that he was forty as of last year.

He loved getting people to dig deep. Everyone was different, and a small step for some represented a milestone for others. Guests left his weekends feeling more confident than they had felt on arrival. Demanding every second of his concentration, they allowed him no time at all to linger over his mess of a marriage. He skipped over the persistent voice in his head reminding him that these weekends were partly to blame for the final breakdown of the relationship less than two years ago, and went to check the kitchen supplies.

Rosie was in the kitchen garden with a broom, beating the curtains which she'd thrown over the washing line. A small cloud of dust puffed from each wallop, and Gareth made a note in his folder that Bryn Mawr Lodge needed to be properly cleaned.

Rosie looked like a woman who needed something or somebody to whack, judging by the expression on her face. Gareth told himself he was assessing her fitness levels, and to be fair, she must have reasonable muscle tone to keep that level of pummelling up. The sun's lowering warm rays caught her glossy auburn hair and outlined her round, pretty and determined face. The vivid green hillside that sloped away behind the bunkhouse was streaked with the same warm golden tones. His photographer's brain framed the shot. Rosie took a breather and looked up at that very minute, spotting him at the window. He dodged back, feeling as if he'd been caught leering at her. Why had he done that? He could've just waved! Now she'd think he'd been spying on her.

He was scrupulously professional on these weekends, although he'd had many offers. His wife – his *ex*-wife – had never been able to level any accusations of philandering. He had plenty of other flaws for her to fixate on anyway.

Suppressing the sigh that always accompanied thoughts about his ex, he pulled out the supplies list, ticking items off as he stashed everything away. By the time he'd finished, he could see that the men had clustered in the garden and had taken over the curtain bashing. Nothing like a damsel in distress to bond them. About to go out and lend a hand, he was thwarted by the other girls wandering into the kitchen in search of tea and coffee. At least he was able to get to know them a little before the meeting at five, but his ears pricked at the sound of laughter drifting in from the garden.

In the old stone-walled Common Room, his audience, on the variety of cosy mismatched leather sofas, armchairs and footstools arranged around the wood burning stove, regarded him, and each other, speculatively.

He introduced himself again, along with the fire exits and safety procedures. 'Are there any questions?' There always were, now they'd had a think about it. What time for this, how do they, where will they, for how long. Was there Wi-Fi? There wasn't. There was a mixed response to this and he tried not to laugh at their crestfallen faces. A weekend getting close to nature was one small way of weaning them away from their electronic devices.

'Right, that's it. Pub now.' There was a cheer and they

jumped up to collect coats and possessions. The Lodge was named after the hill, Bryn Mawr, and translated from Welsh as Big Hill. Gareth grinned as they sped downhill, looking forward to their meal. It wouldn't be nearly as fast on the return journey.

They sat at a long table with their drinks, in the ancient stone pub and ordered their food. As they waited, Gareth said, mostly to divert them from the pub Wi-Fi which they'd all availed themselves of, 'I already know some of you, but could you just tell us who you are and one fact about yourself.' He nodded at the girl to his left to begin.

Between them they'd evidently swum lakes, walked Machu Picchu, climbed mountains, run and kayaked – or they wanted to. Rosie had shredded a paper napkin by the time it reached her.

'Hello, my name's Rosie. My, er, I, um ...' She swallowed. Her eyes darted round at them all. Gareth felt the table's attention waver and was about to rescue her when she said, 'Apparently, I own a fire engine.' Rosie eyed them, hesitantly. Well, that had got their attention. She carried on. 'I've got my grandfather's fire engine. It was in the letter the postman gave me as I left the house. I only remembered to open it on the train. My brain hasn't processed it at all.'

Gareth's eyes rested on her with interest. That had made them all sit up a bit, after blathering on about all the things they were going to climb up or throw themselves off. He wondered what she was going to do with it when she said, in answer to someone's echoed question, 'I don't have the faintest idea. Yet.'

Everyone's asleep. But of course, I forgot – okay, I didn't read it properly – I didn't bring a sleeping bag. And I got a right bollocking off the instructor. So – haha, I took the curtains down and now I'm sleeping under a curtain. Not sleeping, that is.

I'm forty-seven, in a female dorm in a freezing hostel in Wales, in a curtain. In all my clothes.

I nearly turned round and went straight home. At least, I would have, if I'd had my car with me. And in reality, it's Keira's words that are keeping me here. What have I got to go back to? And yes, I know I should be at home hunting down a job. I'm not ready for that yet. I don't even know what I want to do.

So we have the ubiquitous hunky instructor. Talk about a cliché. He must be about ten years younger than me and two feet taller.

I feel like an elderly hobbit next to him.

His name's Gareth. I even got that wrong. I called him Graham. He doesn't even look like a Graham. I was just a bit flustered about not having my sleeping bag, that was all. He's very tall. He lopes. As if he's about to bound up a cliff face or something.

And, I've got to say, he's got the best arse. Not that I've been looking or anything. Who am I kidding? Every female in this dorm has been having a gander. I bet he thinks he's chocolate, away with all these women for weekends. I saw him staring at me when I was bashing curtains in the garden. I don't know what to think about that. He could've come and helped me instead of peering at me! But he dodged back and made it look like he was hiding from me. Weirdo.

But, the thing is, his face – those deep-set, dark brown eyes, and that bit of a kink at the bridge of an aquiline nose ... It's a bit hawklike. And he has a scar. It runs across his left eyebrow – dark again, he has black hair – and down his cheek. You can't miss it. I know we all looked at it.

He said, 'It's a shark bite.' And everyone laughed, because it was obvious that it wasn't. But it was quite clever, because it addressed the scar, and also told us that he wasn't going to tell us any more about it. It doesn't detract at all from his attractiveness. I'm saying this purely in an objective way, obviously. Because of course, he's married. You can tell, not that it matters. I am not having a middle-aged crush. Why on earth would I? What has a man ever done for me?

There is one thing though – he really listens when I speak. Nobody else listens to me these days. Keira never has. Mum's nurses and the Parkinson's specialists used to, right up to ...

He doesn't smile much. I see him watching everyone. But he seems kind. Nice hands. Big enough to pull me out of the ditch I'm bound to fall into tomorrow.

Sleepy now. Good night, from my curtains. X

Oh, and PS I forgot to mention the fire engine. Something else to worry about. What the hell am I going to do with that? Why is this the first time it's ever come up? Nobody has ever even mentioned a fire engine in the family that I can remember.

PPS The Circle said we shouldn't go back and edit. They say, "We can't go back and edit our lives, and we shouldn't edit our journals".

Why are they "journals" these days? What's wrong with "diaries"?

Chapter Four

Hello Diary/Journal. Quick scrawl while the girls put their make-up on. Although why they need to put make-up on to go rock climbing beats me.

We've all been up since the crack of dawn. Picking mushrooms! Scuffing about in the garden getting soaking wet feet in the long grass. And I'd only just warmed up after barely two hours sleep in the curtains.

All the girls were out there fawning over G, (I can't keep writing Gareth alias Graham every time) and all the blokes were posturing and trying to outdo him on the testosterone levels.

Anyway. G said, over breakfast, that today, we were "blank pages". That it didn't matter what we'd done before, because this weekend was a new and original experience. To open our minds to it. That what might be a tiny step for some would be a huge leap for others, and for everyone to help each other.

'Blank page?' I said. I was a bit surprised to hear myself speak. 'I'm a blank book!'

Everyone laughed. I'm not used to being funny. But G studied me with his serious hawk-face. He said, 'I'm sure that's not true.' And the way he said it, he made me want to unsay the funny thing I'd said earlier. I think you say funny things because if you said what you really meant, you'd cry.

He said, 'You've got children, haven't you?'

And I said that I had, and I managed not to say that one of them wished I was dead. I said that Tom was clever and kind and saving the rainforests in Borneo and that Keira was beautiful. Which she is. Even though she's a weapons-grade bitch.

And one of the girls said to me, 'I can't wait to have

children.' And another one said, 'You don't look old enough to have grown-up children.' Which was another surprise.

And by the time we were back in the minibus, the girls were chatting to me about their love-lives, which mostly sounded even grimmer than my non-existent one, and the guys were clustering round Gareth, writing on their "blank pages" with all their prowess and gung-ho.

As he drove to the climbing wall, Gareth ran through the gear list in his head and tried not to tune into the conversations going on behind him in the minibus. Rosie had, apparently without trying, united all the girls in the back seats, like a mother duck in outlandish, sunglasses-requiring neon patterned leggings. There were a lot of laments from the women about "bloody men", so he thought it probably best to keep out of it. She had the potential to be a bit of a troublemaker, that Rosie.

The men were sitting at the front of the bus, testing him, and each other. Fastest run. Furthest travelled. Lots of joshing each other. Keen to prove themselves.

It was what these weekends were about, building people's confidence and having a bit of fun. He wasn't expecting them to climb Snowdon, although many did go on to pursue tougher versions of his very basic tuition. Many kept in touch too. Facebook or Instagram or just plain old email. Like when you go back to your old school as an adult and see your teachers.

It was one of the things his wife – *ex*-wife – had complained about, all these demands on his attention. She'd complained about a lot. In the end, it had been hard to know what to do at all. These weekends were only the tip of the iceberg. He missed his kids terribly though.

He drew the minibus to a halt in the familiar-to-him car park and watched his charges tumble out like puppies, their expectant faces turned towards him. The colour had drained from Rosie's face and she was staring fixedly at him. Interesting. All that fake banter and bravado gone. Her eyes were very green, he noticed.

Dividing up the climbing ropes and harnesses and cool boxes between them, he sent the group on ahead.

'Leanne! You know where you're going – wait for me there!' he shouted to her, and grinned at the banter that returned.

'Old man! Can't keep up, poor old bloke.'

They set off at a good pace. Rosie loitered at the back, looking a bit lost. He adjusted his stride, slowing so that he could stroll alongside her.

'Tell me what you're looking for from this weekend, Rosie.'

'I, er, I ...'

He looked ahead, silent.

'My daughter, she—' She gulped and was silent again. He sensed the words piling up behind her mouth. Finally, 'You know what I said about that blank page? Well it's true. I've spent so long being Mum to my kids and then a carer to my'—she swallowed—'my mum and putting everyone first that now—' She stopped again and he felt her glance at him. 'These leggings look stupid, don't they? I only bought them because Keira ... she ...' Her voice petered out on a lengthy and exasperated huff. She trudged on with her head down.

Into the long pause, Gareth said gently, 'Adventure? Increased fitness, maybe? Improved confidence? Fun? Or all the above.'

'All the above. Yes.' She tipped her head towards him, her mouth compressed into a determined smile. He saw a sprinkle of freckles across her unmade-up face. She nodded firmly. 'Yes. That's it. All the above. The last adventure I had was trying to fit a wheelchair into a taxi. Is that okay?'

'That sounds perfect.' Gareth quickened the pace a little, and was pleased to see that she kept up. 'Come on, or Leanne will be doing my job for me and demanding a discount. Tell me about this fire engine of yours.'

'Oh, that. I haven't even seen it. The letter arrived just as I was leaving. Apparently, it was bequeathed to a transport museum and now they're having to close due to lack of funds. And'—she took a breath—'did I want it back?'

'Do you?'

'I don't know. It must be really old. What the hell would I do with it?'

'It could be fun deciding.'

'Yes. I suppose.' Out of the side of his eye he saw her throw him a penetrating glance. 'I need to start thinking about things in a different way, I think.'

'That could be fun, too.' He saw the group ahead, and Leanne beginning to set out the equipment. He grinned. 'You'll enjoy this, I promise you.' He hoped she would. 'And the leggings are awesome.'

I don't think I can do a whole weekend of this. I'm wrecked. I have aches in places I didn't even know I had. My thighs are burning. I might have to hide until it's all over. There's not even a phone signal or I'd call a taxi. My legs won't even get me to the road to hitch a lift. If I could reach it, I could sit in that pub all day tomorrow. By myself.

What a day!

We got to this "rock face". I just thought it was a weird little cliff sprouting out of the ground in a wood, but it was a "rock face" and we were going to climb it. I was wearing my new, neon pink (I'd put my hand on the black ones but I could hear Keira's voice in my head shouting the B word so I put them back) activewear leggings so I reckoned I'd at least nail it, clothes-wise.

Gareth explained how we'd be harnessed and paired up so that one person climbed, and the partner "belayed".

My new word of the day! Belay.

Basically, it means that the climber is hauled up the rock face by the partner, who stands at the bottom of the "cliff face". Sort of. The climber has to climb. You're not supposed to just dangle there and let your partner do all the work. Although I did dangle. And I screamed. A lot of screaming and dangling, all in all. I can't decide if I'm ashamed of the screaming or proud of myself for even attempting it because I am not good with heights. Not At All. Weirdly, I can go UP – but I get in an absolute funk about going DOWN. So the abseiling day is going to be a killer. Today though, I am astounded to say, was fun!

G shouted at me, 'Get off your knees, Rosa!'

I shouted back, 'It's Rosie! And I can't see anyone else here over forty doing this so shut it, Graham!'

He laughed. He laughed! And he said, 'Except me. And it's Gareth!' So he's not quite as young as I thought he was.

I laughed too then. And so did everyone. I'm getting to be quite the funny girl.

I got to the top and I rang the bell. Then I had to go to the bottom and belay my partner. Leanne. She's way taller than me and fierce and has muscles wider than my arse and she climbed up there like a monkey. I had to go some to belay as fast as she climbed. She rang that bell and was down in a wink of an eye.

G said, 'Well done Leanne,' and she blushed. She fancies him. He doesn't seem to notice though. Maybe he's gay.

I'd been looking forward to a little rest, but Leanne's speed meant me having to climb up again straightaway. G shouted, 'Get on with it, Rosa!' as I fell off the first ledge.

I told him to 'Get lost, George!' as I dangled there and I heard him chuckle again. I can't think of any more names beginning with G to tease him with. At least I hadn't screamed that time. And – I wasn't the last one to ring the bell!

My legs were wobbling by the time I got to the bottom

though. I was glad to have a break and lunch. Which turned out to be some weird veggie stuff that I'd never had. Fajitas and hummus and tahini and wraps and dips and flatbreads. And raw vegetables and fruit. I was starving though so I ate it. I quite liked it actually, but I wasn't going to tell G that. He's just a bit too pleased with himself all the time. So I said, what was wrong with sandwiches?

'I suppose you'd have brought along fairy cakes and pork pies?' He fixed me with those dark brown eyes as he hunkered onto a tree root, with his long legs angled. I couldn't sit like that. Not if anyone wanted me to get up again.

'I could do healthy food, if I wanted to,' I said, standing up to eat, and pretending that's how I always did it.

'You need to feed your body, as well as your soul,' he said, making crinkles at the corner of his eyes. I rolled my eyes, watching everyone lean in to feast on his words. I think he sees himself as some sort of guru.

'Have we got Cadbury Mini Rolls to finish?' I knew I was being cheeky, and I was listening, really. The food was delicious. So many new tastes. I'm going to try them when I get home. After all, no one there to please but me. I'll be able to do whatever I like, whenever I like.

After lunch, we went for a walk. Sorry, a "hike". Not just a "walk". I needed a belay to get me back. We all had to do stretches in a big circle and I fell asleep in the minibus. I expect I drooled too. God. I am so unfit.

They've all gone for a run now. Lunatics. As if they haven't done enough exercise. I'm in the bunkhouse garden with a cuppa.

Gareth wiped his hands on a tea towel and stepped outside to pick some bay leaves. Rosie had found herself a sunny spot in the wild and overgrown garden and was scribbling in a pink notebook. With her copper hair lit by the warm golden afternoon sunbeams, and those patterned magenta leggings, she looked like an exotic bloom. Lifting her head at that moment, she spotted him, and he felt obliged to speak. Just in case she thought he made a habit of staring at her from a distance.

'Rosie. You didn't fancy the run then?'

'Nah. I didn't want to show them all up.' She smiled, snapped the book shut and wound the brown lace around it. She eyed him. 'Don't you ever stop?'

He flicked the tea towel. 'This is for dinner. Pizza.'

'Wow – do they deliver all the way up here?'

'Rosie.' He shook his head at her, straight-faced. 'Home-made pizza.'

'Really? It's been years since I made real pizza. Correction. It's been years since I actually even *ate* pizza. A moment on the lips etc.'

'Everything in moderation.' Gareth nodded.

'More like desperation, in my case.' As Gareth tipped his head to one side and wrinkled his brow, she grinned to take the power out of her words.

He said, 'Want to help out?'

She leaned forward and groaned. 'Gimme a hand up. I'm an old lady, you know.'

He reached out and clasped her small hand, pulling her upright. 'Stop saying that. You're not old.' Her hand felt nice in his. Strong but soft. He let it go with reluctance, feeling his brows drawing together.

Bending to massage the small of her back, she glared at the ground. 'Oh, spare me the hippy New Age shit. I'm the oldest one here, and right now, I feel it too.'

He smiled. 'Come and pummel some dough. You'll enjoy it.'

'You said that about the rock climbing.'

'I was right, wasn't I?'

There was a long pause.

'Nobody likes a smart-arse, Graham.'

He chuckled silently. She was funny, although she didn't seem to realise. He'd enjoyed the rock climbing so much today, what with all her snippy comebacks. The others were all just a bit too in awe of him. Well, she wasn't. Not one bit. She'd listened though and she'd tried hard. He'd spotted her, fast asleep in the minibus on the way back, oblivious to the chatter.

In the big kitchen, Gareth showed her where the dough ingredients were and they set about making more. There was already one pale, mounded form covered in a tea towel on the countertop. Nine hungry adults could eat a surprising amount, and they could have any leftovers in the picnic lunch the following day. He watched her floury forearms getting stuck in and saw the frown of concentration, and had only half decided to speak when he heard himself say, 'When did your mum die, Rosie?'

She jerked slightly, and then slammed the dough onto the table, sending flour into the air. His instincts were right then. 'Just a few weeks ago. Feels like yesterday.' She glared at him, but he could tell she was only glaring in his direction, not *at* him. 'These people who tell you that it gets better with time. They're talking bollocks. It doesn't. It's like a knife in your gut, every time you think about it.'

It was. He knew. 'What did she die of?'

'Parkinson's. Evil, bastard, horrible disease. It stole her away from us, just as ...' She stepped back, lifting her hands. 'Bugger. I don't want to cry into the dough.' She tipped her head back and sniffed. He ripped a few sheets off a kitchen roll and folded one round her nose.

'Blow.' She did. And again. He threw the paper into the bin and washed his hands, thoroughly and matter-of-factly.

'You've got children. Only a dad knows how to blow someone's nose like that.'

'Two.' He returned to his dough. After a pause, he said, 'I lost my brother.'

'Oh.' She stopped kneading and studied him intently with those green eyes. 'I'm so sorry.'

'Thanks.' He nodded. It was his turn to stare at his bowl. 'And you're right. It never goes away.' They kneaded in silence for a few moments and then Gareth surprised himself again.

'So, um, your mum has just died and you've come away on a weekend like this.' He gestured around the kitchen with his head.

'What sort of weekend should I have gone away on?' Rosie addressed the dough.

Gareth was momentarily flustered. It wasn't like him to ask such personal questions.

'Erm, well, er ...' He lifted his shoulders in what he hoped was an expressive shrug which would excuse him from further explanation. She fixed her eyes on him, pitiless. He felt compelled to clarify himself. 'I would've thought, ah, maybe a spa weekend? Some sort of pampering thing or something like that. I'm sure you deserve it ...' His voice trailed off at her stony expression.

Punctuating her words with vicious clouts to the dough, Rosie said, 'When one's beloved daughter'—*whack*—'tells her friends at one's mother's funeral'—*thump*—'that one is so *boring*'—*bash*—'and that's why one's husband left you'—*smack*—'one tends to want to escape. Anywhere. As soon as possible. Your brochure was at the Art Café. Short notice vacancy, so I booked it there and then.'

'Ah. Hence the not reading it properly and arriving without a sleeping bag.' Looking down, Gareth continued to stretch and knead until it occurred to him that his were the only hands working.

Recalling in an instant his less than empathetic reaction to what was doubtless a hideous and emotionally wounding experience, he winced, expecting a couple of pounds of dough to bounce off his head.

Eyes shut, her mouth was stretched open in silent mirth. Either that or she was weeping. Gareth cursed himself and his thoughtless big mouth. 'Rosie? Are you okay?' The snorting intake of breath and helpless, wheezing giggles that followed reassured him and he grinned in relief.

When she could speak again, she gasped, 'Oh dear, I bet you wish I'd never booked at all. What with my domestic dramas, the sleeping bag, the curtains, the screaming and dangling and getting your name wrong … oh dear me … I'm so sorry …' She collapsed into laughter again. He unravelled some more kitchen roll and handed it to her. She toppled into a chair and gradually, the laughter subsided into hiccups.

'Ah dear me. I'm sorry. You probably think I'm completely bonkers. You'll never have to clap eyes on me again after this weekend. But thank you for letting me get it out there.' Getting up with a groan, she looked down at the table. 'I think the dough's done.' She cleaned her hands at the sink. Still facing away from him, she said, pensively, 'I still don't know whether people actually want to know, about how you really are after the death of a loved one.' She turned to lean against the sink, drying her hands. 'You can see them, avoiding you. Not knowing what to say. But, death is a fact of life, isn't it?'

'Yep.' Gareth nodded, his own memories flooding back as he cleaned the bits of sticky flour off the table and his hands. 'Right, now we make the tomato sauce for the base.'

'I'm guessing it's not in a jar, then …' Rosie looked around the kitchen in the same expectant way that she looked for a spare sleeping bag.

'Cooking's not your strong point?'

'It used to be. I love to cook. Haven't for a long time now though. Not what I call proper cooking. Surprising, considering I do like to eat.' She prodded her ample thighs and he levelled a gaze at her.

'Criticising yourself gives permission to everyone else to do the same.' He leaned back against the big table. 'Sorry if that's a bit hippy New Age shit again, but it's true. Your legs got you up that rock face, didn't they? Even with all the screaming and dangling, as you put it.'

'I think Leanne pulled me up most of it, she's amaz—'

Gareth folded his arms and eyed her. He needed to do some serious confidence building on this woman if she was going to get anything out of the weekend. '*You* are amazing, Rosie. You got up that cliff. You could have stayed at the bottom and made excuses, but *you* got up there. *You* rang that bell. Didn't that feel good?'

A flush rose in her cheeks as she stared at him, her green eyes brilliant. He thought again how much he'd like to photograph her.

She nodded. 'It felt fantastic, if you must know. I haven't had this much fun since ...' She glanced out of the window, chewing her lip. 'Since I can't remember when, to be honest. And I'm trying really hard not to feel guilty about having a good time after—That's pretty sad, isn't it? Even when I was screaming I felt, y'know, *alive*.'

'And more opportunities for screaming tomorrow.' He winked at her and she chuckled easily. It was good to hear her laugh. It seemed to surprise her and he imagined that the months, years possibly, of caring for an increasingly bedridden mother didn't offer much opportunity for levity. Laughter was good for healing the soul.

'See all these tomatoes?' He gestured at the sack at the end of the worktop. 'That's our pizza base.'

'I'll get the kettle on.'

He was surprised and must have looked it, because she laughed.

'Believe it or not, but in my dim and distant past, I

actually properly learned how to cook. For lots of people.' She continued in a "presenting voice". 'Number one. How to skin tomatoes. Cross on the top, boiling water, skins peel off easily.'

'That's exactly right.' He was about to ask her what she'd meant when his attention was caught by the sounds outside. 'Hello – catering reinforcements have arrived.' He ducked his head out of the door to greet the returning, panting runners. 'Hi guys! Just in time too, looks like rain! Rehydrate and grab a shower. Make sure you all stretch properly. Then come on in and give a hand with dinner, okay? No exceptions – there's a job for everyone. No job, no food!'

Snatches of their shouts floated in to them. 'Oh aye – he's gonna have us out there shooting our own dinner now!' and 'We'll have to carve our bows first ...' There was laughter as they disappeared to their dorms and Gareth returned to the warm kitchen containing the industrious Rosie, with a smile on his face.

By the time the runners presented themselves, Gareth had set up a few tasks for them to complete. It seemed a bit primary school, but nobody had ever complained. One pair were cooking and sieving the tomatoes that Rosie had painstakingly skinned, others were grating cheese, cubing halloumi, slicing mushrooms, charring peppers and fennel bulbs and prepping potatoes for a mountain of spicy wedges.

'Do you make this stuff at home?' One of the girls wanted to know. 'I mean, it's great to make the effort for a party like this, but would you bother doing it all the time?'

'I come from an Italian family,' Gareth said. 'My grandmother would have been scandalised at the speedy sauces we're making. She would've started them this morning at the latest, letting the ripe tomatoes release their flavour slowly, the sauce bubbling gently, fresh herbs and garlic, all grown in the Mediterranean sunshine of their own garden.' He spoke slowly, lingering over the words until Rosie could see it in her mind.

'Wow. Does your mum still do that?'

'No. Mum buys tinned tomatoes, jarred sauces and dried pasta and has no time for "all that nonsense".' Gareth laughed. 'I had to teach myself to cook.'

There was a rumble of surprise around the table. 'Wow. It must be in your genes. How did you end up with a name like Gareth? Shouldn't you be a Giorgio or something?'

'Don't give Rosie any ideas. She can't remember my name as it is!'

'This needs a good glass of red wine,' Rosie said, when they'd stopped laughing.

There was a collective shocked intake of breath, and Gareth was aware of them all awaiting his reply. As if he'd shake his head and announce that it was an alcohol-free zone. As if.

'We used to provide alcohol on the weekends,' he told them. 'But it was difficult to work out a price plan. One year, the rain was apocalyptic and the group just stayed in and got bladdered. I couldn't really blame them. The path down to the pub ran like a waterfall. They turned all of the board games into a drinking game.' Their mixed expressions made him laugh. Some disapproving, others mulling it over and clearly thinking that the group had had the right idea.

'A glass of wine sounds nice. The pub's only at the bottom of the hill,' someone said from the group skinning the charred peppers.

'Eurgh, I forgot about that hill ...' Rosie groaned. 'I've just become teetotal.'

'Anyway. You don't need it.' Leanne shook her head. 'Empty calories.'

'You sound just like my daughter.' Rosie pushed herself

away from the table, stretching her legs with a groan. 'So I'm definitely having one now. Anyone else care to join me? Just the one. Or you'll have to roll me *up* the hill.'

Gareth assessed the murmurings. If they went to the pub now, they'd be there all night drinking on empty stomachs and be too hung-over to kayak the following day. Or was he not crediting them with any sense? They weren't children. But they did need to eat, and soon. 'What about a visit to the pub after the pizza? A walk before bed helps you sleep ...'

Rosie nodded. 'In that case, I'm setting my phone for a ten-minute snooze. I didn't sleep too well in my curtains last night. I think I've done my cooking chores, Gareth?'

The lift at the end of her sentence sounded as if she was inviting him to go with her. To bed. He had a vivid picture of being held by that soft, rounded body and was astonished to feel his body respond.

'Er, yes, course, Rosie! You'll hear the dinner bell, I'm sure.'

Yawning, Rosie stretched. 'Don't worry. Nothing keeps me away from food. See you all later.'

When she'd gone, there was a sense that the air had gone out of the room.

Time telescoped in that kitchen and I was back at my catering course. The course that I'd begun with such joy and enthusiasm, and which had been curtailed with that positive pregnancy test. I have forgotten so much over the years. Forgotten or deliberately sidelined.

Toddlers have no requirement for cheffy food, and neither did Chester. He was a curry, pasty, and chips man. Half of it used to be left to go cold on the plate while he followed up another riff. Mum, and then Keira, used to be on one faddy diet after another, in the continual search for eternal thinness.

I had to leave them all in that kitchen tonight. I looked around at everyone working together and I thought, I can't wait to tell Mum about it.

Then the "Oh God I'm going to cry in front of all these strangers" feeling. I felt the tears dragging at my eyelids. I'd already spilled my innards to poor G. He probably thinks I'm completely unstable. So I made a joke. Like I do. I said how much I'd love a glass of wine, just to stir them up. It worked too. They clearly regard me as the resident lush.

But I mustn't do that – labelling people. I'm not giving them a chance, I know. I can't help it. There's no room for anyone here in my head but me and Mum. I didn't even ask G about his brother who died, or his kids or anything. I'm so selfish. I can only seem to think about me me me.

What I wouldn't give for my own bed now. Ten mins isn't going to be enough ...

Gareth rang the kitchen bell at quarter to seven, drawing them away from their just started board games and chats. He could see that some had already bonded. He should rebrand these weekends as Lonely Hearts. Several lasting relationships had been born within the confines of the bunkhouse, over the years.

He envied them a little. There wasn't a weekend for divorced, "still in love with the wife" outdoor pursuits instructors, and he *did* still love Hannah. She'd been part of his life for a dozen years, and he adored his children. According to Hannah, he put everyone's needs before hers. In a last ditch effort, he'd cancelled all the outdoor pursuits weekends away and stayed home. They'd spent that time in either strained silence or screaming at each other. Two years ago, Hannah had found someone to replace him and left.

There was no sign of Rosie and he guessed she'd slept through her optimistic ten-minute alarm. He asked one of the girls to go and check on her and she returned promptly with the words, 'dead to the world'.

'Not actually dead, I hope.' Gareth was only half joking. It had happened on other instructors' weekends. The girl shrugged, her eyes on the food that was coming out of the oven. It smelled of warm herbs and fresh tomatoes and melting cheese and he just knew that Rosie would kick herself if she missed them. He beckoned Leanne and she detached herself from the feeding frenzy.

'Could you come with me so I can check on Rosie? I just want to make sure she's still alive and I don't want to be accused of indecent assault.'

Leanne nodded. Her face was very red. He hoped she wasn't coming down with something or they'd all get it. It *was* hot in the kitchen though.

He sent Leanne in first, just in case Rosie had actually got up and half dressed. Once again, his imagination sent a fleeting image of Rosie in her bra and knickers, like a ripe and juicy plum. What the hell was wrong with him!

Leanne returned with the news. 'She's alive. I took her pulse. She didn't even notice me. Just knackered, I reckon.' She jammed her hands into her pockets and shrugged her powerful shoulders. 'Too many carbs, probably. She's carrying too much weight.'

Gareth recalled the conversation he'd had with Rosie over the pizza dough. He said, diffidently, steering Leanne back towards the kitchen, 'I think Rosie has spent a lot of time looking after other people. Maybe it's time other people looked after her, for a change. We'll save her some food for when she wakes up later.'

Leanne shrugged, pushing the kitchen door open into a hubbub of noise. Gareth reached over and filled his plate, squeezing himself alongside them on the benches lining the table. Leanne stayed at the other end of the table, nibbling at some salad.

He'd also kill for a pint, right now. He hoped Rosie would be awake in time to go to the pub later. Or he'd have to stay here while all the others went.

It was nearly eight o'clock when Rosie surfaced. Yawning, she padded into the silent kitchen in her socks, rubbing her eyes. Gareth, dozing in the rocking chair by the pot-bellied stove, opened his eyes and watched her for a moment.

'Morning.'

She jumped. 'What? I didn't see you there. It'd better not be!' She glared at the clock. 'Bugger.' She looked around at the spotless worktops, which only recently groaned with food. 'Why didn't someone wake me? I'm starving!'

Gareth scrubbed his face awake with his hands. 'Are you normally such a heavy sleeper? Leanne was all for resuscitating you with electric paddles.' He tried not to stare at her, but she looked warm, soft and sleepy. Her auburn hair was a mad cloud that rose in all directions, and she was still wearing the pink leggings. A soft, pink, knitted sweater came halfway down her thighs.

Thighs. He admonished himself for even thinking the word.

'Has everyone gone to the pub?' She filled the kettle with a questioning raise of the eyebrows.

He yawned. 'Uh-huh.'

'I'm sorry. And you've been stuck here because I've been asleep.' She reached for two cups and hovered her hand over the teabags and coffee with an enquiring expression.

'Tea for me, please,' Gareth said, watching as she dropped a bag in each cup and flicked the kettle on. She leaned back against the counter and folded her arms.

'My mum would be at the pub now, holding court. She'd be lining up the shots and dancing on the bar while she drank them. And there's no way she would've missed the fun by sleeping through it.'

'She sounds like a character,' Gareth said, neutrally. He wondered what it would be like to have an overactive octogenarian on the course.

'She was. A total one-off.' Rosie made their tea and pushed the teabags about with a spoon. 'I'm not like her. You probably noticed.'

Another self-criticism. In the short time that he'd known Rosie, it was as if several personalities were fighting for dominance. He was beginning to wonder if her mother was quite as amazing as Rosie made her sound. 'I saved you some pizza, if you want it.' He nodded at the tall fridge and grinned as her eyes lit up. She put his mug on the table near him and practically skipped to the fridge.

'Aw, you even put my name on it!' She brought the package out, the greaseproof paper, Sharpie-labelled "Rosa". 'My mum made everything into a party.' She inspected the toppings in her parcel. 'Interesting combos here. Was this one Leanne's choice?' She waved a triangular slice that consisted of the tomato base with a tiny smear of cheese and a lot of rocket.

'There seemed to be a lot of that one left over, yes.'

Rosie carried on where she'd left off. 'And I just seemed to end up as Mum's audience. Which was fine,' she said hurriedly. 'I adored my mum. I still can't really believe she's gone.' She chewed in silence for a few moments. 'In the beginning, when she moved in, we did everything that she wanted to do. Her bucket list.' She made a snort that could have been a laugh. 'You have no idea, with Parkinson's, how long you're going to get. She was well for so long, we actually thought they might have misdiagnosed her. You don't know when the symptoms will worsen. Mum never complained, never let it get her down, she just lived for the day. Every day. Every night I wake up wondering whether I did enough for her.'

'It sounds a bit exhausting for you.'

Rosie stared at him. 'Nobody has ever said that. It feels so selfish to acknowledge it. And I wanted every minute of the time she had left to be wonderful, so of course I went along with it. We had some fabulous times. She would've loved all this.' She swept an arm around the kitchen, and he understood her to mean the weekend. Not just the kitchen. 'And she adored young people.' She put the pizza down and swallowed hard. 'It's so unfair. She should have been dispensing sage advice into her nineties and making us all laugh. No wonder Keira said—' She jumped up and ripped off a sheet of kitchen roll, blotting her face. He'd seen the tears though.

'Keira – she's your daughter? You mentioned her earlier.'

Rosie nodded. 'Mmm. Beautiful face and an ugly soul.' She fixed him with eyes made emerald from her tears. 'I am the only one allowed to say that. I'd kill anyone else who said it.'

Gareth raised his eyebrows and hands, palms up, in a gesture of submission.

'She said she wished I'd died instead of Mum.' Her voice was almost a whisper and he leaned forward to hear. He blew out a long breath. 'That was harsh. But had you had an argument or something?'

Her eyes flicked up to his and he could see the effort it took not to collapse into tears. 'She said it at the funeral. To her friends. And I overheard.' Her tissue was pressed into service with a long blow and she scrubbed at her eyes. Attempting a smile, she added, 'They do say eavesdroppers never hear good about themselves.'

Gareth was aghast. The daughter sounded like a hateful little bitch. He couldn't say that, so he tried for a neutral tone. 'People do say strange things when they're grieving. And they blame.'

She jerked her head in a kind of shrug that could mean anything. 'It was like a knife to the heart. On top of the being boring thing. And it's made me assess my life.' She slumped onto the bench, her elbows pushed forward, palms covering her eyes. 'What there is of it.'

'My ex-wife thinks I'm boring.' Gareth heard the words coming out of his mouth and surprised himself. He'd never admitted that. Not to anyone. Opening her hands, Rosie made a tunnel from them and stared at him through it, her mouth open.

'You are kidding me.'

He shook his head. 'She wanted me to be home all the time and cut the grass and go to garden centres on a Sunday.'

Rosie sat up straight. 'Oh.' She blinked. 'I mean, I like a good garden centre, 'specially if there's a café. And they do cake, and it's chocolate, but I wouldn't have said that was your thing. Not. At. All ...' There was a long silence in which Rosie wore an expression of disbelief that Gareth found quite comforting. Then she jumped to her feet and startled him. 'Dammit! Let's not be labelled by anyone. Let's get our sad arses to the pub and show those kids there's life after forty.' She narrowed her eyes at Gareth, assessing him. 'If you are over forty.'

'I am. Forty. Just.'

'Excellent. I'll just get an ibuprofen and my jacket.' She reached out to the package marked "Rosa". 'And I'll just have another one of these.' Walking towards her room with the slice of pizza, she said over her shoulder, 'You have to line your stomach when you take ibuprofen y'know, and there's no way my legs are going to get me down and up that hill without help from prescription drugs.'

Gareth rolled his eyes, unsure whether to laugh or not. Was this a good idea? His body seemed to have made its own mind up though and he saw his hand reaching out to lace his boots and grab a coat. And some head torches. It was going to be pitch-black coming back up the hill. And a soft, drizzly rain was falling. He mentally checked the contents of the First Aid Box as he waited for Rosie. Would she be putting on make-up, having a shower and doing her hair? She appeared at his side in a moment, her preparations obvious in the woolly hat pulled over her mad hair.

'Come on, Gareth alias Graham. I'll buy you a pint for listening to my whining.' She was still wearing the neon-pink leggings.

Maybe he wouldn't need the head torch after all.

Fri/Saturday middle of the night, whatever.

Thirsty. I just chugged down a pint of water so that means I'll be up and down to the loo for the rest of the night. I really shouldn't have had that second large glass of red. That's nearly half a bottle, isn't it? I'm turning into a complete lush. This weekend was supposed to be about turning my life around and getting fit.

No.

No, it totally wasn't, Rosie Bunting. It was a knee-jerk reaction to being labelled by your daughter. So up yours, Keira Bunting.

I actually looked over my shoulder when I wrote that in case she happened to be lurking here in the dorm. It's not normal to be scared of your own child, surely.

G and I had a bit of a chat on the way down the hill – which is the only time I can talk on that blasted hill. Not only is he divorced, he doesn't appear to have anyone special in his life. I was very surprised. But of course, I don't actually know him. He might be a nightmare to live with. Maybe he dusts all the time or something. Who knows.

When we walked into the pub, they were all huddled round a table looking serious. They waved us over when they saw us and one of them shouted, 'Yay, "Rosa" and "Graham"!' and that made me laugh. I can't believe they've picked up on us messing about with our names. Leanne looked bloody furious though. She'll be flexing her muscles at me tomorrow. I'm steering clear in case she tries to drown me. Why doesn't she just tell G she's interested in him? I hope she doesn't think I've got designs on him. Because I haven't. Even though he's apparently single.

I mean, I would, in a parallel universe, because let's face it, he's utterly gorgeous with his black hair, scarred hawk face and those deeeep brown eyes and that mouth that isn't hidden at all by his short beard that I can just see some silver in when I stare and trust me I HAVE been, shame on me, BUT I would have left school before he'd left primary! It would be ridiculous. And undressing – eurgh, I'd probably look all saggy next to his perfect body. I'm sure it is perfect. I can see quite a lot of it through those stretchy extreme sports type T-shirts that have little holes and breathing panels and things all over them so you know they're not ordinary T-shirts (I bet Leanne has them too) and those climbing trousers with pockets he wears.

Listen to me. I can't believe I'm even allowing these thoughts to have brain-space. Keira would think I was off my trolley to be thinking about myself and G in the same breath. And anyway, he wouldn't be interested in me, with my chubby thighs. I wouldn't be able to climb mountains with him. I had to be practically towed up that hill back to the bunkhouse tonight.

That bloody hill. It's enough to make anyone give up drinking for good. And it was still raining, that soft rain that soaks you before you've noticed. There was a lot of laughter though, on the way up (I was gasping for breath. I let them think I was laughing) and they all sang, although I didn't recognise most of the songs. Not that it mattered, because I didn't sing. I said, I can walk, or I can sing. I can't do both. They laughed. More because they were all a bit pissed than because I'm funny, I'm sure. It was that kind of night.

It was kind of G to stay behind while the others went to the pub though, while I was in my sleep-coma. So I couldn't let him miss out. There's something a bit sad about him. Sad, as in unhappy, not sad as in, Keira-speak, lame, dull, boring. He's very concerned to make sure that everyone is safe and having a good time and yet he's the one who has no one to properly speak to.

I suppose you can't let your guard down on these weekends. You've always got to be in charge. There can't be accidents. It just seems a bit isolating for him. I wonder what his ex is like if she thinks he's boring. You never know what people's lives are really like do you?

We're kayaking tomorrow morning. I hope I wasn't supposed to have brought my own wetsuit because I don't even own a wetsuit and I am definitely not baring this nearly fifty-year-old body in a swimsuit amongst all these slinky young malinkies. Gareth would tell me that I'm not nearly fifty, that I'm forty-seven and I should be living for the day or something. Next to this bunch of kids though, I definitely feel nearly fifty.

The rain had been heavier in the night, and the river rushed and swirled and surged in a living brown foamy tumult over and around the lichen covered rocks. Gareth eyed it with foreboding. Exclamations of delight from the group had greeted the log cabin kayak centre, with its deck over the river bank. It really was very picturesque. They were currently striding along the river's edge, watching experienced paddlers slaloming expertly between the suspended flags.

'We actually have to get into that, do we?' Alongside him, Rosie peered at the water from a respectful distance. 'Not that I'm being boring, or cautious, or anything ... but ...' She glanced at him and then back at the river. 'But, I'd rather not, thank you. I won't even ask for a discount. I'm happy to watch.'

'Mmm.' Gareth privately agreed with her. This was not

suitable for beginners. 'Back in a mo. Don't fall in. I can't swim.'

'You wha—?'

He grinned over his shoulder at her as he strode off to find Dylan, the manager.

'Gareth! I've been trying to ring you, mate.' Dylan hailed him from behind the long counter of the log cabin. 'This won't be any fun for your bunch.'

'No. So what have you got for me?'

'Well, they'll still want to get wet, right?' Gareth nodded. He knew that Dylan would have something up his sleeve. 'Okay, follow me.'

Dylan, a short man composed of solid muscle, led the way behind the cabin to a racking system stacked with sit-on-top kayaks; singles and doubles in ice-lolly bright colours. Made of indestructible polyethylene, they were comfortable, virtually unsinkable, broad and stable with open cockpits and were ideal for every size and skill level.

'You cannot sink these. No worries about rolling and getting stuck. If they capsize—'

'—they just fall out. No need to teach them to eskimo roll, or pull themselves out of spraydecks. Brilliant.'

'I suggest using the side pool for some games. Helmets and buoyancy vests, obvs. What d'you reckon?'

The side pool was a bit tame but for those who hadn't kayaked they'd still get a taste of it and have a lot of fun.

'If there are some real kayakers in my group, would you, or one of the other guys, take them down the river course?'

'Sure. I reckon we can sort something out. For a small fee ...' He grinned. Gareth knew he meant a slab or two of beer for his lads.

Feeling happier, he returned to the group. 'Change of plan – we're giving the rapids a miss this time.' Relieved faces were covered up with loud banter to cover fears and apprehensions.

'We're not leaving though, are we?' Leanne sounded dismayed.

'Nope. We're taking the sit-on-top kayaks over to the side pool instead. They require a fair bit more exertion than the slalom kayaks, but they're great fun and surprisingly nimble once you get the hang of them.' He flicked a quick glance towards Rosie to see how she was coping with the thought of it. To his surprise, she seemed quite relaxed. He sent her a mental thumbs up and said to the group, 'If you'd like to go over to the log cabin you can collect your wetsuits and get changed and I'll meet you all out on the deck. Okay?' He watched them troop away and went to get changed into his own wetsuit. It would take them a while to get their sizes sorted, and he sat on the deck to watch the river and wait.

Silent in bare feet, Rosie sidled out wearing a self-conscious expression. Her curvy figure was accentuated in the black neoprene, and he took in the generous hips and breasts and surprisingly small waist while trying not to stare. Her hair had been tamed into a ponytail which hung jauntily from the back of her helmet. She acknowledged his surprise with a chuckle.

'I told them my real size, so my wetsuit fitted me straight off. The other girls are arguing the toss about being a size 8 in Superdry and H&M. I just said, fat bird size for me please. Their faces were a picture.' He wanted to say yet again that she shouldn't put herself down because frankly, she looked gorgeous, but she carried on. 'So most of them are stuck inside their wetsuits trying to do the zips up or trying to get out of them without the others seeing them.'

Feeling disloyal to the girls in the group, he suppressed a laugh with difficulty. 'So, are you okay about this?'

'Yep. I love the water.' She shrugged simply and he nodded. It was good to see that she was at last in some sort of comfort zone.

'Have you kayaked before?'

She waggled her head from side to side in a so-so gesture. 'I've done a bit of most things water-based. We holidayed in a friend's boat when I was young. I wouldn't have baulked at those rapids then! But'—her eyes slanted left and she made a slow shrug—'stuff got in the way and I gave it all up.'

'Are your kids close in age?'

'Tom is twenty-seven.' The smile on her face said everything about her relationship with her son. 'Keira's twenty-one and the way she's going'—she affected a movie gangster voice—'she ain't gonna see twenty-two.' Her lips tightened to a thin line and she took a deep breath. 'How old are your children, Gareth?'

'Seven and five. Boy and a girl, in that order. Jack and Lily.'

'Nice names.' She nodded. 'That's a cute age. Do you get to see a lot of them?'

'Not as much as I'd like.' Gareth stared into the leaping river. 'Divorce doesn't make it easy. However civilised you are'—*and he and Hannah weren't*—'you miss out on the bedtime stories and the day-to-day stuff.' He was saved from maudlin as wetsuited figures appeared en masse on the deck, each of them appraising the others. Gareth grinned to himself at the stomach sucking-in, and the muscleman posing and laughter.

The kayaks and paddles were already lined up on the man-made sand and pebble beach, and people gravitated to their favourite colour. Allocating the appropriately sized paddles, Dylan showed them which way up to hold them, how to paddle forwards and backwards, and the rudiments of steering.

'Want to come in and play, Dyl?' Gareth called over, knowing how much he hated being inside, tackling the endless admin that came with running an outfit of this size.

'I thought you'd never ask.' Dylan's eyes lit up and, in

a flash, he'd pulled his shorty wetsuit out of the van and changed into it. His colossally muscular calves never ceased to fascinate Gareth, and were having the same effect on the group.

'How the hell do you get calves like that?' Several of the guys had also spotted them.

'I used to be a sprinter. I ran for Wales.' Dylan grinned.

They were all ranged expectantly before him so Gareth went into instructor mode.

'Two teams, one ball, two goals. Me and Dylan are the goalies. We're both shit-hot at this so you're gonna need to work hard to get past us!' There was a ripple of laughter and jeers, now he'd set them an objective.

'One two, one two, one two.' He walked along the short line counting them and then said, 'Number ones, you're Team—?'

'Dolphin?' said one of the girls.

'Storm! We're Team Storm!' Leanne yelled, standing before them. '*Raah*!' She lifted her paddle like a spear. The rest of the team chanted 'Team Storm, Team Storm!' although the girl who'd offered "Dolphin" looked a bit put out.

'And you lot of number twos ...' Dylan emphasised the words with a wide grin on his freckled face. 'Are Team—?'

'Wolverine?'

'No. That's copying them.'

'*Aquaman*!'

'That was a shit film.'

'Yeah, but we are number twos ...'

This was shouted down by a universal "*NO!*" to much hilarity.

'I got it. *The Incredibles*!'

'You can't be Team *The Incredibles*. It doesn't make sense.'

'*Deadpool*?'

'Ew. Bit macabre ... but ...'

'I loved that film.'

'Yay! Team *Deadpool*!'

'Team Storm have already won while you've spent the whole day deciding on a name,' Dylan said, rolling his eyes. 'You'd better make your decisions faster than that out there!' Picking up his kayak he threw it into the water and leapt into it. 'Bagsy I'm goalie at this end!' Scooping his paddle he flicked water at Gareth. 'Come on, old man, get in!'

'Have you got the ball, Dyl?' Gareth regarded him with his hands on his hips.

'Oh, bollocks.' Dylan twisted to scowl at him. 'Back in a mo!' Paddling smoothly and speedily into the shore, he hopped from the kayak to his van. Gareth slid into his kayak, beckoning Team Storm to do the same. Throwing the plastic football he'd hidden behind his back, he paddled towards the other end of the pool and hurled it at the bank where it bounced back into the middle of the pool.

'*Gooooaaal!*' Team Storm set up their chant, despite the fact that most of them had barely left the beach entry point. Gareth laughed, flicking his wet hair out of his eyes with a shake of his head. He looked for Rosie, who was in the "Number Twos" and saw her paddling competently and quickly towards the ball with a determined expression on her face.

Dylan was already back in his kayak and steaming towards them. 'Cheats! C'mon guys! Let's get 'em!' It was an old trick that he and Gareth had played a million times, but it never failed to get everyone going, and sure enough, any anxieties about not being able to steer or paddle properly were soon forgotten as the two teams battled each other to get to the ball first.

It really *was* a battle. There were no holds barred as boats were rammed and the ball bounced off helmets and everyone fell in. Rosie's face was split in either a ferocious grimace of determination or a huge laugh. Nobody had any idea who'd won or how many goals had been scored, and once they were all panting and warmed up, Gareth called time.

Slowing the action down a little, he and Dylan demonstrated how to turn and paddle backwards, and then they set up a follow-my-leader game. Dylan paddled behind them after a count of ten and if he caught someone, they had to paddle all the way to the front and be the leader. They were kids' games and silly fun, but you had to work hard to keep in a line and steer, and with the element of competition, nobody dropped out.

They'd been out there for a good hour and a half and Gareth could see they were tiring. 'Coffee and KitKats!' he yelled. 'First one back gets seconds.' He laughed at the renewed energy and spray as everyone bumped into each other like water dodgems. It was one of his favourite parts of the weekend.

Paddling slowly behind them all to encourage any tired stragglers, he spotted a little posse who had sneakily paddled to the far shore and pulled their boats up on the bank. One was already jogging towards the gravel beach, another was fooling about with his paddles twirling like a majorette. He frowned, shading his eyes with his hand and resting his paddle across his thighs. Leanne was there; she should know better than to let them mess about on the water's edge like this.

'Oi!' he yelled, cupping a hand around his mouth.

And then he saw – as if in slow motion – the twirling paddle connect with the side of Leanne's head. Crumpling, she tumbled head first into the water. He saw her unzipped buoyancy vest fly loose. His heart jolted.

Heels and hips braced against the vessel, his muscles strained as he pushed his paddle against the resistance of the water. He heard the shouts for help and saw Dylan running.

But another kayak was closer than him and speeding towards the scene, a curly ponytail bobbing through the paddler's helmet. Rosie! Arriving at the spot she flung her paddle aside, slipping into the water. Gareth held his breath. Two of them in the water. This was bad. His pulse thundered in his ears.

Less than a second later, she bobbed to the surface just as he got there. Leanne was propped against her shoulder, eyes shut and there was blood.

'It's okay, Rosie. I've got you.' Reaching out, he gripped the back of Rosie's wetsuit. 'Well done.'

The centre's lifeguards arrived on the scene at full speed, carrying a spinal board and rigid neck brace.

Between all of them they brought Leanne carefully onto the bank. Her eyes flickered and opened. Her forehead puckered.

'Ow.' Her hand fluttered towards her head, where a thick dressing now stemmed the blood flowing from the wound.

'Leanne!' On his knees, Gareth leaned in to reassure her. 'You're okay, you're on the bank now. We're just checking you over. Can you hear me? Don't try to move your head.'

The rest of the group had hurried over and were anxiously grouped around.

Gareth hoped the ambulance would be quick.

Chapter Five

'Oliver. You total *arse*. You owe me big time for this.' Leanne's voice was strong, which was a relief. The group let out a collective sigh of relief, along with a ripple of laughter and a few ragged choruses of, 'Go Team Storm!'

She tried to get up and the lifeguards explained why she had to stay where she was. Oliver stepped forward with a hanging head and an abject apology.

Dylan returned with the news that the ambulance would be there in ten minutes, and he'd sent someone up to the main road to signpost them in.

'You did brilliantly, Rosie,' Gareth said, as they waited. 'That was a pretty awesome paddle.'

'Cheers.' Rosie nodded, her ponytail bobbing. 'I think I was on auto-pilot. I expect I'll pay for it later and won't be able to move.'

'Thanks, Rosie,' Leanne said, swivelling her eyes as far as they'd go without moving her head.

'Does this mean I can have wine with my dinner tonight?' Rosie said, with a smile.

'Empty calories ...' Leanne said, with a weak smile.

'That does it. I'm having a whole bottle to myself.'

Leanne made a thumbs up with a weak grin as the unmistakeable sounds of the ambulance sirens wailing could be heard.

The paramedics were efficient and cheery, transferring Leanne onto a spinal board with a neck brace "just in case", despite Leanne's assurances that she was absolutely fine and she'd be back to kick Oliver's arse.

'What about my clothes and my phone?' She held up her wrist and one of the paramedics peeled off the wristband that enabled her to claim her locker.

'Don't worry,' Gareth said. 'We'll sort that and bring them over to you when they let you out. We'll follow you to the hospital once we're all dressed.'

'I'm sorry – I've messed up your plans! Did Team Storm win?' Leanne made a hopeful face which made everyone laugh. 'How long am I going to be at the hospital? I don't want to miss tomorrow's abseiling!'

The paramedic laughed. 'You're a girl, you are! Come on lovely, sooner we get you there, sooner you'll be out. She'll be at the Brecon Hospital, mate.'

The ambulance left to a tatty chorus of 'Bye Leanne!' and 'Team Storm!' and they watched it navigating slowly towards the main road.

'Right guys,' Gareth said, taking charge as inertia settled over them. 'That's kind of put a dampener on the day. I suggest we all shower and get dressed and—'

'Cup of tea,' said one voice.

'And cake,' said another, with feeling.

'—we'll head into Brecon. The hospital is almost in the middle of the town so we can find you a nice café.' Gareth ran his hand through his damp hair. 'I'll go to the hospital and you guys can have lunch and do some shopping for the afternoon. Sorry it's not what we'd planned but I've got a duty of care to all of you to make sure you're safe.'

'Okay boss. No worries.' There were nods of agreement, and he paired them up to return the kayaks to the trailer that had brought them here. Dylan eyed Gareth as they loaded the kayaks onto the trailer.

'You all right?'

'Me?' Gareth jerked his chin upwards in a gesture that wasn't a yes, but showed that he was fully aware of all the considerations from the accident. 'Yeah, fine. Thinking about the paperwork. I need to go and ring her next of kin now. You?'

'You can use the landline here. The mobile signal is rubbish. I dunno.' He tutted with a self-deprecating air. 'You risk assess for every bloody thing and someone manages to cock it up. Note to self, no taking off helmets or buoyancy vests until they're back at the cabin. I'll have to drill it into their foreheads! You tell the kids and you sort of think the adults would have more sense. Not to worry. Looks like she'll be okay, and she's a tough nut.'

'Yeah. Thanks for your help, mate. I'll keep you posted, obviously, so you can fill out your own forms.'

'No worries, all in the day's work. Good thing Rosie turned out to be a super paddler though.'

'Yes indeed. Quite a surprise, our Rosie.'

The minibus was uncharacteristically quiet on the way to Brecon. Oliver looked chastened and stared out of the window, and everyone was lost in their own thoughts.

Gareth had rung Leanne's next of kin, her older sister, who had answered his introduction of himself with a breathy, 'You're Gareth? *The* Gareth?'

'Um, ye-es. I'm Gareth.' He'd explained the circumstances and promised to keep her posted.

'She won't want to come home,' the sister said in a confiding voice. 'These weekends are the highlight of her year, you know.'

'Ah.' Gareth nodded at the phone, realising belatedly that Leanne's sister couldn't see him. 'That's good,' he added, lamely. 'It's always nice to see her.'

'Tell her I love her, clumsy cow.' A child wailed in the background, and she added, hurriedly, 'If she needs collecting I'll have to ring someone to get her. I can't get away. It's too far.'

'Okay. Thank you.' Gareth had rung off thinking that despite Leanne attending numerous weekends, he actually didn't know much about her. Opinionated and brash, she was certainly fit, with not an ounce of spare flesh on her, but she never volunteered anything about herself. At the introductory chat in the pub, she'd only ever say that she'd completed this or that challenge or event, never volunteered anything personal. How had he never noticed? He'd engaged more with Rosie in a couple of days than he had in a dozen weekends with Leanne. But Rosie was warm and interested in everyone. Not trying to be Superwoman or best at everything to get his attention. He located her in his driver's mirror. Asleep again. He smiled to himself. She needed to recharge her batteries after her turbocharged paddling sprint. He recalled it. Amazing.

Brecon was a quaint and pretty Welsh farming town, once prosperous and now, like most rural towns, struggled for footfall. It was still interesting to potter about and there were plenty of cafés, outdoor clothing shops and history to keep everyone interested. Gareth dropped everyone off at the Brecon Basin, a picturesque canal-side arts centre with café, only half a mile from the hospital.

He checked that everyone had his number in their phones and that he had theirs, and set up a WhatsApp group to broadcast to them all.

'Okay. Good luck and send our love to Leanne.' They waved him off, and he steeled himself for the hospital.

Waiting for coffee and diet cake, haha. This morning made me realise how much I miss the water. I miss so many things that I've given up, over the years. I need to get back to being myself. Except what was right for me then isn't necessarily right now. I don't want to be who I used to be.

I want to find out who I want to be now!

My cake has arrived and it looks lovely but everyone else is having some sort of big bowl of veggies. They said it's a

Buddha Bowl. I have no idea what that means but it looks good, actually.

I need to eat better and get fit. And do things that make me happy. Like getting a job. I've sent millions of applications out but absolutely no one has got back to me. Sigh.

I keep thinking about Keira, after the Leanne thing. Are they similar? Similar in age, maybe. Both judgey bitches, bless 'em. But Keira's still my kid. I'll text her now ...

Oh, well, that was so worthwhile. I don't know why I even bothered. K didn't even ASK where I was. She isn't a bit interested in me. Because evidently, her father is back in the UK.

Well, she's welcome to him. They can both stay away from me. I never ever want to clap eyes on him ever again. I don't even want to give him diary space.

He's history. Gone. Out of my life for ever. And good bloody riddance.

Chapter Six

Gareth introduced himself at the hospital reception and was treated to the evil eye as he wasn't either next of kin or a relative.

Leanne's accident triggered his anxiety about his children. It was the beginning of the school half term and they were away on holiday with their mother and her boyfriend Ian. He texted Hannah.

How are the kids? G x

They're fine. We've only just got here!

No problem. Just asking. He sighed. Surely it wasn't a difficult request.

You're not the only one who can parent you know.

He blinked. Then typed carefully, *Hope you're all having a nice time.* After a pause, he added, *Give kids my love. G x*

Mouth breathing to avoid the terrible, antiseptic hospital smell with all its memories, he'd read his way through two dog-eared and ancient magazines before her reply pinged. The screen showed a simple thumbs up. Although she'd taken the trouble to scroll across and find the tanned thumb, and not the usual cartoon yellow one. Another text pinged. He squinted at the screen. It was from Rosie.

I bought a sleeping bag. How's Leanne?

For one more night? No idea re L. Still waiting. They won't tell me anything. Not allowed in. He sent it, stopping himself typing "I can't wait to get out of here. I hate hospitals".

It was in the sale. Always handy. Want some company? I'm outside.

With relief, he typed, *Come on in.*

Burdened with a huge carrier bag emblazoned with the name of a local outdoor store, Rosie marched straight in, ignored him and stood at the reception desk. He was half on his feet to beckon her over when he saw in amazement, that she was being waved through the double doors. He texted rapidly.

How did you do that?

I lied.

She had the cheek of the devil that one, she really did. He breathed a short laugh through his nose and shook his head. He didn't have too long to wait. Rosie reappeared weighed down with another vast plastic bag marked "patient belongings" and sat beside him.

'Very naughty of you,' he leaned forward to whisper. 'But well done. What's the news?'

'Just waiting for results. She's conscious, starving and fed up with wearing a hospital nightie.'

'Sounds like Leanne.' He smiled, feeling relieved. 'Was she surprised to see you?'

Rosie chuckled. 'She was, rather. I played it safe and said I was her aunt. Everyone has an aunt somewhere. But she's a switched-on cookie and she played along. I might be doomed to be Auntie Rosie for the weekend now though.'

'It could be worse!' Gareth laughed. 'What's everyone else doing?'

'We had lunch in a fab little café. Lots of veggies. You'd be proud of me.' She fake-coughed and added, 'After the cake.' She grinned at him. 'But I've bought some veggie cookbooks and I'm determined to get fitter and healthier.'

Gareth nodded, smiling. 'What are they all doing now?'

'Shopping. And there's that great museum about the Welsh Guards and the Zulus, evidently. Most of them have gone there. I thought I'd come and find out how my rescuee was doing.'

'Oh, and there I was thinking you were feeling sorry for me.'

'Nah. This is your job, isn't it?'

'*This*'—he waved a hand around the waiting room—'happens a whole lot less than you'd think. Thank goodness.'

'Yes indeed.' Rosie pushed the big plastic bag at him. 'This is her wetsuit. Sounds as if she took it off by herself. I think that shows that she's okay. If she was that poorly they would've just hacked it off her.'

'Fingers crossed. I've got her clothes here.' He handed the bag over.' Would you mind doing the honours?'

'No probs. I told her you were out here, waiting.'

Gareth nodded. 'Okay, thanks.'

I'm in Leanne's bed space. If you can call it a bed. It's a trolley. She's gone off for another scan or something so I said I'd wait for her. She looked scared to death.

Maybe she's not as similar to Keira because I don't think I've ever seen Keira scared of anything. She came out of me and bonded instantly with her father. I was treated to her most judgemental glare, and she's been honing it ever since. How different children from the same parents can be. Tom is, and always has been, a delight. And I often feel guilty when I think about him because I don't think about him. I'm too busy angsting over Keira.

Leanne was disappointed that I wasn't G. The nurse said "someone to see you" and her face just collapsed when she saw me so I knew she was expecting G. She's so transparent. I'm not going to mention that I know she fancies him.

Moving on. I sent Lucy from the Art Café a message to thank her for looking after me the other day, and told her I was on the course she'd suggested for the "friend". She's so nice. She sent me a coupon for an afternoon tea. I'm definitely taking her up on that. Looking forward to trying out my sleeping bag tonight. I am so tired that I could curl up in it right now. I could stretch out on Leanne's trolley and have a power nap. I did save her life. She wouldn't mind.

Haha, who am I kidding? She'd probably push me straight off.

This journal is a good idea. I wish I'd done it years ago. The times I instinctively go to tell Mum something and then I'm overwhelmed with tears. I'll just write it down instead.

Mum would've said, "Try harder, Dozy Rosie".

So.

1. I'm alone, but now I can make my own decisions. I can listen to my own music. Eat my own food.

2. I ~~could, maybe~~, I will start making my felt jewellery again.

3. I must stop using "maybe". I must just do.

There. Not perfect, but it's a start.

The wound had been small enough to glue, and with no other injuries, Leanne was pronounced well enough to stay at the bunkhouse until the end of the weekend. As they left the hospital and walked to the minibus, she told him that it would be more peaceful than going home to her sister, two of whose four children were under five. Gareth nodded in empathy, wondering about her home life at the same time. He'd been guilty of making assumptions about her. He'd imagined her in a neat and terrifyingly organised apartment.

'Your sister sent her love.'

'You rang her?' She froze, looking faintly horrified.

'Well, yes, she's down as your next of kin, and we didn't know then how severe your injuries were …' He tailed off. Should he not have rung?

'What else did she say?' She fixed him with an interrogative eye.

'Nothing really.' He recalled the phone call, and said, carefully, 'She said you enjoyed these weekends.' Leanne's mouth was a straight line and her eyes bored into his. A deep flush stained her cheeks. Gareth added, 'She rang off when one of the children started crying.' Leanne nodded, relaxing a little.

'Yeah. Those kids are a nightmare. No discipline.' She grimaced. 'Which is why I get away as often as I can.'

'Fair enough. I think it would be best if you gave the abseiling a miss tomorrow though.'

'*Awwww*, that's the best part!'

Just as Gareth opened his mouth to remonstrate with her, she grinned. 'Of course I won't be abseiling. I can still help though, can't I?'

Gareth would much rather she sat somewhere safe and just watched but he knew that wouldn't happen, so he agreed. Over her head, he met Rosie's knowing gaze and rolled his eyes just a little. Rosie's mouth quirked into a smile.

'Oi.' Catching them, Leanne huffed in mock exasperation. 'Pack that in. You're not my parents.'

'No, sweetheart,' Rosie said in a loudly conspiratorial voice, her eyes twinkling. 'Oh dear, that must've been a really nasty head wound. I'm your *auntie,* remember?'

'I wish you were, actually,' Leanne muttered, in an uncharacteristically unguarded moment. She didn't even flinch when Rosie stretched her arm out and caught her into a hug.

Picking everyone else up where he'd dropped them off, Gareth drove back to the bunkhouse with solicitous care, checking Leanne constantly in the driver's mirror. Having assured him, and everyone on the minibus, for the umpteenth time that she was "completely fine", she met his next mirror check with a sticking out tongue and a ferocious glare. He grinned in relief. But he'd still be watching her.

Rain speckled the windscreen as he pulled up in front of the bunkhouse. The temperature had plummeted, as it often did in the hills, despite the coast enjoying a heatwave. He gazed up as everyone disembarked, chatting and sorting out their shopping. Swirling low cloud obscured the tops of the mountains, and bleached the saturated colours of yesterday into pale sages and ochres. Trickier to photograph, but rewarding when you got it right. The forecast said tomorrow would be a fine, sunny day.

'Reporting for kitchen duties!' Rosie was alongside him, her auburn hair bright against the grey landscape. She followed his gaze. 'Looking a bit grim up there, isn't it?'

'I was just thinking how beautiful it is. And how much I'd like to photograph it.'

'Oh. Really?' Rosie squinted up again.

'Philistine.' Gareth eyed her, feeling a grin tugging at the side of his mouth. 'I've actually sold a few shots like this, I'll have you know.'

'Judgemental,' Rosie shot straight back. 'My mother was a photographer. I'm used to all that "staring at nothing" stuff.'

'Now who's being judgemental?' He smiled down at her. 'Right, better crack on with food now, then.'

'What culinary delight do you have planned for us tonight?'

'Pasta. From scratch.'

'Ambitious. I'm impressed.' Rosie patted her bags. 'I'll check on Leanne and see you in the kitchen. I bought a nice bottle of red. Everything in moderation, huh?'

Chapter Seven

It looked like the same rocky outcrop as before, to Rosie. When you've never seen them before, one rocky outcrop looked very much like another. You see one, you've seen them all.

Her mind twirled in crazy and inconsequential clichés as she battled to distract herself from the idea of throwing herself over the top of this perilously vertiginous cliff in the middle of a forest. The previous evening, Gareth had demonstrated pasta making from scratch, which was delicious, followed by a night walk, listening to the sounds of the wildlife. Hearing the eerie sound of the fox screaming had given them all the shivers and made them laugh at themselves. She'd felt a real sense of camaraderie.

The constricting harness she wore this morning reminded her of the wedgie-inducing underwear from her mother's funeral, the helmet strap bit into her neck and she failed to recall a single one of Gareth's instructions. Climbing *up* the rock face had been so much easier by comparison. Because you could *see* it all. This was like blind faith, this business of just chucking yourself over the side. Up was one thing but like a cat stuck in a tree, she'd never been very good at the descent. At age eight, she'd climbed up the open-framed dome in the school playground and then frozen in fear at the top. A teacher had to climb up there and talk her down. Gareth would have said, 'You'll be *fiiiine*. Trust me.'

'You're quiet this morning, Auntie Rosie.' Leanne nudged her, as they grouped ready to walk to the top of the cliff. 'You're not scared, are you?'

'Me?' Rosie tried out a laugh which came out sounding a lot like the fox bark they'd heard last night. She winced.

'*Naaaah*. Course not.' Her palms stuck to the padded gloves they'd been issued with.

'This is my favourite bit of the whole weekend,' Leanne said. 'I wish I was doing it. I'll be at the bottom though, waiting for you all. And taking photos.'

Rosie wasn't sure which was scariest, as she plodded along the narrow winding path to the top of the cliff, jangling with mysterious but prettily coloured carabiners. Leanne would be sure to take the most hideous photo of her terrified expression as she hung, petrified, perched on a lip over the chasm below. Only the thought of Keira's derision kept Rosie's feet moving, one after the other, to join the group.

It was the last day. Surely she'd proved herself. If she was boring, she was past caring, in the face of plummeting to her death over a rocky outcrop. Keira could get knotted. The thought was liberating, and surprised her tired and trembling legs into motion.

Gareth went through his safety talk again. Rosie nodded and smiled and took nothing in at all. She was desperately thirsty, but they'd left their belongings at the bottom so she couldn't have a drink.

'Are you cold, Rosie?' Gareth singled her out, his dark eyes resting on her face.

'No.' Rosie stared at his broad chest. Her jaw clattered uncontrollably. She couldn't meet his gaze. 'I'm terrified.'

He was as immovable as the rock they stood on. 'Trust me.'

Rosie took a deep breath, inhaling the fresh, woody scents around her. Or perhaps it was his scent. She nodded and felt her heart clanging painfully against her ribs. Pressing her hand over her sternum, she said, 'Let me go first then. Or I'll never do it. Please.'

'Okay.' His voice was light and encouraging, unperturbed, as if it was no big deal, and she was grateful for that. 'Let's go then.'

On rubbery legs she followed him to the front. Nobody called her out for queue-jumping and she guessed that they were as apprehensive as she was. The knowledge was strangely comforting. Here she was, she told herself, the oldest one, and she was going first. If a chubby middle-aged woman could do it, then they could too.

'Rosie's going first,' Gareth said, a smile in his voice. 'So she has time to come back and do it again.'

Rosie huffed. 'Fat chance.'

'They all say that ...' Positioning her before him, gripping her harness at her abdomen, where it fastened, Gareth knelt to check it. She looked down at the thick, dark hair where it curled into the back of his strong neck, and his muscular shoulders and wondered what it would be like to have those powerful arms wrapped around her. He straightened up and winked at her. A shard of pure emotion pierced Rosie's soul and flooded her body with heat. At that very moment, she would have done anything he told her to do. Her brain took a snapshot of him and lodged it into her memory files. She knew she'd never forget this moment. He checked her harness and the equipment again, and spoke to her slowly and directly, as if she was the only person on this clifftop. She concentrated, his words slotting into place this time.

'Lean out. Horizontal to the ground. Take it slowly – you have the brake, remember? We practised it earlier.' She did remember, to her astonishment, and showed him. 'Walk down, one foot at a time. You cannot fall. I've got you. Okay?' She was. She nodded, her eyes fixed on his.

'Wait!' Rosie lowered her voice. 'I'm heavier than I look – you can't hold me all the way down! We'll both fall!'

To his credit, Gareth didn't laugh. He turned his head slowly so that she could follow his gaze, and pointed at a vast and solid tree behind them, around which was wrapped a complicated system of ropes and pulleys. 'That's what'll be holding you.'

'Ah. I totally knew that.' Rosie nodded, a bubble of laughter rising in her stomach. How had she not noticed? 'I was just checking that you knew.'

Gareth grinned at her. 'Good thing you reminded me. It's the same system that belayed you *up* the rock face. But instead, you're going *down*.'

Suddenly it all made sense to Rosie. 'Okay. I'll try not to scream and dangle this time.'

'I'm sure it wouldn't be you if you didn't.' His mouth quirked up at one corner, creating a dimple in his scar that Rosie found herself wanting to touch. 'If you're ready?'

Tiny backward steps took Rosie closer to the edge. It was *waaaaay* higher than a house up there. Her heart clattered like a pebble in a can. Gareth kept talking to her in a low voice, encouraging, positive, until she was pivoted, suspended by the rope, her head out over the drop. Her eyes fixed on his. He was all she could see.

'Let some more out, until you're horizontal with the ground.'

Every instinct screamed that this was lunacy, but his voice overrode her fears. She trusted him.

'Perfect. Off you go. Keep it slow. And enjoy it.'

Enjoy it? Was he completely bonkers? She heard him instructing her all the way down, simple, encouraging repetition. It didn't occur to her to be astonished while she was actually doing it. She watched her own feet walking down the cliff face as if they had nothing to do with her body. Time stood still as she committed to memory the colours of the rock strata. She saw the tiny yellow flowers and grasses clinging to life in the crevices, recorded in her brain the tension of her body suspended in space, and finally felt the textures through the soles of her feet.

She stepped onto the brilliantly emerald green grass at the base, staring upwards in astonishment, hearing the birds chorusing in the trees. Sunshine pierced the clouds and sent a beam of light over the scenery. The fresh scent of the pines filled her lungs. The world around her blazed in vivid colour. She'd abseiled down that! Gareth waved at her and gave her a thumbs up, and she heard a cheer from the group. Someone patted her on the back, told her well done and released her from the rope. She turned to see a fit young man, dressed similarly to Gareth. He'd been there all morning and she hadn't even noticed him.

'Thank you,' she told the man, who smiled back at her. He'd probably done this a million times, she thought, and was curious. Did climbers keep this sense of wonder? Was that what kept them doing it? 'Can I go back and do it again?'

'Sure! You did good. First time?' Rosie nodded, noticing that her mouth was now in a permanent grin. 'You're in safe hands with Gareth. He started us all off!'

'OMG Rosie! You did it! Wasn't it awesome?' Leanne jigged about beside her. 'It was, wasn't it? You did so well! You didn't scream once!'

Rosie stared at her in surprise. 'I didn't, did I?' She thought back. 'I was too scared to scream, to be honest with you. I think I held my breath all the way down.'

Leanne pealed with laughter. 'You did better than me. I was terrified. I didn't even do it the first time. I was in a total funk.'

Rosie blinked. 'Really? But – you always seem so confident about everything ...'

'Yeah, well, that's Gareth isn't it? He makes you feel like there's nothing you couldn't do.' She sighed and blushed crimson. Rosie's thoughts flashed back to that moment as she hung out over the crag. She would have done anything he'd told her to do.

She felt her own face heat. Oh God. She'd just joined the Big G fan club, hadn't she ...? Along with someone nearly half her age ... One of the other girls was inching slowly down the cliff now. Pink-cheeked and exhilarated, she landed lightly and gracefully onto the grass and was liberated from her clips by Gareth's assistant.

'That was so brilliant!' She bounced over to join them. 'He's amazing, isn't he? I feel like I could do a skyscraper now. I'm having another go. You coming Rosie?'

Rosie smiled and nodded and acted enthusiastic all at once, but inside, she felt suddenly old and silly. For that fleeting moment, she'd fallen totally in love with her outdoor pursuits instructor, along with probably all the women in the group and very possibly some of the guys. She really was a walking cliché. And a younger man, with an ex-wife and two young children was the very last thing she needed to be mooning after. Like a mantra she reminded herself: job, life back on track and finish the house before winter.

Gareth was delighted to see Rosie reappear at the end of the line for a second turn. Her earlier terror had been visible. She could never play poker. Her emotions played across her features as if her skin was transparent. It made his job easier though. He didn't have to be a psychologist to guess her feelings.

Conquering her fears this weekend had made a difference to her, he knew. In these few days, she'd noticeably relaxed and become more confident, having discovered what her body could actually do, if her mind would let it. He sincerely hoped that she would return home feeling more able to face the challenges of her life.

The thought that he wouldn't see her again after tomorrow sent a curious double thud to his usual slow, reliable heartbeat. He ignored it. Rosie had added another dimension to the weekend. She was a bit different to the usual run of course attendees, that was all. He would have forgotten her after a few days. He would have forgotten that heart-piercing connection as she'd stared up into his eyes, on the edge of the cliff. It had just been her fear, hadn't it. Hadn't it?

What he needed was a course like this to attend, to help him unravel the challenges of his own life. The intensity of running these weekends made everything else a bit humdrum by comparison. But doing it full time would let his parents down and his mind shrank from that idea. The family firm meant everything to them, and it had been expected that he would step up to take over the running when the time came.

He knew they indulged his outdoor pursuit involvement as his "little hobby", just waiting for him to get tired of it and give it up to concentrate on the real work. So far, it hadn't happened, and in fact the draw became fiercer with each successful course. His head overflowed with ideas to improve and expand the courses. But it wasn't his business, and the owner had his own ideas, so Gareth just did his best. The informal cookery lessons were his own idea, and he used his own equipment. Ditto the night walks. He'd bought all the head torches out of his own pocket.

He would love to add coasteering around Gower and West Wales, and walks on Cefn Bryn, the backbone of Gower, with all its natural history and tales of Arthur's Stone. But all those things required research and investment, and even if he could raise the finances required, it would mean him making a decision that would rock his parents' world. And after his brother ... He wrenched his thoughts away from his dreams and focussed on his job.

'Hello Rosie. Nice to see you back for another go.'

'Oh, I'm hooked now. Try keeping me away!' She beamed up at him, and that double thud of his heart responded.

Chapter Eight

Everyone abseiled down the rock face at least twice that morning, some faster than others. Famished, particularly as she'd been too apprehensive to eat breakfast, Rosie devoured her picnic lunch, perched on a convenient rock. When had Gareth had the time to make it, she wondered, before realising that his helper had obviously brought it with him in the cool bags. Not as inventive as the first day's picnic, she noticed, with more sandwiches and pastry items and even crisps, which led her to believe it had been ordered from a catering company.

'I would've thrown myself over the cliff edge for a crisp on that first day.' She held the crisp up and inspected it. 'Now, I don't think I actually want it.' There was a ripple of throaty laughter amongst the silent munchers.

'Who are you, and what have you done with my Auntie Rosie?' Leanne said, cocking an eyebrow in her direction.

'Really though. Can your taste buds change that quickly?' Rosie was still staring at the crisp. 'I didn't even open that bottle of wine I bought!'

'Oh, you're scaring me now.' Leanne's eyes sparkled with laughter. Gareth reached out a long arm and plucked the crisp from Rosie's fingers. He popped it into his mouth with his eyes on hers, and she watched his tongue lick salt from the corners of his mouth. It was a good thing Rosie was sitting down, she thought. Her nether regions had gone a bit wobbly.

'Everything in moderation,' he told her, with a wink.

'So, is this your main job?' Rosie tried for a conversational tone, to disguise the butterflies that were doing a can-can in her tummy.

Gareth shook his head. 'Sadly, no.'

'Isn't it?' Leanne sounded taken aback, and Rosie was surprised that she didn't already know that, given the number of times she'd been on these weekends.

'No. I would love to be doing this all the time, but, y'know ...'

'Life,' Rosie said, succinctly, into the silence. 'So ...?'

'I'm in haulage.'

There was a pause. 'I did not expect you to say that.' Leanne's voice was disappointed.

'What is it you do, Gareth?' Rosie asked.

'I can do everything, although I don't. It's our family firm. As kids, my brother and I learned young. We could both drive trucks as soon as we were big enough to reach the pedals. We were like monkeys up and down the loads. The drivers had to check for us before they left.' Gareth laughed shortly. 'They must have got so fed up with us, but of course, we were the boss's kids so they had to put up with it. I think that's where my passion for climbing started. Kids have no fear.'

'So, are you driving long distance now?' Rosie was beginning to see the problem that his ex-wife had had. An absent husband during the week, who ran courses at the weekends ...

'No. I keep my qualifications up to date, just in case.' It seemed that he wasn't going to say more, but then he added, almost reluctantly, 'I retrained in Health and Safety.' Rosie digested this information with interest, wondering how much had been influenced by his family needs, but Leanne burst into laughter.

'You run courses that encourage people to jump off cliffs and stuff, and you're a Health and Safety officer? Isn't that a complete contradiction?'

Gareth said, good-naturedly, 'With all the weekends you've been on, this is the only time we've ever had to go to hospital, isn't it, Leanne?'

'Sorry again!' called Oliver. They all laughed.

Gareth said, 'It's not really a contradiction. You have to be a risk-taker to know how to risk-assess. I know most of the ways to get into trouble doing all this stuff, because I've done them. And I have the scars to prove it. But I'm still here – and I know how to keep you all as safe as possible now. While still, hopefully, having fun and learning. Get all the safety procedures sorted right at the beginning, and it's ingrained when you progress to bigger experiences.'

Rosie nodded. 'So, what's today's agenda again?'

'Some more abseiling.' Cheers greeted this news. 'Then a circular walk to take in some of the fabulous scenery, and then back to the bunkhouse. Dinner at the pub tonight.'

'Shame, no boot camp cooking school?' One of the guys accompanied his comment with a grin to show he didn't mean it.

'And then, sadly, home tomorrow morning, after breakfast.' A chorus of "*awww*"s.

Rosie's stomach lurched. She felt panicky, suddenly. It was nearly goodbye. She stared at the sandwich in her hand, her appetite gone.

'But you can all book to come back and do it all over again,' Gareth wound up. 'If you've enjoyed it. You'll be getting emails for events and special offers now that you're on our email list.' He ran his eyes over them as they sat munching. 'Would any of you come back and do it again?'

The scattered replies came back with the same kind of agreed responses: that they'd enjoyed it and had more confidence in their ability to do it again. Gareth nodded, his face giving nothing away.

'This weekend has been a complete game changer for me.' Rosie's voice lifted above the hubbub of general chatter. She spoke spontaneously, on impulse. 'I booked it, last minute, as a reaction to something—' She gulped. Shut up now. Do *not* air your dirty linen in public, as her gran would have said. 'Something horrible that had just happened. I needed to get away, and I needed something that would be completely unlike anything I'd ever done before. I arrived without a shred of self-confidence, or a sleeping bag.' She looked round at them all with a wobbly smile. What on earth had prompted this? She wasn't usually prone to making impromptu speeches. 'Apologies to my roomies for the lack of curtains …'

'I should think so!' Leanne chimed in, with a pretend pout and hands on her hips.

'I never would have thought I'd be able to rock-climb at my age, and I'll admit that I was completely terrified, but …' Rosie directed a smile at Leanne. Out of the corner of her eye, she knew Gareth was watching her. If she looked at him she wouldn't be able to continue. 'Gareth made it okay to be scared and to do it anyway, no matter how bad I was.' She flicked her eyes towards him. His intense gaze pinned her where she sat. Her stomach bounced like a pebble skipping water. She stuttered on, 'Yesterday I was much more in my comfort zone—'

'Thank goodness.' Leanne's voice was heartfelt.

'—um, but you know, it's easy to do things you're not scared of. This morning, my comfort zone was nowhere to be seen. I thought the rock climbing was scary, but this—'she waved a hand at the cliff face they'd been playing on all morning—'*this*, was paralysing.'

She looked around at them, anxious that she might be going on a bit, but their faces were turned towards her. She wondered how many of her experiences reflected their own, but they didn't want to lose face by admitting to it. 'Nobody was more surprised than me when I got to the bottom … and ran back to the top for another turn.'

There was a ragged cheer and grins all round. 'You all'—she waved an encompassing arm, feeling suddenly and ridiculously like a Winston Churchill impersonator—

'you showed me a different way to be. In just a few days. From eating and fitness, music and just your attitudes, I've learned a lot.' She wound up on a high note. 'So if any of you are visiting South Wales, I'm on the coast between Llanelli and Swansea. Do look me up. I have a huge house with a gazillion bedrooms and it's not finished yet, so I could always do with a bit of muscle around the place. In exchange for B&B, of course!' She smiled widely. 'So yes, not only would I do this again, but I'd recommend it to anyone else. Top weekend, Gareth. Thank you.'

There was so much more she wanted to say, but nerves had dried her mouth to sandpaper. Leanne, her self-appointed vice president, was busy creating a group WhatsApp account to "keep in touch". Rosie's skin felt red-hot and she unzipped her fleece, fanning herself with one hand as she hunted for her water bottle.

Gareth's hand rested lightly on her shoulder as she rummaged in her rucksack. She felt his touch burn through her clothing. Straightening up, holding her water bottle, she attempted a beaming smile. Her emotions bounced and collided in her head beneath his serious gaze.

'Thanks for that, Rosie.'

'My impromptu and no doubt, incoherent speech? Haha.' Rosie knew she was gabbling. It was as if she'd reverted to being fifteen. She took a deep breath, and cleared her throat. 'You're very welcome. I wanted to mention the cookery classes too, but I think you should always leave your audience wanting more.' There she was again, making a joke out of everything.

'Indeed.'

She fidgeted beneath his steady contemplation. Just as she was about to excuse herself to visit the car park loos, he said, 'I'm so pleased you enjoyed it. People don't like to admit to being scared. Especially amongst their peers.'

'It's easier when you're older, I think.'

'Possibly.'

Emboldened, Rosie said, 'I think you have less to prove when you're older. And if you can't physically do something, you're more likely to accept a workaround without losing face.' She listened to the echoes of her own words, and added, 'Or is that because you expect less of yourself? In my head, I'm still in my thirties.' Rosie remembered her own beautiful, strong body as if it belonged to someone else. It seemed then that there was nothing her body couldn't do. 'And as I'm getting older'—she swallowed, unwilling to admit it, even to herself—'I hate that there are things I physically can't do like I used to.'

'Aging is a process that everyone must endure.'

Rosie rolled her eyes. 'Oh per-lease. We don't have to like it.'

'Many people are physically active right into their nineties. We must age or die. But we don't have to give up.'

Rosie eyed him. 'Are you carrying a little book somewhere with all these sayings in?'

His solemn expression lifted as his mouth quirked into a broad grin. 'No. Maybe I should write one. *Inspirational Quotes. By Gareth*.'

'Let me fix that for you. *Irritating Quotes. By Graham.*'

'Catchy title,' he murmured. 'And with a pen name thrown in.' She peered at him suspiciously. Were those narrowed eyes holding back laughter or did he just have the sun in his face? 'Irritating? Really?'

'Trust me, there is nothing more annoying than someone younger than you, in perfect physical shape, telling you about ageing.'

'Perfect physical shape?' Gareth flicked a glance down at himself and nodded, gravely, with the briefest shrug of his eyebrows. 'Nice of you to say. I shall bear your comments in mind.' Rosie felt a flicker of doubt cross her mind, and she frowned. Then he said, 'It sounds as if I live quite close to you. Would you like a lift home instead of the five hour, convoluted train journey?'

'Oh, yes please! Although I quite enjoyed the train on the way here. It gave me some time to think.'

'You can carry on thinking all the way home, if you'd like to. I promise not to offload any more of my irritating quotes.'

Before Rosie could respond, he straightened up and raised his voice. 'Okay guys, onwards and upwards. Or in our case, downwards. Ten minute call to start.'

Rosie dutifully headed for the loos back at the car park, thinking over that conversation. Leanne jogged to catch up with her. Rosie's heart sank a little, wondering what Leanne would think about Gareth's offer of a lift home.

'I'm sorry to hear about your troubles, Auntie Rosie.'

'Thanks, Leanne. Sorry if I've been weird this weekend. Of course, you don't know me, so you probably think this is normal for me.'

Leanne wasn't put off by her nervous babble. 'What actually happened?'

'My mum died and my daughter said she wished I'd died instead.' Rosie said it fast. With every repetition, it was beginning to feel as if it had happened to somebody else, and she was doubting her reaction to Keira's words. But Leanne gawped. Rosie added, 'At Mum's funeral. She said it then.'

'I'm so sorry about your mum.' Leanne's expression darkened. 'But your daughter! That's bad.' She was silent for a moment. 'I don't always get on with my mum, but I wouldn't wish her dead. She's always saying I should get a proper job and a husband.'

'What do you do?'

Leanne hesitated, fractionally. 'I have an online wool shop.'

Rosie blinked. 'Oh. That's surprised me! Where are you based?'

'Norfolk.'

'Goodness me, that's a long way to come for a weekend. But wool is huge these days, isn't it? Everyone is knitting. I used to do a lot of hand and needle felting. I loved all those fabulous colours and textures. I had to give it up when Mum came to stay. She needed me.' She recalled with pleasure her little workshop, and the rainbow hues of the dyed pure wool fleece. 'I was just starting to get enough stuff together to sell.'

'Send me some photos. If I like it, I could put it on my website to sell. Only if I like it, mind. This is business.'

'Thank you, Leanne! That's really kind of you.' Rosie felt a lurch of excitement. Her mouth watered as she thought about shopping for new colours, and ideas sprang immediately into her head. Was this something she could do as a living? Might Leanne think her ideas old-fashioned? She needed to do some research, see what was out there. Get some ideas down on paper.

It was weird how she'd suddenly noticed all the colours and sounds around her after that first abseil. As if a switch had been turned on in her head. It was very early days, but she felt as if a tiny part of her might be coming back to life after years of being shrouded by grief and duty. There was a definite spring in her knees as she climbed up the cliff face ready to tackle the drop again.

Chapter Nine

Gareth sat at the head of the table in the pub, looking round at everyone. As was usual on these weekends, they were now bonded tighter than ticks. They'd all eaten, exchanged mobile numbers and there were a couple of telltale body language giveaways indicating budding romances. He felt a self-congratulatory rush of a job well done. His eyes rested on Rosie, remembering her nerves at that first pub meal. She was relaxed, curvy in the pink sweater, chatting in an animated way to Leanne, bony in a strappy top. They say opposites attract and these two couldn't be more different.

His thoughts were interrupted by one of the waitresses placing a folder of papers before him. He opened it and hailed her as she stepped towards an adjacent table, carrying more folders.

'What? Wait, tonight?'

She nodded, a grin spreading across her face. 'By popular demand ... It's been on the posters ...' She looked pointedly at an A4 poster blue-tacked to the bar. He hadn't really looked at the bar. He'd just gone through the usual motions of ordering food and focussing on his group. Nil points for observation to him.

'Sorry to hijack your last night,' the waitress said, not looking sorry at all. 'But it won't be for long. We're trialling it to roll out for a weekend. Tonight is just a bit of fun for the locals.' She darted away to distribute more folders.

A bit of fun for the staff, more like. His gaze flicked across the group, wondering what their thoughts were. They were poring over a similar folder with expressions varying from curiosity to delight.

Feeling outmanoeuvred, he ran his eyes down the songs, not recognising many of the titles. He'd never been very good at song titles. Even when he'd listened for hours to the radio in his cab, he could recognise a tune and even sing along to it, but he had no idea what it was called. He wasn't at all sure that this was how he'd want to end his courses. It seemed tacky and downmarket. They didn't have to stay. They'd all eaten, and they could slope off at any time and return to the bunkhouse, sit and chat in the Common Room with hot drinks ... He caught himself in his pomposity. It sounded dull as ditchwater by comparison. He decided to go with the flow. If nothing else, it could be good for a laugh, and that was always a good way to round a weekend off.

It wasn't long before the stage was set. A drop-down screen rolled out the words, and the karaoke machine, complete with speaker, was set in position. The audience watched the set-up with interest, and Gareth looked around him to see who might take up the challenge. No surprise to find one of the staff setting the tone, with a pleasant, light voice that had everyone clapping at the end. Into the grinding silence that followed, the sense of embarrassment in the air was palpable. Gareth stared into his pint, thinking it was all over and that was the end of that idea.

'Come on Team Storm! Team singalong!' It could only be Leanne. Gareth was astonished. They trooped towards the stage, dragging a reluctant Oliver. There was no arguing with Leanne once she had the bit between her teeth. They belted out a song which he vaguely recognised, despite their tuneless but enthusiastic rendition, and sat down, flushed and laughing. He clapped and stamped his feet in applause.

The other half of the group had been huddled over the folder, and jumped to their feet in response to the challenge. Rosie among them. Gareth caught himself studying her. How would she react to this? What song had they chosen?

It was Pharrell Williams, "Happy", which he actually recognised from watching the film *Despicable Me* with his children. As they stamped, clapped, and mangled the lyrics, he felt nostalgic for his old family home. Rosie clapped and sang as enthusiastically as the others. Just a few bars in, she caught his eye, and seeing his lips moving in time with the words, beckoned him to join them. He shook his head, smiling. He'd have to be several pints down to get up there and that wasn't his style. They all seemed to be having a good time, and that was good enough for him. He was happy to be in the audience while they entertained him for a change.

The ice well and truly broken by then, several other people got up to sing. Some of them were surprisingly good, others memorable only by how excruciating they were. Gareth tried not to wince, wondering how they had the nerve to get up there in front of everyone.

The evening passed by in a flash. Looking around at the smiling faces, he realised that they'd rearranged their seats into their "teams", vying each other to see what song they could butcher next. Funny how competitive people could be, he thought, as Abba's "Dancing Queen" had the girls shaking their booties together. Rosie was giving that one her all, he noticed.

Finally, the guys pulled him to his feet, and he allowed himself to be dragged to the floor for the Queen anthem, "Bohemian Rhapsody". Hysteria followed attempts to hit the high notes, and the entire pub joined in after only minor prompting. He couldn't remember when he'd laughed this much. As they left the stage, Rosie high fived them like one of the Three Tenors as she made her way to the microphone. Gareth stopped laughing in surprise, his eyes following her progress as he headed back to the table. Was this another of her rousing speeches, he wondered.

His mouth opened as her low, husky voice began, note perfect, on the iconic, classic song made famous by Frank Sinatra. "My Way". The lyrics appeared on the screen behind her, but everyone knew the words, and it wasn't long before they were joining in quietly.

Her voice sent prickles up the back of his neck and it was a while before he realised he'd stopped dead in the middle of the pub, on the way back to his seat. She improvised lyrics to fit the weekend, and gained a round of laughter and applause from the group.

As emotion overwhelmed her, her voice broke a little and without pause, the whole audience swelled to continue the song to the end. Including him. It was the perfect end to the weekend, he thought, his palms burning as he clapped harder than anyone.

He looked slowly around the pub, taking in the smiling faces and stopped abruptly at one scowl. Leanne. Her eyebrows drawn tightly together, she rotated her gaze towards him, including him in her murderous expression. If a death ray was beaming from her eyes in that moment, he'd be a pile of ash. In an instant, her expression flipped into a tight smile. It happened so quickly, he wondered whether he'd made it up by some trick of the light.

Blinking, he looked away and down, breaking the eye contact, and pretending to look through his jacket pockets.

Chapter Ten

'That's quite a voice you have there.' Gareth glanced across at her from the driver's seat of the minibus. The group had been delivered to their homeward transport, and he and Rosie were now heading west.

She thought about Leanne. Had she been strange this morning or was it Rosie's imagination?

'Did you ever think of going professional?'

'Sorry, what?' Rosie, lost in her thoughts, bobbed her head towards him. 'I was just thinking about ...' She flicked an expressive hand. 'I was wondering whether Leanne would be okay, going home.' She stared out of the windscreen. The minibus had three front seats, and she sat nearest the passenger door, her jacket on the space between them. In his close proximity, she felt awkward, tense and hot. It was ridiculous, she told herself. Her reaction to him up on the clifftop had simply been provoked by adrenaline. That's all it was. He wasn't at all interested in her, other than in a magnanimous, instructor to pupil way.

'With her head injury?' Gareth jerked his chin up, his eyes on the road.

She found herself staring at his hands on the wheel, the sleek dark hair on his tanned wrists where they emerged from the cuffs of his jacket, and imagined it following the lines of his muscular forearms.

'I gave her head a proper look this morning and told her to see her GP if she has any worries. I think she's fine. She hasn't even had a headache since.'

'That's good.' Rosie hesitated. 'Although I kind of meant, in herself.'

He was silent, and she worried that she'd overstepped the mark, criticising one of his cherished followers. Because it was clear that he did cherish them. She had seen how much thought and care he put into these weekends. He spoke then, just as she did.

'Did she seem a bit ... last night ... a bit strange, to you?'

'She nearly killed me stone dead with that look she gave me last night in the pub. I was almost scared to sleep!'

They glanced at each other as their words formed in the air. Laughed. Shook their heads.

Rosie said, '*Naaah.*' The evening flashed back to her in a vivid recall. She hadn't been able to miss Gareth staring at her as she sang. It had made her feel, just for a second, wonderful. Talented. Wanted and admired. She couldn't remember when anyone had looked at her like that. It was like being hugged bodily. And then her brain told her, that's his job, making people feel good about themselves. It's not personal. It's not *you*. It was his "Gareth the Guru" role. Had he looked at Leanne like that once and she'd been obsessing about it ever since?

'She's making another trip over this way soon.'

'What?'

'I did invite everyone over to my house, whenever, remember? And she looked really keen ... especially as she's possibly going to be selling some stuff for me. She said there were some suppliers she could do with visiting.'

'Stuff?'

Rosie explained, and watched Gareth's jaw drop at the mention of the wool shop, just as hers had. 'Yeah, I was surprised too.'

'She's been on several of these weekends, and not once has she told me what she did.'

'Maybe you didn't ask.'

'Point taken. So, what "stuff" is she selling for you?'

Rosie hesitated. He waited patiently. The ideas that were forming in her head were as damp and unfurled as the wings of a butterfly. Chester would have either pretended to listen or dismissed her ideas as worthless. The "idea butterfly", shimmering and lustrous, lit by the first rays of the sun, would beat its wings against the glass walls of her head and fall to the ground, lifeless beneath his derision.

She said, eventually, with a shrug to show that it was all a nonsense, really, 'Just some ideas I have for some jewellery and things.' The colours in her head crowded and jostled for space. Shapes and textures grew together and re-formed. She snatched up the pink notebook and scribbled furiously. When she looked up again, the colours of the hills seemed more vibrant, and the horizon, high against a cerulean and cloudless sky, was punctuated with scribbled, windblown trees. It called to her. With a fluid line, she captured the undulating outline of mountains and trees.

Her stomach plummeted at the idea of going home to an empty house, and she gave herself a stern talking to. She could get out her sketchbooks and do a stocktake on her felting and fabric supplies. The sooner she got into the creative zone, the more likely she'd be to start earning again. She surprised herself with how much it felt like the right thing to do.

'Anyway.' His eyes slid towards her and back to the road. 'That voice. Why aren't you making money out of it?'

'It's limited,' she told him, her stomach jolting at this attention. 'It's pleasant enough, and I know what it can do. No fancy high notes. It's a decent tenor.' He was silent, listening. She carried on. 'My ex-husband is a musician, so our lives were all about music. There were always music makers sleeping all over the house, or in their vans in the yard.'

'It sounds pretty amazing.'

'It was, then. For a long time, it was a wonderful way to live. It's surprising what you can do without, materially, when you're spiritually fulfilled.'

'You've written your own book of quotes, haven't you?'

'Yeah. Mine aren't irritating though.' She grinned, lifting her eyebrows to show that she was teasing him. 'So – I know where my voice is on the scale of things. It's backing singer. Supporting act. Useful, can carry a tune, but not "blow you away" quality. And when your husband is mixing with singers who do have that quality, there's no point at all in'—she crooked her index fingers—'"setting out your own market stall", so to speak.'

Gareth was silent for a long time. 'You have to stop doing this. I realise you're at a low ebb, spiritually, but you make it difficult to even compliment you. Please stop knocking yourself.'

Rosie's fingers tensed white around the pen and she stared down at the little notebook. 'I don't think you understand what's going on here.' Her chest felt tight and her voice was small. 'Your little "bon mots" don't make me feel better about myself, they make me feel judged. Like, I'm not even being allowed to validate my feelings – they're just packaged in a cheesy phrase to print on a mug or something.' She pinched the bridge of her nose where her brows had met. 'I have no job, no relationship, and it looks like I have no family either. I have laid myself out for them, and they've walked all over me. I'm nothing to anybody.' She tried not to gulp. 'I'm not even zero. I'm in negative equity.'

'I'm sure your mother appreciated you.'

'My mother barely even knew I was alive, most of the time. She only came here to die. She used me.' She sighed, chewing her lip. Her throat constricted. 'And I was so desperate to have a relationship with her, that I let her.' She stared fixedly at the dashboard. 'She was ashamed of me. If pushed about what I did for a living, she insisted that I was "in catering".' She swallowed. 'I was a school cook.' Lifting her eyes towards him, she said, simply, 'And you know what? I loved it at the school. I wasn't ashamed of it, but she was. I was "squandering my education", apparently.'

Gareth stretched out a hand and gripped her arm, squeezing it gently. His brows contracted in an expression of concern. Rosie looked at his strong hand, and felt a mixture of comfort, lust and irritation. She couldn't remember when she'd been touched spontaneously like that. Heat rose up her neck. Should she touch his hand? He returned it to the steering wheel while she was still deciding and she was sorry she hadn't followed her instinct.

'The fact that you are able to articulate your emotions so clearly, tells me that you are not "nothing", to use your words.' He shot a quick glance at her before focussing on the road. 'And you're quite right about those "helpful phrases". I'd never really thought about them like that before. I suppose it's a little wardrobe of clichés I've built up so that—' He swallowed and Rosie, watching his expression, carried on for him.

'—so that you don't really have to get involved in fixing other people's dramas and crises. You've neatly flipped responsibility for their issue back on to them.'

'God. Yeah.' He rubbed the back of his neck. 'How have I never realised that?'

Rosie snorted a laugh through her nose. 'Maybe because you have enough problems of your own and you're not being paid to be their therapist?'

His eyebrows shrugged and she watched his eyes narrow, as if he was thinking about her words. Or maybe he was wishing he could listen to the radio.

She said, 'Don't beat yourself up about it just because I've given you a bollocking. Besides, people who don't have any real problems like to hear them. People who do have issues – they're often more complex, plus, they don't necessarily want to be fixed. Not all at once, like that. They want to – need to – work it out for themselves, mull it over. Perhaps sometimes, your quotes give them a different way to think about it.

'You're very wise, Rosie.'

'Yeah. For a woman who can't even read an email properly.' She laughed.

'And you did save Leanne's life.'

'She wasn't really hurt. She would've bobbed up by herself.' She saw his face swivel towards her, with an unmistakable glower of exasperation. 'Oh. Sorry. I'm doing it again, aren't I? Um ... thank you.'

'Well done.' He grinned, showing white teeth.

Some time had passed, when Gareth asked her, 'Who told you that you were a "supporting act"?'

'A woman at the funeral told me that.' Her brow creased as she recalled it.

'I meant, your voice. Who told you that your voice was "backing singer"?'

Rosie shrugged, lifting a hand and letting it drop back onto her lap. 'I suppose, Chester. My ex-husband. But he would know, wouldn't he?'

'Would he though? Or might he have been manipulating you so that he retains the limelight?'

'What? Uh ... no, I don't ...' Rosie swallowed, her throat constricting as she pondered Gareth's words. 'Oh my God ...' Her voice was a croak. 'Would somebody do that?' The past unravelled in knots and catches, like worn-out string. 'But – I had his babies. I gave up everything to support him!' Her mind sheared away from the implications.

'Obviously I don't know him. But that's gaslighting. Emotional manipulation to get what he needed.'

'Me where he wants me ...' Rosie was aghast. 'Well, it's a bloody good job I divorced him then. I'm a free woman.'

Gareth nodded, and his silence allowed Rosie's mind to roam across the last few years of her life.

'You need to believe in yourself, Rosie.'

'I'm sorry to sound a bit negative. While I was away, I felt as if I could do anything, and as I'm getting closer to home, it's crowding back in.'

'Rosie, stop apologising. One weekend isn't going to fix everything.'

'You can stop with the "Gareth the Guru" thing. I'm not paying you now.'

He burst into laughter. 'Gareth the Guru? Is that what you think of me?'

'Oh come on. You love everyone hanging onto your aspirational words of wisdom. You're a one man chalkboard.' After a moment, she said, 'You did a great job of looking after us and bolstering our self-confidence. No one is an island though. Who props you up?'

He was silent and she carried on in a rush, 'Forgive me if I'm being nosy, but you're really, really good at this outdoor pursuits instructor stuff – and you're obviously in your element, and I don't understand why you're tying yourself down to being a health and safety officer. Unless you love it. Do you love it?'

'Erm ...'

'I'm sorry. That really was nosy of me, and I have absolutely no right to pry into your private life. I've been out of the social whirl for so long, that I've forgotten about boundaries and I think the switch on my courtesy filters has slipped to "Off". I just, weirdly, feel as if I've known you for ages. And I care! Forgive me.'

'Rosie, there's nothing to forgive.' Gareth rubbed his chin, and his eyes flicked towards her. 'And you weren't overstepping any boundaries. In an ideal world, I'd love to be running my own outdoor pursuits business.'

'What would you do differently?'

'I'd add coastal walks, with some climbing and abseiling to see the caves in the cliffs. I'd like to lead some mountain bike trails, some sea kayaking and some corporate, team-building stuff, and really use this area to explore and learn more about nature. Does that all sound a bit naff?'

'Not at all. You are obviously very knowledgeable, and

you can put it over entertainingly. I hope you'd add the food element in too.'

'Hell yeah. And now you're going to ask what's stopping me, aren't you?'

'Nah. I'm not that interested.' Rosie grinned at him. 'Of course I bloody am! What *is* stopping you?'

'You're going to tut at me.'

'Oh, like you're scared of me tutting.' Rosie saw his mouth curve in a smile and then tighten.

'My parents would be devastated if I gave up working for the family business. And since Aled is gone ...' He shrugged. 'It's kind of all down to me.'

'Aled,' she prompted gently. 'He's your brother? The one who died?'

He nodded. 'We were paragliding. Motor paragliding. We'd really got into it, both of us. Adrenaline junkies.' He massaged the nape of his neck. 'And Aled was showing off some moves and I turned and suddenly he was there, in front of me.' He finished in a rush. 'And our lines got tangled together and we smashed to the ground. He was still alive when we landed. And I couldn't get to him. My legs—' He cleared his throat and said, matter-of-factly, 'They didn't think I'd walk again. That was twelve years ago. And here I am.' He smiled. 'I had a lot of counselling. I guess that's where all my little sayings come from.'

'Oh God.' Rosie touched her face, mirroring his. 'So the scar ...?'

'Not a shark bite.' He shook his head.

'I couldn't imagine you surviving having your head in a shark's mouth anyway. The halitosis would kill you for starters.'

Gareth laughed. 'I'm gonna need another cover story.'

'Why do you even need a cover story? Why not just say, I had a paragliding accident?'

'Because I can't bear the thought of dissecting it over

and over again, thinking that it was all my fault. If I hadn't turned into his path, we'd both still be here.'

Rosie said slowly, 'And he would have taken over the family business. So you'd have been free to do your outdoor pursuits experiences.'

'Got it in one.' He shrugged his eyebrows. 'Although, to be fair, Aled was a complete daredevil. I'm not even sure that he would've been happy taking over the business. But we'll never know, will we?'

'Oh bugger. That's a tough one.' She was silent for a while. 'So – I'm confused. You have this terrible accident—' He noticed how firmly she pronounced the word accident. 'And I can completely understand the decision to move into Health and Safety now. But I don't understand why you're still instructing what are potentially, dangerous sports?'

Gareth scratched his chin. He took a deep breath. 'No. Neither could Hannah. We'd only just got together when I had the accident. After the struggle to just get out of hospital, she thought I'd give it all up. And maybe I should have.' He drummed his fingers on the steering wheel. 'But it was what got me out of that bed. The thought of not just walking, but climbing … the freedom. Using your body to its fullest extent. That's living. Being fearful of tripping over the kerb because it took so long to rebuild your legs, that's not living. Not to me, anyway.'

'Oh God. And I said that thing about you being in perfect shape, didn't I? I saw you make a face, and I wondered why …'

'Pah. I'm not perfect.' Gareth grinned at her discomfiture. 'But I'm pretty damn close!' He laughed. 'Thanks to a team of bullying physios and a good dose of self-flagellation, I'm as good as before, if not as pretty. If I didn't totally trust my body, there's no way I'd be taking people out like I do.'

'You're a legend.' Rosie shook her head, trying to imagine what he'd gone through, physically and mentally.

'Naah. So. Your fire engine. Do want me to have a look at it?'

She followed the change of subject without missing a beat. 'Would you mind? I wouldn't have the first idea what I'm looking at.'

'I'd love to! I thought you'd never ask despite pointed mention of my family truck company. Where is it?'

Rosie recited the location from her letter, and her heart sank. 'That's miles away!'

'Not really. For today, yes, but'—he tipped a questioning head towards her—'for another day?'

A tiny bouncing bomb skittered across Rosie's stomach. He wanted to see her again! Or, more probably, she quelled her excitement with a firm hand, he wanted to see the fire engine.

Gareth slowed to park outside her house and she focussed with unblinking eyes on her driveway, which contained two cars. A small hatchback, hers, and behind that a bigger saloon.

'Whose car is that?'

Chapter Eleven

Her rhetorical question was uttered in a voice that was thin and harsh.

'It's not yours?' As soon as he said it he felt stupid.

'Of course it's not mine. I wouldn't ask if it was, would I?' Hunching in the passenger seat of the minibus, she peered through the window. 'And there's a light on.' Her hands clutched her leggings. He could see the whites of her knuckles.

Gareth studied the house. It was big. Rambling, in fact. Did Rosie live here all alone now? It seemed very isolated. And a bit derelict in places, if he was being honest. He wouldn't be happy about finding a strange car in the driveway and an unexpected light on after being away either.

'Your kids?'

'I don't recognise it.' Her voice was brittle. 'It's not Keira's.'

He couldn't let her go into her house without checking it now. 'Shall I go and find out?' Asking was a courtesy. Of course he was going to find out.

'Would you mind? I don't like to ask …' She fumbled in her tiny waist bag and brought out a bunch of keys on a ring. 'Sorry. I expect you think I'm being silly.'

'Not at all.' He climbed out, picking up the five cell, sturdy metal torch that he always put under the seat. 'You stay here.' He strode towards the side of the house to look confident for her and then edged his way to the window. His momentary glance told him there were people inside. Talking. He was pretty sure that burglars didn't stand around chatting. Ducking back, he felt in his pocket for his phone to ring Rosie. He nearly dropped it as Rosie herself jostled his elbow.

'God, you scared the bejesus outta me. There are people in—' He jerked his thumb to replace his words.

She stood on tiptoe to see. 'Oh crap!' Ducking down, her eyes wide and bright, she stared up at him. In a conspiratorial whisper she hissed, 'Gareth. Would you mind being my boyfriend?'

He opened his mouth and shut it again. 'I, er ... what?'

'My *pretend* boyfriend! Just for now. Please?' Pointing at the lit window, she carried on, '*That* is my shithead ex. With, I believe, my most recent replacement. And my vicious, betraying, underhand, sneaky, changeling daughter. And why hasn't she got her car?'

'Rosie, I'm more than happy to come in with you, but you don't need a man to validate you as a person.'

Her mouth wobbled, just for a moment. 'Just for once, I don't want to be "pitied" for being "on the shelf". Poor Old Rosie.' She made the speech marks with her fingers. Continuing more like the Rosie he was familiar with she said, 'And spare me the hippy dipshit. I *know* I don't need validating by a *man*. But they don't.' She jerked her head towards the window. 'And I just can't cope with all their judgey shit right now.'

'They'll know it's a fake.'

'How will they?'

Curious, Gareth risked another quick glance inside. The husband, tall, thin, greying hair in a ponytail, short beard and moustache. Trying too hard, he decided. What the hell. He liked Rosie and he'd feel bad about driving off and leaving her to the wolves.

'Okay.' He waggled his head to indicate that he wasn't entirely onside with lying. 'What do you want me to do?'

Rosie hauled him down. 'I don't know.' She threw her hands in the air. 'I can't remember the last time I *had* a boyfriend!'

Gareth felt his mouth tug up at one side. Now that he

didn't have to confront a potentially vicious burglar he'd relaxed.

'Do I look okay?' She shot him a piercing, appraising look and then smoothed her hair down at the sides. It sprang straight back up. 'Answer like a boyfriend.'

'Oh – erm, hang on, er, yes darling you look lovely,' he intoned without looking at her.

Rosie gave him a disgusted look. 'Come on.' She stood up, stretching her back and then stared down at her legs in horror. 'Oh God, these leggings! What was I thinking? I can't go in there with these on!'

'You, Rosie Bunting, have earned the right to wear eye-watering leggings, after throwing yourself over a cliff in them.'

Rosie eyed him for a second. Then her brow cleared. 'Yeah! Damn right.' She straightened up.

'Wait!' Still crouching, Gareth whispered to her. 'Where did I meet you?'

'On this weekend! Where else?'

'Whoa. I'm a quick worker.' He grinned at her, and reached for her hand in an exaggerated way. 'Come on, moi *loverrr*,' he said, in a West Country burr as she turned the key in the door.

'What accent is that meant to be? I've changed my mind.' But her eyes twinkled. 'Thank you,' she mouthed. Then, her forehead puckered. 'Eye-watering?'

He clapped his free hand over his eyes and peered at her through the fingers, grinning. She gripped his hand tightly and they stepped inside.

'Oh – Mother. You're back at last.' She scoured Rosie with a withering look. So this was Keira. 'And what on *earth* are you wearing?'

'I've been on a climbing weekend.' Rosie pulled her spine straight and Gareth felt a surge of pride, as Keira's jaw sagged in response. To his own surprise, he found himself acting like a real boyfriend. He pulled her close and wrapped an arm round her shoulders. In that moment, he registered how right it felt, even though they were only meant to be play-acting.

'Your mum's amazing. She even saved someone's life this weekend.'

Keira's mouth hung open even further. She was, as Rosie had said, very beautiful. Long, perfectly straight, dark glossy hair. Gareth watched her as she slumped to one hip in a pose that looked cute on his five-year-old daughter. He would lay money that she spent a lot of time taking pouty selfies on Snapchat.

The man, Rosie's ex, nodded approvingly at Rosie. 'Good for you. You always were a good earth mother to the crew.' The woman with him darted a furious glare his way. Gareth found himself watching their reactions as if he was at a tennis match. The ex was still studying Rosie with a hungry eye. His feelings for her seemed obvious. Why had he left at all? Gareth felt a curious sensation in the pit of his stomach, but Rosie wasn't swayed by the sudden turn of the conversation.

'Why are you here?' She directed the question at her ex and the woman. The confidence in her voice was belied by the pincer grip she'd renewed on Gareth's hand. He squeezed it gently to remind her that he was still there. And to maintain the blood flow.

'Aren't you going to introduce us?' The man indicated Gareth with his forehead and a raised eyebrow. Rosie stiffened.

'Who is she?' Rosie looked pointedly at the woman who wasn't Keira. And repeated to her ex. 'And why are you here?'

In the uncomfortable silence, Gareth gritted his teeth and said, 'Hello, I'm Gareth.' He held out his free hand to the man. After a pause he shook it.

'Chester.'

A cog dropped into place in Gareth's brain. 'Chester Bunting?' He felt Rosie half-turn towards him. 'Saxophone?'

'Yeah.' Chester nodded. 'That's me.'

Keira's painted mouth and eyebrow slid up at one side in a gratified smirk.

'I heard you at Glasto once, didn't I?' Gareth tried not to be a fanboy but he couldn't help it. He stared at the man, remembering. Fancy Rosie being his ex!

'Yep. We were supporting Whistle.'

Gareth snapped his fingers. 'That's it. Fabulous. Wow. So, you're still playing, right?'

Chester tilted his head in an offhand way. 'Yeah.' He folded his bottom lip over his teeth and scratched at his goatee.

'What do you want, Chester?' Rosie inserted. Her tone was nails on chalkboard now.

'I was sorry to hear about your mother,' Chester said, hesitantly.

'No you weren't. You never liked her. And she didn't like you. I should have listened to her all those years ago.'

Chester threw his hands up in a "what can you do" attitude and in a sudden emotional about turn, Gareth fought an overwhelming and wholly alien urge to punch him. He winced as Rosie dialled her murderous stare up to ten and directed it at Chester. She was terrifying. Why on earth she'd needed Gareth there as backup he couldn't imagine.

'Dad came over to see me,' Keira chipped in.

'After all these years, you show up now.' It wasn't a question, the way Rosie said it. It was a statement of pure outrage. 'Just a coincidence that my mother has just died.'

He shrugged. 'Whatever. Anyway, now I'm here, I thought I'd have a look round my house.'

'This is not your house, Chester,' Rosie said, tightly. 'We're divorced.'

'Ah.' Chester sounded almost apologetic. 'But it is. Because we're not.'

'What? Not what?' Rosie's hand was clammy in his and Gareth felt a hard knot grow in his own stomach in sympathy.

'Not divorced.' Chester tugged his goatee now. 'Sorry.' He shrugged, not sounding at all sorry. He pulled Gareth into his sweeping glance for sympathy. Gareth felt hot. Avoiding Chester, he swivelled his eyes downwards to Rosie. She had turned to stone. Perspiration sheened her skin.

'How—' She gulped. 'How are we not div—' She lifted a hand. 'I sent you the— didn't I?' She sagged against Gareth. Reflexively he tried to loosen her hand to put an arm around her but she maintained her death grip.

'No decree absolute. Sorry Rosie.'

'I sent it to you! I'm sure I sent it!' Rosie's eyes darted around at them all, willing them to believe her. Gareth saw Keira flush hotly, her eyes on the floor.

'I didn't get it. I thought you'd changed your mind.' Chester smiled smugly.

'So my client is entitled to half the property,' said the woman who wasn't Keira.

'I don't know who *you* are, but you can get out of *my* house.' Rosie levelled a finger at the woman. 'And you!' She rounded on Chester. 'You can fuck right off. You abandoned us, leaving us in a, a *shell* of a house! Penniless! To pursue *your* dreams abroad! *I* finished this house! I worked my arse off with three jobs to pay for it, with a child still to feed and clothe *and* I did all the decorating myself – while my mother was dying here!' Rosie was magnificent. Gareth looked around him in admiration. She'd done all this? He looked up at the vaulted, beamed ceiling. The open-plan kitchen/diner/lounge was magnificent. And her daughter thought she was "*boring*"?

'I'm Mariette Arnold. Chester's solicitor. Have you kept receipts?'

'It wasn't a *shell.*' Chester spoke over her. 'You're exaggerating. And I didn't *abandon* you. You knew where I was.'

'*Somewhere in Spain* is not a location! Get. Out.' Rosie snarled. 'All of you. How fucking dare you, Chester. You fucking leech.'

'Half the property,' repeated Mariette Arnold, standing her ground as Chester edged towards the door. 'Plus any monies and proceeds from your late mother's estate.'

Rosie's hand snaked out and a kettle flew across the room in a blur of bright colour. It bounced off the door frame.

'Mind my hands!' Chester yelped.

'That does it.' Rosie tugged her right hand out of Gareth's grip and reached for a chunky ceramic dish on the worktop.

Chester ducked out. Mariette tried for a more dignified retreat, with the words, 'I'll be advising my client about the attempted assault on his person. You will of course be receiving all this in writing.'

'Excuse me.' Disengaging Rosie gently from the heavy dish, Gareth said, 'There was no attempted assault. That kettle went nowhere near him. He was never in any danger of being hit by anything.'

There was a snort from Rosie, pawing the ground like an enraged bull behind him. Gareth wouldn't like to bet on how safe Chester might be from further assault with a deadly kettle. The solicitor stalked away.

'God's sake, Mother. Could you be any more chavvie? I've never been so embarrassed. You, coming in here, dressed like that, with your … your—' She wobbled her head, mouth pursed, clearly searching for something in her vocabulary to depict her utter disgust with her mother, and finally came up with, '—your *twinkie!*'

Gareth raised his eyebrows. *Twinkie?* He said nothing. This wasn't his fight.

'Keira.' Rosie rested a level gaze on her daughter. Her

voice was the sort of polite growl a wolf might give before it gobbles you up. 'I think it's time you left.'

'I'm getting some clothes. And then I'm going back to Peck's.'

'Take them all, for all I care. And don't hurry back.'

Keira's chin sagged and then snapped back. 'What? It's not my fault Dad came over! I didn't know you weren't divorced! It's your fault for being a disorganised slag!'

'So I'm a slag now too, as well as all the other names you've called me?'

Keira's face flamed. 'I don't know what you're talking about.' She tossed her hair and stomped away. Gareth heard her heavy tread on the uncarpeted staircase. Reminded again of his little daughter when she was about three, he felt awkward in the middle of this family crisis. Should he make his excuses and leave?

It seemed only moments before Keira thundered downstairs and crashed out of the front door. Rosie sank onto a nearby chair. He didn't realise she was crying until the first, serrated intake of breath betrayed her.

Chapter Twelve

Her anguish poured from her eyes and constricted her chest. It was everything, all at once. Her mum, Keira, the disputed divorce from that shithead Chester and ridiculously, on top of it all, the bloody kettle.

'Oh Rosie.' Dismissing any thought of sloping off, Gareth folded her into his arms as if she was one of his children and let her weep. She felt him reach out and a tissue found its way to her. Blowing her nose lengthily, she nodded her thanks and turned away a little, getting up to drop it into the bin and snatch another from the box.

'I'm so sorry,' she managed, leaning against the table, blotting her still leaking eyes. 'The kettle was the last straw. It was a leaving gift from the girls in the school kitchen. It sounds mad, but I'd gone on and on about wanting a lime green kettle for the gas hob, and I was spending every last penny on the house, it seemed so self-indulgent. They wrapped it up in a huge box, and then a smaller box, you know the sort of thing. I'm sorry, it's stupid to be so upset, isn't it? It's not like it was rare or anything. I can get another kettle.' Trying to contain the childlike sobs that kept breaking out, she stared at it. 'Pity it didn't break over Chester's bloody head though.'

'I'd like to have seen that.'

'You were his biggest fan a few minutes ago. I thought you were going to ask for his autograph!' Rosie eyed him. 'Rubbish fake boyfriend you turned out to be.'

'Yes, I know.' Gareth slapped his forehead. 'I'm sorry. I don't know why I didn't connect the dots earlier. I'm an idiot.'

'I forgive you. He *was* – still is, I suppose – a pretty amazing musician. Now you see what I meant about the singing.'

'I still think you have a wonderful voice,' he asserted firmly. Rosie's mouth wobbled and tears tracked down her cheeks.

The open-plan room had been positioned to catch the view. Gareth gazed through the bifold glass doors.

'They were a pig to hang,' she said, following his gaze. 'I bought them cheap from a local guy after he made them the wrong size for a customer. And he'd gouged a chunk out of one of the doors. Didn't bother me.' She squared her shoulders. 'And of course, there are no receipts, as I paid cash.' She swept a hand around the house. 'I've scrounged, begged and bartered everything you see here. Skip-ratted. Bought on eBay or the free online sites. I had three jobs going on at the same time. I bartered months of ironing to pay for the plastering throughout the house, plus I cooked for people. Along with my job at the school. I catered and hosted a big anniversary party for the flooring. No questions asked, and of course, no receipts. Everywhere I look, there's a story behind everything. The kitchen – that was free, and I painted it.' As she spoke, waving her hands about to illustrate, Gareth inspected the stone-flagged floor, and the smoothly painted ceiling.

'It looks like one of those home magazines.'

'Do you want the tour?' She jumped up, unwilling to let him go and feeling guilty that she was being needy. He went along with her easily enough and she pushed her feelings of dread about the future aside. 'This bit is all open-plan, dining room and lounge – sorry, I sound like a bad estate agent, don't I? You can see it perfectly well by yourself. This is where I tend to live, really. I love seeing the sun go down over the sea. And it's cosy in the evenings with the wood burner.' She led him out and across a long, wide, flagged hallway, pushing open doors as she spoke. 'This is a little sitting room – Keira uses it a lot with her mates. It's a bit of a mess, sorry.' Having furious thoughts about Keira,

Rosie nearly shut Gareth's head in the door as he peered in. 'This is the downstairs bathroom. Mum paid for it to be made into a wet room and fitted out with everything she needed.' Adjacent to that was the bedroom her mother had used, and a guest bedroom which had been used by the overnight carer, when needed. 'The kids' bedrooms and mine are upstairs.' She hoped he wouldn't want to see them. Hers still had bare plasterboards, although the kids' had at least been painted. 'These rooms'—she indicated the doors further along the corridor—'haven't been done yet. I've been wondering whether to do bed and breakfast or something but I'd need to get them finished and wouldn't the cost of that cancel out what I'd earn? I don't know.' She shrugged. She couldn't get her head round it. Somewhere in the deep recesses of her brain, past the fog of not coping with what was happening, she realised that it was a good place for a B&B, sea views, separate sitting room, plenty of parking. But the thought of looking after other people? She just couldn't. She was running on empty. Barely looking after herself.

'So – how much of the house needs finishing?'

Rosie felt the heat rising into her face. She hated feeling ashamed of the house that she'd worked so hard on, but there was only so much she could do, and as her mum had become increasingly immobile, work had stopped altogether. Her stomach loosened at a sudden piercing memory of her, her mum and Keira emulsioning the big open-plan space over several long weekends and evenings, with loud music, laughter, picnic food and wine.

'Upstairs is – rudimentary. The bathroom works but it's not pretty. The rooms along there – I've done nothing to them at all. I keep the doors shut. Outside – there's my workshop.' She waved a hand that indicated the hopelessness of it all. 'I haven't touched the other buildings.'

'Other buildings? How big *is* this place?'

'Come and have a look while there's still light to see. There's only electricity in my part.'

Collecting a key from its hook, she led him through the back door, wincing as she saw with a stranger's eyes, the messy and unfinished utility area that led off the kitchen. Boxes and crates balanced precariously alongside boots and coats. Outside, there was a bit of patio, which had allowed her to wheel her mum into the garden, and then you had to hop over the broken bits of paving which acted as stepping stones. Gareth, with his long legs, had no trouble with this, she noticed.

'Excuse the garden.' Rosie tried not to look at the masses of frothy cow parsley and pink campion, that had all but swallowed up whatever blooms jostled heroically for space.

'The bees love all that,' Gareth said, with a smile. 'Don't tidy it up too much.'

Her workshop was furthest from the house, which meant they had to pass the unloved and untouched outhouses. Gareth eyed them up speculatively until she stopped and unlocked the workshop door.

'This is a good size.' Gareth walked inside, nodding, his face alight with interest. Rosie looked around too. She hadn't been in here for months now. Her eyes travelled over the plastic storage boxes of bright felt, twirled into balls, and her sewing machine, zipped carefully into its padded bag. The worktable, angled to catch the light from the window facing the sea, was still strewn with bits of material, paper, sketchbooks and photographs, pots of paints, pens, brushes and dyes. She itched to close herself away in there and push the world away.

'Chester designed it as his music room. Which'—she sighed heavily—'is why it has a better finish than the house. Insulated, and soundproofed. He'd even blocked over the window. It was like a cave in here. But he could get up in the middle of the night and come out here to do his thing without waking us up. Or the neighbours.'

'How considerate.' Gareth's voice was flat.

'Yeah. Tell me about it.' She felt fury flowering again. 'But at least I was able to take it over when he walked out. I'm looking forward to getting back in here again.'

'You mentioned jewellery on the way here. What is it you do?' Gareth's eyes were running along the boxes and she was surprised at his interest. Most men she knew would run a mile from things like wool and sewing stuff.

'It's wet felting.'

He shook his head, puzzled. She reached into a drawer and pulled out pieces that she'd already made, laying them on the table and smoothing them with her hand. Patches and strands of exuberant jewel colours fused and merged into a sturdy but pliable fabric. He picked it up, holding it to his eye, his expression mystified.

'I thought felt was that stuff you bought in coloured sheets for your kids to make hideous cards out of, and you have to look pleased when they give them to you. This doesn't look anything like that.'

'No. This is made from washed fleeces.' She bent and lifted the top off a box to show him. 'See how soft it is? It's combed so it all goes in the same direction. It's a long rope and you can break lengths off it, like this.' She teased out a length of emerald green and handed it to him. 'This is from the merino sheep, and it's used a lot because it's long, soft and strong, and dyes well. But there are loads of different types of fleeces.'

'How does it go from this to that?' Gareth was fingering the soft piece of fleece in his hand and holding the fabric she'd made in the other.

'Are you really interested? Or are you just feeling sorry for me?' Rosie eyed him. 'I'm okay, really. I know I had a bit of a meltdown, but I'll manage. I will. Thank you.'

'I'm sure you will. You're a tough lady, and I'm more than impressed by what you've achieved here.' He smiled at her, holding her gaze for a long moment, and her poor, battered heart gave a little skip before she lashed it back into place again. 'And believe it or not, I *am* interested. This is stunning. It looks like the colours of a frosty field when the early sun hits it.'

Rosie stared at him, open-mouthed. She swept her eyes over the worktable. 'Where did you read that? Did I tell you that?'

'What?' Gareth shook his head. 'No – sorry, have I offended you? I just said what popped into my head.'

'No. No! Not at all – it's just – that's exactly what it is. Those plums and siennas are the earth, and that pinky grey is the bits of stones you see, and the pale turquoise of the frozen blades of grass is here …' She slapped her forehead then. 'Of course. You're a photographer, aren't you? I remember.' She stared at him for a moment, and then opened another drawer. 'What do you think this was inspired by?'

'Easy.' Gareth held the piece to the window. 'It's the patterns made on the wet sand, when the tide comes in.'

'Bloody hell,' she breathed, looking up at him as he held her work in his long fingers.

'You could frame these,' he mused. 'What do you do with them?'

'I make some of it into jewellery, sometimes clothing, although that takes time and needs to fit well. Scarves, bags – I loved doing those. I'd got enough stuff together to start selling them and then …' She shrugged, her throat tightening. 'And then Mum.' She swallowed. 'I hadn't thought about framing them though.' She frowned, looking at them in a new light.

'You know the Art Café sell things like this. I've never seen anything this beautiful there though.'

'Lucy's lovely, she sent me a voucher for an afternoon tea!' Rosie remembered, suddenly. 'Do you think she would sell these for me?'

'What have you got to lose by asking her?' Gareth had opened more drawers and lifted pieces out with care to inspect. 'This is the sunset here. Beach again – and you've even got the seaweed in it.' She liked that he treated them so carefully, even though they were actually quite robust. It showed that he respected her art. 'Send her some photos and see what she says. If she says no, then at least you can still have a nice afternoon tea. At the very least, I bet she'll give you some feedback on them. She's always interested. She sold quite a lot of my photos.'

'Really? I might have seen them!' She frowned then. 'Sold, past tense? Aren't you still supplying her?'

'I haven't liked anything I've done for a while.' He ran his hand round his soft dark beard. 'Feeble excuse, I know. I need a kick up the arse.'

'Maybe we could inspire each other,' Rosie heard herself say. 'We seem to see the same sort of things ... and I haven't made anything since ... Mum ...'

Without hesitation, Gareth said, 'That would be brilliant. I'd love to!' His eyes sparkled with enthusiasm. 'Maybe the trip to see your fire engine will inspire both of us.'

'You still want to do that?' Rosie was surprised.

He was still for a moment, his gaze holding hers, and then he said, 'I can't think of anything I'd like better than to spend another day with you, Rosie.'

She fell into his liquid gaze, pulled in by his dark eyes, and stepped closer to him. He held out his arms and she found herself in them, with no recall of moving her legs. Her body vibrated with pleasure, and there was a buzzing in her ears. Gareth stiffened and reached into his jacket pocket.

'Oh drat – it's Hannah. It might be the kids. I have to—'

He pressed the accept button while Rosie stood there feeling like an idiot with her face lifted for the kiss that never came. She moved quickly to put the felt pieces away, trying not to listen to him saying, 'Hello? Hello, Hannah? Are you—? She's gone. Stupid phone.'

'Signal here is appalling. Sorry.'

Gareth swore. Looking apologetic, he made for the door, opening it to find Chester right outside. Rosie wondered if it was possible to hide under the table. She listened to the two men muttering insincere courtesies to each other for a moment and made a decision.

'Gareth, shall we go?' She collected his arm, tugging him outside and locking the door to her workshop in one fluid motion. 'Chester, what do you want?'

'What have you done to my music room?' He peered through the window, with an appalled expression.

'It's not *your* music room any more. You're the one who left. Did you think I'd keep it as a shrine?' Rosie tucked herself under Gareth's arm. It was proving difficult to do when Gareth was fiddling with his phone and they were both trying to hop over the badly spaced stepping stones. She gave up. Chester caught up with her and she walked faster. Why had he come back?

'I was worried about you,' he murmured, with one eye on Gareth.

'You haven't even thought about me in years, until you realised Mum had died.' Rosie spoke furiously and loudly. 'There's no money, by the way. But you're bloody welcome to all the debt.'

'That's unfair. Of course I thought about you. And you are looking mighty fit, if I might say so. Proper gym bunny. You always did have a great arse.'

'Fuck off, Chester. Don't even think about getting round me. You've never been short of female company, as we both know.'

'Aw, Rosie, don't be like that. You know what groupies are like. It always looks worse than it really is.'

'I know what I saw, you two-timing shitbag.'

'I don't like to think of you all alone in this great big house.' The light was fading fast now, and Rosie strained to follow the path.

'I've been all alone in this great big house since you left! I don't know exactly what the difference is now. You're so transparent, Chester.'

'But, you know,' he said, in his weaselly voice. 'I just walked straight in, through the house and out into the garden. You should be more careful. You never know who's lurking.'

She heard the crafty note in his voice, and felt her shoulders tighten. 'I am well able to look after myself, thank you. What would you do, hit any intruders with your saxophone? Rustle a music book at them? Whack them with your music stand? Don't make me laugh.'

Chester sagged like an old balloon. 'Rosie.' His voice went all pleading and she steeled herself. 'Please let me come home.'

Rosie marched past him and attempted to thread her arm through Gareth's. At the exact same time, his phone connected again and he whirled away from her, missing her completely. She heard him calling, 'Hannah. Hannah!' as he went through the house towards the front door, which slammed behind him in the draught caused by the back doors being open.

Chester smirked, following her inside. 'Looks like lover boy has other calls on his time.'

'Chester. Watch my lips. Fuck. Off. You are not coming home. You do not live here. And if you turn up again tonight I will call the police.'

As her legs fizzed with adrenaline, she watched him slouch through the house, *looking* at everything.

'Those kitchen cupboards are wonky,' he said, as he got to the lobby.

'Out!' She raced ahead of him, opening the door and waiting, glaring, as he sloped off.

'You haven't won, you know!' he yelled back at her. 'I saw this place first!'

'I'm double-locking everything, so don't even bother to try and come back!' she shouted after him, turning the key in the lock and shooting the bolt as she spoke. She ran back through the house and locked the back door too, then yanked the curtains across all the windows.

Panting with adrenaline, outrage and pure disappointment, she let out a long snarling howl. The house echoed back at her. She shivered. She really was alone.

Chapter Thirteen

The signal in the minibus was no better. Frustrated, Gareth rammed it into first gear and headed for home. The signal wasn't much better there, but at least he'd have a decent internet connection. His brain flicked back and forth between the various worst-case scenarios and he willed the bulky vehicle faster.

In between visualising unimaginable disaster befalling his children, he thought about Rosie. Where he would be a cool-headed man of action in a disaster, he was utterly confused by his feelings for her. Had Chester not turned up when he did, he was quite sure that he and Rosie would be, at the very least, in a hot-lipped clinch now. In that split second though, Chester's appearance had reminded him forcibly that he was still married to Rosie. And despite Rosie's vociferous disapproval of her errant husband, Gareth was well aware of how many changes of mind occurred during the divorce process. Chester was charismatic and talented, and what's more, their daughter Keira would be only too pleased to reunite them. He'd seen the expression on her face when Rosie was expounding her disbelief that they weren't divorced. She'd had a meddling hand in that somewhere, he'd lay money on it.

He arrived home to his little rented house, and as he parked he remembered too late that he hadn't yet delivered the minibus back to the hire company. Which meant he'd incur an extra day's charge. His loud curse was interrupted by the mobile ringing and he snatched it up, still in the driver's seat.

'Where've you been?' Hannah's voice shrieked in his ear.

'What's wrong? How are the kids?'

'The kids are fine.' She sounded irritated, but he was too

busy being relieved to care. 'It's Mum and Dad.' Her voice caught on a sob and Gareth instantly lost his impatience with her.

'What's happened, Han?' he asked, more gently.

'Road accident.' He heard her swallow noisily. 'They're both in hospital. Still alive, thank goodness, and conscious. We cut the holiday short and flew straight home when I heard. I'm going there tonight. Ian said he'll take me. You'll have to have the kids.'

'I'm so sorry to hear that. Of course I'll have the children.' His heart jumped at the thought of spending time with his kids, even while he was genuinely sorry to hear about her parents. They'd always treated him fairly.

Hannah was still talking. 'I don't have a choice. I can't take them with me, it's so far, where would they go and what about school?'

'Hannah, I said I'll have them. And it's half term still, and with the inset day ...'

'Oh. Yes.' She cleared her throat. 'Okay. Sorry, not thinking straight.'

'It's no problem. Do you want me to collect or are you dropping them over on the way?'

'We'll drop them to you. They're nearly packed.'

'Okay. I can always bring them over to collect anything they've forgotten.'

'We've changed the locks,' she said, flatly.

'I know that.' Gareth tried to relax his jaw. She was stressed, that was all. 'Perhaps you could loan me a spare key.' He could hear her talking to someone away from the phone. She had better not be asking that Ian whether he could have a spare key. Gareth took a deep breath, fighting down his irritation. His house, his children. Just not his wife since two and a half years ago. It was hard enough to ask for a key in the first place.

'When are you dropping them over?'

'Why, are you going out? Am I inconveniencing you?' Her voice dripped with sarcasm and he closed his eyes. He had toyed with the idea of returning the minibus to avoid the overdue charge. If he had to ask his parents to meet her he'd never hear the end of it.

'No. It's fine. Bring them when you're ready.' As she hung up, he couldn't help rewinding the conversation and wondering just why they always ended in this same passive-aggressive manner. It was as if she wanted to punish him still.

He rang the hire company to apologise. They said if he got it back to them before eight thirty the next morning, they'd waive the charge. If they were closed, there was a secure box at the entrance for keys. Thanking them, he turned on the interior light and his eyes swept the cab, checking for any possessions he'd stowed over the weekend. They fell on Rosie's rucksack and sleeping bag at the same time as his groping hand beneath his seat failed to locate the torch he habitually kept there. He'd left it at Rosie's. Aware of the little leap of pleasure that the idea of seeing her again gave him, he messaged her to tell her, but the signal had now dwindled to non-existent. Pushing open the driver's door, he recalled his headlong dash through Rosie's house with his phone held high, and was grateful for the cool air on his face.

Headlights appeared in the road towards the house. Had to be Hannah. They only lived a few minutes down the road, in the opposite direction to Rosie. He climbed down to wait for them.

'*Daddee!*' Lily had her nose and palms pressed to the car window and was pulling a face at him. He opened the car door and unbuckled her from her car seat, lifting her out. She threw herself at his legs, squealing with joy. He bent to hug the bits he could reach. Jack, a very grown-up seven, unbuckled his own seat belt even though he'd been told not to. He waited patiently for his child-locked side door to be opened by his mother.

Ian, Hannah's bloke, unfolded his long legs from the driver's seat of Hannah's "suitable for Yummy Mummies 4×4", bringing with him a bottle of spray cleaner and a mint-green microfibre cloth. His own car was some anti-social two-seater, Gareth recalled, still feeling irrationally irritable at seeing another man behind the wheel of the car that he'd paid for.

'Kids, eh?' he muttered to Gareth with a blokey, long suffering air, as he cleaned Lily's joyous smudges off the windows. 'Who'd 'ave 'em?'

Gareth's chest squeezed. *My kids*, he thought. And *he'd* have them. In a heartbeat. Jack appeared beside him, towing his and his sisters' Trunki cartoon cases that they were able to sit on. Gareth didn't recognise them, and fought down his jealousy that he hadn't bought them. Privately he decided that Jack was a bit too old for those babyish cases, but he couldn't fault the little boy's sense of quiet responsibility. He leaned down to give him a hug. Jack was stand-offish and stiff under Gareth's arms.

''lo Dad,' he muttered, standing slightly apart in an obvious attempt not to be as impulsive as his sister, currently pulling Gareth's arm out of the socket with excitement.

Hannah, collar of her smart coat pulled high round her slim neck, looked pinched and cold as she walked round the car to stand with Ian. Even in the velvet dusk she looked pearl white and the planes of her face were tense. Gareth wanted to pull her into his embrace and make it all better for her. The way he always used to be able to do.

'Any news?' he asked tentatively, and felt guilty as her face crumpled a little.

'Nothing.' She shook her head and dabbed her eyes. 'I'll text you from the hospital and where we'll be staying etc.'

Indicating the children, she became more prosaic. 'I've packed their school uniforms. Just in case I'm not back.'

Gareth tried not to wonder how he was going to juggle work and two children at home. Single mums managed it somehow. Ian dismantled the car seats and handed them over.

Lily was still attached to his leg as her mother blew kisses at them and they all watched, still waving as the car tail lights vanished from sight.

'Brrr.' Burdened with the car seats, Gareth put his cheery voice on. 'It's gone chilly – who wants hot chocolate?'

'Yay!' Lily, bless her, could always be relied on for a perky and positive response. Jack simply shrugged. Gareth's heart squeezed for his firstborn, and they trooped into his little house. Putting the kettle on, Gareth hunted through his cupboards, realising that he'd run out of hot chocolate. His mobile rang. It was Rosie.

'Hi, hello, I've got your big torch, and er, I'm so sorry, um, have you got my bags? Only I can't remember getting them out of the van and I've looked everywhere and I *know* I'm going bonkers and forgetting things lately but—'

'Stop worrying! I've got them, and I'm no better, leaving my torch behind.' Gareth continued the search with his mobile held to his ear. Hadn't he bought some recently? Had they used it all?

'Oh, phew. Sorry, I've gone on about me as usual. Is everything all right? The phone call?'

Gareth explained as succinctly as possible, given the two pairs of little ears nearby. 'Um, so, bit of a change of plan. I've promised hot chocolate and I've'—he lowered his voice—'run out – yes, I'm sorry Lily, silly Daddy, so I'm thinking, I'll drop your bags over to you and—no Lily, that's a tub of gravy granules.'

'You use gravy granules? I'm shocked. I had you down as a gravy-from-scratch man.'

'The kids don't like my gravy. Yes, thank you guys, I know you don't like it. You don't have to make faces.'

Rosie laughed at the sound of his children pretending to retch in the background. 'I've got hot chocolate. You can borrow it. Well, you know what I mean.'

'Really? Oh, thank you, we'll be over to you in a jiffy and we'll swop your bags for your drinking chocolate.' He laughed at how ridiculous that sounded. 'Road trip, guys!'

'Where?' Jack sounded sulky. 'I'm hungry.'

'You haven't eaten?' Gareth tried not to sound shocked but it was way past their teatime. Although they might have eaten and just forgotten. Or hoped to put off the inevitable bedtime.

'Road trip? Yay! Are we going to McDonald's for hot chocolate?' Lily's face lit up, and so for once, did Jack's. Gareth juggled his thoughts.

'Um, Rosie ...' he began. 'Sorry to be a nuisance, is your car drivable and does it have four seats? It does? Um, could I ask you a really, really huge favour?'

Chapter Fourteen

Headlights swept into the drive and Rosie flung open the door, zipping her jacket against the chilly evening, and glad that she'd changed out of the leggings and into jeans.

'Hello Rosie!' Three voices chorused at her from the minibus as Gareth opened the driver's door. He climbed out, carrying her bags, leaving the door open and the cab illuminated. She waved at the children, smiling as they waved back.

Gareth put the bags in her hallway and beamed down at her as she handed his torch over. 'Thank you. Are you sure you're okay about this? I could always order a taxi—'

'And miss out on a Maccy D?' Rosie felt her face smiling and remembered to fish her purse out of the rucksack and put it in her handbag. 'Everything in moderation, that's what you told me. Shall we go?' She stepped outside with him, locking the front door. 'To tell you the truth, I'm glad to go out. I'm on pins expecting Chester to waltz back in again.'

Gareth frowned. 'Would you like me to change the locks? I could probably do it tomorrow evening.'

'Isn't that illegal if ...' She lowered her voice, still shocked by the news, 'we're still married?'

'Only if you withhold a key from him. And maybe you just can't find it ...'

'Oh. Really? Then yes, please. If you're sure. Thank you. That's very kind of you.'

'One good turn deserves another.'

'I'm glad to hear that Motivational Man is alive and kicking.' Rosie smiled. 'So, I just follow you to drop the bus off, and then we all go for diet chips.'

Gareth headed towards the bus, where Lily and Jack,

still belted in, watched them. He looked back at her with a nod. 'That's it. You won't lose me. I'll be going slow. And it's really not far.'

Rosie sincerely hoped he was right. She blotted her clammy hands on her jeans and pasted on a cheery smile. 'Let's go!'

He turned back towards her and laughed. 'Diet chips?'

She winked and climbed into her car, trying to look devil-may-care and confident. The effect was spoiled as she stalled twice following the bus out of the drive and then shot into the road like a bullet out of a gun. Thank goodness there was no traffic. She unzipped her jacket and fanned her hot face, forcing herself to relax as she saw the big white shape of the minibus in front, and saw the brake lights illuminate as Gareth slowed down for her to catch up.

By the time they arrived at the van hire centre, her back felt as if she had a metal pole rammed up it. She was wearing her shoulders as earrings and didn't remember breathing even once during the entire journey. She prised her fingers off the steering wheel and massaged them to get some feeling back. Gareth appeared at her window.

'I just need to put the car seats into the back of your car. I'll go and get them now.'

She hadn't thought about those. It was a long time since her children were small enough to use them. And they'd walked everywhere anyway, hadn't they? She hoped Gareth didn't expect her to put them in. She climbed out, attempting to look useful and together and mainly to hide the fact that in her state of nerves she'd had a brain fade about which button opened the side window. Good thing the car had four doors.

She tried not to follow his long legs with her eyes as he loped back to the bus. It was slightly weird to see him in father mode after being with him all weekend in instructor mode. He lifted his little daughter out, and she recalled her own children at the same age. Lily held her arms up to him and planted a kiss on his face. His son scrambled out on his own, evading assistance, his drooping head contrasting with his sister's perky cheerfulness. He plodded behind her and Rosie wondered what was going through his mind. She'd always warmed to the little boys at the school. She always thought that little boys were like big dogs. They needed lots of exercise and food, and didn't always communicate their feelings as well as little girls did. Certainly, Keira had never had any problem communicating *her* feelings, however negative they were …

'These things are like those infernal puzzles you get in Christmas crackers.' Gareth rested the seats on the ground beside the car, leaving the children with her. 'I just need to check everything is out of the bus and drop the keys into the box. I'll be back!'

'Hello. I'm Lily,' announced the snub-nosed little girl with Gareth's dark hair and eyes. She held out her hand and Rosie, enchanted already, reached down to shake it solemnly.

'Hello, Lily, I'm Rosie. Pleased to meet you.'

'Pleased to meet *you!*' She indicated her brother with her head and said in a conspiratorial tone, 'That's Jack. He's sulking.'

'I'm not! Shuddup Lily.' Jack glared from beneath floppy hair that was a lighter version of his father's but identical in its soft, wavy texture. He was a mini clone of Gareth, his features rounded where his father's had grown angular.

Rosie decided not to get involved in the children's bickering and instead, as Gareth wrestled the booster seats into place, said, 'I don't remember the last time I had a McDonalds. What do you recommend?'

'You can choose from the screens. And pay for them there too,' Jack said. 'Did they have them when you were there last?'

Rosie blinked. 'No! Oh dear, I'm hopeless with technology. Don't real people take your order now?'

'Sometimes. If you don't have a card.' He made it sound as if it was the worst transgression he could imagine.

'Do you think you could help me?'

Jack nodded, his expression earnest. 'Don't worry, I'm sure you'll manage. A lot of old people do.'

'Oh. Thank you.' Rosie tried not to laugh, both at Jack and at Gareth's look of horror. He gave the car seats a hefty experimental tug and buckled his two charges securely.

'Ian says I'll be big enough soon not to need one of these,' Jack said. Rosie concluded from Gareth's briefly clenched jaw that Ian was the ex's current squeeze. She hoped for the children's sake that he was nice.

Gareth rubbed his hands together. 'Right, onwards to Maccy D! Do you know where you're going?' The question was directed at Rosie and it took her a moment or two to realise as her heart was pounding so loudly in her ears.

'Not. A. Clue. Would you like to drive?'

'Me?' Gareth frowned at her. 'But it's—' She watched understanding dawn in his deep brown hawk eyes. 'Would you prefer me to?'

'Yes, please.' Rosie was out of her seat belt and standing on his side of the car before he'd barely unclipped his own belt. She handed him the keys with a smile that she felt through her whole body. 'Thank you!'

'No problem ...' In the few minutes it took Gareth to adjust the driver's seat, mirrors and acquaint himself with the car's instruments, Rosie felt her blood pressure restore itself to normal. She breathed out slowly. Gareth turned the key in the ignition. The radio, windscreen wipers and heater blowers sprang into action on full volume and speed.

'Are we expecting rain?' Gareth enquired to a chorus of giggles from the back seat, as he switched everything off. Rosie couldn't bring herself to explain that she'd pressed everything in her panicked attempts to open the side window. She just laughed with the children.

'This car is like Herbie the Love Bug,' she said, twisting to speak to them. 'The car that was alive? Have you seen the films?'

The children looked mystified, shaking their heads with blank faces.

'Alive? Like Transformers?' Jack said.

'Um, no, not quite that high tech, to be honest, Jack.' Rosie faced forward again, feeling ancient.

'Tell me that *you* remember the Herbie movies ...' she muttered to Gareth.

'Not personally,' he said, straight-faced, pulling smoothly away. 'My gran told me about them though.'

'What?' Rosie stared at him, open-mouthed. 'Oh well, I mean, I wasn't born when they first came out, I was—' Out of the side of her eye she caught him grinning. 'Oh, you are mean! You're teasing me!'

'That was for sabotaging the car.' He cocked an eyebrow at her, and then checked the driver's mirror before indicating. At least, that's what Rosie presumed he'd planned to do as once again the windscreen wipers flew manically across the glass.

'Other side,' she murmured.

'Yes, thank you. I got that.'

'You don't know how to drive this car, do you Daddy?' Lily's piping little voice carried clearly towards the front.

Rolling his eyes, Gareth cancelled the wipers and indicated. 'I *do* know how to drive it, sweetheart. It's just strange to me, that's all. Not all cars are the same.'

'I still haven't got used to it,' Rosie confided. 'I'm always squirting water on the windscreen instead of beeping the horn. I spent ages trying to open the boot before I worked out that it was on the key fob thingy.'

'Silly Rosie,' said Lily, paying attention from her little perch in the back.

'Yes, very silly,' agreed Rosie.

'Don't be rude, Lily,' said Gareth, automatically. 'When people make mistakes it doesn't mean they're silly. We're nearly there now. Please make sure you go to the toilet and wash your hands properly before you eat.'

'Yes, Gareth,' said Rosie, smiling as she heard the children giggle.

Gareth put on a stern face. 'Yes, you too!'

'Yes Gareth!' Lily said.

'And it's Daddy to you, young lady,' he replied, mildly. 'Who can see the golden arches? First one to see gets to, er, order from the touchscreen!'

Rosie didn't want to show herself up on this new-fangled screen gadget so she inspected the contents of her bag instead. She was relieved when Jack shouted, even though Lily heartily disputed his claim.

'You can show me where the toilets are, Lily,' she said, in a mollifying tone. Gareth shot her a grin.

'Is this taking you back in time?'

'Ha, yes. My own and the kids at the school.'

'Are you a teacher?' Lily wanted to know, and Rosie was reminded how sharp children's hearing was.

'No, sweetie. I used to be a school cook. Do you and Jack have school dinners?'

'Yes.' Lily nodded emphatically. 'What do you work as now?'

'I haven't quite decided,' Rosie said, after a pause.

'Stop interrogating poor Rosie,' said Gareth, and then, seeing his youngest extricate herself from her car seat, added, 'and you're not supposed to be able to do that.'

'Ian says it's okay as long as the car has stopped.'

Gareth grunted and remained silent. When they were all out of the car, he locked it and handed the keys back to Rosie. She didn't take them. 'That's okay. You did a much better job of driving than I could have done.' She avoided his puckering forehead and headed quickly for the brightly lit entrance, where she was confronted immediately with the tall, colourful touchscreens headed "Order Here", as Jack had promised. He darted in front of her, importantly.

'Now, do you want a Meal?'

Rosie was confused already. Of course she wanted a meal. What else would she be here for? Jack's arm shot out and he pointed out the various options. 'And if you add chips here, see? That makes it a combo meal. And then you add a drink. What size, regular or Large?'

'Um ...' Rosie's eyes scanned the photos of the food.

By this time, Lily was hopping beside her. 'I'm having a Happy Meal. Look, it's there.' She pressed her option and Jack growled at her, reaching up to brush her questing fingers away.

'We're not allowed chips, Lily. And stop pushing in. *I'm* doing it.' Shielding the screen from his sister he tipped his head to one side, awaiting Rosie's instructions. Lily wailed, 'I want chips! Hate carrots.'

'You don't hate carrots, Lily.' Gareth's voice close behind made Rosie jump. 'What takes your fancy, Rosie?'

'I have no idea.' Rosie shrugged, still trying to make sense of it all. It was like stepping into a foreign land. 'What do you have?'

'The veggie wrap, usually.' He shrugged. 'Or the chicken salad.'

'I'll have that then.'

'With extra salad?'

'God no. Chips. That's a Welsh salad, you know.'

'Chips are full of fat, Mummy says.' Jack's tone was reproving.

'Did I say chips? I meant salad. Yes. Salad please.'

'Don't let them bully you, Rosie,' Gareth murmured in her ear. 'Stick to your guns.'

'Chips then. And a diet coke please.'

'Coke rots your teeth,' intoned Jack.

'Everything in moderation,' said Gareth to the little boy. Rosie smothered a smile. 'But it will keep *you* awake this late at night. So – juice or milk?'

'Milk, please.'

Rosie was led through the wonders of paying by card, despite Gareth insisting on footing the bill. Their order number flashed up on another screen above what used to be the order counter.

Following Jack's running commentary, they collected straws and napkins and little paper pots of different sauces, then colouring-in posters and pencils. They found a table that wasn't covered in the rubble of the previous occupants' meals and sat down to wait, in between the obligatory visits to the toilet. Girls first, then the boys, to reserve the table. Lily chattered throughout.

Jack industriously coloured in, tutting as Lily went over the lines. Rosie wished she'd picked one up too. Conversation in the hubbub of noise was tricky.

'I think these two will sleep tonight,' Gareth murmured, keeping an eye on their order number on the screen by the till, his voice only just audible over the background music and general chatter. 'Thanks so much for the lift.'

'You're welcome. And you drove, anyway.'

'You not keen on driving?'

'No.'

'Any particular reason why?' He was diffident, folding his paper napkin into an aeroplane. Rosie eyed the children, knowing of old how they could assimilate information without ever seeming to be listening.

'Constant criticism causes conflict.' She hoped it was a sort of code that he might understand.

'What's conflick?' asked Lily, casually. 'And critti thingy?'

'What's five plus two?' Rosie asked her, changing the subject.

'Seven of course. Easy-peasy,' Lily said, triumphantly.

'Clever girl. How about ...' Rosie pretended to think and gave the little girl several sums, most of which Jack answered first.

'*Ja-ack*! S'not fair!'

'Here's a hard one for Jack.' Gareth leaned forward. 'Two foxes, a badger, a ladybird and three rabbits are having a picnic. How many mammals are there?'

Lily gasped and looked at Jack with awed reverence as he thought and answered correctly. Rosie felt her mouth forming an O.

'Crikey. Don't give me any sums. I'm rubbish!'

'Rosie makes things like this.' Gareth held up the tiny mermaid made from felt that was attached to her car keys and Rosie saw Lily's face light up.

'That's so *cuuute*! Can you make me one?'

'Please, Lily,' Gareth prompted.

'*Pleeeeease?*' Lily's expression was heart-meltingly beseeching.

'I'm sure I could, Lily,' Rosie said. 'Although it's been a while since I made them.'

'Food's ready, I'll go.' Gareth jumped up and strode to the counter.

'Are you Daddy's girlfriend?' Lily wanted to know.

'Lil-*leee*,' growled her brother, lifting his head long enough to pin his sister with a furious scowl.

'No, sweetheart. I'm just your daddy's friend. I only met him this weekend.'

Undaunted by Jack's reproving glare, Lily continued, 'He likes you though. I can tell.' Jack rolled his eyes and huffed loudly. 'And can I have a mermaid with dark brown hair like mine please? And can I make one for Mummy? She has blonde hair and she's really pretty. We could have a whole family of mermaids. Are there mermen? And merdogs? I'd really like a puppy but Mummy says no.'

'I think mermaids might have fishes as pets. Or crabs.'

'Eww. You can't pet a crab! Ooh, here's Daddy!' She jumped to sit up straight with her hands out in front of her and knocked all the colouring pencils onto the floor.

'Lil-*leee*!' Jack scrambled down and banged heads with Lily as she climbed off her chair at the same time. Laden with a tray of red and yellow cardboard boxes, Gareth arrived back at the table to tears and bruised heads.

'I was gone for two whole minutes!' He shook his head and inspected his children. 'No one's bleeding. I'll get some ice. Sit still. Don't move.'

'I'll get it.' Rosie leapt up, forgetting that the seats were bolted to the tables and narrowly missed upsetting the tray of food. It lifted at one end and the children and Gareth chorused an "*aaargh*" sound. Rosie scurried away wishing she was eating her food in the car. Or at home. Silent munching had replaced whingeing by the time she'd ferried back a cardboard cup full of ice and a thick handful of napkins.

The meal was punctuated by, 'I'm dripping, Daddy. My jumper is all wet now.'

'Use another napkin. You can take the ice off now, anyway. You're fine.'

'I'm not dripping. You're making a fuss, Lily.'

'I am not! I'm not, Daddy!'

'That'll do. Nobody is dripping now.'

'Can I have more sauce?'

'You have plenty of sauce. Finish that first.'

'I got the wrong sauce. I wanted tomato.'

'I'll swop with you. Stop prodding your sister.'

'Can I have more salt?'

'No. Lily, stop waving that around and eat it, please.'

Rosie groped in her bag for some paracetamol. A headache hovered behind her eyes.

'Jack's got chips. Why couldn't I have chips?'

'He's got some of mine. Here you are.'

'Eurgh, what's that green thing?'

'It's a gherkin. And it's not in *your* food so stop worrying about it.'

'What are we doing tomorrow, Daddy?' Sucking hard through her straw, Lily squeezed her drink with both hands and the milk shot out of the lid, showering her and the table.

'Oh.' She stared at them all as milk dripped from her hair and chin. '*Sorreeee*.'

'Lil-*leee!*' Jack had got his reproving tone to a tee.

Lily's milk- and sauce-stained mouth opened in a silent wail that threatened much higher decibels on the next intake of breath.

Rosie fought down her instant nausea. 'I'll get something to clean that off,' she muttered, scrambling to her feet. Gareth got up and began to dry his daughter off with whatever he could lay his hands on while Jack pretended to be sick. Rosie knew how he felt. The smell of milk turned her stomach. It had since she could remember. She brought back a huge roll of blue absorbent paper and eventually, something like peace was restored.

'Uh, so, tomorrow?' Gareth replied to Lily's earlier question. 'You're coming to work with me.' Both children eyed him, silently. He added, heartily, 'And Nana and Grandad will be there, too.'

'But they're always busy!'

'And it smells of lorries all the time!'

'I know, sweetheart.' Gareth's voice was gentle. 'But your mum and me, we couldn't really plan this, could we? You were meant to be on holiday and …' Rosie saw their faces crumple. 'It can't be helped. I'm sorry.'

'I miss Mummy.' Lily's bottom lip trembled. Mouth breathing, Rosie reached over and patted her little pudgy, tomato sauce and milk daubed hand.

'I'm sure Mummy won't be away for too long,' she said, with absolutely no idea whether she was telling the truth.

'Perhaps we can video call Mummy before bedtime, if she has a signal,' Gareth said, without much conviction.

Nobody was more surprised than Rosie, to hear the words, 'Can I help out at all, with tomorrow?' All three faces turned to stare at her. 'I need to ring the solicitors first thing, but after that?' She glanced down at the children's colouring posters, and added, 'I could bring over a box of crafts and things to make ...'

'Could we make mermaids?' Lily's eyes were bright, her tears forgotten.

Rosie thought quickly. The tiny mermaid had been made using a technique that involved stabbing the wool fibres continually, with a long and horrifically sharp needle. She had plenty of scrap fabric and bought felt though. 'We could make bigger mermaids, how would that be?'

'Bring over?' Gareth said, his expression quizzical.

'To your place? Presumably, you would want to keep an eye on them, wouldn't you? I mean you don't really know me ...' She looked at their faces as they all stared hopefully back. 'Although, I'm fully DBS checked and everything. I have loads of space at mine, the huge table and a mountain of craft options. And you could ring the school for a reference.'

'So you've sat through the Armageddon of Happy Meals and you're offering to have them at your place?' Gareth blinked. 'Wow. Are you sure?'

His "wow" sounded more like "Have you lost your mind?" Rosie wondered that too.

'I'll pay you.'

'This one's a favour.' Rosie smiled. 'Have they got any allergies?'

'Sugar is best avoided unless you want them to climb the walls.'

'Got it.'

'What's your house like, Rosie?' Jack asked, his head on one side.

'It's huge,' said Gareth. 'And you can see the sea.'

'Wow!'

'It is huge,' Rosie said. 'Way too big for me now. And I'll probably have to sell it. So I'd better make the most of it while I can, hadn't I?' She smiled quickly to hide the lump that lodged in her throat.

Hello again Diary/Journal

I am so tired. It would be easier to hike up a mountain than fit another day in like this one. Was it really only this morning that I was still in the bunkhouse?

I'm still in shock that Chester turned up after all this time. I'm sure Keira has something to do with it. I don't know how but I can smell her guilt.

I'm going to be checking with my solicitor first thing. I wouldn't put it past him to be trying to fool me.

And, I'm telling you, Diary, if Chester hadn't reappeared, would I be on this sofa tonight on my own in my sleeping bag?

All I can say, is that there was a split second of total madness when time and life meant nothing and my lips would've met G's and ...!

I know it's a stupid crush. He's nice, he's handsome, thoughtful and sensitive and I actually really enjoyed being with him and his kids tonight. And G is great with them.

But he's a man nearly a decade younger than me, with his hands full of two small children, and two jobs. He does not have time for a relationship. And I've already brought up a family. Do I really want to be part of another one, with such young children? It's not as if I've done an amazing job with my own. They're cute kids though. I'm actually looking forward to having them over.

It was good to have something to do when I got home too. G made me promise that I'd ring and let him know I was home safe, even though it's only about half an hour away, which says a lot about what he thinks of my driving. I nearly died of embarrassment after I kangaroo-hopped out of his drive.

Anyway, I went into my workshop and packed up a whole stack of child-friendly things to make stuff out of. I really enjoyed poking about in there. I've missed it.

So here I am, snuggled into my sleeping bag on the sofa, with a mug of hot chocolate. And not because, Diary, I really do not want to be upstairs in my draughty bedroom, on my own. I'm not scared. If Keira was here then of course I'd go upstairs. But the sleeping bag reminds me of the weekend.

Closing the notebook, she sent a text to the WhatsApp group.

Missing you already, early night, sleep tight! XX

Replies came through quickly. Amongst others, *Night night Auntie Rosie!* from Leanne. Rosie replied with an emoji blowing a kiss. A direct message appeared from Leanne in quick succession.

Will be down to see you in next week or so if that's ok. Are you free?

Yes! Do you want to stay over?

That would be brilliant if I could, thank you. I can bring my sleeping bag if that helps.

Bring it anyway, but I'm sure I can sort something out. She glanced in the direction of the carer's bedroom and her mother's room. It was time to clear things out. *Looking forward to it! X*

Sleep was a long time coming, despite her weariness.

Chapter Fifteen

When the phone rang at eight thirty the following morning, Rosie was ready for it. Awaking rumple faced and slightly sweaty from the clinging confines of the sleeping bag a couple of hours earlier, for a moment she'd thought she was still in the bunkhouse. She'd showered and breakfasted, then cleared the big vintage dining room table ready for several hours of creative play. Having to boil water in a saucepan for the morning tea was a constant reminder, if she needed one, of Chester's unwelcome re-entry into her life.

'We'll be over for ten o'clock. Can I bring anything with me?'

'Yes, please – milk, whatever Lily and Jack drink. I don't have milk in the house. Ever.' She couldn't help her small shudder of disgust. 'Just the smell of it turns my stomach.'

'Ah. Oh. So, last night ...?' Into the pause in which Rosie, visualising last night's spilt milk, tried hard not to mouth breathe too noisily, Gareth said, 'No probs. Anything else?'

'Are they okay having sandwiches for lunch? Egg or tuna and mayonnaise or something? Or pasta? Egg on toast, jacket potatoes ... I haven't been shopping for a couple of weeks so it's whatever's in my cupboards—'

'You're ruining them.' Gareth laughed. 'And they're not shy about telling you what they'd like to eat. Just don't take any nonsense from them. They eat everything, at the moment.'

'Haha, they all start off like that and then they get picky.' Rosie took a deep breath, hearing herself chuntering on just to keep him chatting. 'I need to make *that* phone call now.'

'Good luck. See you later.'

Rosie's whole body tapped a staccato rhythm as she waited to be put through to her solicitor. She gazed out through the bifold doors, to the slice of shimmering sea that was sandwiched between the jigsaw of creeks and the blue of the far coast.

'Good morning, Mrs Bunting, how can I help you?'

Rosie gritted her teeth. That name was going to be the first to go. Why hadn't she done it earlier?

'Um, could you check that I'm actually divorced?' The whole sorry tale unfolded.

'Hmm.' The solicitor had listened in silence. 'It's not unusual for couples not to go through with the decree absolute, and I can see that we don't have one here, but we can sort that out for you. But it only ends the marriage – not your finances, so we'll need to work on those first if he's contesting them now.' She detailed the documents that she'd need and gave Rosie a date for a meeting. When she hung up, Rosie felt drained and useless. She'd failed. She hadn't even managed to get herself divorced. And the opportunity to look out over that wonderful view from her back garden was under threat. She googled estate agents on her mobile and arranged valuation visits from two local firms. Her mind drifted to the shameful pile of unopened and undealt with mail that had been shoved into a blanket chest in her bedroom. Her mother's bedroom also contained boxes of paperwork that needed to be sorted out, as she'd decided already that she'd put Leanne in there or the carer's bedroom.

This was a wake-up call. She really needed to get to grips with her life. She shook herself like a dog at the sound of gentle taps at the front door. She didn't have to pretend to look happy as she opened it to see Gareth, Jack and Lily there, all wearing what had to be their widest smiles, and in Gareth's case, carrying a litre bottle of milk.

'Good morning!' She stepped back and welcomed them into the big open-plan room. A wave of pride washed over her as she did so. The morning sunshine was just slanting into the room. It looked like a magazine shot. The bright cushions on all the sofas were plumped up and just so, the surfaces that were meant to sparkle did, and the tiled floor was neatly swept. The children stared around them curiously until their gazes fell on the heap of brightly coloured art supplies on the big table.

'Thank you for this, Rosie,' Gareth said, his mouth curving up in a delighted smile. 'What do you say, children?'

'Thank you, *Rosieee*,' they chorused, already investigating the boxes of pencils and sponges. 'What's this? What are we doing? Can we do it now?'

'First things first,' Rosie said. 'Let me show you where the bathroom is.' All three made a walking crocodile behind her as she led the way and Rosie laughed.

'Good plan,' Gareth said as they waited outside the bathroom door for Jack. 'He's at the age when he needs to investigate toilets wherever we go.'

'I remember that with Tom. Trains, shops, hospitals, everywhere, the toilets were a source of constant curiosity.'

'Hurry up Jack,' shouted Lily. 'I'm next!'

'You don't need to shout, Lily, and you went before we came out.' Gareth bent his head towards Rosie. 'How did the phone call go?'

'My solicitor seemed to think I'd changed my mind about being married to Chester,' Rosie said. 'This door can be unlocked from the outside by the way. The kids can't lock themselves in.' She shook her head. 'As if I would change my mind.'

'People do.'

Rosie shot him a sharp look. 'I won't.' She exhaled. 'But apparently, courts are reluctant to divorce couples who still have outstanding finance issues, so sorting the finances is our first priority.' She sniffed as helpless and frustrated tears brimmed on her eyelids. 'Sorry. I need to man up. Money isn't everything. As long as I have my health.'

'You're being very brave.' Gareth focussed on her. 'If there's anything I can do ...'

Jack emerged from the bathroom.

'Did you wash your hands?' Gareth enquired. Jack's eyes wobbled.

Lily said, 'He didn't. He doesn't. Mum is always telling him. Eurgh. He's minging.'

'That's not a nice word, Lily. Jack, go and wash your hands and I don't want to hear that Rosie had to remind you today, okay?'

Transported back in time to childcare of her own, Rosie eventually shooed Gareth away with promises of regular updates.

Once their father had gone, the children settled down, and happily cut out, drew, painted and stuck things for just over an hour before they became restless. Sending photos of their art works to their father, Rosie took them out into the garden where they spent the next hour hunting down bats and balls of all sorts stored in one of the outhouses, to knock about.

As a heavy football that had once belonged to Tom hurtled past her, Rosie reflected that her neglect of the flowers and plants was a godsend. Jack had quite a kick on him. But it was good to see him letting off some steam. An ancient Swingball gave him an opportunity to thwack something, while a well out of whacking distance Lily collected daisies to make a necklace. Or at the very least, a bracelet. For a doll, or something very, very small, seeing as Lily snipped the blooms off with her little fingers just beneath the head, and Rosie had to give her the ones with stems that she'd collected instead. She took more photos and pinged them to Gareth.

The mid-morning sun was surprisingly hot on her own freckled skin, and it wasn't long before Rosie moved them into the shade for a cool drink. The children's dark hair would give them a little more protection than she had as a redhead, but she didn't want to return them to their father glowing fluorescent pink, and there hadn't been any suntan lotion included in the bag handed over with them.

'Time for lunch!' she announced brightly. She ran through their options and was surprised and pleased that they both opted for scrambled egg and triangles of toast, which was one of her favourites too. It was also an easy way to occupy them both with Jack beating the eggs and Lily popping bread into the toaster and finding tomato ketchup. Even the argument about sauces didn't materialise. Either they were genuinely having a nice time or their father had beat them that morning accompanied by dire threats about their behaviour. Rosie was pretty sure that it wasn't the latter option.

She was considering the merits of boiling a saucepan in close proximity to two children she barely knew, for a cup of much needed tea, when a sudden draught lifted the children's drawings and scattered them all over the floor.

Rosie looked expectantly in the direction of the front door, expecting it to be Gareth, finishing work early and come to join in the fun. The smile was wiped off her face by the appearance of Chester. Carrying a large box, he strolled in as if he owned the place and Rosie felt her hackles rise. If she was a dog, she'd bark and chase him out of the house. Her stomach shrivelled as she realised he must still have his old front door key.

'Peace offering,' he said to her dumbstruck face, holding out the box.

'I don't want it. You can take it away with you now. Because you're leaving.' She bent to help collect the drawings that had blown beneath the sofas. The children fell quiet, shuffling the drawing paper and eyeing the newcomer. Rosie wanted him to leave, right now. She didn't want to introduce them to him. This was her life, and he wasn't part of it.

'It's not green, but I hope you like it.' Undaunted by her chilly reception, Chester lifted out a new kettle. Rosie stared at it. It was sunshine yellow, with a polished stainless steel handle. After all these years, Chester could still read her face.

'I knew you'd like it,' he said, triumphantly. 'And look'—he strode towards the cooker and placed it, just so, on the hob—'it belongs here already. Shall I make us some tea?' Rosie blinked mutely, her thoughts scattered, her instinctive reactions hampered by the presence of her young charges. He rinsed and filled the new kettle and turned towards his silent young audience. 'Hello, children. My name's Chester. Looks as if you've been busy today.'

Head down, Lily backed away and went to hold Rosie's hand. Rosie's heart scudded in her ribs at the feel of the little, trusting hand in hers. It was impossible to recall whether Keira had ever done that. Jack glowered at the newcomer. Rosie cleared her throat. She did not want a scene in front of the children. She filled her lungs and made her voice bright.

'This is Jack and Lily, they're Gareth's children. You met Gareth yesterday.'

'Ah. Gareth the new boyfriend!' Chester said in a sly way, and Rosie remembered too late the conversation she'd had with Lily the previous evening.

'I *asked* you if you were Daddy's girlfriend and you said no!' Lily's plaintive little voice showed that she was paying attention. Which was a nuisance.

'Well anyway, Chester is just about to leave. Aren't you, Chester?'

'Oh, well, no, not really. I thought I'd come and have a bit of a look round, seeing as I'm here. You just carry on with whatever you're doing, and ignore me.'

Pins and needles tingled in Rosie's fingers. How dare he just wander back into her life as if he belonged? Her pulse rattled in her chest like a tin full of marbles. Collecting the lunch plates, she stacked them on the kitchen worktop – she'd never been able to afford a dishwasher – and in a steady voice turned to the children.

'Would you like to do some drawing for a little while? I'm just going outside to speak to Chester.'

'I don't know what to draw!'

'That's my piece of paper. I wanted that.'

'When are we going to make a mermaid? I wanted to make a mermaid! You *said!*'

'This pencil has broken. Is there a sharpener?'

'I need a wee.'

'I feel sick.'

Clearly Chester's appearance had unsettled them all, and Rosie wasn't having that. She took a deep breath. 'Right, bathroom first, off we go. Chester, this is not the right time to have this conversation. Please leave.' Lily and Jack raced towards the bathroom, pushing and shoving each other. Rosie could see that it was an accident waiting to happen and took charge immediately, overtaking them and making it into a game.

'You always were a good mum,' Chester drawled behind her. 'But if the kids are bored, maybe we could make some music ...'

'They're not bored,' Rosie said, through gritted teeth. 'We were having a lovely day until you showed up.'

Chester pulled a thin silver flute from his inside pocket and Rosie's heart sank. Jack was agog.

'Wait until they've both been to the loo, at least.' Rosie fixed Chester with a gimlet eye.

'Lily! Hurry up!' Jack shouted. 'The man's got a—' He stopped, flummoxed, eyeing the instrument.

'It's a tin whistle. Listen.' Chester put it to his lips and Rosie saw Jack's mouth round into an O. It was hopeless to resist. The man was like the Pied Piper with any blown musical instrument. Teasingly, Chester lowered the flute and said, 'But it can wait until after you've finished.'

'And wash your hands, please,' added Rosie, shepherding him in and a wide-eyed Lily out. She added, through the closed door, 'We're not going anywhere, Jack. You don't need to rush!' Take as long as you like, she added, in her head. The less of an audience Chester had, the quicker he'd leave.

Chapter Sixteen

Finishing his jobs early, Gareth got into his car and drove to Rosie's. If the photos she'd sent were anything to go by, his children were having a lovely time, and he was going to have to pull his finger out somehow to entertain them for the rest of the holiday. He'd managed to shuffle his tasks about and delegate others so that he had some free time, but he couldn't just take days off without notice.

He'd rung the school she'd worked at first thing. She had offered it as a reference, in any case. It wasn't that he didn't trust her – he thought he was a pretty good judge of character – but because if anything happened, he'd have to explain himself to Hannah, and most of all, his health and safety brain wouldn't allow any other path to be taken. The school had been very complimentary about Rosie, which was good to hear. They even offered condolences for her recent loss. It sounded as if there could be a job if she ever wanted to return. He'd pass that on to her.

Could he ask her to have Lily and Jack again? He'd offered to pay her, and she'd turned it down, but he knew it was an imposition. She had her own life, and looking after two young children was a pretty exhausting prospect, especially when they weren't your own.

Before leaving that morning, he'd inspected the lock on Rosie's front door. He'd bought the appropriate replacement, and collected his tools together. There was no reply to his knock, but he could hear music coming from the back of the house. He smiled. It was a glorious day and he would be out with them in the fresh air too. The wooden door into the garden was a bit stiff but gave easily enough, and he strode through, hearing his children giggling, interspersed with the sounds of percussion and music.

Shading his eyes, he squinted to see his daughter wearing an unfamiliar wide-brimmed hat that kept falling over her eyes. She brandished a long wooden spoon, before a set of saucepans which dangled by the handles from the washing line. He smiled as he watched her nodding head counting the beat before she bashed each pan. Wearing a trilby and looking very natty, Jack faced away from him with a large metal sieve and a wooden backed scrubbing brush. As he watched, the little boy concentrated on making a sound with one side or the other and then bent to exchange it for a sealed tub which he shook to make another noise. A smiling Rosie sat cross-legged before a set of upturned plastic boxes. In her sunhat, with her auburn hair glinting in the sunshine, she looked beautiful. She was beating out a complicated rhythm with her hands. They really were having fun, and it was a good thing they had no neighbours, as the cacophony would drive a saint mad. The only melodious sound was the flute. It played again, and at first, he thought it must be from a recording of some sort. Until he stepped further into the garden.

Rosie saw him first and her drumming stopped instantly. She scrambled to her feet, smoothing her hair, and walked towards him, her smile uncertain. His children, concentrating on their tasks, were a little slower to react. And Chester, the flute player, was oblivious. Eyes closed, his fingers flew along the little holes in the instrument, and the strains of a Celtic tune carried in the warm air.

'*Daddeee*!' Lily had spotted him. Oblivious to Chester's virtuoso flute playing, she randomly bashed the saucepans and Gareth winced. Chester turned towards him, still playing, and gave a little bow. Gareth wanted to bash him like one of the saucepans. What was he doing there? With his children? This man who was still married to Rosie and who in his view, did not deserve her at all.

Jack turned at Lily's shout and scraped the scrubbing brush over his own hand.

'Oww-er!' He burst into tears and Rosie got to him first.

'Ouch, let's run that under the cold tap. Nasty scrubbing brush!' She hurried him towards the kitchen, leaving Gareth facing Chester like a pair of gunslingers. Lily skipped towards him.

'Daddy, this is Chester. He's been playing a magic flute and we've been his band! Do you want to join in?'

'What else have you been doing, sweetheart?' Gareth did not want to join Chester's band, thank you very much.

'Both your children have excellent natural rhythm,' the man said, strolling over the grass with his hand outstretched. 'We've been having a bit of fun this afternoon, haven't we, Lils?'

Lils? The little girl gave a whole body nod, and Gareth clamped down his jealousy. He should be appreciating the time that this musician, whom he had admired enormously until yesterday afternoon, had given freely to his children. He loosened his set jaw and shook the proffered hand.

'Thank you for giving them some of your time. It looks as if they've enjoyed it very much.'

'It's amazing what can be done with a few household objects. Children don't need expensive toys. Just a bit of time, usually.'

Gareth forced his legs to walk towards the kitchen, and his son. How dare this patronising dickhead suggest that he didn't spend any time on his children? And from what Rosie had told him, he'd had precious little to do with his own children. Pulling on his arm, Lily skipped happily, tugging him towards the table and down to sit.

'Look, we did this, and this.' She chattered happily, holding up drawings and writings and sums and puzzles and folded things that looked as if they were meant to be birds of some sort. Rosie was drying Jack's hand gently, blotting his eyes at the same time.

'I'm okay. Thank you Rosie,' said the little boy politely, regaining his composure.

'Not at all, sweetheart. It was an accident. And look, no damage, but it probably feels sore, doesn't it? Shall we have a look for something nice to have with a cold drink, what do you think?'

Jack nodded, holding her hand as she went to the cupboards to search. Gareth, still being harangued by his daughter for approval of her efforts, watched them out of the corner of his eye. Rosie was very good with them. But how long had Chester been there? He had not been part of the arrangement. Although he hadn't specifically said, do not invite your ex-husband over for the day. And as Rosie had offered to have them, did he have the right to control who else was there? Reluctantly, he decided that he didn't.

Clamping down on the surge of jealousy that Chester had been here, sharing quality time with Gareth's children and Rosie, instead of Gareth himself, he responded to Lily.

'Lovely darling! I like all these colours.'

'Rosie likes colours too. Chester bought her a new kettle. He said it was a peas off ring, or something. It's really pretty. It's yellow. Look!' She whirled and pointed with her hands full of pictures and several of them slipped onto the floor. 'Oops!' As she scrambled to collect the paper, Gareth's eyes travelled towards the very handsome new kettle. A peace offering. And not rejected, judging by its proud position on the hob. Why hadn't he thought about buying a kettle?

He had no right to feel jealous. Maybe Rosie still had feelings and hopes for her marriage, and had subconsciously avoided processing that decree absolute. Who was he to get in the way? Might he and Hannah still be married if Ian hadn't got in the way?

Thoughts clattered around his brain. But he hadn't fought for Hannah. Wallowing in the guilt that had dogged him since his brother's death, he'd accepted that everything was his fault, that she would be better off with someone else. And she had been, hadn't she? Ian was a bit of a fusspot, but he bought the children things, and took them on holiday, and the fact that Gareth's life had remained a hollow shell wasn't Hannah's fault.

The creeping knowledge that Rosie was the first woman he'd met in ages who lit even the tiniest spark in his heart, tapped insistently in his head. He couldn't help how he felt.

He put an arm around his son for a hug as Jack joined them at the table, bearing a tin of brightly wrapped biscuits. All of them bore the words, "diet" or "sugar-free" in one form or another. Gareth looked up to find Rosie, carrying tumblers of milk, looking directly at him. She placed them carefully on the table.

'I know what you're going to say. Those were Mum's. I don't think she ever ate a biscuit from a normal packet. I can't bring myself to throw them out. They're still in date.'

'I was going to say thank you.' He smiled as the tension left her face. 'A friend of mine has shown me the error of my ways, and I'm cutting down on my chalkboard psychology.'

Lily stared at them, open-mouthed. 'What's chalk-chalk—?' She gave up and laughed with them. 'Chester said you were Rosie's boyfriend.'

'Did he?' Gareth smiled at Rosie, who was blushing. 'I wonder where he got that idea from?'

'Sorry,' she mouthed. He smiled back at her with a tiny shrug and even as he did it he wondered what exactly it was meant to convey. That he wouldn't mind being her boyfriend? Apart from the obvious flaw that she was still married and her husband was in her garden ...

She was close enough for him to feel the warmth of her skin against his shoulder. The children were leaning across the table, raking happily through the assortment of biscuits, and Gareth turned towards her, his mind photographing her creamy skin, scattered with new freckles.

She leaned towards him. Her smiling green eyes, her soft pink lips, her scent ... her head lowered towards him as his chin lifted for their lips to meet ...

At the same time as Chester said loudly, in a "don't mind me", way, 'I'll put that kettle on again, shall I?' Leaning against the counter, he picked up two spoons and played them with his hands, a bright, fast and clever percussion. Gareth felt his jaw drop and wasn't at all surprised to see his children jump to attention, expectant smiles on their faces.

'No, thank you, not for me,' Rosie said, firmly, standing up straight. Gareth stood too, mainly to look authoritative but also so that he'd be able to see if Chester did the spoons thing again. It wasn't his proudest moment.

'Thank you for the kettle, and for entertaining us this afternoon.' Rosie squared her shoulders. 'The children had a lovely time. It's time you were off though, I think?'

If Chester was at all crestfallen by his dismissal, he didn't show it. 'That's okay. I know where you are. And you don't have a job so you'll be easy to track down for that little chat, won't you?'

'Where is your car parked?' Rosie asked. She seemed so calm, but Gareth could see the tension in her face. 'I didn't hear you arrive.'

Chester made a casual gesture with his head. 'I'm just up the road.' He accompanied his words with a flourish of spoons, running them at quicksilver speed along his fingers and up his arm. Lily and Jack clapped wildly. Gareth was going off the spoons trick and wondered why he hadn't parked in the driveway. There was plenty of space. What was he hiding?

'I'll walk you to your car. You can tell me what you came to tell me then. Shall we go?' Rosie took his arm and to Gareth's surprise, Chester turned to leave.

'Bye Lils and Jacky boy! Keep practising!'

'Bye bye!' called Lily and Jack, waving from the table.

Chester clicketty-clacked once more with the spoons before Rosie yanked them out of his hands and hurled them into the sink. She escorted him into the garden.

'Back shortly,' she called over her shoulder. 'Help yourselves to anything you want.'

'*Awww*,' said Jack, when they'd gone. 'He was fun. I hope we see him again.'

Gareth had to stop himself huffing. He was quite sure they hadn't seen the last of him. The sooner he changed that lock the better.

Chapter Seventeen

'What is it that you want, Chester?' Rosie folded her arms and faced him. Her fingers and toes tingled and her ears rang. 'Cut to the chase.'

'Rosie, Rosie, Rosie. Being so hard-faced really doesn't suit you.' Tipping his head on one side he gave her his practised sad smile and moved towards her. She stepped back. 'This afternoon was like the old days, wasn't it? We had some great times, didn't we? And you know'—he reached a hand up to her face and she jerked away—'when the decree absolute didn't arrive, I thought, well, y'know, Rosie's probably lonely now that her mother has gone, and maybe she wants to make another go of it.'

Rosie felt her jaw drop. The cheek of the man. 'Let me fix that sentence for you. You thought, Rosie's a soft touch. Now that her mum has died, what can I get out of her? Does that sound closer to the truth?'

Chester's eyebrow twitched upwards and Rosie knew she was on the right track. 'Well, look, you've got all this'—he waved an arm back towards the house—'and I'm ...' His eyes flicked towards a battered grey transit-type van parked half on the verge fifty yards away. Rosie followed his gaze. Chester had always preferred a van rather than a car. It meant being able to transport instruments, speakers and whatever paraphernalia his current musical partners required in order to fulfil a gig. Plus somewhere to sleep over when needed. Was he trying to insinuate that he was sleeping in it now?

'I've got all these *debts*, yes.' She pointed at the house. 'And a house that's only habitable in parts.'

Chester's brow puckered. 'What do you mean, parts? Those bedrooms off the hall looked really smart. And the open-plan kitchen lounge is—' He shrugged. 'Your mother paid for all that, I suppose.'

Rosie could barely speak. 'You're unbelievable,' she managed, eventually. 'My mother's funeral was *last week*'. She swallowed down the lump that formed whenever she mentioned it and glared at him. 'You couldn't be bothered to get back in time for that but you've had a good snoop about to try and work out how much you can get out of me – I suppose that was Keira's doing, and clearly, she didn't take you upstairs, didn't you wonder why? Did you really think I've done nothing since you've been gone?' She uncrossed her arms and planted her hands on her hips. 'And where did you get the idea that Mum paid for everything?'

His eyes slid away from hers. He mumbled, 'She was rolling in it, last I saw. *Heard*.' He corrected himself quickly. 'Last I *heard*.'

'How would you know? You never spent any time with her. You were never here! You left me to be a full-time carer to her. What happened to "in sickness and in health"?' The sun beat down on Rosie's shoulders and her skin burned. 'And Keira was devastated when you left. How could you?'

Chester fidgeted. 'Me and Keira are fine.' Realising that she didn't have a clue about her daughter's relationship with him, clearly better than her own as she presumably hadn't wished *he* was dead, Rosie took a different tack as another thought struck her.

'If you're entitled to half the house, then I'm entitled to half of whatever property and investments you've made while you've been abroad.' Chester's startled expression almost made her laugh. Surely, he couldn't be that stupid? How could he have thought this was a one-way street? Did he really think it was all take, take, take? Adrenaline coursed through her.

She continued without pause, 'Well, never mind, I'm sure your "solicitor" will advise you. If she really *is* a solicitor.

You must be paying her well for her to come out with you on a house call like she did. And if you've got enough to pay her well, then half of that money is mine, I think you'll find.' She watched his face working but other than a noisy swallow and a glower, he remained silent. After a long moment, she turned to go.

He said, loudly, to her back, 'You must get lonely in that big place. Is it safe for an older woman, all alone? You need to watch yourself.'

There was nothing caring about his tone, and it was the second time he'd said something similar. The smiling musician of the afternoon had gone. His words hung in the hot, still air. Rosie's legs stopped moving. One more step would pitch her forward onto numb hands. She clutched her throat.

Turning on her heel, she glared at him. 'How dare you threaten me! Don't come here again, you shit!' Her voice wasn't nearly as strident as she would've liked and he strode away, showing no signs of hearing her. She steeled herself not to watch him leave. He liked an audience. Today, she'd watched him transform, before the adoration of Lily and Jack, into the Chester she'd very first met. There had been a moment when she'd mused wistfully on what life might be like if they got back together. It made her feel dirty.

She licked her lips. Was it too early for a glass of wine? Because she definitely needed one right now. She stalked back on legs that felt alien to her to where Gareth and the children were clustered at the front door. She wondered if they'd heard.

'Daddy is fixing your lock,' said Lily, in her important voice. 'And we're helping.'

Gareth glanced up with a look of apology. 'I thought I should—Oh! What's up, Rosie?'

'Excellent timing. Thank you so much, that's really kind of you.' She wiped the tears that wet her cheeks and surprised her. 'I'm fine. I'm just angry, that's all.'

'Are you sad that the music man has gone, Rosie?' asked Lily, kindly, holding her hand.

'No sweetheart, I most definitely am not sad that he's gone.'

Lily pondered the double negatives and settled for an, 'Okay.'

'So, can I help with this at all?' Rosie was in dire need of a distraction. And company.

'Not really. I won't be long.' Gareth's expression was sympathetic.

Desperate to talk it over with him, but not in front of the children, Rosie hovered, feeling like a spare part. Adrenaline hurtled through her veins. She marched into the kitchen, washed up with furious energy and filled the hated kettle with water to make tea. That kettle would have to go. It would shout his name at her every time she saw it.

When Gareth came to find her, she'd tidied the children's artwork into two neat piles, and put all the craft supplies back in the box. Gareth held out the keys and folded them into her hand. She stared at them, unable to stop the tears that plopped into her palm.

'Take one off now, and put the spares somewhere safe and out of the way.'

Lily and Jack were inspecting their pictures and fidgeting. It was time they had their dad to themselves.

'Thank you. That's a really kind thing to do. How much do I owe you?'

Gareth's face was gentle and she couldn't bear it. She much preferred the lustful expression of earlier when their lips had almost met before bloody Chester had barged in and hogged all the attention as usual.

'Let's call it part payment for you entertaining the kids today, shall we?'

'They were a pleasure to have. Honestly.'

There was a pause, when Rosie felt they both had things to say, but somehow couldn't.

'I'd invite you for dinner, but we're booked in at Nana and Grandad's tonight ...' He smiled, ruefully. 'And I need to clock up the brownie points to get some time off with the kids.'

Rosie nodded, stretching her face into a smile. 'Thank you, but I've got lots to get on with.' She forced a bright, carefree tone. 'It was Mum's funeral only last week and I've been away since, on a changing-my-life weekend, doncha know, and I've got some eye-watering leggings to wash, a pile of admin, and other exciting things like that.'

Gareth wasn't convinced, she could see. His dark brown eyes rested on hers for a long moment.

'If you need anything, you know how to get hold of me. And I haven't forgotten that we need to visit the you know what.' He bent swiftly and left a light kiss on her cheek. Rosie's stomach skipped with lust. 'Lily, Jack, we're leaving now. What do you say to Rosie for your lovely day?'

They both chorused a well-practised '*thaank yooo Rosieee*' and gave her a spontaneous double hug which made her eyes water.

'Hope to see you again soon!' she called, dabbing her eyes surreptitiously as she waved from the front door until they disappeared from view. She went out and scanned the lane in both directions. No grey vans. Closing the front door, she turned the new key in the lock, and then did as Gareth suggested and slid it onto her mermaid key ring, slipping the old one off at the same time and tossing it in the bin. She hid the other two separately. It made her feel anxious that she was having to do this, and she wondered what Chester's reaction would be when he realised he didn't have access the next time he tried to saunter in. Keira would just have to come in when Rosie opened the door to her. She was very far from forgiving her daughter for her perfidy.

She slid the stiff and barely used bolt across the back gate, and collected up the items the children had played with in the garden. Rotating a selection of her favourite female singers on the bulky and now old-fashioned music centre, she set to sorting out her washing, hoovering and clearing up the mess that lay untouched since the funeral.

Hunger pangs caught her by surprise. The contents of her fridge, freezer and cupboards yielded a jar of pesto, a lump of parmesan and some dried pasta, and she threw it together in a few minutes. It was a far cry from the handmade and delicious pasta of the weekend. Pouring herself a large glass from the bottle of wine she'd brought back unopened from Brecon, she took the bowl of pasta to the big dining table, opened her pink journal and started a list.

Complete divorce.
Sort out mail.
Clear out Mum's room.
Make stock and ask Lucy, Art Café to sell it.
Fire engine.

It was some list. She closed her mind to the knowledge that each item it contained was in fact a heading, representing even more time and energy. Nobody else was going to do any of the things for her, and the sooner she got to grips with it, the better. She couldn't face paperwork right now. Not that it had ever been her thing. Her body fidgeted with pent-up energy. It was time to tackle Mum's bedroom.

Chapter Eighteen

While Jack and Lily hugged their grandad, Gareth wandered into the kitchen in search of his mother, Carol.

'Can I help?'

'Hello, darling.' She tilted her face so that he could kiss her cheek. 'No, don't worry. I'm faking it, as usual. You know how terribly busy we've been.' She waved an arm at the packets which lay discarded on the counter, from which Gareth deduced they were eating lasagne and garlic bread. Two plastic bowls of salad joined them from the fridge. Gareth opened his mouth to say that he could have cooked and shut it again. He knew better than to suggest such a thing.

'I brought wine. One of each.' Opening the fridge, he stood the bottle of white inside the door.

In her early sixties, his mum was still slim and smart and showing no signs of slowing down. His parents worked harder than anyone he knew, and never complained about the six thirty morning starts and long days. Guilt about his own truncated day gnawed at him, despite the fact that he told himself it had been because of Lily and Jack. Or had it been the desire to see Rosie?

'Have you heard from poor Hannah?'

'Briefly. She video messaged the kids last night. Her parents are more or less conscious. Whiplash, concussion, her mum has a badly broken leg and other injuries, and her dad has a head injury from something that went into the car or was in the car, I didn't quite get that. Possibly chest injuries? I haven't got all the details but I think she'll be down there for at least the rest of the week. Probably longer.'

'What about their work?'

There we go. It was always about work. He shrugged.

'They were all in Spain somewhere until yesterday so I guess they're still on leave.'

'And the children are on holiday this week. What arrangements have you made? Can you lay the table, please?'

'There wasn't time for me to "make arrangements", Mum. I'll have to take annual leave.' He piled the dinner plates together and counted out the cutlery. 'What else can I do?'

'What did you do with them today?'

Do with them? As if they were a pair of dogs that needed boarding? 'A friend looked after them.'

His mother shot him a look. 'A friend? Who is this friend?'

'A lady from my course this weekend. She's very nice and she happens to live quite close. And she offered.'

'Did she indeed? Does she have children too?'

'She does. I'll just go and—' He tried not to hurry into the dining room. His father was holding the children's attention in a simple game of Snap, and Gareth smiled as he laid the table around them.

At the dinner table, once Lily and Jack had been supervised for toilet and handwashing, his mother said, 'Did you have a nice day today, children?'

Lily nodded, dropping her cutlery to the floor in her enthusiasm and making Jack laugh. Gareth went to the kitchen to wash them. Returning, he overheard Lily holding court about drawing and kettles and how they didn't make a mermaid because the music man came but Rosie had said they could do it another day and did his mother think there were mermen and merdogs?

'Goodness me. Who is this music man?'

Jack said, breathlessly, 'He showed us how to make a beat, and we used—'

'I had saucepans! In the garden!' Lily interrupted, earning a scowl from Jack.

'And he could play the …' Jack dried up, frowning.

Gareth, standing behind Lily and using her clean knife and fork to cut her food into smaller pieces, squeezed his shoulder and supplied, 'Flute. He played the flute. And the …?' Gareth prompted, without quite knowing why.

'Spoons!' yelled Jack, desperate to get in first. 'He played the spoons! Can I practise playing the spoons, Daddy?'

'Maybe later,' Gareth promised. It was great to see Jack so animated, but annoying that it was Chester who had inspired it.

'Goodness me,' repeated his mother. 'How lucky you were. Did your friend hire this music man, Gareth?'

'Not exactly.'

'Rosie isn't Daddy's *friend*,' said Lily, scornfully.

'Oh?' His mother leaned forward, her expression interrogative.

'Rosie is Daddy's girlfriend!' Lily chortled with delight, staring round the table at them all.

'I see.'

Sitting back at his place, Gareth eyed his mother, waiting for the inevitable interrogation. He had a sudden memory of Rosie popping a paracetamol during the McDonalds Happy Meal and he wished he had one too. He caught himself fingering the scar on his face. He could never forget what had happened. He only had to see his reflection in the mirror to be reminded.

He wished his mother would just go for him. Shout and scream that he'd taken their oldest son. The one who really loved the family business. Whereas he not only preferred running these courses which paid him peanuts really, but he hadn't even been able to keep his wife. Yet she remained strung as tight as a rope on an abseil.

The analogy brought his mind straight back to Rosie,

and their shared eye contact as he'd urged her over the edge of the cliff. Since then, he'd thought about her non-stop. Seen so much of her, and had his parents not issued the "come for dinner" edict, he would probably have been cooking her and the children a handmade pasta this evening which they could all have made, maybe with some simple poached salmon and crème fraiche, a salad and a glass of chilled white wine. Although there was no room in his little house for her to stay over, so she might have had to ...

His mind snapped back to the present as his mother said, 'Well, if she's so wonderful, this Rosie, can't she look after the children for the rest of the week? And you can carry on working. Doesn't *she* work?'

'She's been a full-time carer for her mother for years.' He saw his mother's eyes hood over and said, firmly, 'Sadly, her mother died recently. It was the funeral last week. Rosie is exploring the idea of being self-employed.'

'How *interesting*.' How did she make it sound as if it was the least interesting thing in the world? She'd somehow crushed the idea of Rosie's ambitions as small and silly. Not big business like the haulage world. 'So is she qualified in any way?'

His father leaned towards them. 'The HGV that came back from Newcastle today has lost a strapping clip. And the driver—'

'Is that Blethyn?' interrupted Gareth, keen to jump off the track of his mother's cross-examination. 'Yes, he mentioned the sidelights needed sorting too, and it's due for MOT end of the month. I've put it on the schedule already.' He knew his father was already aware that he'd attended to it, and guessed he was also heading his mother off at the pass. He thought desperately of a subject that would interest both them and the children and somehow the words spilled from his lips.

'One of the ladies on my course this weekend has

inherited something unusual.' He had been about to mention the fire engine but had to explain inherited for the children, and that led to a detour about how their haulage firm had been passed down since 1935 from his great-grandfather. His mother jumped up to show them photos and to his surprise, she began to tell them some stories of the company's history.

'We didn't have big shiny lorries then, like we do now,' she said. 'Look – I know the photo is in black and white, but can you see how different they were then?'

'They're not so high,' said Jack, nodding. Lily, seeing as there were no mermaids or her current crush, unicorns, stared at the photos and said nothing.

'That's right.' Carol nodded. 'And do you know what the highest, the tallest thing we ever transported on our lorries was?' The children shook their head wide-eyed. 'It was a giraffe!'

Gareth had heard this story a gazillion times. It was still a tale worth telling though.

'The giraffe had to go from where he lived, in a zoo up north, to another zoo down in Kent, which is a very, very long way away. It meant going under a lot of bridges. And are giraffes very tall?'

'Yes!' squeaked Lily, eyes alight, food forgotten. 'We did giraffes in school. They're up to here!' Springing off her seat, her hand stretched to the sky, she tipped her dinner so that it slithered onto the polished dining table. 'Oh!' She stared down in dismay, her eyes flicking to her grandmother's steely gaze. Gareth and his father jumped up, scooped the food back onto the plate and wiped the table down in an instant, wiping Lily's tears at the same time. They high fived each other and transported the plate and debris into the kitchen. Carol cleared her throat, and clearly decided the story was the better option. Gareth, with relief, heard her continue as if nothing had happened.

'We had to build him a very narrow crate so he couldn't fall over, because they can have heart attacks and die. So how do you think the giraffe was able to go under the bridges?'

'I don't know!' chorused Lily and Jack.

'Well. The giraffe's keeper – that's the man that looks after him. A sort of carer, really ...' Gareth heard her from the kitchen and stiffened.

'I don't know if there's any pudding,' said his father, Cled, making a show of hunting in the fridge.

'Don't worry, Dad. I know what she's like. It doesn't matter.'

'I'm sorry, lad.' Cled lifted his hands and dropped them again. Gareth had only ever heard his father speak lengthily about the lorries he loved and lived for, never about his own feelings.

'Did you always only want to work in the family firm, Dad?' Gareth knew the answer already. Historically, the boys in the family took over the haulage company. And Aled, the elder son, had been the shining light. 'Only I was wondering, whether there's any way that I could step back a bit, you know? Still be involved,' he added hurriedly, 'but have more time to pursue my ideas for the courses that I do? Maybe set up my own business?'

Cled's firm mouth compressed in a line, but kindly, as if he knew what was in Gareth's head. Gareth wished *he* knew, too.

'Shall we go back for the rest of the story?' Cled squeezed his arm, and Gareth allowed himself to be led back into the dining room. He'd sown a seed. Maybe his father would consider it.

'So,' said Carol, evidently stringing the story out to gain the maximum audience. 'So the keeper, who the giraffe knew, was in the cab, with a whole load of apples! The giraffe's favourite food! And every time they approached a bridge, the keeper held out an apple, and what did the giraffe do?'

'I don't know!' squealed Lily.

'He bent his neck to eat the apple!' yelled Jack, delighted with himself. 'And then the lorry could go under the bridge!'

'That's exactly right, clever boy,' said Carol, smiling. 'Do you know, when your daddy and his brother were about your age, they already knew how to drive a lorry?'

Gareth felt his thighs tense. 'Things were different then, Mum.'

'Teach me, Daddy!' Jack jiggled in his chair.

'Looks like we have the next generation of Merwyn-Jones right here, Carol!' Cled smiled. 'Give it a few more years, young Jack. Plenty of time yet.' Gareth saw his son nod. Time telescoped back to conversations exactly like he and his brother had all those years ago. The carefree little boys who wreaked havoc beneath their parents' noses.

He felt sick just thinking about Jack clambering about on the HGVs now. Not for the first time, his parents' anguish at the death of their firstborn settled heavily on his shoulders.

How could he abandon their dreams?

Chapter Nineteen

Stripping the bed had been the easy part, and Rosie still shed a bucket of tears over it. She'd opened the wardrobe door, scanned the contents and like a film director shouting 'Action!', each item of clothing had reminded her of when her mother had last worn it.

The soft, beautifully-cut charcoal grey lounge trousers had been the only things she'd worn repeatedly for the past year. Two pairs that had been washed and dried daily. Other trousers, she endured, but never loved like these ones. Beautiful cashmere sweaters in purple and lilac and royal blues, that enhanced her pale, Nordic colouring and long slim limbs. It was as if she was still in them.

Rosie backed onto the bed, staring at them. She couldn't do the wardrobe. It would be like throwing her mother away. Blinking back the tears that returned so easily, just when she thought there could surely never be any more, she shut the wardrobe doors and turned her attention to the dressing table.

Bottles of Clarins cleansers and toners remained lined up and gathering dust. Scented body lotions had long ago given way to prescription emollients as her skin became paper thin and dry as an autumn leaf, but they remained there, tightly capped, along with the perfumes that she'd stopped using since her sense of smell had deserted her. Jean Paul Gaultier. Rosie had always thought it was the sculptural bottles of beautiful women that she loved, not just the perfumes. She unscrewed one and sniffed, at the same time wondering why she felt the need to torture herself like this. Tears ran freely down her face and she sat, in the darkening room, on the unmade bed, surrounded by her mother's ghosts.

The CD had finished a while back and so the sound of

her mobile ringing echoed around the empty house. It was an effort to get up and find it. The screen told her it was Leanne. She smiled. If anyone could, Leanne could help her sort this room out.

'Hello!'

'I'm sorry, I know it's late—'

Was it? Rosie glanced at her watch, surprised to find that it was nearly ten o'clock. 'Are you okay? It's not your head, is it?'

'No,' Leanne said, her voice sounding nasal and congested. 'It's my shitty sister. Um, I'm just outside Swansea, and I could find a hotel, but I wondered, um, if you were up, and if you'd um, mind, if I …'

Rosie pressed her ear to the phone. Was Leanne the toughie crying? She couldn't imagine it.

'Leanne, come straight here. Whatever it is, we'll sort it out. Okay?'

'Ok-*aaay*. Tha-ank-you,' the girl stuttered, openly crying now. She hung up, and Rosie stared at the phone for a few seconds, wondering whether she'd been cut off, or gone through a tunnel or something. Eventually, she put the phone down and blew her nose fiercely.

'Get a grip, Rosie,' she told herself, marching into the carer's bedroom. It would take Leanne around half an hour to get to her, if she didn't get lost. And she couldn't imagine that for one minute.

Vacuumed and with fresh bedding, the room only needed a quick wipe over of the bedside cabinet and lamp for it to look welcoming again. Luckily that room had several sets of bedding that matched the curtains, as it had been used by so many different people. She headed into the garden with the torch on her phone, to hunt for any flowers that had survived not only her neglect, but Jack's hefty kicks, and was pleased to find a clump of marguerite daisies. They'd closed their faces to the sun, but they'd open again in the morning. She'd only just arranged them into a little ceramic vase beside the bed, when she heard the sound of a vehicle in the drive. Hesitating for a moment in case it was Chester, before reminding herself that he would want to surprise her by sneaking up on her like earlier, she opened the front door.

Leanne, lit by the hall light, appeared in the doorway. She looked just as when Rosie had last seen her, in skinny jeans and the same jacket she'd been wearing at the weekend, carrying her rucksack. But her demeanour was very different. A tremulous smile wavered on her mouth; her eyes and cheeks were pink and sore looking.

'Aw, sweetheart.' Rosie held her arms out and Leanne stepped into them for a long, sniffly hug. It was a bit awkward as Rosie was shorter than her, but it didn't seem to matter. Rosie shut the door and bolted it behind them. 'Come on in. Tea? Wine? Something stronger? I think I've got some brandy somewhere ...'

Leanne had stopped dead in the open-plan room and was staring around her. 'Wow. This is – wow. It's so, so *you*, Rosie.'

'Oh. Thank you.' Rosie waved an arm towards the sofas and went to fill the yellow kettle. Blasted thing. 'Tea? I've opened a bottle of wine, if you fancy it?'

Leanne hesitated. 'Tea, I think, first.' *First?*

'Do you want anything to eat? Although I think toast is the only option, and I know what you think about carbs and—'

'Oh, yes please, tea and toast would be wonderful. Let me help you.' She unfolded her long, lean body from the sofa. Crossing the stone flags in a few strides, she began to flap the cupboards open and closed, peering inside them.

'Er, toaster is on the counter, here.' Rosie pointed. 'And the bread is in the bread bin, just by there. Cutlery in this drawer, plates in that cupboard there. Teas, coffee and sugar here by the cooker. It's a gas kettle, so it does take a little while.'

'Nice kettle,' Leanne nodded. 'Is it just me for toast or—?'

Rosie considered it. But she'd just had pasta and she wasn't actually hungry so she'd just be eating to keep Leanne company and was that a good enough reason to eat? She caught her train of thought, astonished at herself. 'No, I'm fine thanks. I'll stick to the tea.' She thought longingly of the wine and pushed the thought firmly to the back of her mind. Leanne already thought she was a lush.

Watching Leanne demolish four slices of toast with two mugs of tea, Rosie asked her, 'Did you eat at all on the way here?'

The girl shook her head. 'I couldn't. My stomach was just—' She clenched both her fists and Rosie knew exactly what she meant.

'Do you want to see your room, and go to bed? Or do you want to talk about it?'

'Oh, Rosie.' Leanne's face crumpled and Rosie guessed the room could wait. 'My sis-sister ... She's pregnant. Again!' She raised a tear-stained face. Rosie attempted a neutral expression. There had to be more. 'She's already got four of the little shits, and now this. They're like *rabbits!*'

Out of her depth already, Rosie tried to work out whether she was referring to the children or the parents. Wisely, she said nothing, settling for a sympathetic intake of breath.

'I can't even lock my room. They're always in there, pulling things out, using it for hide-and-seek, taking my things ... I caught one of them *in my actual bed!*'

Rosie thought it sounded very typical of family life, but the expression on Leanne's face told her this was the worst transgression of all. 'Oh dear,' she managed.

'They don't even *like* me! They're always taking the piss out of my weights corner, and my running, and these courses.' Leanne waved an arm around as if she thought she was still in the bunkhouse, and as her own eyes followed the arc of Leanne's arm, Rosie wondered if that's why she'd felt so at home last weekend. This high ceilinged room had once been a barn. Wait. Her *weights corner?*

'And, and so, my sister told me about the—' She described a burgeoning belly with both hands. 'I suppose I was kind of—' She waggled her head from side to side. Rosie felt as if she was in a game of charades.

'Upset?' she guessed.

Leanne nodded. 'Yeah, and she went right off on one. God! She started going on that I'd have to help out a lot more, that I only looked after myself, and all that. And I said, well, what about *him?* Lazy git! *He* doesn't do anything at all! Other than stick his cock in you and, and make more little bastards that neither of you know how to look after!'

Rosie blinked. 'Ah.'

Leanne's head drooped. 'Yeah. So that's when she told me I could eff off. And, she said, take all that effing wool with you …'

'Oh.' Rosie's glance flicked towards the drive. Did that mean …?

'So I bunged all the wool into my van. It took me ages – and I buggered off.' She stared sadly into her empty mug. 'I didn't know where I was going, really. I thought I'd just find a hotel. And then I thought, and what do I do after *that*?' She gulped. 'And that's when I thought of you.' She wrapped her arms around herself, dismally. 'I've never met anyone like you.'

Rosie, staring at her as if she was watching a play, groped for an appropriate response and came up with nothing. Luckily, it seemed that Leanne was happy to do all the talking.

'You know, the outdoor pursuits courses come easily to me. I keep myself really fit. But for someone like you, it must be so much harder, and you were so much *older* than all of us! But you never gave up. And you kept on smiling, and you made us all laugh too.'

Rosie was still grappling with the implications of the "someone like you". Oblivious, Leanne continued on her own trajectory.

'And you saved my life when that twat Oliver nearly killed me. *And* you came to visit me in the hospital. Not even Gareth did that!'

'Well, to be fair, he was *at* the hospital. They just wouldn't let him see you as he wasn't a relative or anything.'

'How did you get in then?'

'I told them I was your aunt.'

Leanne stared at her. 'Oh yeah. See though? See? You even lied for me! Even in a weekend, you did more for me than my own family!'

'Um ...' Rosie's mouth puckered for want of that second glass of wine. 'So – have you thought about what you want to do next?'

'I knew you'd ask me that.' She sat up. 'So, I've got this supplier to see, and there are a few more I can see too – Wales being a land of sheep. And alpacas, as it happens. And if I can help you with things around the house – cos I could see that it was quite a mess in places as I drove in – then maybe I can find somewhere I can afford to live. And have a shop. Maybe. Although, I know you won't believe it, but I'm not sure I'll be all that good at running a shop. You know. People, and everything.' She gave a small shudder. 'A lock-up would do. Or just a couple of rooms where I'm renting. Wool just needs to be dry. It's not heavy or anything and it doesn't smell. And I love all the colours. You like colours too. That was another thing.'

'I'm going to have a glass of wine,' Rosie said, firmly. 'Would you like one?' She was astonished when Leanne said she would. 'And it's a beautiful clear night. Would you like to sit outside with the firepit? It doesn't take long to fire up a few logs ...'

'Really? Wow.' Leanne's eyes shone. 'That would be so awesome.' She jumped up.

'Come on then. Let's brush the chairs down, find some old throws and look at the stars. Nothing ever seems so bad when you can see the stars.' Rosie heaved herself to her feet. Her legs still ached from the weekend plus the long day spent with the children and then throwing herself into the cleaning. This would be a lovely way to unwind. It ticked nothing off her list, but it healed the soul.

It wasn't long before they were sitting cosily before the crackling logs. Leanne had put herself in charge of poking the fire and adding wood, and Rosie was glad of that as it meant she didn't have to keep getting up. She'd found another bottle of red lurking at the back of the cupboard, and was enjoying the moon's reflection, gilding the edges of sea and land.

'This would be a great end to Gareth's weekends. There's something really elemental about a fire.'

Rosie didn't say, well, fire *is* one of the elements. She was too busy being on alert at the mention of Gareth. She "*mmm*"-ed in reply.

'Have you seen him since the weekend?'

Oh God, she'd seen him almost every waking hour since the weekend. She had to be honest. She'd told Gareth off about not being honest with her.

'I have,' she said, sipping her wine to disguise her anxious swallow. She stared into the fire through the ruby liquid. 'I looked after his kids today.'

'Gareth's got *kids?*' Leanne sounded aghast. 'God. I didn't know that. I thought he was single.'

'He *is* single. Divorced. I wonder though, if he might still be in love with his wife.' The thought had only just occurred to her, and the wine loosened her lips.

'That makes sense. I mean, I've been throwing myself at him for two years now, and'—she stabbed a log with the poker—'nothing. No interest at all. I was beginning to think he was gay.'

Rosie swivelled her head to look at the girl, hunched morosely over the flickering flames that were illuminating the sharp planes of her face. She *knew* Leanne had a thing about Gareth. She bit down the gurgle of laughter that threatened at Leanne's supreme confidence in her ability to attract Gareth. She could do with a bit of that confidence herself. And yet, Leanne seemed to know nothing about Gareth. She hadn't known about his kids, or his job. She would bet her last bottle of wine that she knew nothing about Gareth's accident.

'Do you find it difficult to meet men?' She made her voice casual.

'I find it difficult to meet *anyone!*' Leanne laughed, and with astonishing self-awareness said, 'I've got bigger muscles than most blokes, and I run an online wool shop!' She got up and placed another log, just so, on the pyramid she'd already made. The fire would be burning until dawn at this rate. 'And there's you'—she waved an expressive hand at Rosie, currently twirling the stem of her almost empty wine glass and contemplating a refill—'and you already know Gareth's kids, where he works and where he lives!'

Rosie eyed her. 'Er ...' She shrugged, as if it was no big deal.

'You know everything there is to know about me! How do you do it?'

'I didn't know there was an "it"!' Rosie gave in to the refill, holding the bottle out to Leanne. 'I'm just interested, that's all.'

'*I'm* interested!'

'Why don't you ask then?'

'I don't know! It just seems to come out like a—'

'An interrogation?'

'Yes!' Leanne pushed the top log off her pyramid and it tumbled into the flames. 'Can you teach me how to talk to people? Please Rosie? *Ple-ease*?'

Rosie laughed. 'No. You're only asking now because you're a bit pissed and you're upset. Tomorrow, when you're sober, you'd whack me with that poker for telling you how to talk to people.'

Leanne laughed. 'Probably,' she agreed.

On an impulse, Rosie said, 'Do you fancy coming to the Art Café with me while you're here? I've got a voucher for an afternoon tea. I probably have to book it, and it's all cakes and sandwiches, lots of carbs and sugar and stuff and you probably wouldn't like it, but it's a really interesting place and I'd like to sell some of my stuff there.' Too late, she remembered that Leanne had also said she'd sell her stuff for her, but it didn't harm to spread your wares about. Plus, she needed to sort out her workshop and decide what she actually could sell ... 'I've got things to do over the next couple of days. And you're going to see your supplier. But, you know, when I work out when I'm going, if you—'

'Yes. I would. Yes please. Thank you.' Leanne turned a shy smile her way. 'Am I learning?'

Rosie laughed. 'Yes indeed. Well done.' Should she warn Gareth that Leanne had designs on him? Or just not interfere ...

Chapter Twenty

Gareth had brought along the children's pyjamas, and once they'd dropped off to sleep, he was able to have an adult conversation with his parents, resulting in him having some time off, if he promised to maintain a watch on his mobile and be in contact at all times. He acquiesced to all their demands, kissed them both on the cheek and he and his father carried a child each out to the car, popped them carefully into their car seats and buckled them in, still fast asleep.

'Gareth, think about what you really want, lad. Sometimes the grass on the other side – well, it's just grass.' His father eyed him for a moment before he pulled him in for a quick, hard hug.

'I will. Night, Dad. Give my love to Mum.'

'I will. She – you know. She does love you.' He chewed his lips as if he had something else to say, and settled for a, 'You'll be okay with those two?'

Gareth looked into the back seat at his sleeping children. He nodded. 'Yes, thanks, Dad. We'll be fine. Thank you.' When he drove away, his father remained in the rear-view mirror for a long time, his arm lifted in a farewell wave.

Having tucked them into bed, he flicked the cap off a bottle of beer and picked up his phone to text Hannah. The only person he wanted to properly speak to right now, was Rosie. He wanted to rant, and he knew that Rosie would listen, and give him plain-speaking advice.

In his text he asked Hannah how her parents were, and told her that Jack and Lily were fine, that they'd had dinner with his parents and everyone sent their love. He added an X as a kiss after some deliberation before sending. The word "Read" appeared beneath his message, but there was no response. It was a long time before the phone rang and he grabbed it before it woke the children.

It was Rosie. Whispering sibilantly. 'Is it too late to talk? Sorry, it is, isn't it? I didn't look when I picked up the phone. Shall I go? I'll go.'

He grinned at the phone. 'Hello Rosie. I'm still up. Are you a bit drunk?'

'No! I'm *very* drunk.'

'But you're okay? No sign of Chester again?'

'Yes. I mean, no.' She snorted a laugh. 'I rang to tell you ... you'll never guess.'

He couldn't guess, but he hoped it had nothing to do with Chester. She carried on.

'Leanne! She's *here*! In my spare room, downstairs. I think I got her drunk.'

'Good God.' Gareth could hardly believe her.

'I *know!*'

Gareth took another sip of his beer, picturing her snuggled up in bed with the phone to her ear, her auburn hair spread across the pillow. Their giggly, murmured conversation was how it might be if he was beside her, his arm across her breasts, holding her soft warm body curved into his.

'Yes! I told her I'd looked after your children today – was it only today? Well, yesterday now, you know what I mean. No wonder I'm so knackered and ...' Rosie giggled, breathily. Gareth smiled. The story unfolded. He wheezed with silent laughter as she recounted it.

'So, what's going to happen next?'

'If she and her sister haven't made up, she's going to rent somewhere, and continue her business.'

'Makes you wonder why she hadn't done that already.'

'I wondered that too. I don't think our Leanne is quite the toughie she makes herself out to be. I think she needs a bit of propping up.'

'Don't we all.'

'How was dinner tonight?'

'Apart from Lily throwing her meal over the polished table and my mother interrogating me? Fine, thanks.'

'Poor Lily. All five-year-olds are like that though. Your mother should be used to it by now, surely?'

'You'd think so, wouldn't you? Jack can do no wrong in her eyes. God, she was even encouraging him to learn to drive the lorries tonight. He's *seven!* Even *we* weren't driving them then!'

There was a pause, and Gareth wondered if sleep had claimed Rosie's ear. Then she said, 'Really, though? You already told us you'd both been terrors in the yard. I bet the cab wasn't out of bounds.'

'Okay. Outed. But that was then. And we didn't actually really *drive* as such. I mean, we couldn't reach the pedals for a start.' Gareth lifted his bottle. Empty. He didn't dare have another, much as the idea of a night of oblivion appealed. 'I just couldn't bear the thought of Jack being hurt.'

'Mmm. Your children are connected to you, viscerally, from birth. I know that's true for women. I don't know about men though. Although Chester always adored Keira. Sometimes it felt as if I'd only given birth to her so that I could hand her over to him.'

Gareth digested her words, reflecting on his mother. Eventually, he said, 'I'm planning to take the kids to the beach for the day while this weather holds out. If you're not busy, maybe we could meet you and Leanne there? Would Friday, day after tomorrow, be good for you? Lily can be relied on to throw her ice-cream over herself and be revolting, bless her. Also, I've been checking the weather, and it looks as if this warm weather is set to continue. Maybe it'll be a heatwave. I've managed to wangle some leave while I've got the kids – as long as I stay in touch and don't leave the country. A sort of working from home, scenario. Perks of being the boss's son. I thought that maybe, we could all go and see your fire engine as soon as? The kids would love it, and we can work out the best way of getting it back. What do you think?'

'It would be lovely to see you all. And with Friday, what about the beach at the Art Café? I've asked Leanne to come with me for the afternoon tea and she said yes. We could do Friday and see you then. Would you mind being on the beach by yourselves for a little while? Or perhaps we leave the afternoon tea to another day. Sorry, I haven't thought this through at all, have I?'

Gareth's cheeks lifted at the headlong rush of her words. 'That would work great. The beach there is glorious and Jack and Lily would have a wonderful time.'

'Are you sure? I'm still reeling that Leanne said she'd come. I even told her how many calories there were in an afternoon tea! Well, not exactly, but y'know, I mentioned sugar and fat and carbs in one sentence and it didn't put her off.' She paused to breathe. 'You're very good to remember my fire engine, thank you. And I'd love to spend another day with you and your children.'

'I look forward to it. I'll make a picnic for me and the kids for when you two go for your posh tea.'

'Ah but Graham, would it be pork pies and Cadbury Mini Rolls?'

'No, Rosa, there'll be wraps and hummus and carrot sticks.'

She chuckled, sleepily. 'I might let you teach me how to do some of that healthy stuff, one day.'

They chatted on for a little longer before Rosie began to yawn prodigiously and they said goodnight.

Gareth wasn't as tired as he would have liked to be. Opening up his laptop, he saved a new folder as Grass, and began with a spreadsheet of estimated costs. He worked long into the night, surprising himself with how much he actually knew.

Chapter Twenty-One

Leanne was up, washed and dressed by the time Rosie blundered sleepily into the kitchen.

'Morning! What do you usually have for breakfast?'

'Coffee.' Rosie eyed her. 'You look way too perky for a late night and too much wine.'

'Should I not tell you I've been for a run, too?'

'*Ohhh.*' Rosie slumped into a chair at the dining table. 'That's just wrong.' She sat up suddenly. 'The front door is locked, isn't it? What did you do with the key?'

'I took it with me. I wasn't out for long, and I didn't know where I was going anyway. I just needed to stretch my legs after driving all day and ...' She sighed. 'I enjoyed it. There are some really smart houses around and yours is letting the side down a bit, if you don't mind me saying, but with some TLC it could be—'

'And the front door is locked now, is it?'

'Um,' said Leanne, her forehead creasing in thought. Rosie got up to check. It wasn't, and she turned the key in the lock. Chester could have just barged in while she was asleep and be sitting here at the table, probably attempting to charm Leanne.

'Leanne, could you make sure the door is locked all the time, please?'

'Really? I thought these rural places were so safe!'

Over coffee and toast – she really needed to do some shopping – Rosie explained her dilemma with her semi-detached husband. With a fierce expression on her face, Leanne said, 'So if I find him hanging around here, I can bash him with something, can I?'

'I'd rather not have a conviction for murder hanging over us, to be honest.' Realising with Leanne's literal turn of mind that she might need to completely qualify her words, she said, 'No physical harm. If I can't work out the finances so that I can keep the house, however derelict it might be, then it will either have to be sold, or Chester will have to live in it with me. That's a ghastly thought.'

'Sell it, and we can find somewhere to live together. How cool would that be? I could sort out your diet and get you fit, and we could talk about wool!'

Rosie swallowed a too hot gulp of coffee and choked. 'So, are you off to see your supplier today?'

'Yep, I'm leaving in a mo. I'll probably be out all day, so you don't need to worry about me.'

'I'll give you a spare key. Just remember, even if you're in the house—'

'Lock the door. I get it. What are you doing today?'

'I'm keen to make some felt – the colours of the moon and the reflections last night when we were outside. I'm thinking deep purples, indigos, emeralds and streaks of magenta with whites and lilacs. I've also got a stack of ideas from the weekend.' Her mind floated over the yellows and pinks of the tiny flowers in the crevices of the cliff face before she saw Leanne's raised eyebrows. 'Um – and I need to sort out what to take to show Lucy at the Art Café tomorrow.' She paused. 'And then I have to clear out Mum's room. I had a go at it last night, but I didn't get very far.'

'I expect it would be easier to just lock the door and not have to deal with it,' Leanne said, with a rare flash of insight. Rosie blew her nose and nodded.

'I could help you. I mean, I didn't know your mum, so her things wouldn't upset me. Are you planning on keeping any of her clothes?'

'I don't know.' Rosie threw her hands in the air. 'They won't fit me, that's for sure, but there are some beautiful garments in there. And when I look at them, I can see her in them.'

'You need a system. Rags, charity shops, sell, keep.'

'That's a good idea.'

'I can help you with that,' Leanne said, cheerfully. 'We can have a crack at it tonight. The sooner we start, the sooner it's done.'

'Great. Thank you. What do you fancy for dinner tonight? I'm hoping to do the shopping tomorrow, if you don't mind? I've got some chicken breasts in the freezer and I can defrost them and— do you eat chicken?'

Leanne nodded. 'Not very often, though.'

'Sorry, I have nothing in the fridge, no veggies or fruit now.'

'I can pick some stuff up on my travels today.'

'Thank you.' Rosie guessed they would be having grilled chicken and kale or rocket for dinner, and decided that actually, it really didn't matter. It was good to have company, and Leanne was so straightforward and positive about everything, that tasks which had overwhelmed Rosie became doable.

When Leanne left to do her visits, Rosie locked the door behind her and took a mug of coffee into her workshop, where she spent several hours making felt and as that dried, turning some of the felts she'd already made into jewellery and some little pictures that she thought would look cute framed.

Lunch was the last egg, poached on toast, and she returned to her mother's room in a much more positive frame of mind.

She left the top of the dressing table untouched, and concentrated on the drawers and cupboards. These contained her mother's financial matters, photo albums, and memorabilia. By the time Leanne returned from her wanderings, she'd managed to move all the boxes into her own bedroom, upstairs. The photo albums, she'd opened one at random, but had closed it as emotion threatened to overtake her again. They weren't going anywhere, and she could look at them whenever she wanted to. But not right now. The boxes of memorabilia held importance only to her mother, but Rosie felt obliged to keep it all, so they took up residence along with the photo albums, destined for the attic.

Her mother's files were full of bank statements, meticulously filed, right up to the last few months. Rosie wished she'd been as scrupulous with her own finances. She stacked the boxes of files out of the way. She never threw anything like that away. You never knew what the Inland Revenue might want to look at.

Resolutely, she yanked open the deep drawer that bulged with her own haphazard filing system. Unopened mail, bank statements higgledy-piggledy, and pulled them out, onto the floor. She could hear Leanne's words in her head. She needed a system. So, statements here, receipts there, household bills over there, anything relating to the house renovations in this pile on the chair. It was a start, and she felt so much calmer for exercising some control over the mess.

Her eye rested on the wonky pile of bank statements and she recalled Chester's words about her mother "rolling in it". Certainly, her mother had made money in her lifetime. She'd paid to renovate the bedrooms and bathroom for her care. And she'd been generous about giving Rosie money for her own keep, so much so that Rosie had been able to continue to pay the mortgage, modest as it was. It was one less debt hanging over her now.

But her mother had sold her own house, and Rosie hadn't asked where the proceeds of that money had gone. It had been her mother's business, and who knew what debts her party- and holiday-loving mother had run up? She frowned, shuffling her statements in order. First things first, she thought, hearing Leanne retuning. She headed down to find out what they would be eating that evening.

'I *was* going to do us a nice nettle soup, with almond flour flatbreads,' Leanne told her, and then pealed with laughter. 'Your face!'

'Very funny.' Rosie eyed her house guest with a raised eyebrow. 'Please tell me you didn't change your mind in favour of kale soup instead?'

'Ooh, kale soup. That's an idea. I'll have to try that. I love kale.'

'Why does that not surprise me ...?'

'We're having spinach—'

'Yuk.'

'—sweet potato and lentil dahl,' Leanne finished, firmly. 'It's delicious, I promise you. And I bought real naan breads. To go with the fresh mint raita we're going to make.'

Rosie brightened up. 'Oh, okay. Sounds lush. What can I do?'

They prepared dinner between them, chatting about Leanne's visits and plans, with some background music. A mighty thundering on the door disturbed their peaceful chatter. Rosie froze. Was that Chester?

'If that's the shithead ex, give me the key,' hissed Leanne. Rosie blinked at her quick reactions. She trudged towards the door and unlocked it, making a mental note to get a spyhole installed. Keira burst into the hall, her beautiful features contorted and tear-stained. She was instantly on the offensive.

'Why couldn't I get in? Why was the door locked? Who are you? What have you been saying to Dad?'

'Leanne, this is Keira. My daughter.'

'Ah,' said Leanne. She turned, expressionless, and walked back to the kitchen without another word. Rosie watched Keira's dumbstruck face with a certain amount of guilty satisfaction. She could learn from Leanne.

'I thought you collected everything you needed last time you visited.'

'Visited?' Keira's jaw dropped. 'I *live* here!'

'Not since you said you wished your mother had died, you don't,' Leanne called from the kitchen, stirring the saucepan.

'I—what?' The colour drained from Keira's face. 'I didn't.'

'I heard you,' Rosie said, noting with astonishment, how even her voice was. 'I heard you telling your friends, how boring I was. And how you wished I'd died, instead of my own mother. I heard you as clear as day. You have a loud voice, Keira.'

All the energy had drained from Keira. Her unblinking gaze focussed on a space somewhere to the left of Rosie's ear. If it wasn't for the pulse visible in her long, smooth neck, she might have been a marble statue. Rosie strode into the kitchen, leaving her standing there.

Hiding her shaking hands, she pretended to hunt for chutneys. The front door clicked closed. She went to look. Keira had gone.

Chapter Twenty-Two

Lily spotted Rosie first. The beach was already filling rapidly with families staking their claim on their little bit of sand, and Gareth made sure he did the same. He ensured that both children knew what their parasol looked like, where they were on the beach relative to what was around them, and he grilled them thoroughly about their safety.

'If someone you don't know comes up to you and wants to give you an ice-cream, what do you do?'

Jack was quick off the mark. 'Shout "NO" really loud, run away and find you and tell you.'

Lily's eyes were round. 'But I like ice-cream.'

'Yes sweetheart, I know that. And we will have ice-cream today. But *I* will give it to you. Or the person in the shop. Or perhaps Rosie will, but—'

'I like Rosie too!' Lily nodded. 'Rosie and ice-cream!' She waved her spade in the air and whacked Gareth around the head where he knelt on the beach mat beside her. 'Oops! Sorry Daddy.'

'That's okay, darling.' Gareth rubbed his eyebrow, feeling as he did so, the long scar that dented his face from eye to mouth. He ploughed on. 'So if you see someone you don't know, and they've got a puppy with them, and they say you can stroke their puppy, what do you do? And yes, I know you like puppies too ...' Out of the corner of his eye, he saw Jack prompting his little sister to "*run away!*"

'I run away and I say "NO" in a loud voice.'

'Yes. Good girl. You're not going to be on your own, because I will be with you all the time.' But God forbid, they should become separated on the crowded beach ... 'Do *not* go into the sea without me. Or Rosie. Okay? And *stay together*!' He eyed them both fiercely, waiting for them to focus on him, and not the delights of the beach. He'd done this earlier but there was no harm in reinforcing the message.

'I can see Rosie!' squeaked Lily. Forgetting everything her father had just said, she set off at a run towards the figure with auburn hair, wearing a wide-brimmed sun hat and a cobalt blue sundress that the breeze toyed with. She was carrying a cool box, and a brightly striped bag was slung across her back.

'Jack, fetch!' Jack took off like a rabbit, his legs a blur. Gareth wasn't far behind, just close enough to pluck his daughter off the sand that his son rugby-tackled her onto. He hauled her onto his hip, wiping the tears and sand and snot off her face with his hand. 'Aw, Lily! What did I say to you? You can't just run off like that. What if you get lost and I can't find you?'

'But Rosie will find me!' Lily sniffed, with the unassailable logic of a five-year-old, pointing over his shoulder, to where Rosie had put down the cool box and was waving. Behind her was Leanne, loaded up with beach chairs and a parasol. She wore a little sunhat, a pair of tiny shorts and a cropped top. Gareth lifted a hand and the three of them trekked over the soft sand towards Rosie and Leanne.

'Hello! Shall we set up beside you, or would you rather we found our own spot?' Rosie smiled up at him, her eyes made aqua by the sunshine. 'Hello, Lily.' She looked down to the little girl now hopping excitedly beside her. 'Hello Jack. Lovely to see you again.' She bent and gave him a hug first, and then Lily. 'This is my friend Leanne. She's staying with me for a while, and she's also a friend of your daddy.'

'A'right?' Leanne encompassed them all in one nod.

Gareth watched his children studying her. She looked like a volleyball player in her skimpy outfit. Her six-pack was better than his. Eventually, she held out an awkward hand

and they took turns to shake it. It was clear that she wasn't very comfortable around children, and he wondered, with a sinking feeling, what Lily was going to say to her.

'You look like my Barbie dolls,' she said. 'Except for your hair. Have you got any hair?'

'It's short.' Leanne hefted her burdens into her arms and followed them over the sand to their encampment.

'So,' he said to Rosie, taking the cool box from her. 'Is this full of sausage rolls and Mr Kipling?'

'Nope. On the basis that we're having afternoon tea, it's water and fruit.'

'Oh well. You'll probably be pleased of it later when you're all dried up and full of cake.'

'That's what I told her,' Leanne said, catching up with them and setting the chairs onto the sand. 'I need a swim. See you in a bit.' She ran, heels high, towards the sea, and Gareth felt them all watching her. She floated effortlessly over the sand. A natural athlete. Picking up a bucket and spade, he scooped up some sand and made the first sandcastle. Rosie followed suit, and it wasn't long before Lily and Jack were industriously creating the biggest sandcastle known to man.

'Everything okay?' he asked Rosie quietly, when the children were out of earshot. 'You seem a bit, subdued.'

'Mmm. I suppose I am. Keira turned up last night spoiling for a fight. Leanne told her that I'd overheard what she'd said.'

'What?' Gareth was aghast. 'Surely that wasn't for her to say? What happened?'

'Well, once it was out there it couldn't be unsaid. Keira tried to deny it, but not with any conviction. And then she just, kind of, walked quietly out. No door slamming. No shouting and screaming. A silent withdrawal. It wasn't like her at all. I haven't heard anything from her since.' She smacked the upturned bucket of sand, and lifted it. The soft sand crumbled away, leaving a formless heap. 'I don't know what to do now.' She sat back on her heels. 'I'm quite glad to be away today. I'm driving myself mad, feeling guilty about her.'

He put a hand out and squeezed her arm. 'Families are hard work, aren't they?'

'No life-fixing quotes for me?'

He shook his head. 'I wouldn't dare.' He pulled her upright and she brushed the sand off her legs as they moved closer to where Lily and Jack had chosen to excavate industrial quantities of sand. He felt her warm bare skin through his thin T-shirt. 'Do you think she's just licking her wounds somewhere? After all, she did say those things, and now she knows that you heard her ...'

'Yeah, that's what I'm thinking too. It's just – you know, it goes against the grain to hurt your children. You're somehow supposed to shake it off if they're horrible to you. It's the price of parenting. And you're always meant to be the grown-up, no matter what.' She filled a starfish mould and smoothed the top. 'But does that mean being a doormat to your children for ever?'

'Do you think Leanne did you a favour by bringing it out in the open?'

Upturning the mould deftly onto the sand, she lifted it to reveal a perfect starfish.

'Maybe. It's where we go next that's bothering me. And I can't help chewing over *why* she said it! It's true that she was always Chester's daughter – it was always a bit of a standing joke when she was small. But aren't little girls always the apples of their father's eye? I didn't even know my dad. He died when I was little. I have no memory of him. Just photos.

Mum didn't even talk about him. So I'm a bit short on my own family experiences. And I don't have anyone to talk to about her. Anyone who knows her, that is. Apart from

Chester, of course. And he wouldn't exactly be a neutral referee.' She made a second sand starfish and Lily came over to admire it.

'Make me one for my Princess Tower, Rosie!' She stood close enough to bury her toes in the tentacles.

'Please,' said Gareth automatically.

'Please Rosie,' said Lily, giving the starfish a casual shove with her toes before scampering back to her own building site. Rosie shovelled the sand back into the plastic mould, her hands on autopilot.

'But as you say,' she continued, 'the wound has been opened and now we have to try and heal it. Maybe we'll never have a wonderful mother-daughter relationship. God knows, it took long enough for me and my mum.' She stood and navigated her way to Princess Towers where Lily bossily directed her to place her creation. Gareth shaded his eyes and squinted at the sea, looking for Leanne. He could see a figure with a strong overarm stroke swimming parallel to the shore and guessed it was her. She was another enigma. Strong of body and yet vulnerable. And it had taken Rosie to see that, despite Leanne attending so many of his courses that she could probably run them herself. The thought seeped into his brain, not quite catching onto anything, but settling, to be considered later.

'Argh, *Lil-eee*!' He knew the peace had been too good to last. Jack stood, red-faced and close to tears. 'Look what she did to my drawbridge!' He stuck out a skinny arm. Gareth looked hard, but it all just looked like sand to him.

'Maybe you could build it again?' he suggested. 'And you could tell me about it as you're making it?'

'Don't want to. She'll only kick it over again.'

'Who wants a paddle?' Rosie stood, beating a rhythm on the starfish mould. 'We could make a sand tower and see how long it lasts before the waves wash it away!'

'*Okaaay*,' Jack said, with all the tiredness of an old man.

Gareth hid a grin as, clearly not wanting to be left out, the little boy added, 'Can I do that too, please, Rosie?'

Rosie jumped back and lifted the starfish high. 'You have to catch me first!'

Lily demolished Princess Towers as she jumped to her feet. She wouldn't care a jot about that, Gareth knew. Jack was fast and nimble and Rosie had her work cut out keeping in front of him. She dodged and weaved and Gareth smiled at the three of them laughing. He clicked off some shots on his phone. Rosie's blue dress contrasted with the pale sand and the sunshine threw lilac shadows across the children's all-in-one striped sunsuits.

Tucking the phone into a waterproof case, he jumped up, buttoning it into his shorts pocket.

'First one to the sea gets their feet wet!' he yelled, taking off at speed and then circling behind his giggling children and scooping them up, one under each arm.

'Pick me up too!' Rosie laughed, catching the skirt of her dress up with one hand.

Gareth ran back to her and set the children down.

'Hold hands! All together, ready?' Like a paper cut-out, all four of them ran into the shallows, kicking up the water so that beads of diamond-cut spray hung, sunlit, in the air around them. 'Not too deep!' He watched Jack wading out a little further, pulling on Rosie's arm. Beside him, holding tightly to his hand, Lily jumped and splashed and landed heavily on his left foot. Rosie could swim, of course she could, she'd saved Leanne. He still moved closer to them, feeling the cold water swirl around his legs.

'D-daddy!' shrieked Lily in a mix of excitement and fear. 'Jump! Jump the waves!' The waves were tiny, and he obliged, making a big deal of lifting her in front of him and swinging her over them. Rosie's dress was caught up to reveal a length of lightly tanned thigh, reflected in the sparkling sea. Jack was demonstrating his manly prowess by jumping the waves alongside her. His sunsuit was soaked, and his face was alive with laughter. Gareth relaxed a little, still watchful. He was so busy watching them that he didn't even see Leanne wading towards them until she was close, water streaming over her taut muscles. She slicked her hair back with one hand and regarded them with bemusement, as if the water was just another workout, not for *fun*.

Rosie had made it fun for them, Gareth realised. He wanted Leanne to feel it too. He held his hand out. 'Jump!' Lily, seeing Leanne as only another facilitator to her needs, held up a trusting hand and Gareth bit back laughter at Leanne's look of horror.

'Jump!' Lily insisted, and Leanne didn't seem to have a choice. Lily dropped onto her knees, signalling that they lift her over the waves. Luckily Gareth was strong enough to lift her by himself, which was a good thing, as it took Leanne until the next wave to work out what she was meant to be doing. Had she never played with her nephews and nieces?

However warm it was, it wasn't the Mediterranean, and soon he felt Lily shivering, although she denied strongly that she was cold.

'Time for a snack!' he decided.

'Yay!' yelled Rosie. 'C'mon Jack, where were we sitting? Can you see?'

Gareth was pleased that the little boy knew, and he and Leanne followed them, swinging Lily between them. He was able to watch Rosie's hips swaying in the thin fabric of the dress. She hadn't mentioned anything about her divorce. Was it wrong of him to be hoping for a quick dissolution? He wouldn't make a move on Rosie until he was sure about what she wanted. He knew what he wanted. And he could be patient.

Chapter Twenty-Three

Grateful for her sunglasses, Rosie surreptitiously eyed Gareth's lower legs, stretched out on the beach mat, and goosebumps prickled over her skin as she tracked the telltale silvery scars that criss-crossed and pockmarked his shins and knees. What huge determination he'd had to overcome those terrible injuries. And how lucky not to have lost his legs altogether.

Fanning her face, she wished she hadn't booked an afternoon tea in this weather. Although her stomach had been rumbling for the last hour, and watching Gareth's hungry children tuck into his delicious-looking picnic had been torture. She'd messaged Lucy back and forth, and was determined to show off her new work. She was so proud of it, and had laughed at Leanne's expression when she'd shown her.

'I wasn't expecting something like this,' she'd said.

'What were you expecting?'

'Something old-fashioned, I suppose.'

'I see. These were made including scraps of silk.'

'Wow. Really?' Leanne squeezed the richly coloured felted baubles that made up the necklace, and then picked up the buttoned cowl. 'Even I would wear this.'

'Praise indeed.'

'You're teasing me, aren't you?'

'You're learning.' It had given Rosie a huge boost to hear Leanne praise her work. She hoped that Lucy would be as honest. The stock she'd brought was carefully rolled in a felted bag in her capacious beach bag, and she was clock-watching for her appointment. Even the idea of visiting the café again since the funeral was making her pulse rage. At 1.45 p.m. she stood up, brushed herself off and announced her departure. It would give her time to freshen up.

'Good luck!' Gareth gave her a thumbs up. 'Not that you'll need it.'

'Sorry, Rosie, do you mind if I don't come after all?' Leanne said, shading her eyes to look up at her. 'It's too hot to eat sticky cakes.'

'Oh!' Rosie blinked and stared at her, where she was stretched out on one of Rosie's beach towels, alongside Gareth. Her concave stomach was a rebuke. 'Um, no. Erm ...' Inside, she seethed. Why only say it now? If she'd mentioned it earlier, they could perhaps have cancelled. Rosie was too hot to eat sticky cakes too, but they would have been sharing. And she'd wanted to show off the Art Café, show Leanne the artist-led gifts there.

Gareth said, 'Maybe they'll give you a doggy bag, for later?' Rosie nodded, feeling let down and irritable and once again, somehow taken for granted. It was clear to her what Leanne's intentions were, whether Gareth had picked up the signals or not, and what made it worse, was that she had no right to feel jealous. Gareth had been nothing but a good friend to her since the weekend and Leanne had known him for much, much longer than she had. Not to mention her being completely on his wavelength with all the climbing and sporty stuff. She nodded, hoping she didn't look as hot and cross as she felt, and tried for a graceful exit, tripping over her flip-flops instead.

'Oops-a-Daisy!' called Lily, and she heard them all laugh. She forced herself to lift a cheery arm, and plodded over the sand. Haha, funny old Dozy Rosie.

She was hot and sticky and ready to call it a day by the time she walked into the cool of the café loos. The mirror confirmed her worst fears as she removed her sun hat. Freckly faced, ginger hair hanging in frizzy coils; sticky marks on her dress, courtesy of Lily. She went to the loo and sat there, thinking, hearing people coming and going.

Whatever was going on out there on the beach was not

in her control. Gareth would do what he wanted to do, and so would Leanne, and nothing she did would change that. She could change herself though. This was the beginning of being what and who she'd wanted to be for so long, and she was going to give it her very best shot. Otherwise, it was back to the school canteen. It was probably best that Leanne wasn't there. She could just be herself.

She washed her hands and her face, blotting it with a paper towel, and then eyed the marks on her dress with a rueful eye.

'Pretty dress,' remarked the lady at the next basin, in knee length shorts and T-shirt. 'I wish I'd worn something like that. You look very cool and elegant.'

'Oh, thank you so much! I was just wondering whether I'm going to make these stains worse by trying to wash them out.'

'It's so hot out there, I'd say it would dry in no time. But anyway, you can't really see them until you stretch the material flat. I wouldn't worry about it.' She left with a smile, and Rosie decided she'd leave the marks as they were. She might end up with a bigger patch of wrinkled fabric and look even worse. And in any case, Lucy had seen her in a worse state than this, covered in tea and sobbing. At least now she looked "cool and elegant".

The café was as full as she'd imagined, although it was cooled by the gentle breeze from the open doors overlooking the veranda. The one where she'd overheard Keira …

The staff directed her to Lucy's desk in the gift area. She took her stock from her bag, and spread it carefully on the empty desk, arranging it just so. As she was fussing with it, she was aware of somebody at her elbow, and stepped back, thinking it was Lucy coming to see her. It was the woman from the loos, earlier.

'Oh my. These are gorgeous! Are you selling them?' She put out a tentative hand.

Rosie beamed. 'Thank you! I am hoping to sell them here, yes.'

'Do you have a card? Or a website?'

'No – oh goodness, I hadn't even thought of anything like that! It's been such a long time, and I'm quite out of touch really, and—' *Stop talking Rosie!* 'Which ones do you like the best?'

'I love this collar thing. I mean, it's too hot right now to wear it, but it's so beautiful. I might not even actually wear it. Just have it on my dressing table. It looks like—' She put her head on one side, her mouth pursed. 'This is going to sound a bit mad, but it looks like a sort of journey? I love the silvery strands and how it could be dark but there are all these colours in there ...'

Rosie clutched herself with joy. It was the piece she'd made after sitting outside by the firepit with Leanne. It had evolved into a kind of scarf-type cowl when she'd found some buttons that looked right, and held it against her neck to see. A voice at her elbow made her jump.

'It sounds as if I'd better snap all these up before somebody else does!' Lucy smiled at her. 'Hello Rosie, it's lovely to see you again!' Giving her a brief hug, she turned to the woman who was still studying the collar. 'Good afternoon – you have very good taste. It's stunning, isn't it! I might have to fight you for it.'

'I have more stock, and I'm making again, now that, er ...' Rosie was almost holding her breath, feeling the now familiar lump rise in her throat. Lucy caught her eye and nodded. *Now that Mum has gone ...*

'How much is it?' The woman had the collar in her hands and held it to the light.

Rosie made a pleading face at Lucy, who rolled her eyes at her and mouthed back the word, *seventy*? Rosie nodded, her heart drumming. God, she was so unprofessional. And how much commission would Lucy take from that?

Why hadn't she found out beforehand? The woman loved it so much that Rosie would have given it to her. Useless businesswoman she'd be.

'That one is ninety-five pounds,' Lucy said. Rosie tried to look cool and nonchalant, despite her jaw dropping inside.

'I only came in for a cup of tea,' the woman said, and Rosie's heart sank. 'You take cards, I hope?'

'Of course.' Lucy smiled. 'Shall I wrap this for you?' Enclosing Rosie's work in coloured tissue paper, and tying it with ribbon, she dropped a contact card into the paper bag that bore the Art Café logo, and handed it over with the receipt. 'Thank you so much. Have you had your tea?' The woman shook her head, and Lucy said, 'Show the staff your receipt, there's a nice discount. Lovely to meet you.'

Rosie wanted to hug her first customer. 'Thank you!'

'Thank *you!*' the customer said. 'It's wonderful to meet the artist in person when you buy something. I'll be watching out for new stock.'

When she'd gone, Lucy said, 'Well, I think that speaks for itself. Well done. Have you got any more like that? I like these necklaces, and these cute little brooches too. No price list though. Tut-tut.'

'I'm so sorry. I was dying a thousand deaths when she asked how much it was. I didn't have a clue.'

'Never mind, you're not the first one. So, I included my commission on that sale. A bit less, as you'd already hooked her, and I just reeled her in. We'll sort out the prices that you want, and add commission, okay?'

'Okay,' Rosie agreed. They sat at Lucy's desk while she patiently listed Rosie's stock and they worked out prices.

'I expect you to do this the next time though. A proper list, with titles and prices. And photos too, in case they get mixed up.' Lucy grinned. 'Making the stuff is sometimes the easiest bit. Are you on social media? A website?' As Rosie shook her head, she continued, 'Customers like to find out about you. Your qualifications. Your inspirations. Your aspirations.'

'Crikey,' Rosie said, faintly.

'Tell me what inspired you to make that piece you just sold.'

'I was in my back garden a few nights ago with a friend and a nice red wine.' Rosie let her mind drift back. 'The firepit shone through the glasses like rubies. The moon was silvery over the creeks where the tide left flickers of colour.'

Lucy slapped the desk. 'You're made. You live overlooking the sea?' Rosie nodded. 'Take photos. Start a blog.' She looked so enthusiastic that Rosie felt her own excitement begin to fizz.

'A blog?'

'Like a diary, but online, so people can read it.'

'Okay. I've been writing a diary since Mum died. I don't think I'd want people to read it though. There's a lot of swearing in it.'

Lucy looked sympathetic. 'The best blogs give some personal stuff away, but don't feel you should lay yourself out there for the public. Talk about the things you see, like you just told me. How they make you feel, and what you make out of them. You don't need a posh camera, your mobile will do for the internet. Make a little film of yourself creating. Nothing fancy, get someone to hold the mobile over your hands as you do it. Really short, leave them wanting more. Have you got a name for your business?'

'I hadn't thought about it.'

'It all adds to the image ... Maybe your house name? Or the beach?'

Caught up in the moment, the words spilled from Rosie's mouth. 'I've inherited a fire engine. What about, Fiery Felts?'

'What about, Fire Truck Felts?' Lucy's eyes sparkled. 'Are you going to convert it into a camper van or something? How exciting!'

'I haven't even seen it yet.' Rosie laughed. 'It might be a wreck.' She delved into her beach bag and brought out her pink notebook. 'Can I show you my ideas for the next lot of felts?'

Lucy leaned forward. 'Of course! I love to see other artist's sketchbooks.' Opening it to show her, Rosie thought of that delicate, damp, butterfly of creation, the one that Chester had always snuffed out before it ever took flight. She saw it soaring into the blue sky, iridescent in magenta and violet, streaked with emerald and cerulean blue. Now, *that* would make a fabulous cowl.

'When I was abseiling at the weekend, that's what unlocked it all. It was as if I suddenly started to see again.'

'How amazing. Put that in the blog too. Make notes.' Lucy made them for her on a piece of paper and passed them over. 'Sorry, I'm very bossy aren't I?' She laughed. 'I am so excited for you.' She paused for a moment. 'Do you have enough money to buy supplies? I know how expensive this stuff is when you're starting out. I'll pay you cash now for your sale, but usually it's at the end of the month. I pay straight into your bank account. You can sort that out later.'

'Wow, thank you! I was also wondering about putting some of the little pieces in frames?' Rosie ventured, as Lucy wrote her an invoice and counted out her cash. She pulled out her felt roll and handed it over. 'I didn't put them out with everything else because they might just look like unfinished bits.'

'Oh my God, I even love this! You're so clever.' Lucy fingered the piece of felt that Rosie had used to wrap her other creations in. She nodded at the small pieces. 'Yes. I love them. They'd be gorgeous in white mounts and frames. Do it.'

'Goodness.' Rosie leaned back, overwhelmed. 'I just want to rush home and make more stuff!'

'Aren't you booked in for an afternoon tea? With a friend?'

Rosie shrugged. 'She decided it was too hot, and stayed on the beach.'

'Oh.' Lucy eyed her. 'Her loss. It *is* hot though. I can give you a takeaway box to take some of them back with you. We're trialling the idea for posh picnics!'

'Really? Gareth said you might, but I didn't want to ask in case you thought that was cheeky.'

'Gareth – from the outdoor pursuits course?' Lucy's mouth slid up on one side. 'He's – *phwoaarrr*.'

'You noticed.' Rosie grinned, feeling the blood rush to her face. 'We've seen a bit of each other since the weekend ...'

'And he's on the beach with you?' Rosie nodded. 'And this friend decided to stay there at the last minute. With him.' Rosie nodded again. Lucy ran her tongue over her teeth. She tutted.

'But it's okay,' Rosie said. 'She's known him much longer than I have. And she's all muscles and action and long legs and everything I'm sure he'd want. And I'm just ...' Rosie shrugged.

'Rosie, I used to be like you. And if I've learned anything, it's that you've got to be your own woman, your first priority. You love yourself *first*.

'If he's worth his salt, he'll find you. And if he doesn't, you'll find someone better. Someone worthy of you.' She fixed Rosie with a stern eye. 'Now then. Let's get your afternoon tea sorted out.' She held her arms out for a quick and spontaneous hug. 'I'm so glad you came back. I've been thinking about you. But you've blown me out of the water with these. Enjoy your cuppa.'

'Oh, thank you. I really will.' She couldn't wait to tell Gareth and Leanne.

Chapter Twenty-Four

They'd trekked over the beach for an ice-cream. They'd looked for creatures in the rock pools and they'd built an entire town out of sandcastles. Or at least, Gareth, Lily and Jack had. Leanne had abstained from the ice-cream, and had trailed behind them in the rock pools doing her best to look interested.

Lily, having been ousted from her brother's latest construction, said in her best wheedling voice, 'Will *you* play wiv me, Leanne?'

'No.' Leanne, performing some complicated stretches, was matter of fact.

'That's okay. I'll wait for Rosie to come back,' the little girl said, sadly. 'Rosie will play with me.' Gareth swivelled across towards his little girl.

'Lily, shall we make a sand unicorn?'

'*Okaay*.'

Later, Lily and Jack snoozed under the shade of the parasol and Gareth was at last able to read his paperback. The tide was coming in fast. They'd have to pack up soon and move up the beach if they were staying.

In his peripheral vision, he saw Leanne stand on one leg, perfectly poised. Placing one foot in front of another she sank into a cross-legged yoga position and watched him as he read. He turned the page without taking the words in and without looking up.

'You're not keen on kids then?' he said. She sighed by way of a reply. 'It'll be different when you have your own.'

'Ew. I am *never* having kids.'

'You might change your mind when you find that special person to have them with.' He thought with a pang about Hannah. How they'd thought they would be for ever.

'No.'

'Wow. I adore my children. I hate being a part-time parent. If I could, I'd have them full time.'

She made a noise that sounded like "bleurgh", and then muttered, 'I wish I'd gone with Rosie now.'

'Why *didn't* you go with Rosie?' He gave her a sharp look.

'I er, I thought you might sort of, *notice* me more ...' Her voice was hesitant and not at all like the Leanne he knew.

'Huh? I've always noticed you. I think you're amazing!'

'Yeah, for being the first up the cliff face, the fittest one, the reliable one. You don't notice me as a—' The muscles in her face twitched and worked but no words followed. She mumbled, 'I thought you might have a no shagging rule on the courses, so, on the beach, it might be different.'

'What?' As the implications of her words sank in, he dry washed his face with his hands and eyed her over his fingers. 'Oh, Leanne. I do have a "no-shagging rule", as you put it, it would be totally unprofessional – but look – I'm sorry if I ever gave you the impression that I, er ... because I don't.'

Looking at her stricken expression, he added, 'Not that you're not gorgeous and everything, because you have a fantastic body, and you obviously take a lot of care of it.' He hurried on. 'But I, oh God, I-I'm sorry but, I don't fancy you. You should wait for someone who will fancy you. And they will, I'm sure. Just—' He'd come to the horrible knowledge that he should have stopped while he was only slightly behind. 'Not me.'

'What is "shagging"?' Lily asked, curiously. Gareth knew, with a sinking feeling, that she'd been spectating for some time. 'I need a wee, Daddy.' She added helpfully, 'I can wee in the sea.'

Relieved to get away, he took her little hand and said to Leanne, 'Can you keep an eye on Jack please? He's still asleep. I won't be a minute.' Leanne looked lost and wrapped a towel around her shoulders and knees.

How could he have missed the signs, he thought, listening

with only half an ear to Lily's chatter as she skipped beside him the short distance to the sea. All this time? He was an idiot. Or blind. Had he noticed and ignored it? Had he noticed and, oh God, been *flattered?* How long had she been carrying a torch for him?

Half-remembered incidents bubbled to the surface and he winced at his dim-witted oblivion. He glanced over his shoulder towards their camp and saw Leanne staring back at him, her arms hugging her knees.

His gaze took in Rosie walking towards them, the breeze moulding the blue dress to her curves and twirling her auburn curls.

'Rosie's back!' he told Lily. She whirled around to see where and overbalanced, face first. Spluttering and wiping her eyes, she charged out of the water with him in hot pursuit. He grinned at her sturdy figure. She was growing up so fast. It seemed such a short while ago that she'd screamed full into his ear with terror when he'd first paddled in the sea with her.

'Phew, goodness me, it's hot out there.' She beamed at him. 'Better put these in the shade!' Rosie held a large cake box out to him, and Lily immediately took possession of one of her available hands, chattering about the ice-cream and the rock pools. He popped the cake box into his almost empty cool box and waited while she settled herself beneath the shade.

'So, did it go well then?' Gareth asked when Lily took a breath.

'It certainly did. I actually sold something! To an actual real customer! That cowl, collar thing that you liked, Leanne, the one I made the—' Her head swivelled between them, and her eyes narrowed. 'What's going on? Have you two had a row?'

'No,' said Leanne.

'Erm,' said Gareth, at the same time.

'They have,' said Lily, nodding wisely. 'What's in your box, Rosie?'

'Not a row, exactly.' Gareth put his hand on the cool box, protecting it from his daughter's inquisitive fingers. 'Perhaps a misunderstanding. That's Rosie's box, sweetheart. Not yours.'

Leanne remained silent and hugged her knees tighter. He wanted to make it all right again for her, wanted the old Leanne back. It reminded him of how he'd felt when he saw Hannah last, when she'd dropped the children off. The same way he reacted when his children fell over and hurt themselves. It *was* love, it was *caring* – but that didn't make it the sort of love that he knew Leanne wanted.

Jack awoke into the silence of the tension between them, knuckling his eyes and yawning. 'Thirsty.' Leanne reached into their cool box, unscrewed a bottle of water and handed it to him.

'Thank you.' Jack nodded, still yawning.

'Thank you,' said Gareth to Leanne. It wasn't the right time to mention reusable bottles, so he didn't.

'Could I have one of those too, please, Leanne?' Rosie asked. 'Thanks, lovely girl. I'm parched.' Gareth watched her throw her head back to drink, watched her throat and followed the skin down to the tan line on her rounded breasts in the sundress. She licked her lips and beamed at them all.

'I bring gifts! Gareth, would you do the honours, please?' Gareth opened the box towards them. 'Look! What can you see?'

'Cakes!' yelled Lily. 'I see lots of little tiny cakes.'

'What're they?' A still drowsy Jack pointed at the wrapped packages.

'Sandwiches! All different kinds.' She encompassed them all with her smile and said, 'This is a generous afternoon tea for two people. It's not going to go far between five of us, so it's just a little nibble each of something nice. I think we should eat them all now, before they dry up in the heat.'

She put the box onto the beach mats, and Gareth found some napkins, holding back his voracious offspring until Rosie and Leanne had made their choices.

'Lucy's given me a ton of ideas about how to promote myself,' Rosie said, wiping cream from her fingers. 'And she was so enthusiastic that I nodded as if I understood everything. But I don't have a clue! Leanne, you're pretty hot on your website and social media, can you help me?'

'Course,' said Leanne, trying not to look pleased. Rosie smiled her thanks.

'She also suggested I name my business after my fire engine. I said I hadn't even seen it, but she thought of Fire Truck Felts, and, well, I really like it. Even though I haven't seen it – it might be a total wreck ...'

'We'd better go and get it then,' Gareth said. 'Shall I ring tomorrow and make some arrangements?'

'That would be really kind of you, thank you!'

'Fire engine?' Jack was agog. Rosie looked at him and back at Gareth with an enquiring eye.

'Let me see how the land lies with it first, Jack.'

'This has given me so much confidence.' Rosie stretched her legs out in front of her, wiggling her toes. 'I'm powering on with the divorce – he can't stop that happening. And if I have to sell the house, well, then I have to sell it. But I'm going to do my best to fight for it. Even if I have to take lodgers or something.'

'I'll be your lodger,' Leanne said, quickly. 'Please. I really love it here. I'll pay the going rate, and if I can also pay for storage for my stock, that would be brilliant.' She eyed Gareth, and his stomach sank, wondering what her motives were. But she added, 'I hardly know you, Rosie, but you seem fair, and you're always honest with me.' She ducked her head. 'I know I'm not ... very good at making friends,' she mumbled. 'But I will try.'

'We can be your friends,' said Lily, patting her smooth

thigh with her sticky, cake-crumby hand. Leanne lifted her hand away with pincer fingers and a pained expression. Both Rosie and Gareth pealed with laughter. Even Lily and Jack joined in, although they almost certainly didn't know why they were laughing.

'What?' Leanne said, her brow puckered.

'You'll be fine as long as your new friends are over eighteen, then ...' Rosie chuckled, and went on. 'I've got some ideas about running workshops and classes on felting, and sketching, getting inspiration out of doors, that sort of thing. I did a bit of googling. If they're set up well, people are prepared to pay properly.'

'Your house will be perfect for that.' Gareth nodded, thoughtfully. 'Lots of parking, great position just off the main road, terrific views.'

'Maybe I can do something like that with the wool,' Leanne said, and looked around at their faces. 'What? I can tell people what to do. I'm good at that. We could have felting for half a day and knitting for the other half. Or felting for most of the day and an hour of knitting.' Her eyes roved along the horizon as she thought, and she shrugged. 'Or I could just offer a discount on yarns ...'

'... and we'd do lovely home-cooked lunches,' said Rosie.

'If we could finish off those other bedrooms and those outhouses, people could stay. Make a weekend of it.' Leanne was warming to her theme. Gareth thought about how much those renovations might cost and kept his mouth shut. Now wasn't the time to pour cold water on their dreams. He wasn't exactly pursuing his own dreams, was he? But he could visualise theirs actually happening.

'I think now might be a good time to pack up,' he pointed out, having looked up. 'Before we're swept away by the sea – and have you seen those clouds?'

Chapter Twenty-Five

The cloudburst had been sharp but mercifully short, and between navigating that, and with her head bursting with ideas, Rosie hadn't realised how quiet Leanne was for quite some time. She studied her in the passenger seat where she sat staring straight ahead.

'Do you want to talk about it?'

'What?' Leanne stared out of the windscreen.

'This row you didn't have with Gareth.'

'It wasn't a row.'

'Even Lily could see something had happened between you.' Rosie glanced in the mirror, her pulse increasing as she changed lanes. Even though she knew this route so well, driving was never going to be her favourite thing. Talking with Leanne took her mind off her fears. 'You don't have to tell me, but I'd like to stay friends with both of you, and at the moment I feel like the pig in the middle.'

'Uh, *o-kaaaaay*!' She waggled her long neck. 'I should have gone with you. I was wrong and I'm sorry.' She huffed a long exasperated sigh. 'But Gareth just wanted to make sandcastles, and look for crabs or something.'

'Sounds like fun to me!'

'Oh well, you *would* say that.'

'Explain to me.'

'I can't do all that!' Her feet beat a nervous tattoo on the floor mats. 'All that *pretending* that kids want you to do. I don't know how to!' Her voice fell to a mumble. 'So I waited until they were asleep ...'

She fell silent, and Rosie's rapid, sideways glance confirmed that Leanne's red face wasn't sunburn. After a long pause, Rosie said, 'You came onto him, didn't you?'

'Yes.' Leanne buried her face in her hands. 'He said he

didn't see me like, like *that*. How will I ever go on another course with him again?'

'Oh, Leanne.' Rosie had nothing to offer. She could see how excruciating it would be for them both. 'Um, so, I'm going to ask – was it the courses that you enjoyed? Or the thought of seeing Gareth?'

Leanne peered through her fingers, considering the question. 'Both, I suppose. I've always really enjoyed the courses. But it wouldn't be the same without Gareth there.'

'Well, maybe you could try some different courses, and widen your circle of friends.' Rosie laughed suddenly, surprising herself. 'That's how I found you! Lucy from the Art Café said something a bit like that during Mum's funeral party ...' She paused, struck by the term, "party". It was how her mum had always referred to it. Not a wake. 'Too dismal, darling', she'd say. Rosie wrestled herself back to the present, and carried on where she'd left off. 'I booked myself onto the course straight away. You have already changed my life, Leanne.

'And, you know, Gareth has a lot on his plate right now, what with juggling his children, his two jobs, and his loyalties to his parents. Not that I'm telling you to keep trying,' she added hastily, and then, as the thought occurred to her, 'You didn't ask to be my tenant so that you could keep seeing him, did you?'

Leanne turned a scornful expression her way. 'Oh, per-lease. I've got *some* pride. I'm not *chasing* him. He's had his chance.' She pulled one arm into an overhead stretch, and added, as she stretched the other, 'And I hadn't factored kids into it.' She gave a shudder of disgust. Rosie, about to say how lovely Lily and Jack were, kept her counsel.

'Shall we stock up on the food shopping?' she suggested instead. 'I want to crack on and make stock, and all the million and one other things we talked about, and I don't want to be fannying about to the shops every ten minutes.'

Later, emptying the loaded trolley into the back of the car, Leanne said, 'You should be growing your own veggies, and some fruit. That would save you loads. It's good for you and you have plenty of space.'

'I've never actually thought about that. Do you know anything about gardening?'

'A bit. But we could learn. What else have I got to do, right now?'

'Aw, sweetie. Don't be down. I understand that you're disappointed, but there will be someone who is just right for you.'

'Yeah. I s'pose. I feel like a bit of an idiot though.'

'I really don't think you need to. I don't know Gareth very well, but I bet he doesn't think you're an idiot at all.' She sincerely hoped so, as her heart constricted at the thought that he might avoid *her* in the process of avoiding Leanne. And then she felt *really* mean.

Gareth was as good as his word, and contacted the museum about her fire engine. He dropped in a couple of days later, along with Lily and Jack, to let her know. Rosie and Leanne were dying wool in huge buckets.

'How are Hannah's parents now?' Rosie asked, as she made blackcurrant squash for the children.

'They're out of hospital, but she's staying down there until either they get someone else in, or they can manage themselves, I suppose. She's managed to get leave and Ian has gone back to work, but he went home on the train so she's still got the car. I guess Mummy will want these two monsters back home with her soon!' Lily and Jack obliged with monster faces and noises to make them laugh.

'How have you managed with your work?'

'I'm in a more executive health and safety role now. I'm not as hands-on as I was and can arrange my hours to suit me more.'

Lily was unable to contain herself. 'Rosie, Daddy is taking us swimming now and then we're going to visit Nanna and Grandad.'

'On the basis that swimming will wear you both out and so you'll be really good for Nanna.' Gareth winked at his daughter who hung on his arm and pretended to be cross with him. Rosie watched, remembering Keira at the same age with Chester. She'd adored him, and he could do no wrong. And he'd abandoned her. Only returning when Lana had died. She frowned. There was some connection, but she couldn't for the life of her think what it was.

'Anyway, we popped over to tell you that we can collect your fire engine!'

Rosie squeaked an 'Ooh! Oh my goodness, how exciting. I can't wait to see it. When?' They agreed on an upcoming Saturday. 'And, um, how much is it going to cost to get it here?' Rosie held her breath.

'Well, that could be up to you.' He tapped his chin. 'It's driveable. So it doesn't need a low loader.'

As his words sank in, Rosie's pulse began to hammer. 'So, who would drive it?'

'Well, you could.'

'Me?'

'You can drive, Rosie!' Leanne said. 'And you'd be driving it anyway. Why not start now?'

'But, I, er, I …' Rosie floundered, reluctant to say that she was scared. 'Hang on a minute. I don't have a HGV licence. How can I drive it?'

'Well, this is the best bit. It's like a mini fire engine.'

'Oh. I'm not sure whether I'm disappointed or relieved.'

'It's still beautiful. I don't think you'll be disappointed.'

'Um.' Leanne leaned forward. 'I drive my big van everywhere. I could drive it, if you wanted me to …?' She paused, and Rosie saw her thinking. 'I've got a satnav. We could take turns?'

'It would be lovely to have somebody with me,' Rosie said. 'Could we do that?'

'Why not?' Gareth smiled at them.

'Are we coming, Dad?' Jack asked.

'Of course you are!' Gareth said. 'You want to see Rosie's fire engine, don't you? We're a Team!'

'Team Bedelia,' said Leanne, unexpectedly. She looked around at their enquiring faces. 'Bedelia is the mythic Celtic goddess of fire. Rosie has red hair, she got her inspiration for the first piece she sold, from the firepit the night I arrived.' She shrugged. 'So the fire engine is called Bedelia.'

'Wow,' said Gareth.

'I love it,' Rosie said, slowly. 'That's genius, Leanne. What made you think of it?'

'I read it once. I don't forget things. And, I like patterns. The firepit and the fire engine and that thing Rosie made, it's all a pattern.' She shrugged as if it all made perfect sense and how hadn't they seen it?

Gareth promised to pass on details for insurance and they confirmed that they'd meet early, so that, should the weather still be as hot as it was, they could travel in the cooler morning.

The museum was tucked away amongst the most southerly villages of the Cotswolds, down a narrow lane, bordered with high hedges. An elderly man emerged from the direction of an expansive shed that was emblazoned with a huge metal banner. He looked as if he'd stepped from a bygone age, in long boots and britches, with a tweed jacket and gamekeeper hat. White hair and a thick moustache and beard completed the ensemble. He looked like an out of season Santa.

'Hello, a lovely day for it indeed. So, one of you ladies is Rosabeth Bunting?'

'That'll be me.' Rosie stepped forward to shake his outstretched hand.

'And Gareth Merwyn-Jones.' Another handshake. 'My name is Brian Brimble.'

He turned to Leanne, who kept her hands firmly in the pocket of her shorts. She mumbled, 'I'm not anyone, I'm, just, er …'

Brian Brimble gave her a little military nod to replace the handshake, and repeated the manoeuvre to Lily and Jack, who gazed back, wide-eyed.

'Thank you for coming along so promptly. We weren't sure if you would. Some people would prefer not to have a fire engine dumped on them, what?'

'What?' Rosie responded automatically, realising too late that this was a figure of speech from another era. She added an 'Ah,' feeling unequal already to owning this vintage vehicle.

They all trooped after Brian as he led them around to the back of the big shed. She felt Lily's little hand creep into hers and gave it a squeeze. Despite not knowing anything about cars, Rosie felt sad that it was all closing down. It had been someone's dream.

Gareth, holding Jack's hand, was asking Brian all sorts of intelligent questions and she was glad he was there. She hurried along behind them, listening to Leanne and Gareth discussing fuelling with Brian, along with tyre conditions, certifications for this and that, what equipment was included, on and on. The fire engine was tucked behind a tall hedge.

'Wow.' Gareth stared at the glossy red flanks of the creature before him. 'Wow.'

'Oh.' Rosie stared too. 'Where's the rest of it?' She swept her gaze from one end of the scarlet vehicle to the other. It didn't take long. Even though Gareth had said it was a miniature version, in her head, she'd still envisaged a huge Dennis fire engine, somehow full of handsome, hunky firemen, hauling their hoses and tipping their helmets back to reveal brilliant white smiles in sooty faces. It was clear that her imagination had over-revved somewhat. The fire truck before her was – well, it *was* pretty. Pretty small. The smallest fire engine she'd ever seen.

She whispered to Gareth, 'Did it want to be a real fire engine but got turned down for not meeting the height requirement?'

Brian boomed with laughter. 'This, my dear, is a 1979 Ford A series, powered by a petrol Ford 3000cc V6 engine. Bodied by Bridge Coachworks of Ealing, London. It has a 200 gallon water tank and Godiva 500 gallon per minute pump. Originally supplied to the Royal Ordnance factory in Bridgewater, Somerset then later served at Rugeley Power Station.' Rosie could feel her mouth hanging open. She clamped it shut. Brian powered on.

'A few A Series were used by public fire brigades, mainly as small emergency tenders, but there was no Home Office approved specification for a light pumper, so the A series pumpers that did get built went to private industrial, factory or institutional brigades. Presumably this is how your grandfather came by it. This is a splendid example. We were delighted when he bequeathed her to us.' He reached out a familiar hand and patted it gently. 'I'll be sad to see her go. She was always very popular with the visitors. Bye-bye, girl.' He wiped a tear from his eye.

'We're going to call it Bedelia,' said Leanne. 'After the goddess of fire.'

'Wonderful!' Brian clapped his hands and nearly dropped his clipboard.

'Why did grandfather buy it? I had no idea it even existed!'

'I understand that he had plans to turn it into a sort of "gypsy wagon", but they didn't get off the ground.'

'Ah. That explains everything. Nana would never have entertained such a thing.' Rosie laughed and stopped abruptly. This vehicle was an embodiment of her beloved grandfather's hopes and dreams. Could she pick up where he'd left off and convert it into a modern day version of a gypsy wagon, a camper van?

Rosie had a flashback to her grandfather in his big shed, always working on some contraption or other. She felt a little sad that he hadn't been able to go adventuring in his little fire truck. She stepped closer to it. 'Does everything still work?'

Gareth had explored its outer flanks and was currently delving into the cubby holes and shutters like the boy he undoubtedly was, beneath all that health and safety gravity. 'The hose is still in here – and the pump and look at this! Look – it goes right through to the other side!' Rosie shook her head, nonplussed. 'You're going to drive this!'

Rosie gaped. 'But, but, it's *huge!* I can't drive *that!*' Could she? Her thoughts jangled together. She was insured to drive it, along with Leanne and Gareth, so there was nothing to stop her. Just her own lack of confidence.

'Oh, you were saying how ridiculously small it was just a minute ago. Make your mind up.' Gareth's brown eyes twinkled at her and she glared back at him. He was enjoying himself enormously, she could see. He addressed Brian. 'It's all ready to drive away, isn't it?'

'Oh yes.' Brian nodded. 'All the vehicles are drained of fuel while they're in there'—he waved a cheerful hand towards the enormous shed—'it would go up like a fireball if they weren't ... But yes, she's all ready for you, as we discussed. We've put new tyres on, and checked the brakes and all the other things you asked for.'

Rosie made a mental note to ask how much it had cost to make the vehicle roadworthy. But she was still reeling at the prospect of driving it.

She glanced over to see that Leanne wore a similar expression of enchantment to Gareth. Rosie sucked her teeth. This was another adventure, right? Hadn't she walked over the edge of a cliff? She could do anything now. She could. Totally. Do. Anything.

Her imagination conjured up a picture of Gareth, tall, strong and capable in a fireman's uniform, and she had to swallow hard past her suddenly dry throat. She turned to Brian, assuming a practical air as a thought occurred.

'How much would this be worth?'

Brian tipped his head to one side. 'Difficult to say. There weren't many of them made so they're quite rare – but the value depends on what someone might want to pay for it. As I said, it could be converted – some people have used them as gin bars. I'm quite partial to a tot of gin myself, and as round the world tour buses, and for weddings, and hen parties, that sort of thing. They're sturdy beasts, and they haven't usually done much mileage, seeing as they're kept on sites and not used much. I don't know, in its current condition, say somewhere around five grand?'

'Okay.' Rosie tried not to look too disappointed. For a moment, she'd wondered whether it might save her fortunes, pay for the remaining house renovations, keep her in a manner to which she could become accustomed.

'Do you have room for her at your house?' Brian asked, as if the fire engine was a puppy going to a new home.

'Well, I do, as it happens.'

'Although she's going to live in my yard while we do some renovations on her,' Gareth added with a faintly proprietorial air.

'Well, then you don't have to make a decision about what to do with her straight away. It's a piece of history. And she's beautiful.'

'It, *she*, is, actually …' Rosie stared at the poppy red beast again, thinking about her grandfather. The vehicle seemed to be smiling at her. She *was* part of the family, she supposed. And it was pointless having it if she was too scared to drive it. It, *she*, whatever, would just be a big red, white elephant, stuck in Gareth's yard, waiting for something to be done to it. That couldn't happen, she decided, firmly. She needed to man up.

Chapter Twenty-Six

'I can't do it.' Rosie backed away from the beckoning open door to the cab.

'Just try sitting in it,' Gareth said, quietly, standing alongside her. From the corner of her eye, Rosie was aware of Lily, Jack and Leanne watching.

'Don't worry Rosie. I'll drive,' said Leanne, in her "shall we get on with it" voice.

It was just the motivation Rosie needed. She swung herself into the cab.

'There's no power steering,' said Brian, helpfully. 'And you need to double de-clutch on these older gear boxes, and—'

'—so you get a workout at the same time,' Gareth interjected smoothly, as Rosie's jaw began to slacken in alarm. 'And I can show you how to double de-clutch. It's easy.'

On her lofty perch, Rosie let their words drift over her. Her pulse settled and she ran her hands up and down the wheel, feeling the smooth, worn surface. When had her self-confidence thinned and wavered so that she'd become a prisoner, trapped by her lack of self-belief? She squared her shoulders. Enough.

'Is Rosie going to drive us home?' Jack peered up at her, bringing her thoughts back to the present. 'I want to be a fireman when I grow up.'

'I want to be a fireman too!' squeaked Lily.

'Is there a siren?' Jack wanted to know. 'And blue lights?'

'Sadly,' Brian said, 'we've had to disconnect them, or you wouldn't be allowed on the road.'

'Boo!' wailed Jack and Lily. 'We'll make the siren noises ourselves. *Bee baaa, bee baaaa …*'

Gareth climbed into the cab beside Rosie, grinning down at his children. Rosie turned the ignition key. The engine rumbled to life. And then, it was just like abseiling down that cliff. Gareth's calm voice soothed the jumping beans in her. She heard Brian cheering as she pulled away. A little jerky, but no kangaroo hops.

Rosie licked her lips, feeding the steering wheel through sticky palms and checking the wing mirrors. 'I can't believe I'm driving this.'

'And you're doing really well too! Very impressive.' Rosie glowed with pride. 'Just take it all nice and slow.' All too soon, it was time for Leanne to take her place.

'I don't want to get out,' Leanne said to Rosie when they'd stopped. 'Isn't she gorgeous? You are so lucky.'

'She *is* gorgeous.' Rosie nodded. 'I think I'm in love.'

After the initial terror of being on the narrow country roads, she began to relax, and Leanne was a non-judgemental passenger, content to watch the scenery. As passing drivers waved at them, she began to feel like the queen. It was quite noisy in the cab, and there was no radio, so they sang instead.

Stopping for fuel, and later, something to eat and to swop over, they began to realise what a draw their vintage fire engine really was.

'I'm starting to feel really envious of you two,' Gareth said in the motorway services, after several people quizzed them about what it was like to drive, and how cool it was.

'Yeah, and I am.' Jack pulled a face. 'I wish we could have a go.'

'Can't we go wiv Rosie, Daddy?' Lily pouted.

'I'm sorry, guys. There aren't any proper seats for children in it.' Gareth tried to mollify his disgruntled children.

'I'm sorry too. But I promise that you can sit in the front seats when we get it home, for as long as you like.' Rosie hugged herself with joy. 'To think I was terrified of driving her this morning.'

'It's pretty slow going though,' Leanne admitted.

'What? Don't listen to her, Bedelia,' Rosie turned to gaze at the engine through the window, where they could see her parked.

It took them nearly three hours to make the return journey. They stopped off to buy marshmallows and wine, and returned to a little flurry of people, clustered around the fire engine. Rosie almost burst with pride. Closer to home, Gareth overtook them and led them to his yard, and it was a tired but jubilant Rosie and Leanne who climbed out of the cab. Jack and Lily clambered straight into their vacated seats and jostled for the steering wheel, under their father's watchful eye. As Rosie stretched, a tall, slender woman made her way towards them, with a tall, greying man who reminded her of Gareth.

Gareth introduced them.

'Thank you so much for letting me store this old girl here,' Rosie said.

'Show us round her then.' Cled grinned in delight, his eyes raking the old vehicle. 'She's in great nick. You drove her all the way then?'

'Well, we fought over the driving ...' Rosie smiled. 'And I know this is just a baby compared to your monsters, but I loved being up so high. It must be amazing in the cabs of your HGVs.' She looked around her. 'My ex-husband is a musician, and I never ceased to be amazed by the hauliers who brought the staging for the really big concerts. The way they manoeuvred those enormous trucks about. Amazing.'

Carol walked around the fire engine as Rosie talked. 'Presumably you'll be machining some new valves to change her to unleaded?' She directed her questions at Gareth, and Rosie felt a little miffed. Not that she knew any of the answers, she acknowledged. Cled, like his son, had returned to boyhood, investigating the lockers and pumping equipment, with excited accompaniments from Jack and Lily who didn't want to be left out of anything.

'Congratulations,' Carol said, 'she's a cracker. What are you planning to do with her?'

Rosie began to explain her plans and then tailed off. 'We're going to order some pizzas this evening, and light the firepit in celebration ...'

'And toast marshmallows!' said Lily.

'And um, I wondered, if you'd like to come over too?' She was aware of Gareth, silent and stiffening with tension, and the long pause seemed to indicate that the reply would be a no. 'It's only about twenty minutes away.'

'Well, it's not a school night,' Carol said, eventually, 'so why not? Thank you for inviting us.'

'Do you want me to come back and collect you?' Gareth asked them. 'I'm dropping Rosie and Leanne back now.'

'That would be lovely.'

Gareth said, 'About six, I should think, to give us all a chance to freshen up.'

Rosie and Leanne patted the fire engine goodbye.

'See you soon, Bedelia.'

On the short journey home, Leanne shared the back seats with Lily and Jack and watched whatever cartoon they were watching for the millionth time. Gareth said quietly to Rosie, beside him in the passenger seat, 'Thank you for that.'

'What?'

'Mum. She's – she used to be so different. She was so much fun. But since Aled went, she's replaced him with the business.' He sighed and her heart broke for him. He couldn't fix this one, but it wouldn't stop him trying. 'And I'm pretty sure that Dad is thinking about retirement for them, but ...' He shook his head and she saw him swallow.

Driving the fire engine had brought all her senses to the

surface. Just like the abseiling had. If she closed her eyes now she could still see him clearly, the black hair and close beard that framed his resolute chin, and the charcoal grey polo shirt that hugged his lean body.

'Does she have any hobbies? Or things they do together?'

'Nothing. It's all about work.' He threw her a glance. 'And I think she sees my courses as a self-indulgent hobby.'

Rosie nodded, beginning to understand. 'And why should you have a hobby which you enjoy, when her life as she knew it is over …?' Impulsively, she reached over and squeezed his bare arm. And even though her intention was to offer him some comfort, her heart flurried at the feel of the hard muscles beneath his warm skin. 'I read somewhere that time is a great deadener of grief.'

His full lips compressed briefly, and then he smiled at her. 'It's been a brilliant day. Looking forward to that pizza!'

'Me too. I hope it cools down a bit though, or there's no way I'm lighting the firepit.'

She narrowed her eyes, squinting ahead. 'Oh *fuuu*—for goodness' sake. We've got a visitor.'

Chapter Twenty-Seven

Chester, glaring at the door, spun around as he heard the car pull up. Rosie blew out a long, weary sigh.

'Just who I wanted to see. Not.' She climbed out, straightening her back, and stalked towards her ex-husband to be. *Be the fire goddess Bedelia.* 'Can I help you?'

'You've changed the locks!' His tone was incredulous.

'You'll be pleased to know that my solicitor informs me that the decree absolute will be served on you any day now.'

He barked a laugh. 'Good luck with that. You don't know where I live.'

'*I* don't need to know. Your solicitor will handle that.'

'I've sacked her.'

'That's your problem. And if I have to pay for someone to find you, that money comes out of the pot.'

'I want my pound of flesh.' White beads of spittle collected in the corners of his mouth. 'I'm not walking away without what I'm owed.'

'What is it you think you are owed?' It was her turn to sound incredulous.

'We were together for twenty years!'

'Well, you haven't given me a thought for the last what, six years? And you spent the ten years before that, shagging your way round the music circuit! I should've divorced you a whole lot earlier!'

He windmilled his arms around, marching around her. His shoes crunched on the gravel drive. She was aware of Gareth, Leanne and the children in the car, watching and listening. She'd just co-driven a fire engine all the way from England. This man could not hurt her any more.

'That's the business, innit? It's what *happens*. It's not *personal*.'

She still reeled at his callousness. There was a time when his words would have thrust a burning spear into her heart. When she would have cried for days. When he made her feel as if she was wrong, and he was right, and how dare she expect anything different. And she'd carried on working, and cooking and cleaning and pretending to the children that everything was normal.

He said, wildly, 'Your mother – she knew what it was like *out there* though. That's why she—' He stopped dead, his face twitching.

'Why she *what?*'

'Nothing!' He lifted his arms extravagantly, palms up. Fleetingly, she wondered if he was high on something. His eyes hooded and with a leer, he added, 'But I bet there's more where that came from. I know you're holding out on me.'

'I have no idea to what you may be referring,' she said, crisply. 'But I've had the house valued, and I have passed all my receipts on to my solicitor. If you still wish to contest our financial obligations, then it will need to go to mediation and you must also make a full and final disclosure of your finances too. And then court, if necessary. I'm not afraid of going to court. I've got nothing to hide. Have you?'

His eyes disappeared in the folds of his face as he glared down at her. 'You *bitch*.' Spit flew out of his mouth and she wiped her face. She heard the driver's door open and Gareth's tread on the gravel.

'I don't care what you call me now, Chester. You'll get what's fair, and not a penny more, when the time comes. And maybe, it will be that you owe me money. I bet you've had your finger in a few pies, knowing you.'

She saw his expression change. His lip curled upwards on one side, pulling one eyebrow with it. Oh, leopards never change their spots! Since she'd met him as an emerging musician at a talent show he'd always been keen to put money on “the next big thing”, the next big band or musical venue. And she’d backed him in the beginning. After all, he was brilliant and he could be charming, and you had to take a few risks in this sort of business, didn’t you? And some of his hunches paid off, and they’d have holidays and pay off the most pressing bills. But before she could save any of it, he’d have slapped it on the next thing. They’d limped along like this for years. He would never change.

‘So what’s the next big thing, Chester? Got any tips for me?’ His mouth opened and closed like a fish and his face shut like a trap. She said, matily, ‘Is it a new band? A big show? Have they asked you to back it? Come on Chester, you’re brilliant! Who wouldn’t want you on their side? And you’ve got money, haven’t you? You’ve always got a few bob tucked away …’ He preened for just a second, but she saw it – that now he was desperate. ‘So who’s after you? How much do you need?’

‘Fifty grand!’ he roared. His windmill arms flailed again and he paced back and forth and then stopped to look at her. ‘Get me fifty grand and I’ll go. I’ll sign your bloody papers.’ He shot a glance at Gareth, hovering nearby, his brows knitted and looking surprisingly menacing. Leanne was now leaning against the car, arms folded in a tensed “lemme at ’im” pose. ‘And I’ll leave you alone. I’ll sign anything. I did it before, didn’t I? I kept my promise. I’ll be gone.’

‘I haven’t got fifty grand!’ Rosie shook her head, trying to clear the buzzing inside her brain. What was he talking about?

‘Well, you’d better find it!’ He screamed into her face and Gareth crossed the space. Chester stepped back. ‘You’ve got four weeks. They’ll find me – and then they’ll come for you.’

‘Don’t you dare threaten me!’

‘I’m calling the police.’ Gareth towered over him.

‘Don’t bother. I’m going.’ Chester rolled his eyes insolently and slunk away. They watched him go.

'Looks like I got away without giving him a key, then.' Rosie made an attempt at a grin, rubbing her tight chest with the heel of her hand. Wordlessly, he opened his arms and crushed her to him. Their bodies touched in a single unbroken line for a long moment. His heart thumped solidly against her ear. Her arms folded around his lean waist.

Squeezing her in return, it felt like a wonderful, comforting oasis of time before he relaxed his grip and looked down at her. His brown eyes bored into her soul, and there was no denying the concern in his expression.

'Shall we go and collect the rest of the team?' Legs wobbly from the adrenaline fizzing through her body, she was glad of his hand around hers as they returned to the car. Leanne's face was fierce, and for a moment, Rosie quailed, remembering too late Leanne's obsession with Gareth.

Until Leanne said, 'I heard every word. You should have joined the police.' She reached out and gave Rosie a quick, hard hug. 'How did you stay so totally cool? You didn't even swear!'

Rosie snorted. 'Oh, trust me, I wasn't that cool when I found him here that first night home after the weekend. Poor Gareth will testify to that. I think he thought I was going to burst into flames.'

'See? The fire goddess.' Leanne's mouth curved upwards. 'So what happens next?'

'I want to write down the things he said, so I can think about them. Would you guys help so I don't forget something? I know we're on a deadline.' She glanced at her watch.

Gareth said, 'We can cancel tonight, if you like ...'

'Not on your life. I am not letting that shi—' She glanced into the car. Lily and Jack continued to watch their cartoon, oblivious to the drama outside on the drive. She edited herself to: 'I'm not letting that *charlatan* spoil our celebrations.'

Half an hour later, their notes written down, Gareth sped off with his children to collect his parents and pizzas, and Rosie and Leanne put a colourful oilcloth on the garden table, strung fairy lights wherever they could, then made sure the public areas of the house were spick and span.

Making some mixed salads and hunting out bamboo skewers for the marshmallows, Rosie thought about that long, wonderful hug on her drive. She could still feel the imprint of Gareth's long, muscular body against hers, and she wanted to feel it again.

Showered and in a fresh, floral tea dress which she'd made herself some years back, Rosie opened the door to Lily and Jack and their grandparents.

'Nana, look, this is the kitchen ...' Lily tugged on Carol's hand.

'And the toilet is there ...' Jack pointed. Rosie hid a smile.

'And Rosie did all the renovations herself.' Bringing up the rear, Gareth smiled over several boxes of pizza and handed her a bag, clanking with bottles. 'She's a woman of many talents!'

'Very impressive.' Gareth's parents looked around them and Rosie felt a glow of pride, mixed with embarrassment at the unexpected praise.

She said, 'Gareth is being kind. There's still so much to be done.'

Lily and Jack tugged their grandparents into the garden.

Gareth dipped his head to leave a kiss on her cheek. 'You look lovely. There's some juice and lemonade for the kids. Mum and Dad sprang for the wine. They're on the red.'

'Thank you. That's kind of them. I'll take them some out.'

They were both in the garden. Cled was kicking a football about with Jack and Lily. Carol, in neatly fitting black jeans, an animal print shirt and a bronze knit slung around her shoulders, gazed out at the view. At its best under the soft sky, the ebbing tide reflected the turquoise, corals and pinks.

Rosie handed her a large glass of red wine and left Cled's on the table.

'Thank you.' Holding it up to the setting sun, she said, 'It's very peaceful here. Have you ever been flooded?'

'No, thank goodness. It used to be a farm, many years ago but the ground is too boggy to graze or to grow anything, and it fell into disuse. That's how we were able to buy it so cheaply. The sea has receded over the years, and we do have some pretty high tides, but they've never come close enough to affect us. You can't walk to this bit of sea from here though, it's so marshy. But the public beach is close enough.' She excused herself to bring out the salads and nibbles.

'Pizza!' Gareth called, bringing the boxes out and spreading them across the table.

'Yay!' Lily and Jack were first to sit. Leanne appeared, hair slicked back with a sparkly clip, wearing a pair of skinny jeans and a glittery vest top, and Lily stared at her in awe. 'You look like a princess!' she declared, and Leanne blushed.

'Oh. Thanks.' She lit the firepit, prompting a lecture from Gareth to his children about staying well away from it. The wine flowed, and the sky became pinker. The sun blazed liquid gold as it slipped into the sea, and they toasted its journey with marshmallows, toasted over the fire. Rosie brought throws out to drape around everyone as the temperature dipped. Flickers of fire lit their faces and the soft night settled around them all. Lily leaned sleepily against Leanne, her newest best friend.

'Wonders will never cease,' Gareth murmured to Rosie, nodding at them with a smile.

'So, talk us through your plans,' Carol said, sipping her wine. 'Gareth says you make felt. I have no idea what that means.'

'I'll bring some to show you.' Rosie slipped away from the table, switching on the fairy lights on her way to her workshop. She returned with a selection of pieces and showed them briefly how the process worked.

'Could you work with alpaca fleece?' Leanne leaned forward to look more closely, the throw around both her and Lily slipping off. Lily whimpered and Leanne dipped backwards awkwardly to tuck it around the sleeping little girl. Carol pulled off her bronze knitted sweater, passing it over to Leanne and snuggled up to Cled. Rosie's gaze swivelled to Gareth, whose eyes crinkled in a smile. People, weaving themselves together with kindness.

'Absolutely. It's beautiful to felt with. And alpaca is completely ethical, whereas merino wool isn't always. Even now. Maybe we have room for a few of our own alpacas!'

'These colours are astonishing.' Carol lifted a ball and fingered it, thoughtfully. 'Have you made a business plan?' she asked.

'Uh – I don't know how to.'

'I can help you with that.'

'Thank you! I need all the help I can get right now. Would you like to see my workshop? I've got so much more in there, and designs, ideas ...'

'I would.' Carol stood, holding out her glass. Gareth topped her up, and Rosie caught the smile on his kind, handsome face. Her breath caught in her chest as she looked around at them all. She was so lucky. How her mum would have loved this gathering. Maybe, somewhere, she could see them all and be happy for her. She was glad of the dark as she picked her way over the ragged paving slabs to her workshop.

'Are you all right?' Carol said. Rosie wiped her eyes as the lights flickered over the rainbow of colours in her workshop.

'Oh, yes, Sorry. My mum died not long ago, and she always loved a party. I miss her.'

'I expect Gareth has told you about his brother. You seem very close, considering you haven't known each other long.'

Rosie tensed. What did she mean by that? 'He has told me. I can't imagine the pain of that, as a mother,' she replied, honestly. 'You watch over your children when they're small, and you hope and pray that they look after themselves when they're grown up. My son is on the other side of the world working with orangutans. I can only hope he's safe. But I think about him all the time.'

Carol's face crumpled, for a moment so fleeting, that Rosie wondered whether she'd actually seen it. She took a sip of her wine, and Rosie wished she'd brought her glass with her too. Or maybe not. They might both be bawling, at this rate.

'I want Gareth to be happy,' Carol said. 'But I'm not sure that he knows how to be, any more.' Rosie moved a pile of sketchbooks from an old wheel back chair and waved her on to it, pulling a stool out and settling herself down. 'He blames himself for Aled.'

Rosie nodded silently.

'And God help me, I blamed him as well. For such a long time. And he's my son too. But he was always the careful one. Aled – he was wild.' She shook her head, a smile playing on her lips. 'Such beautiful boys. We always thought they would take over from us. Gareth loved the driving, always so steady and reliable, but Aled saw the way the company could move forward. Different types of business, you know.' Carol seemed to shake herself. 'I'm sorry. I didn't come in here to—'

'They say that time is a great healer. But it's not, really, is it?'

Carol squeezed Rosie's arm and gathered herself together. 'We have to make some sense of it. It's the one thing we know is certain. Apart from taxes. So, enough of this sad talk. Show me your plans.'

Rosie had no idea how long they'd been in there until Gareth tapped on the door.

'Um, the kids are asleep. That's okay, they'll sleep through anything, and I've got their PJs, but I didn't know how long you wanted to stay?'

'Oh, I'm so sorry. I've monopolised your mum! And I have space – you could have stayed if I'd got myself organised.'

'Maybe next time then? And don't forget that business plan. Call me.' Carol clambered off the stool a little unsteadily and Gareth hurried to help. 'Thank you, my darling,' she said, snuggling under his arm. Rosie saw Gareth's look of pleased surprise and her heart squeezed for him. If she could help in any way, she thought …

Chapter Twenty-Eight

Carol is amazing. She sent me a stack of business plan templates and followed them up with phone calls to see if I'd completed them. I was groaning and moaning and said that it was all just a wish list, wasn't it, really? She told me wishes would never come true if you didn't make them in the first place. And I suppose she's right, isn't she?

I do love these long, sunny evenings. I haven't seen that much of G since school started back. Between Jack's football, Lily's gymnastics, the pair of them swimming after school, and his work, life is pretty hectic there.

He took me and Leanne on a beach barbecue after he collected the children from school today though – and not with one of those eco killing disposable barbies, he actually built a little fire amongst the pebbles! I just love fire. It doesn't matter what you eat, it always tastes better cooked outside. G makes everything into an adventure. I feel quite honoured that he invited us, as he's so busy.

It's nearly the school holidays again though, so perhaps I might see a bit more of him? The thing is, I know this is such a one-off, having his kids full time and to himself, and I don't want to butt in. And they're all so cute together.

I'm busy too. Sales have been good at the Art Café, and Lucy has passed on some commissions too. And Carol is going to host a party for me, for people making a start on their Christmas shopping. It seems far too hot to think about it! She says not to leave it too close to Christmas or they will have spent all their money. She's thinking end of September.

So the idea is that she invites her friends, pours wine down them while I set up my stuff and give them a little demo on how I make it, and they buy it. Hopefully. I don't want to let Carol down. I've got loads of time to make stock though.

Leanne has helped me with social media. I didn't have a clue. But I'm on there now as Fire Truck Felts, which is so exciting. I've got posts already on my photos!

Since Leanne's shown me how social media works, I've started stalking Keira. I'm not proud of it, but at least I know she's okay. I don't know how we're going to fix our relationship, I'm still so hurt by what she said. And the fact that she denied it! Although that's her all over. I don't know why I'm so surprised.

I don't know what bloody Chester is playing at. He's still not disclosed his finances. I suppose mediation is the next step but I can't even see him coming along to that. He really is an arse. We're going to have to go to court, aren't we? I'll have to start looking for a smaller house. I'm trying not to care. After all, G lives in an ordinary little rented house since his divorce. It doesn't seem to bother him. I just need to suck it up and get on with it.

I shouldn't even be thinking this, but I could live with G in a tiny house. I wouldn't care how tiny it was as long as he was in it with me. Him and me, in a cupboard, pressed together ...

I'm becoming obsessed, aren't I? I will crack on with some more work and put him out of my head.

School holidays and it's sunny! Unbelievable for Wales.

We went to see the flamingos in the Wetland place up the road here, the other day, and today we've had fish and chips at Tenby. All of us. Me, Leanne, him and the kids. And it's lovely and all but ... I feel so guilty, complaining here. I'd just like to have a bit of time with him. Just the two of us. I know, I'm being selfish.

But I'm so confused about him. I hardly see him, what with all the kids stuff, and then, this, today:

When he dropped us off after the trip to Tenby, he stood at the door after Leanne had gone inside and he put his hands around my face – he has such lovely long fingers – and he looked into my eyes for such a long time as if he was thinking of something.

I know what I was thinking. I was thinking if the kids and Leanne weren't there I'd drag him upstairs and ravage him. Sigh.

He dropped the lightest kiss on my lips and off he went. I stood there like a fool, feeling his lips on mine still, even after they drove away. Is he just a really slow burner? I have no idea.

In the end, I decided, we might not be lovers, but we are friends. Mates. I'd rather have that than nothing at all.

It doesn't stop me hoping though.

'I feel like I have my own business mentor,' Rosie told Gareth one afternoon, when they'd all dropped over on the way back from a kids' club. 'Your mum doesn't let me get away with a thing. I know my costs down to the last penny. She's fantastic.'

'She is. And I'm so lucky to work for my parents.' They both watched, smiling, as a giggling Lily and Jack kicked a football around in the garden.

'They've been really good at letting me step back from the job a bit while I have the children.' Gareth rubbed the short hair at his chin. 'It's nice that I've been able to let Hannah have the time with her parents. Her work have been very good about giving her leave, even though it's unpaid now.' He swirled the melting ice around in his glass and eyed her. 'And I'm learning too. I've been considering the idea of running my own courses, and you've made me realise that I've just played at it. No written costings, no projections, marketing budget, cost of hiring other instructors, insurances – the list is endless.'

'Would you like one of my templates? I have a selection box, courtesy of your mum ...'

'Yeah,' he said, to her surprise, turning to face her. 'I would, actually. If I want my parents to take my ideas seriously, then I have to get serious. Otherwise, I'll be spending my life wondering whether I could have done it. Life is not a dress rehearsal.'

'And just like that, Cliché Man is back in the room.' She chinked her empty glass against his and he laughed.

After a pause, she grimaced. 'Leanne is another slave driver. She said to me, "If you have to sell this house then I'm homeless too. I am brilliant at paperwork and numbers, and you are not, so I'm helping." Bless her though. We've tackled just about all of Mum's paperwork.'

Gareth laughed. 'Oh dear. Don't mince your words, Leanne, just say it as it is. And?'

'Nothing. A few small investments that I didn't know about, so that's welcome, but it's not anywhere near fifty grand. I am so angry with him. How the hell could he have got himself into that much debt?'

'You've only got his word that he *is* in that much debt.'

She regarded him with narrowed eyes. 'That's very true, actually. I'm still brainwashed by him, aren't I? He seemed so desperate – but the one thing I know about Chester is, he's a good actor, and he *loves* an audience.'

'Hmm. And the three of us gave him an audience that time.'

Rosie ran her tongue over her teeth. 'You must think I was mad, hooking up with him in the first place.'

'Not at all. You forget what a fanboy I was when you introduced us. I've seen him on stage. He's got presence. And my children thought he was wonderful.' He looked over at Lily and Jack. 'You don't just stop loving the person you made children with. Every time you look at your children, you remember.'

Rosie did *not* think of Chester in that way at all. Her eyes slid towards Gareth and then away, and in her tummy, butterflies took flight.

Turning back to her, he said, 'I should let you know that the valves have been changed on the fire goddess, so she's drivable on unleaded now on a permanent basis. Are you still thinking about converting her?'

'Thank you! I'd love to convert her, but I can't see how I will ever afford it. Speaking of which, please don't forget to give me a bill for all the work you've done so far.'

'Rosie, you've given me so much already. I have a better relationship with my mother, and I've found a wonderful friend less than half an hour away who my children love.'

Rosie felt that strange thudding sensation in her chest again. A wonderful *friend?* She wanted to be more than his friend. Was she mistaking those occasions when he'd kissed her, and almost said more? She knew he wasn't the type to string her along. Was he waiting for her to make the first move, perhaps?

She caught sight of her reflection in the bifold doors. Her hair was a cloudy frizz, still in her spattered work apron that she'd forgotten to take off, and dyes ingrained in her fingernails. No wonder he still hankered after his ex and only thought of her as a friend. Her throat snagged and she sipped her water, swirling the almost melted ice cubes.

Chapter Twenty-Nine

They'd reached the end of the boxes of her mother's papers. There was nothing. Rosie sat back on her heels, staring at them.

'Let's take a walk,' Leanne said. 'Let's not sit, looking at this stuff.'

There had to be a way to keep the house and put her plans into action. But no matter which way her brain twisted and turned, she couldn't see how.

As they returned to the house, Rosie's spirits sank even further as she saw a familiar car in the drive. Keira. She was determined not to be browbeaten by her own daughter, and pinned a determined smile to her face. After only a few more steps though, she didn't need a fake smile.

'Tom!' She ran towards him, her feet floating over the ground and she enveloped him in an enormous hug. She'd forgotten how tall he was. Her head was at his chest! He hugged her back, laughing.

'Hello, Mammy.'

'Oh Tom! I can't believe you're here – what a lovely surprise! Are you staying? I do hope so. Your bedroom is just the same. How did you get here?' She whirled around. Keira sat in the driver's seat of her car, watching. When she met Rosie's eyes she looked away, and leaned forward to turn the key in the ignition. Rosie marched towards the car, and opened the door.

'Keira – thank you for bringing Tom home.' She stalled, her mind a blank. 'Could we, maybe ...'

'Come *on* Keira,' Tom called, waving his arm. 'Oh. Hello.' He looked towards Leanne, who had frozen on the drive like a frightened doe, and then looked away at the same time as he said, 'Are you one of Mum's friends? I'm Tom. Pleased to meet you.'

Rosie was astonished to see Leanne step towards him. Although he *was* extremely handsome, she acknowledged. His deep tan and the beard she hadn't seen before made his green-blue eyes, so similar to hers, as bright as the sky. She hurriedly unlocked the door and held it wide. 'Come on in! Excuse the mess ...'

Tom marched in behind her, leaving Keira and Leanne eyeing each other on the drive. Rosie left them to it after a moment and put the lock on the latch. Her son stood in the open-plan room and dropped his bag with a thud, his eyes everywhere.

'Wow, Mum! This place looks amazing!' He turned to give her another hug. 'I'm so sorry about Gran. I wanted to come back for the funeral.' He hung his head. 'Getting out of the rainforests isn't that easy. And yes, I'm staying. If you think it rains a lot in Wales ... nothing ever dries in the rainforests!'

'I can imagine. Never mind. You're here now. We've a heatwave! And I can't tell you how pleased I am to see you. Have you eaten? We're about to have some lunch. There's plenty for everyone.'

'Sounds great. Tell me how I can help.' He pulled a chair out, well away from the papers strewn over the table. 'Looks like I've caught you in the middle of something here.'

'It's a long story,' Rosie said, from the depths of the fridge, pulling food out. Bent over like a hairpin to reach the furthest reaches of the cupboard, she became aware of a pair of bare feet in all terrain sandals which she recognised as Leanne's, quickly accompanied by her daughter's sparkly flip-flops.

'In the garden?' Leanne asked. 'I'll put the tablecloth on.'

'I can do that. You can carry things. That looks like your thing,' Keira shot back.

Somehow, the food was transported to the table, and along with the jug of iced water, Rosie set out a bottle of wine. It *was* a special occasion after all.

‘I’m driving,’ Keira said, putting her hand over her glass.

‘You could stay,’ Rosie said, not putting too much emphasis on her words. Keira shrugged without answering and filled her glass with water. ‘So, what have you been doing, Tom?’

Her lovely son dispelled the awkwardness of the conversation, telling them stories about the animals he helped to care for, the places he visited, the people he’d met. He brought his world alive for them.

‘It sounds amazing,’ Leanne said. ‘Is it something you always wanted to do?’

‘In a way,’ Tom said, turning his full attention on her. ‘It’s rewarding and it’s good to give something back.’

Keira snorted. ‘All hail my saintly brother.’

‘Shut it, you,’ Tom said, mildly. ‘So. Lots been going on here then, apparently. I’m going to jump right in and say that I know Dad’s been back …’

Rosie hesitated, wondering what to say and how much he knew. Leanne stood up, clearing her plate and any other empty plates. ‘I’ve got some orders to sort out,’ she said. ‘It’s been nice meeting you, Tom.’ She completely avoided Keira and said to Rosie, ‘Thank you for lunch.’

‘You’re welcome, sweetie. Please don’t feel you have to leave.’

‘It’s okay.’ Rosie noticed both her children following Leanne’s progress into the house. Tom’s brows rose in interest, while Keira’s lowered in a frown.

‘And, apart from this thing with Dad,’ Tom continued, breezily, turning back towards Rosie, ‘I believe there’s another *thing* with my little sister. Isn’t there, sis?’

Keira glared at him and then focussed on the table. ‘I’m sorry, Mum.’

Rosie turned her gaze from one offspring to the other. More than anything in the world, she wanted her relationship with them to be wonderful. But she would not be walked over.

'When you were an adorable little girl, Keira, about three, you poured a bucket of water all over the floor in the kitchen. I had to get the mop out to clear it up, and you stood there, staring at me, with your hands on your hips and your little chubby legs wide like a cowboy.

'Daddy said to you, "What's Mummy doing?" And you said, cute as a button, "Wiping up!" He said, "What do you say?" And you said, "*Sor-reeee*". Just like that. And he said, "Are you really sorry?" And you said, with your whole body ... "No!"' She paused, remembering. 'And we had to try so hard not to laugh, because you were so cute, and so naughty. Like little children usually are.'

'Except me. I was perfect in every way,' said Tom, nudging Keira with his elbow.

'I don't remember it like that,' Keira said, returning a tremulous smile.

'Well, the thing is, it was cute when you were so little, those easy "*Sor-ree"s*,' Rosie said. 'But you got older, and you did and said whatever you liked. And you're so beautiful, Keira. So everyone forgave you for your casual apologies that you never actually meant.' She took a deep breath. 'But you hurt me. On the day of my mother's funeral. When I could not have been lower.' She sipped some water, her hands shaking. But she held her daughter's gaze. 'I understood why you might have thought I was boring. And you know, having spent my life looking after you and your brother, working three jobs if you remember, I took in ironing and catered as well as working at the school, to find the money that your father squandered, and then nursing Mum, right to the end, I guess I *was* pretty boring to you. I'm sorry if I didn't give you as much attention as you think you deserved. What I do not understand is what I have done to you, that you would wish that I was dead, instead of my mother.'

Keira looked stricken, and Rosie thought that she might

walk away. Let herself out of the front door again, never to return. She held her breath. Tom sat, motionless. She couldn't meet his eye. Hell of a homecoming. What if he thought that she was horrible, and unforgiving? What if both her children left, and became estranged? So that her entire life's efforts would have been a complete waste of time. She'd just begun to find herself, only to lose them in the process.

'Mum, I-I, oh God ...' Keira put her face in her hands and then spread them before her. 'I wish I could turn back the clock. I hate myself for what I said about you. How sad I've made you. And it's taken me ages to work out how I felt.'

Rosie said after a moment or two, 'I'm listening.'

Keira's voice was quiet and halting. 'I was Dad's favourite, and he left us. I couldn't have loved him any harder – but he still went. Tom has been gone for ages, and yes, sorry Tom, I love you too even if you are a total shithead.' She gulped as Tom put his hand over hers. 'Granny died, and I *adored* her. I couldn't stop her dying.' She swallowed, and a fat tear made its way down her smooth cheek. 'And I love you, Mum, and you're all I've got left.' Her tears fell faster. 'And I-I couldn't bear that you would go too, so I made it seem like I didn't care. So it wouldn't hurt when you left me too.' She sobbed, and her words spilled in ragged gasps. 'And you're always so strong. You carried on like always when Dad went, and when Granny got worse and worse, you never changed. I thought it was just me missing everyone. I had nobody left ...'

Rosie filled Keira's glass with water and pushed it towards her, with a clean paper napkin. She waited while Keira blew her nose, her mind reeling. Keira had been going through hell, and she hadn't even noticed. How could she have been so blind? Pushing herself away from the table, she jumped up and put her arms around her. Keira leaned into her and broke her heart.

'Oh, sweetheart.'

'I always thought Dad would come back. I couldn't believe it when you started divorcing him. There would be nothing to bring him back home if you did that! I'd always thought, that even if he wouldn't come back for you, he'd come back for me. I can't believe how stupid that makes me sound. And I didn't understand *why* he'd gone. Why *now?* It wasn't as if he'd changed or anything. He'd always been the same, as far back as I could remember – brilliant and fun on one hand, and lazy, selfish and immature the next. I thought you just accepted him as he was.'

'I did. For a long time.'

'So I waited, and waited, but he didn't come back. He didn't send for me. I got texts – he promised me he'd bring me over to live with him, when he'd paid off this, or that, and he'd send photos of these fabulous places he was living in and say, you'll be able to come and live with me. He kept me hoping all the time. He kept saying he couldn't return because of Granny.'

'You intercepted my mail, didn't you?' Rosie was beginning to understand. 'You sabotaged my divorce.'

'I'm so sorry.' Keira hiccupped. 'I wanted him to come back and everything to be like it used to be. Not him to come back, take everything and go again.'

Rosie squeezed her eyes shut. What a mess. 'I'm sorry you've only just realised what a liar he is. Don't take all the blame though. He's always been at his best in front of an audience.' She held her daughter tight. Her beautiful, difficult daughter. Mothering was never over, no matter how old your children were. Thinking of Gareth's mother, Carol, she resolved to be better at it. At least she still had both her children.

'And,' Keira blew her nose. 'There's something else. I'm pregnant.'

Chapter Thirty

Gareth arrived later with Lily and Jack, who were wide-eyed at the new visitors, and even more astonished to find out they were Rosie's children. Rosie threaded her arm through Gareth's and introduced him with pride to a tall young man, with a deep tan and eyes as turquoise as a warm Caribbean sea. Gareth shook hands with Tom, liking him on sight. It was hard to imagine Chester as his father. But no mistaking Rosie as his mother. He had inherited her wide, mobile mouth and ready smile.

'Mum tells me you climb – I've done quite a bit in France and in Patagonia,' Tom said, diffidently. 'I'd love to have a chat with you about it. I'm considering a change of career, and I'd like to do some instructor training.'

'Patagonia? That sounds pretty awesome. Tell me what you know about instructing already.' Gareth could have sat and talked to this young man all evening, but Keira sidled up to them, and Tom and Rosie diplomatically stepped away. Red in the face, Keira stuck her hand out.

'I need to apologise to you,' she began, hesitantly as if she'd rehearsed it and still wasn't sure of the script. 'I was very rude to you when we met last.' Gareth was aware, at the corner of his eye, of Rosie watching them while pretending not to, engaged in conversation with Lily, Jack and Tom. He remembered quite clearly the only time he'd met Keira, the day he'd given Rosie the lift home from his course and become her "fake boyfriend". Keira had insulted Rosie, horribly and referred to him as Rosie's "twinkie". The memory made him consider what role he occupied for Rosie now.

'I'm not bothered, for myself,' he said, carefully. 'Just for your mum.'

'Oh.' She swallowed. 'That's nice of you. I suppose I'm expecting a lot really, that everything is forgiven.'

'Your mum is a really special person.' He accepted the small, soft hand she held out and shook it. 'If anyone can work this out, then she can.'

'Yeah. I'm getting that.' She nodded, and chewed her lip. 'Everything I thought I knew has turned right round and bitten me on the arse.'

'Life has a habit of doing that.' He smiled at her. 'And I hear that congratulations are in order.'

'Oh. Yeah. Thanks. I'm bloody terrified though.'

'That sounds normal.' He eyed her. Stripped of make-up and posturing, she seemed prettier and more natural. He wondered how long it would last. The afternoon had been a pretty intense emotional trawl, from the way Rosie explained it. He was pleased that she'd involved him in this, really quite private part of her life. Although he'd included her in his, right from the beginning.

Glancing over to Rosie now, where she was making squash at the kitchen sink for his children, he felt his mouth curve into a smile. He said to Keira, 'You might as well get used to that feeling. Your kids carry on terrifying you even when they've grown up.'

Thoughts of his brother catapulted into his mind, and his eyes rested on Lily and Jack. How would he react when they went to college? Travelled, like Tom, all over the world? And it looked as if that young man was still looking for adventure.

'I wish you luck,' he told Keira, sincerely, wondering where the baby's father was, whether he was supportive, and treacherously, whether Keira had made such desperate overtures with her mother in the hope that Rosie might become the unpaid, full-time mother to her child, while she pursued her own life as before. Keira drifted away to her brother with a murmured 'thank you'.

Giving himself no time to think, Gareth strode over to Rosie, slipping an arm around her waist and kissing the back of her neck. He'd wanted to do it for so long, but Rosie's married status always stopped him. No matter that she insisted it was just a matter of the legalities, there was always that possibility that they could get back together. Their family rifts were healing, and Chester's was now the only piece out of alignment. His heart skittered at the thought of Rosie going back to that man. So many times he'd been on the brink of telling her how he felt about her. But was that unfair? If Ian had let him and Hannah sort themselves out, might they still be married? Still be a family unit?

Startled, she blushed, spinning in his arms to face him. He used her nickname. 'Rosa.'

He held her tightly and she settled into his embrace as if she'd always been there. His heart drummed a bass beat.

'Hello, Graham.' She smiled up at him, and he looked down at her tanned, heart-shaped face, seeing how the freckles had all but joined together now. 'I'm so glad you came over,' she said. 'Thank you.'

'I'm glad too. Thank you for inviting me. It was great to meet Tom. I can't stay long,' he said on a sigh. 'The kids have an early start tomorrow – they're going on a day out with their friends. I've got things to get ready, some washing to do, packed lunches to make and all that stuff, but I'd love to have a longer chat with him.'

'I *knew* you two would get on,' she said, triumphantly. 'I just need to winkle Leanne out of her cave next. She and Keira have been skirting round each other. I don't think Leanne quite believes the sudden personality transplant.'

Gareth felt guilty. He wasn't sure he did, either. He hoped that their anxieties were unfounded. He released Rosie reluctantly and went to round up his children.

Dear Diary/Journal,

My boy is home! I am beyond thrilled to see him. He looks so strong and handsome.

And Keira is pregnant. She's due end of October. I did my best to look happy, but ... I'm so worried for her. She tore at my heartstrings today. I could kill Chester for what's been going on in her head all this time. He's always been selfish. And I guess the pregnancy hormones were raging at the funeral, so maybe that explains her behaviour? I can't process all this today, honestly. I'll think about it later...

I invited G and the kids over to meet Tom, and to celebrate Keira returning to the fold, and also I suppose, to show Tom and Keira that G and his family are part of my life. Even though we've never shared anything more than a friendly kiss, he's in my thoughts all the time. I'd kind of accepted that that was how we were. He got on really well with Tom. I thought he would.

So anyway – I'm leaving the best bit till last, Diary, so pay attention – when I followed him out to wave them goodbye he waited until Lily and Jack were in the car, and then he caught me up in the most wonderful hug, and we were so close, and he said – ready, Diary?

He said, 'Rosie, I've been holding back, waiting for your divorce to come through. I know you're still married and I didn't want to be in the way in case you thought about getting back with Chester. But I think I know you well enough to know that it's over between you. I don't want to wait any longer. And I hope you feel the same way, because ...'

He cleared his throat, still holding me so tight, and well, I was flabbergasted. And that's a word you don't see very often these days, outside of those ancient Carry On films. God. I'm gibbering. And G carried on talking, while my brain pinged like a bagatelle machine, and I was thinking that I don't ever want him to let go of me, because it feels so exactly right.

And he said, 'Because I don't want to lose you, Rosa. And

I know it's impossible right now with both our houses full of our children, but I want to be more than a fake boyfriend to you.'

And, oh GOD, I'm cringing now, because I started to wonder out loud whether people our age are still called boyfriend and girlfriend and I carried on gabbling, 'I've been wondering about why you haven't – er, y'know. And you kept talking about us being "friends", and I thought I'd misread the signals ... but there is no way on earth that I am ever getting back with Chester.'

Shwizz! Whooo! Peeeyoingshweee!

That was the fireworks going off in my brain because then he properly kissed me. And Diary, his lips ... God, I'm so hot just thinking about them ... I don't even know if I can write it down ... they were just perfect.

You know, apart from a bit of tooth collision – because I am SO out of practice – and we laughed but then ... oh.

It was – it was ... exactly right, you know when you see those perfect kisses in movies and you go all swoony and they look so totally right for each other?

Well, our kiss felt how those movie kisses look. I can still feel him. All over. And on my mouth. And my nose can still smell him. What does he smell of? He smells of all the colours of the rainbow.

Swoon. I've got it bad, haven't I? But the thing is, I don't want him to be without his children, once Hannah is home, because it will be like seeing only a half of him, and I know he's going to miss them so much ... but oh. Is it so selfish of me to want him all to myself?

A week later, on another hot afternoon in the garden, Gareth and Rosie watched Lily and Jack sloshing about in the inflatable paddling pool that he'd brought with him. Having worked solidly since the cool of the morning, she was glad of the break, and of course, delighted to see him.

They laughed and then yelled as a direct hit from a water gun soaked them both.

'They could play in your garden,' Rosie remarked, enjoying the feel of the cool water.

'They could. But we like it here.' He pulled his shirt front away from his wet skin and Rosie's pulse rocketed as she caught a glimpse of his muscular torso, the soft dark hair meandering from side to side and then down ... 'Your garden is so much nicer than mine, and the company is better. Oh, talking about gardens, Mum also has some ideas for yours.'

'Leanne is planning an allotment.'

'It'll be like one of those garden makeover programmes on the telly. You'll have to choose between them.'

'God, I hope not. They both scare the pants off me.'

He raised an eyebrow, holding her gaze, and she toppled into the deep pool of his dark eyes ...

'*Da-deeee*! Jack has got both the guns and he won't even let me have one!'

'I knew they were a bad idea.' Gareth grinned at her and the moment was gone. 'Jack! You need both hands to work one of those, so play nice!' He turned back to her. 'I've got another course booked.'

'What about Lily and Jack? Because I could ...'

Gareth's eyes rested on his children. 'They'll be back to school on the day my course finishes. Hannah says she'll be back beforehand and she'll collect them. They'll be so pleased to see her. She's a good mum.' He stared towards the bright sea. 'And I'll revert to being a part-time dad.'

She reached over and squeezed his hand. 'Oh, Gareth, I'm so sorry. I know how much you've loved having them.'

He cleared his throat. 'Yeah. Little monsters.' He grinned but his eyes were sad.

Gareth wondered how single mums managed. It made him more determined to help out more with his children, when Hannah returned. The long school holidays, packed with activities, sunshine and laughter, were almost over. Outgrown shoes and uniforms were bought and Hannah had ordered their school sweatshirts weeks back so that was sorted.

Trying to fit in time with Rosie, with whom he was desperate to spend some close contact time, was tricky too. If she wasn't being mentored about social media and websites, or combining her deliveries with a trip out with Tom, she was flat out creating. Mindful that this was her only source of income, he tried not to distract her for too long.

Leanne let him in when he dropped over on the off-chance one day after collecting some parts for work and while the children were at a kids' club. The workshop double doors were propped open in the relentless heat. Rosie was surrounded by sketches and torn scraps of photos and magazine spreads pinned onto boards and she was rolling the felt, wrist to elbows, back and forth, back and forth. With her chestnut hair caught up on the top of her head and wearing a thin cotton dress, he thought she looked delicious.

'Oh no!' she said, seeing him at the doorway, her hand going instantly to her hair.

'Nice welcome.' He grinned.

'But I look a total mess!'

'You look beautiful,' he told her, stepping towards her and wrapping her in his arms, their mouths finding each other, their hot bodies fusing together. His hands ran over the curve of her bottom and he pulled her into him. He felt her touch on his back and at the waistband of his works trousers, and he groaned, feeling his body responding to her fingers. Gathering up the thin cotton of her dress he stroked her soft skin, and she pressed herself against him more urgently. He was on the verge of hurling everything off her big table and making love to her there and then when his mobile rang.

'Leave it,' Rosie panted, her eyes wide.

'I can't. I'm so sorry. What if it's the kids?' It was work, needing him back for a meeting. There never seemed to be any time for *them*. He pocketed the phone. 'Drat. I have to go.' He reached out and coiled a lock of her hair around his fingers. 'Rosie, I love you but we never get a minute to ourselves! So, erm, what do you think about coming with me this weekend. My course? I was thinking, instead of you sleeping in the bunk beds, we could maybe, y'know …' He cringed. How desperate did he sound?

'What happened to your "no shagging" rule?'

'Oh God. Did Leanne tell you about that?' He groaned.

'I would love to come on your course and be your co-shaggee, Gareth,' she said, her expression mischievous. He eyed her cautiously.

'I'm sensing a "but" coming.'

'Yes, there is. I'm drowning in work – not that I'm knocking it – but more to the point, I don't want you to take your attention off your guests.' She swivelled to face him. 'One of the things that impressed me most about you, was how much you cared about them. How much you wanted them to have a really good weekend.

'It was you who turned the key for me, when I was at rock bottom. It was you who gave me back a love for proper cooking, and it was you who gave me confidence in what my body can do. I have my children back, and a flourishing business that is earning me proper money at last, and that's all down to you.

'So, I thank you from the bottom of my heart. And because I know how much you care about the success of your courses, I will not allow my desires to distract you from your job. I will still be here, when you come back. And we'll have all the time in the world then.'

He leaned forward to kiss her roundly. 'You're the most amazing person I've ever met, Rosa. And thank you.' He wanted to tell her about his plans – but it was still all just on paper. Spreadsheet dreams. She was actually doing it, and succeeding. 'I am so proud of you. And I can be patient.'

Chapter Thirty-One

Waiting for food at the pub at the bottom of the hill on the Friday night, Gareth checked the weather apps on his phone, as he always did. With severe weather warnings blaring at him from every one, he excused himself from the group, and dialled his boss, Ben, to talk it over. Ben rang him at the exact same time.

'Hi Gareth. I've seen the forecasts. What's it like there?'

'Well, nothing at all here right now ... but the landlord is filling sandbags. He's preparing for the worst. You know what it's like after a long spell of dry weather, the rain will come off the hills like waterfalls.' Gareth sucked his teeth, thinking. 'So kayaking will definitely be off, if the river is flooded like they say we won't be able to go anywhere near it.' He thought about Dylan. He was bound to have all the kit ready to take up to higher ground. 'The climbing and the abseiling *could* still go ahead, but it won't be very nice if it's absolutely chucking it down, and there's the risk of the roads flooding so access could well be a problem.' He paused. 'And then there's the clients' own properties. If they're in potential flood zones, they'll probably want to get home to them, just in case. Plus, do we want to risk the possibility of flooded roads here, meaning we're stranded?'

'Hmm,' said Ben. 'And then if the forecast is wrong, the whole weekend is cancelled for nothing. And they have been wrong before.'

'Yeah, I know. And it's fine and dry here right now. It's hard to imagine that it's going to be that bad.'

'Right, well Gareth, you're the Health and Safety man on this team! If you need to cancel, we'll issue credit notes for them to rebook. What about your house?'

'My rented place will be fine, but my ex's house is in a

dip and that could be a problem. She'll have her bloke there though, so they're not on their own.' *But there's nothing between Rosie's house and the sea, except half a mile of dried-up creek.* His stomach pitched and he licked his lips. He should ring and warn her, in case she hadn't seen any forecasts. She wasn't much for the TV, or social media, unless she was checking her own work posts, so she might very well be completely oblivious. When the call ended, he rang Rosie straight away.

'Hello – how nice! I wasn't expecting to hear from you.' He could hear the smile in her voice and his own mouth lifted in response. 'Is everything all right?'

'Yes, we're all fine, but have you seen the weather warnings for this weekend?' It was no surprise to him that she hadn't. 'The pub is sandbagging. They're talking about evacuating if it's as bad as they're saying.'

'Oh no! Oh, poor things. If they're correct, it will really affect your weekend, won't it?'

'I'm just going back in to talk about our options. But Rosie, please, please be careful there.'

'I'll keep an eye on it, of course, but we've never been flooded here. The sea would have to go uphill to get to us. And you know what the forecasts are like. It might just blow over. Fingers crossed it does.'

'I hope so too. But you look after yourself. I don't want to have to swim out to you for my homecoming hug.'

She laughed, blowing a kiss down the phone. 'You look after yourselves too. Looking forward to that hug. And more ...'

'Oh, me too. Me too. Night, Rosie.' He hung up reluctantly and went back to the group. The waitress went to get his food, and he outlined the options to their upturned, expectant faces.

Rosie was, as usual, in her workshop on Saturday morning.

The day had dawned as hot as before, and she wondered just how reliable the forecast was. It had been lovely to hear from Gareth last night, and she wondered what decision he'd come to. She kept the radio on for updates, and her mobile nearby. Just in case he rang again, and there was enough signal to hear him. Slow, fat raindrops plopped onto the roof, and it was such a long time since they'd had any that she went to the door to watch it. In a moment, the few drops turned into sudden sheets of rain, drumming onto the hard packed, parched earth and bouncing upwards. It was exhilarating. The earth gave off a thankful scent, as it rejoiced in the long-awaited water.

She stood in the doorway, taking photographs and videos, which she sent to Gareth, with *Raining at last, hope you're all okay!* She knew there was no signal, but he'd get it eventually.

Then she texted Keira with, *hope you're okay, might be flooding?* The reply returned instantly: *We're fine, uphill! X*

It was as if the world had been varnished, the deluge washing away the dusty tones and replenishing them with glossy greens and blues, the dry earth into rich plums and deep reds. She couldn't resist pulling out a sketchbook and making some colour notes.

Time slid away from her and she felt a sudden, sickening fear as she saw with a start that the ribbon of the incoming tide had crept closer than she'd ever seen it. For a moment she was paralysed, suspended in a sliver of time. Her first thought was of Gareth, and she prayed that they were all safe in the mountains.

Lightning sliced through the leaden sky and she cowered as a furious thunderclap roared overhead. She cursed herself. Gareth had warned her and she'd doubted him. The words "we've never been flooded" as she'd said them to his mother returned to her. Her stomach constricted. With fumbling fingers, she wrapped her precious work, her sketchbooks and her paints, stuffing them into a huge bag. Everything else, she stacked as high as she could manage. Then she unplugged everything. Locking the door to the workshop, she was soaked just hurrying to the house, the big bag banging against her chilled, bare legs. Tom and Leanne returned drenched and laughing from a run, to find her tearing around the house, moving books and photographs upstairs.

'Check the sea,' she panted at their bewildered faces.

Tom tore through the house to look. 'Closer than I've ever seen it, but still a way off. We need to fill some bin liners with earth and use them as sandbags by the back doors. Then we should lift the furniture.'

Leanne said, 'There's a pile of bricks out the back – can we use those?' Rosie was so glad Tom and Leanne were there, strong, calm and practical. In the garden, eyeing the encroaching sea with scared eyes, they shovelled earth into as many plastic bags as they could find, dividing them between her workshop and the back door of the house. Leanne carted the bags of compost she'd bought for her allotment and they layered those against the back doors along with whatever else they could find. They locked the doors and Leanne sprinted around the house to re-enter through the front door. They carried the big dining table as far back as possible, put it up on bricks, and repeated the exercise with the sofas and the storage units.

'My wool!' Leanne said, stricken. There was a mountain of it in one of the untouched downstairs rooms, luckily most of it in plastic wrappings and neatly labelled boxes. They carted the whole lot upstairs into Keira's bedroom. It covered the floor to a depth of several feet, including the bed.

'Keira won't be happy with me,' Leanne said.

'Keira isn't here.'

Panting, the three of them grouped at the glass doors and

stared out over the expanse of creek as it inched ever closer. And still the rain fell.

'I guess we have to be prepared to shut off the electricity and gas. Maybe even the water? I read something about putting the plugs into the sinks and weighting them down in case it comes up through the drains. Should we do that too? What are the roads like?' Rosie's mind skittered from one thought to the next. 'I suggest we all go and have a hot shower while we can and put some warm clothes on. Pack a bag each, just in case we have to evacuate.'

Wide-eyed, they did as she suggested, and Rosie went upstairs to follow her own advice, although the thought of leaving the house to the vagaries of nature went against the grain, and where would they evacuate to? She collected some throws together, in case they had to head off to some draughty village hall. Her sleeping bag might be useful, she thought, so she made sure that was handy too.

'Bring your bedding upstairs!' she yelled to Leanne, as she raced up and down the stairs, throwing wipes, paracetamols, bottles of water and some food that didn't need heating, into an insulated bag. Just in case. She plugged her phone and her laptop in to make sure they were fully charged in case the electricity went off. Candles. Matches. Torches. Where the hell were the batteries?

She went to look out of her bedroom window. Fearful of what she might see, but terrified not to know. The wind howled and whistled around them, sliding thin, biting fingers through the gaps in the eaves. They were on an island, marooned in a silvery sea ...

All they could do now was wait. And wonder what was happening to Gareth.

Chapter Thirty-Two

It had begun to rain in torrents on the bunkhouse around midnight and it hadn't stopped. Everyone was up early, staring out of the rain-lashed windows and trying to get a signal on their mobile phones.

'I'm going down to the pub to find out what's happening on their Wi-Fi,' Gareth said. Several of the group wanted to come too, and it wasn't long before everyone was trudging down the hill with him, slipping on the path that already looked more like a riverbed.

'I'm so sorry, guys.' In the car park at the bottom, Gareth faced them all after seeing that the forecasts looked, if anything, worse than the previous day. 'But I'm going to have to cancel the weekend. You'll get a credit note to rebook. I know we were hoping that the forecast might be wrong, but we can't run the risk of being stranded here, and I'm sure you'd all prefer to be at home and not stuck on public transport, or in a flooded car. We can have a quick breakfast but I think we should get packed and moving as quickly as possible now.'

Apart from one grumbler saying that the flooding wouldn't be that bad, everyone else accepted the situation. There wasn't a thing Gareth could do about it anyway, and he made a mental note to think through his policies in the event he was faced with the same dilemma. Breakfasted and packed to a soundtrack of the relentless rain, he delivered his guests to their chosen public transport. Even the grumbler was silenced by the sight of fields that had become lakes, and the many dramatic waterfalls cascading from the mountains. It was with relief that Gareth turned towards home.

As the phone signal improved, message after message

pinged and flashed onto his screen, so many that he pulled over to read them.

Hannah's text shrieked at him.

House flooded staying with neighbours, help!

There were photos: a lake in the road rising higher and higher, the kitchen flooded with filthy water, them in the kind neighbour's spare room, surrounded by duvets and bags. Lily and Jack looking like tragic, homeless orphans.

'Oh, shit,' he breathed, rapidly thumbing through them before ringing her.

'Oh Gareth!' He could hear the wind blowing across the phone. She must be outside. 'Oh God, it's such a mess. I don't know what to do! I-I-I'm so useless!' She sobbed.

'Where's Ian?' He glared through the rain-streaked windscreen, drumming his fingers on the dashboard.

'We, we – we had a row last week,' she wailed. 'He's not here.'

Why hadn't she told him that? 'Are you all safe?'

'Yes.'

'I'm on my way. Just stay at the neighbours. Text me the door number so I can find you.'

'*Ok-k-aay*,' she stammered. 'Thank you.' She hung up. He rang his parents next, explaining what had happened.

'Anything we can do, just let us know,' Cled said, his voice reassuring. 'We can put them all up here, if the house isn't habitable?'

'That would be great, Dad. I should be at their house in a couple of hours or less. Could you meet me there? I think I might need some help, see what we can do. Hannah and Ian have had a row and he's walked out, by the sounds of it.' He heard the anger in his voice, and tried to calm himself. It didn't help the situation.

Rosie's photos were accompanied by cheerful reports that they were fine, not to worry, and lots of "phew" emojis. He returned the same emojis, and a row of kisses, and the words: *Hannah and kids flooded out. Ian has buggered off. Me and Dad going to help.*

She replied immediately with, *Oh no! Let me know if I can do anything. Good luck XXX*. He smiled at the phone. Dear Rosie. So calm and strong. He was so pleased she had her family around her now.

He arrived at his old house, parking behind his father's car. The front door was open, and as he walked towards it, the hall looked as neat and tidy as ever. Until the smell hit him. Raw sewage. He gagged, holding his hand over his mouth.

'Gareth!' His father hailed him from the pavement. 'Saw you arrive. It's pretty grim in there, lad.'

Gareth joined his father, breathing in lungfuls of clean air. 'God, Dad, that's revolting.'

'Sewers,' his father said, shaking his head. 'Come up and speak to Hannah. She's in bits, bless her.'

At the neighbour's house, Hannah leapt to her feet as Gareth and Cled arrived. Jack and Lily were watching the telly in the lounge, and managed a laconic, ''lo, Daddy,' barely wrenching their gaze from the cartoons. Hannah was more forthcoming. Throwing herself into his arms, she sobbed. He couldn't understand a word she was saying, and smoothed her hair, making shushing noises. He guessed this wasn't her first meltdown, as neither his father, the children, or the neighbour took any notice. He couldn't blame her though. Holding her gently, he led her into the hallway so that he could speak to her. The neighbour made the universal sign for tea, and he nodded with a smile. That was kind of her.

'Tell me what happened.'

Hannah stammered out her tale. It seemed that they'd been watching the rain, thankful that it wasn't flooding into the house. Then Lily had shrieked that water was coming out of the toilet, and her immediate thought was that Lily had put something down it, a toy, maybe. Until she saw it, gushing upwards.

'The smell was just terrible,' she sobbed. 'I couldn't stop it. I grabbed the kids and legged it up the road.'

'Okay, okay, we'll sort it. You did the right thing.' He rubbed her back in a circular motion. 'Have you contacted the insurance company?'

'Of course I have!' Her body tensed, and she glared up at him. 'I'm not completely useless. I went back and collected the big file with all the important documents in, plus the computers and photos.'

He took a long, silent breath. She was stressed. Under the circumstances, she had every right to be. 'Mum and Dad said you can stay with them.' He thought quickly. 'Alternatively, you could have my house, and I'll move in with them.'

'Maybe that would be best. It would be familiar for the kids, and wouldn't impact on your parents. You know what they say about visitors and fish.'

'Yeah, they both stink after three days, but I didn't think you'd want to talk about smells in the circumstances ...' He tried for a joke, but she jerked away from him.

'Do I smell?'

'No Han, of course you don't! Sorry, not a good time for jokes.' He scratched the back of his neck. Of course it wasn't! what had he been thinking? 'What else do you need from the house? If you make a list I can go and collect everything for you. I can be here for the claim assessor, if you like. Or maybe Dad could, if you'd prefer?' It was like tiptoeing on broken glass, steering his way in an effort to avoid offending her.

'I'm sorry Gar. I just don't know if I'm on my head or my arse right now. I was so looking forward to coming home, and then I had this stupid row with Ian and he stormed off. And now this!' She looked so dejected that he put his arms around her and pulled her in for a comforting cuddle, just as he would Lily or Jack. She stayed there, sniffing, and then looked up at him with a disarming smile. 'Thank you. I've always been able to rely on you. I'll make that list now.'

It was a long list, but between them, he and Cled managed to find almost everything. He steeled himself to search through Hannah's clothes in the bedroom she shared with Ian. It had been *their* bedroom. They'd bought a new bed, at least, he noticed. The stench pervaded the house, and Gareth hoped they didn't have to wait long for the claim assessor. Should he open all the windows, or might that invalidate their contents insurance if they were burgled? He had no doubt that Hannah would be nagging them to get the house sorted out, so that she didn't have to live with him for too long.

Not *with* him. In his house, he corrected himself.

Chapter Thirty-Three

The television news for the next few days was full of the storm damage. Rosie was shocked to see that the Art Café had been destroyed. She cried. And then rang Lucy.

'Oh God, Lucy, I've just seen what happened! You poor things!'

'It was so sudden,' Lucy told her. 'One minute we were moaning about how hot it was, and the next, bam!'

'It must have been terrifying. I still can't believe the café has gone. The photos are just shocking.' She heaved a sigh, shaking her head. 'The sea came into the garden here, freaked us out, then the tide turned and it went away again. We've never come that close to being flooded. A scary few hours, and the garden's a mess, but we're all okay. I can't imagine what it must have been like for you.'

Lucy cleared her throat but Rosie couldn't miss the sob. 'We've lost all the stock, Rosie. I'm so sorry.'

'Oh Lucy, please don't worry about that. It was all insured.'

'We've not given up though. We've been approached by someone with an interesting business idea, and we're taking advice. It was only a building, after all.' Her voice shook. 'Nobody died,' she added. 'Please do keep in touch. I haven't seen your fire engine yet!'

Rosie promised to, then she dialled Gareth's mobile.

'Hello?' said a high, young voice.

'Is that Jack?' Rosie guessed, smiling. 'It's Rosie. Are you all okay?'

'Yes! We're back in Daddy's house cos our house stinks!'

'Oh no! You poor things. Is it really awful?'

'Yes. It smells of poo. But it's nice to be back at Daddy's. Do you want to speak to Lily?'

'Well, yes, but I'd like to speak to your daddy, if he's—'

'Hello?' said a female voice. Rosie had guessed the ex-wife might be there.

She said, politely, 'Hello, could I speak to Gareth please?'

'Jack, stop pulling at the phone!' Hannah yelled. Into the phone, she said, 'I'm sorry, Gareth isn't here at the moment.'

'Yes, he is, Mummy!' Jack contradicted in a shout. 'He's in the garden. I'll go and get him. He'll want to speak to Rosie!'

'No, leave it Jack. I'll tell Daddy and he can ring back.'

'He's here, Mummy,' Jack said, and then as if she was listening to a radio play, Rosie heard the little boy calling his father. There was the sound of the phone exchanging hands and a sarcastic sounding, 'It's your girlfriend on the phone,' from Hannah.

'Yes, hello, who is this, please?' Gareth's voice sounded uncharacteristically crisp.

'It's me. Rosie. Have I called at a bad time? I was just wondering how you're getting on.'

'No, no, it's fine, hello, hi. Erm, yes, it's as bad as we imagined. Worse, actually. So, um, Jack and Lily have moved back into my house.'

'And Hannah.'

'Yes. That too.'

'Have you told her about me?' Rosie's stomach knotted with dread.

'Well, I er …' He cleared his throat.

Rosie didn't know what to make of that.

She heard Hannah calling him. 'Gareth! I need you here a minute.'

'Look …' Gareth's voice lowered. 'This isn't a good time to have this conversation. I'll er …'

'Is Rosie coming to see us?' Jack's high voice asked. 'I miss Rosie.'

'Gareth!' Hannah again, with an unmistakeably barbed edge.

'I'm on the phone, Han.' Rosie frowned as she heard the telltale rustle of him putting his hand over the mouthpiece. She heard his muffled voice. 'What's the problem?'

'I need you to help me with something,' Hannah said, her tone imperative.

Gareth spoke back into the phone, 'Rosie, sorry, I'll ring you back.'

'Okay. I won't ring again. I'll wait for you to ring me. You've obviously got your hands full.' She waited for him to laugh and agree with her.

He said, 'Yep. Okay. Bye.' He disconnected.

Leanne came out of her room and caught Rosie glaring at her phone.

'Wassup?'

'I have a horrible feeling that Gareth has got back with his wife.'

Leanne's jaw gaped. 'No. Surely not. He adores you.'

'Hannah's broken up with her bloke and I think she's got her hooks back into Gareth. And isn't it what he always wanted? Back to being happy families? I'm not coming between them.'

Their eyes met in silence. Then, 'I'll get the wine,' said Leanne.

'Read this one, Daddy,' commanded Lily, snuggled into her Frozen Elsa pyjamas, and waving a Peppa Pig story.

'Agh,' Jack huffed, from his bed on the other side of the room. 'Not that again. I want Horrid Henry!'

Gareth, folded onto a stool between the two beds, could only think of that awful, stilted phone call. He'd hung up and gone to see what Hannah wanted. She'd spun some rubbish about needing a bit of furniture moving and then she'd kissed him as a thank you. Not an on the cheek kiss. An on the mouth kiss. He ran his fingers through his hair and tried to concentrate.

'Peppa Pig for the first ten minutes, Horrid Henry for the next ten.' He must've sounded sharp, as they both gave in straight away. He read for longer to make up for it. Lily was asleep before he'd finished. Jack's brown eyes stared owlishly back at him over the covers.

'Are we going to live here forever?'

'No, sweetheart. Just until your house has been cleaned up.'

'And you'll be ...?'

'I'll be here for you, as I always will be.' Disingenuous, he knew. He tucked the covers around his son's lean body.

'Will we see Rosie soon? I want to show her my drawings.'

'Rosie is really busy at the moment, sweetheart. But I'm sure she misses you too.' That at least was true. 'Do you want to listen to a story CD for a little while?'

Jack nodded. 'Yes please.' Gareth put a CD into the old style player that they'd kept for this purpose, and set the volume to a quiet murmur. Kissing them both goodnight, he switched off the light and looked back at them, illuminated from the hallway. Jack snuggled onto his side, his eyes closing drowsily already and Lily, flat on her back, one arm flung across the pillow.

They could be a family again. He could do this every night. He plugged the little night light into the socket on the landing and switched off the landing light. Wasn't that what he'd always wanted? He would be a better husband, a better father. Banish his ideas of running his own business, and focus on the haulage instead. It wasn't as if he hated his job. He didn't, and that was the hardest part.

But running an outdoor pursuits business felt like an indulgence because he *loved* it. Loved the challenges, the people, the fresh air and the feeling that he was making a difference to people's lives.

And what about Rosie? He slumped quietly onto the top

stair, elbows on his knees. Rosie had made sure she'd never come between him and his children. Never complained that he didn't make time for her. She simply understood how important time with his children was. Look at what had happened to Keira because her father had deserted her. He wouldn't just bugger off like Chester had but wouldn't Lily and Jack prefer it if they were a family again? He raked his fingers through his hair and crept down the stairs to avoid disturbing the children.

Hannah was stretched across his sofa, her eyes glued to his TV set. He rested his hands on her shoulders and she put her hand up to catch his. It was just like old times. 'Come and watch this with me.'

'Tea? Coffee, wine?' He hovered near the kitchen.

'Coffee in the night time? Are you mad? And wine, God no. Too many calories. Just sit down, for God's sake. You're like a bear, prowling about. Come on, it's Corrie. Just started.'

His limbs twitching with pent-up energy, he did as he was told, trying to focus on the television. He couldn't make head or tail of the storyline and his mind slid away from it. On the infrequent times he watched TV, it was for the type of real-life series that showed cars being done up, survivalist stories Bear Grylls style, and men sawing down trees to build houses for their families to live off grid. He rather liked that idea. Soaps weren't on his radar at all.

He remembered with a sinking feeling that Hannah had always been addicted to them. Had Ian shared her passion? Visions of balmy evenings watching logs burning in Rosie's garden with a glass of wine pushed themselves into his head.

'Would you like a firepit?'

'Ssh! What?' She turned her head fractionally towards him. 'What on earth for?'

'We could sit in the garden, and ...'

'How would I see the telly? And what's the point of

paying for heating and then sitting outside in a freezing garden?'

'I just thought it might be, um, nice?' God, that sounded lame.

'You are funny.' She gurgled with laughter, flicking the remote to the next channel. 'I love this. You don't mind if I watch it ...'

'Course not. I'm going to go for a run. Bit fidgety, y'know.' The restlessness was more in his head than in his legs. Memories surfaced of the fire picking out the copper tones in Rosie's hair. What on earth must she think of him? He could ring her. What the hell was he going to say? He didn't even know what was going on in his own mind. Apart from the feeling that he was obliged to do his best for the family. A creeping sense of failure settled over him. He'd failed at being a husband, failed at being the son his parents wanted. Rosie deserved better, didn't she?

Hannah was already watching her next programme, and he climbed the stairs to get changed, feeling weirdly like a stranger in his own home. He didn't know where he belonged any more.

Chapter Thirty-Four

I went back to The Circle this week. I thought I'd finished with it. But this thing with Gareth has knocked my confidence. He's gone back to his wife. It's been two weeks now. He hasn't rung me since THAT phone call and I have more pride than to ring him again. I could hear how awkward things were and I get that his family had all moved in on him but where is he sleeping? With her? On the sofa? Where? I feel guilty that I'm thinking the worst of him, but why hasn't he called me?

I talked about it a bit in The Circle. I could see some of them looking at each other. Someone said that maybe I'd read more into the friendship than there was, and also that perhaps I'd fallen into it because I was lonely after Mum dying. I don't think I was wrong, was I?

I don't know what to think any more. So I'm working. Leanne helped me set up some online workshops, I've set up a trade account to get materials at trade prices, and I've put together a starter pack of felts plus the necessary equipment to go with them.

And Gareth's mum rang me, just like always, as if nothing had happened between me and Gareth. I didn't ask after him, although I was screaming inside to know, and Carol didn't offer.

She said, in her brisk voice, 'I still want you to come and sell your work at my house. I know my friends would love it, and they'll have parties in their houses for you, I'm sure. Bring some felt along and do a little demonstration of how you make it. You could have some "here's one I started earlier" examples. I'm sure I've got a display stand somewhere – we could put photos up of you working, and people wearing your jewellery, things like that. Perhaps your friend Lucy could help with those, if she has a list of your customers?'

I wrote it all down. I need all the help I can get. She reminded me about business cards, an order book for commissions, and one of those machines you can take card payments on.

Tom has been looking at courses to train as an outdoor pursuits instructor. He'd talked to Gareth about it a lot and now, he doesn't mention it at all. I expect he thinks it will upset me. He's got the perfect temperament to be an instructor. I wonder what that means for Leanne. They've become inseparable and she is so happy. They're very well matched. I'm pleased for them but I hope he doesn't break her heart and leave her behind when he goes off travelling again. That boy has itchy feet for sure. I can't see him ever having a house of his own. He's never in one place for long enough. But that's up to them. You give your children roots to grow in and wings to fly.

Keira is blooming and beautiful. She comes over for dinner now, bringing Peck. I think my first impressions of him might have been a bit unkind. Or maybe he's relaxed a bit but he was really good at explaining about display. He works in electrical sales. He was actually pretty switched on. Geddit? I made a joke. Sigh. I didn't laugh either. Sorry Diary.

Anyway, the money has started to come in from the workshops so that's good. There's been no sign of that shithead Chester, and we've looked everywhere and there are no piles of money hidden away as he seemed to think.

Worst case scenario, I'll have to sell the house. I'd better start getting used to it but I worry about Keira and Peck and a tiny baby.

Thank goodness I have my work. I can't sleep properly, so I go down to my workshop and work. The wool shows me where to go. I'm painting my life by the sea. Those drawings

I made of the Welsh hills after that weekend away? Never used. And not likely to be either.

And oh God, not long before I'm a granny! I'm not old enough to be a granny. I wonder if this is how Mum felt? Talking of Mum ... she used to call her room her apartment. That, plus the little sitting room opposite would be perfect for Keira and the baby. Like a little flat. They can be a bit independent, apart from the kitchen. And, of course, Peck, although I don't know if he has a lease or anything where he's living. That's up to him. I'll get the family dream team onto it, bless them. At least I have my family around me now. Which is all that Gareth wanted for himself.

So I can't really blame him.

I suppose.

Hannah had decided that it was a good time to redecorate her house, as it would have to be done anyway, and have a new kitchen. They spent hours poring over brochures and trailing around kitchen showrooms but with opposite tastes, they never seemed to come to any decisions. Did Gareth truly want to live there again? Doubt racked him. He loved Rosie's open plan living space, the open shelves, quirky colours and textures that made the place cosy. Hannah's glossy white, hi-tech look repelled him. It suited her, though. And of course, she'd get her way.

When Hannah wasn't out with her mates, either at the gym or socialising, Gareth ran, or took his camera out and created atmospheric photographs of yellowing leaves falling in the twilight. But they reminded him of Rosie, who was the only person he knew who shared his ability to see the abstracted beauty of their surroundings. He showed some of the photos to Hannah, and she pronounced them "gloomy".

Scrolling past the densely packed thumbnail prints on his computer screen, he spotted the photos he took of Rosie playing with his children on the beach. It was that day she'd sold her first felts at the Art Café. He lingered, remembering, and forced his fingers to scroll past, his stomach contracting with guilt and indecision.

He never missed reading a bedtime story to Lily and Jack. But pounding the streets he pushed himself to his limits, his music playlist blaring in his ears, pushing away awkward thoughts that were always about Rosie. On those nights, Hannah had a calorie-counted ready meal, and watched the telly. He'd make himself a bowl of noodles and veggies when he came home, always offering it to her too.

'You know I don't like coriander.'

'I can leave the coriander out.'

'I hate those little sweetcorn things too. They're like fingers.' She shuddered, theatrically. 'And mushrooms are so slimy in your mouth. Eurgh.'

'So that's a no from you, then,' he'd say with a laugh. She'd eye him with a tiny frown and her gaze would slide back to the television.

In his dreams about them getting back together, he'd visualised them shopping together, days out with the children, eating as a family, waking up in the same bed and having the children coming in to snuggle up with them at weekends when they weren't working. Somehow, he hadn't visualised the sex.

They'd been apart for so long, that now the whole idea seemed wrong. She slept in his bed, and he slept on the sofa. They were companionable, considerate of each other's feelings, they were the parents of their children. It was a week before she instigated a move in his direction. Pulling off his sweaty running T-shirt before a shower one evening he caught her proprietorial scrutiny. She trailed her finger down over his chest, and he shivered.

'The kids are asleep ...' she said, following her finger with her tongue. 'Hurry up in that shower.'

When he emerged, she'd stretched herself alluringly along the bed, and plucked at the towel around his waist in a playful way.

'Let's see if you've still got it, big boy.' Her lips curved upwards as her eyes closed. She was still beautiful. He remembered the days when they hadn't been able to keep their hands off each other. He'd been obsessed with her.

Propped on his elbow alongside her he gazed at her. She was offering herself to him ... and his body completely failed to respond. He squeezed his eyes shut – and saw only Rosie, round and luscious as a peach, smiling up at him. His body answered *that* call and he felt Hannah's touch as she reached for him. He'd almost fallen out of the bed, he'd yanked himself away from her that fiercely. He couldn't do that to Rosie, he just couldn't. And he couldn't use Hannah in that way, with Rosie in his head. Neither could he explain to her. In anguish, he'd apologised to her sullen pout and stalked away to sleep on the sofa. They hadn't tried again.

After that, she went out more and more frequently. He never asked her where, and she didn't volunteer any details. He prowled the lounge and flicked, unseeingly, through the TV channels. It wasn't going to work. Their time was over. Even her breathing irritated him – who'd have thought that could happen? He'd made a huge mistake – and now he was stuck with it. He'd blown his chances with Rosie and he couldn't even escape to anywhere. Idiot. *Idiot!*

He *knew* Hannah! She hadn't changed, and neither had he! What, in the name of God, had made him think they could make a go of it again? What madness had possessed him? He'd wanted so much to be a full time dad but this was so wrong. He buried his head in his hands. So. What was he going to do about it? Who could he talk to?

Next morning they got the kids off to school without saying very much to each other. Hannah went to work and Gareth went to see his mum.

Chapter Thirty-Five

The main office was like a global planning department with added pot plants. There were huge maps on the walls, charts and stickers and chalkboards with the HGV identification numbers and drivers, filing cabinets and shelves stacked with ring binders, all orderly and neat. His gaze swept across the walls. It was like a story – who was going where, with what and from whom – and he read that story easily because he knew it too.

His mother had her desk at the rear of the room. She'd never wanted her own office, preferring to be in the thick of things, unlike Cled, whose office was more reflective of his personality. His door was never closed and drivers, managers and mechanics alike trekked back and forth in the certain knowledge that he always had an ear for them.

Carol was holding a mug and hailed him as he entered.

'Good morning, darling! Coffee? I've just made it – the pot is hot.' He stooped to kiss her cheek and went for coffee. Typical of his mum to make the coffee for the staff.

He sat at her desk, wishing that for once, she did have her own office so that he could talk to her privately. He could have gone to the house, but Hannah and the kids would want to come too.

'Mum – I think I might have ballsed up.'

'What? Where?' He saw her scan the wall charts, reassuring herself that everything was as it should be.

'Not the HGVs, Mum.' He allowed himself a small smile as she visibly relaxed. She'd been a whole lot more approachable since – and here it was again – since she'd met with Rosie and been mentoring her, but the business still drove her. 'On a personal level.'

She threw him a sharp look. 'Cled's at the workshop this

morning. His office is empty. Let's pop in there. Bring your coffee.' His father's office was comfortable, and devoid of pot plants. Signed rugby photos shared the walls and shelves with photos of himself with Carol, together with family snaps of Gareth and Aled as children and generations of Merwyn-Jones's beside their beloved fleet of HGVs.

'Is everyone okay?' Carol asked, sliding a coaster along the desk that bore countless coffee cup rings.

'Yes. Everyone is fine.' He scratched his ear. Where to start?

'How's the house coming along?'

'Um, yes, it's okay, we've been told not to even think about decorating for at least three weeks after the walls have dried out. Hannah is talking about colours and having a new kitchen.' He groaned inside. Why was he talking about the bloody kitchen? Rubbing the heel of his hand into his forehead he said in a rush, 'It's not working out for me and Hannah.'

'No.'

'I'm so sorry. I know how disappointed you were about us splitting up in the first place and—what ...? No?'

'I mean, no, I can see that it's not working for you both.'

'Oh.'

'So, what are you going to do?'

His eyes travelled over the photos again. There was one of him looking young and carefree in the driver's seat of a lofty HGV, giving a thumbs up through the open window.

'I'll rephrase that. What do you *want* to do?'

'I've made a mess of everything, Mum.' He dry washed his face. 'Since Aled, I ...'

'Since Aled died, you've worn the mantle of blame on your shoulders for everything.' She leaned forward, fingers interlinked over her crossed knees. 'And that shouldn't have been your cross to bear. Gareth, it was an accident. And it was twelve years ago. Time we all moved on.

'Aled was a tearaway, and even though you were the younger one, you were always so careful. You weren't the risk-taker, he was. But I needed someone to blame, and you were there.' She uncrossed her legs and rotated her shoulders. 'It's taken me years to come to terms with that. Aled was the future of this company. I always guessed that you weren't as interested. And then we didn't have Aled, but we still had you …' She stared out of the window. 'And you seemed to throw yourself into the business, so we let you. I did, anyway. Your dad had reservations. And then you married Hannah, and the kids came along and you seemed as happy as anyone else did … and at least it was a secure business. You were never going to be sacked, that's for sure!' She stretched her mouth into a mirthless grin that was gone as quickly as it arrived. 'I closed my eyes to your outdoor courses. Your dad said you needed a hobby, and it's kept you fit.

'But I never understood why you did it. In my head'—she moistened her lips with her tongue and avoided his eye—'you'd killed my eldest son, and here you were, still doing all those things.'

Gareth forced a breath into his tight lungs. He'd guessed some of this, of course he had, he wasn't stupid. But his mother had never said it out loud. He couldn't believe how much it hurt. Words, even if he had any, would never get past the lump blocking his throat. Tears misted on his mother's eyes.

'I am so sorry, sweetheart. Because I was wrong. I was so wrong. You were always such a sweet child. There was never an ounce of malice in you. You always cared for things. While Aled crashed about, taking chances and stomping all over everything, you'd be behind him, mending them. I see a lot of you in Jack.'

Gareth nodded, slowly. 'While Lily is a mini Aled. Sweet but a bit careless. And completely fearless. Aled would have loved her.

'He loved you, too. You made a great team, you know. Like opposite sides of the same coin. You balanced each other out. And I've come to terms with the fact that it was a tragic, awful accident. An accident. Not your fault. No doubt he was trying out something reckless, just like he always did. We were lucky that you survived, darling.' His mother smiled, her eyes gentle.

Gareth gulped, his throat tight. 'I still miss him, Mum.'

'He would have talked you out of going back to Hannah, you know.'

'Why didn't *you*?'

'Would you have listened? Besides, we all have to learn from our own mistakes. I'm learning from mine.' She drained her coffee. 'So tell me, is Hannah happy?'

Gareth chewed his lips. 'I don't see how she can be. We're like strangers in the same house. We don't row – we don't really even communicate. It's horrible. We're cooped up in my tiny little house for at least another month – and it's all my fault. I've offered her this alternative and made everything ten times worse.'

'There you go, taking responsibility for everything again.' Carol raised her eyebrows at him over the glasses that she wore more and more frequently. 'She might feel trapped too – she has nowhere to go, and she doesn't want to throw you out of your own house. Instead of making assumptions, you need to speak to her properly.' She stretched her back. 'And yes, I know I'm a fine one to talk about making assumptions. As I said earlier, I'm learning from my many, many mistakes.' She leaned forward and touched his arm. 'Darling, you know we have a spare room. It's yours whenever you need it. You and Hannah are both sensible people. I'm sure you can come to some kind of arrangement.'

'Thanks Mum. Thank you. And the other thing is—'

'Rosie?'

He stared into his coffee. 'Mmm. And I—'

'I think that's something you need to sort out for yourself.' She studied him, making a conscious effort to drop her shoulders. 'I'm sorry, I jumped the gun a bit there. You were about to say ...?'

'I want to start my own business.'

'Do you?'

'I've filled out my business plans, and worked out my costings and I've even started on some market research. I've researched the current business model for the courses I'm doing and I think I can deliver a unique experience.'

'Excellent.'

'What?'

'Gareth, I might have been the mother from hell these last years, but I'm not blind.'

'Oh Mum ...' He reached out and put his hands over her slim, nervy ones, feeling how much thinner the skin was now, assailed by a sudden memory of his hand in hers as a child, skipping alongside her, chattering non-stop. 'The trouble is, it will take a while to establish, and winter isn't the best time to entice people onto these types of courses, so there'd be no money coming in.' He took a deep breath. 'And I'm not thinking about myself here, but—'

'Maintenance payments?'

'Yes. I would never see the kids going short because I'm pursuing my dreams.'

'Gareth, I heard something the other day and I wrote it down. It was, "Memories are better than Dreams". Your father and I have plans too, you know.'

'For the business?' His heart sank.

'No, darling, for our retirements.' She rolled her eyes at him. 'And we're hanging on here, while you're dithering, in case you decide to take over the haulage after all.'

'I don't understand.'

'You've been hinting at your outdoor pursuits business idea for ages now, but never taking it anywhere. We didn't know whether this was an idle dream or real, and you never seemed to get any further forward with it. Merwyn-Jones Haulage has made us a lot of money over the years, and we've both loved it. It's been our lives. But I don't want us to keep going like a pair of desiccated old sticks, dying at our desks. We want to travel and have adventures too. While we still have our knees.'

'Why didn't you tell me any of this?'

'Well, I have to say, this has been on the agenda fairly recently. Since coming to terms with Aled's death, really.' Her grey eyes met his. 'Rosie helped me a lot. She's a pretty special person. And in return, I helped her with her business ...'

'And indirectly, you knew that might help me with my ideas.' Gareth shook his head. Rosie again. 'Genius. Sly, but genius.'

'At the very least, I hoped it might make you focus on what you wanted.'

'It did. And then I messed it all up by hooking up with Hannah again.'

'Stop beating yourself up for everything. She could have said no too! It was clearly something you both hoped would work. It hasn't and so your way ahead is clear.'

'Except for the finances. And Rosie.'

'Yes. Well, you need to work on how you approach Rosie yourself. But there might be a way out of the finances. We've had an offer on the business. It's not quite what we're looking for, but it's made us focus too and so we're refining what we want.

'Now, you and Aled were both shareholders, as you know. Dad and I were thinking, how would it be if we put Aled's shares into trust for Lily and Jack. You'd retain your own, so you could invest in your business, and whatever happened to that, you'd always know that your children would be financially independent.'

Gareth digested her words slowly. 'Oh my God. Mum, would you really do that?' He leapt to his feet and hugged her. 'That would be – I can't think of the right words! That would be so wonderful. Thank you so much.'

'You're so welcome. I only wish we'd thought of it sooner. I suppose everything has its own time.'

Back at his house, Gareth packed the things he'd need. He could always pop back later if he'd forgotten anything. Hannah eyed the bags and said nothing until Jack and Lily were in bed. He took a deep breath, having rehearsed what he was going to say.

'Stay as long as you need to, Han. I'm moving in with Mum and Dad.' He swallowed. 'I'll always love you – but not in that way any more. I can come over and have the kids whenever you want to go out, but I'm sorry, I—'

'I've been seeing Ian. We're getting back together again.' Hannah cut through his speech. Gareth blinked. 'I'm sorry, but me and you, we're different people aren't we? I don't know how we stayed married as long as we did. I loved you too. Who wouldn't? And after the accident ... But Ian gets me. His idea of a weekend away is a luxury spa whereas yours is some shed halfway up a mountainside.' She flashed a quick grin at him. His stomach flip-flopped with relief. And irritation, with himself and her, that either of them had thought it could work out a second time. We learn by our mistakes. Rosie would have rolled her eyes at the cliché, he knew.

'I'm pleased for you both.' He nodded, his mind whirling.

She seemed to have done a better job of thinking it through than him though, because she said, crisply, 'Shall we sort out a better arrangement with Lily and Jack, while we're at it?' Gareth eyed her cautiously.

'In what way?'

She put her head on one side. 'You did a fabulous job of having them while I was with Mum and Dad. I know how much you adore them and I wondered if you'd like them more often than the current every other weekend and odd days in between.'

'What are you thinking of?' Gareth held his breath.

'Well, we'd have to talk it through with them, but maybe you could have them every other week, or a fortnight at a time, something like that?'

'I'd like that.' He'd make it work, somehow.

'And um, this Rosie person.'

'What about her?' Gareth's heart thudded.

'Why didn't you tell me about her? The kids talked about her all the time and I felt like a right idiot. You knew about Ian! You should have told me.'

'Well, there's no point now. I've cooked my goose with her.'

'Oh Gar. Make it up to her. I could tell her we didn't sleep together or anything!'

'Uh, no, thank you. I don't think that would help.' Rosie wouldn't be so easily swayed, he knew. He'd let her down horribly. He had serious doubts about his ability to sustain a relationship.

Chapter Thirty-Six

Rosie knocked at the door of Carol and Cled's house, swallowing down her nerves. She ran through her list in her head as she waited. Stock – all priced. Display cubes, boards with photos, her laptop with her website, photos and videos, little bags with her stickers on for sales. Her payment machine, change for cash sales and a receipt book with business cards. Lastly, a few little packs of felts and materials as a starter pack to sell alongside the courses she'd set up online, and her demonstration materials. What a long way she'd come in a few short months. She only hoped she didn't disappoint Carol's faith in her.

The house was just as she'd imagined. Big. Expensive. Well maintained, with manicured lawns at the front and bay trees in huge stone pots on either side of the porch. Detached, with beautiful trees around the perimeter. The carpets would be thick and cream coloured, and the sofas deep, she was sure. Carol's voice floated to her through the door, 'Would you get that for me, darling?'

The door opened, and her pinned-on smile fell away in shock. Gareth looked just as startled.

'Rosie! Uh ...'

She hadn't seen him for almost three weeks. Two weeks and four days, but who was counting ...

'Good evening, Rosie, my dear.' Carol bustled past him, planting a kiss on Rosie's surprised face. 'Gareth, would you be a darling and help Rosie with her stock, please.'

He stepped outside looking dazed and she clicked the boot open on her fob. She had enough on her plate coping with her first party, without him hanging about. He made her *feel*. Made her feel exposed. Vulnerable. And she didn't want to. Not about him. Was Hannah here too? Would they meet and Gareth would be all awkward and formal, introducing Rosie as his "friend"? Why couldn't he just go?

'I can manage. Really. You don't have to ... oh. Okay.' Stacking the many boxes one atop the other, he lifted them as if they were weightless and took them inside without a word. Feeling more awkward than she'd ever thought possible, she removed everything else and stacked it just inside the front door, and locked the car. You can do this, she told herself. He might just be visiting. He'll go now, surely. Why prolong her humiliation? The discarded girlfriend, still sniffing about.

He looked thin, she thought. His biceps were much more defined in the short-sleeved polo shirt. Strained. But of course, he hadn't expected to see her. He probably felt as awkward as she did. Naughty of Carol not to warn either of them. He returned as she was trying to restrain the gangly, wayward display board, and eased it calmly away from her. Their fingers touched and she felt her heart contract. Angry that she didn't snatch her hand away, she grabbed up the few lightweight bags and followed him along an oak-floored hallway into an enormous lounge. It seemed to stretch on forever. There was a table at one end and her boxes were stacked beside it. She was glad she'd remembered to bring an oilcloth, and even more relieved that the expected carpeting hadn't materialised. The thought of splashing water onto it had been enough to send her blood pressure rocketing.

'Would you like some help setting up?' Gareth asked her. His formal tone sent icicles into her heart. Just go away!

'Of course Rosie would like some help,' Carol said, briskly. 'I would too. There's another table in the snug that I need in here, to put people's drinks and nibbles on. Could you carry it through for me, Gareth?'

Rosie spotted Gareth's restrained look of exasperation and felt her mouth lift at the corners despite her anguish.

Who was he meant to help first? Sending her a helpless half-smile, he plumped for Carol, and bobbed in and out with various chairs and stools and cloths and lights for the next fifteen minutes.

Rosie was glad of the time to herself. It gave her the breathing space she needed to set the table up how she wanted it. Arranging her stock on the Perspex display cubes, she made sure they were all priced, and placed price lists for commissions in another Perspex holder. Photos and videos played from the laptop which she plugged into an extension lead and then into the nearest socket, and she plugged her clip-on spotlights into the same extension lead, angling them onto her work for the best effect.

She'd had a small range of greetings cards printed from her work to test the market and they had their own display too. Cute, chunky white frames stood on miniature easels on top of the upturned wooden crate that the cards lived in, to give them height.

'That looks fantastic, Rosie,' Gareth said from behind her, as she inspected it critically and took photos for her social media sites. She'd practised this so many times on the dining table at home.

'Oh! Thank you.' She whirled to face him, feeling her face heat. Her pulse thrummed in her ears and she heard herself say, 'Do you think there's enough? I didn't know how much to bring, so, I brought it all. I've got more in the boxes. Should I put it out? How are you? How are Jack and Lily? And Hannah?' She reined herself in with difficulty. Relief that she'd set up. Nerves about the next couple of hours. Not at all her proximity to this tall, gentle, handsome man she'd allowed herself to fall for. Who'd cast her aside in favour of his ex-wife. She steeled herself to hear his happy news about his lovely family. She was strong. She could do this.

'Me and Hannah – um,' he began. She forced herself to

look away and set up her demonstration materials. La-la-la. She'd asked but she didn't want to hear. People would be arriving soon. She needed to be calm and in control, and having Gareth standing there "umming" about him and Hannah, wasn't helping at all. Were they planning to remarry?

Eventually, she took a deep breath and eyed him. In the same headmistress voice she remembered using on him to ask for help taking the curtains down at the bunkhouse, she said, 'Yes?'

'We're not together.' The words landed in a rush. 'It was stupid of me. I'm so sorry I upset you, Rosie. I've missed you every single day. I loved seeing Jack and Lily as a full-time dad, but not—' He stepped towards her, put a hand on the table, and everything wobbled precariously, like an avalanche about to happen. 'Agh, oops, I'm sorry, I'll um, I'll go, shall I?'

His words sank in slowly. Rosie wasn't quite sure she'd been listening. 'You and Hannah – not together?' He'd missed her every single day? She reached out to prop up the fallen display and her treacherous hands shook so much she knocked over everything next to it.

Gareth reached over and, with his long, strong fingers, delicately repositioned everything to where it was meant to be. She stared at his fingers and in an agony, wrenched her eyes away. 'No. I'm staying with Mum and Dad until the house is ready to move back into. How is Keira doing?'

'She's fine. On maternity leave and staying in Mum's old room. Four weeks to go now. She's pretty huge already.'

'Only four weeks! That's not long.'

'No. She didn't know she was pregnant at the funeral, and she was quite a way on.'

'I see.' Gareth looked downcast. 'I'm so sorry about … everything …'

'Gareth, you did what you felt you had to do. And please

don't expect me to turn back time and have everything as it was – because what you did made me feel like second best.' She lifted her chin. 'And I can't take any of this in right now, because I have a job to do, and this is how I earn my living. Okay?'

Gareth lifted the palms of his hands in surrender. 'I never meant to make you feel like you were— I'm sorry. I keep saying that, don't I? I really am, though. At the time, I thought that I did have to try again with Hannah, but we were over a long time ago, and I had never rid myself of the guilt of my failure. I've learned a big lesson. I'm *still* learning. Please don't write me off. Tell me I'm an idiot, but I'm an idiot who loves you.'

'That looks wonderful, Rosie. Well done. My ladies will love it all.' Carol turned to her son. 'Gareth, be useful or be gone.'

'I can be useful.' Gareth nodded firmly.

'Good man. Go and answer the door please, my darling. A glass of pink Prosecco for the ladies. Cled will host their men in the snug with the rugby and they're all on soft drinks so none of the ladies is driving home. Off you go.' Gareth went.

Reassembling her face, still slack-jawed with shock from Gareth's news bomb, Rosie said, 'Does anyone ever say no to you, Carol?'

'Many have tried,' Carol said, her eyes twinkling. 'Right, I've finished matchmaking you two, people are arriving.'

Rosie's eyebrows lifted at the same time as she heard the first ring on the doorbell. 'You knew – about ...?'

'Of course, my sweet. Someone had to give the pudding a stir. You two would have just ended up skirting around each other forever and time is too short, isn't it? Also my grandchildren miss you. Right. Are you ready for the onslaught?'

Rosie nodded faintly. 'I am. Bring it on.' She took a

steadying breath, looking around at everything Carol had done for her. 'And thank you!' She greeted her first guest, escorted by Gareth, with a smile she hadn't used in far too long.

Gareth, clearly well trained by his mother, was kept busy handing out pink bubbly with a smile and showing male guests to the snug. Her eyes followed him greedily, taking in his broad shoulders, the hair that needed a cut, the leather belt gathering the jeans that hung around his lean waist. Her hands longed to hold him, touch his warm skin, smooth his hollowed cheeks, but despite all that, she was hesitant. Scared. Was she clinging to the idea of a dream?

He brought her a big glass of chilled sparkling water, tinkling with ice and lemon. She felt the electricity fizz between their fingers as she accepted it and heat flooded through her body.

'Good luck,' he said. 'Although you won't need it. I've already heard the ladies discussing what they're going to buy.'

She watched them crowding around her table, peering through their specs at the prices and lifting pieces to look at their reflections in the mirror over the fireplace. She answered their many questions. Just one sale, she thought. One sale would settle her, give her confidence. And not a pity purchase from Carol, either. Carol introduced her, and Rosie stepped forward to speak, legs, hands and voice all quaking in symphony.

'Good evening, ladies, thank you so much for coming ...' She faltered, scanning around the room. Each of them with a glass in their hand, watching her expectantly. She took a steadying breath and smiled. 'And a huge thank you to Carol, Cled and Gareth for hosting me!' She raised her glass of water to them. 'If they keep giving me gins this big, I'll be buying all my own stock!' There was laughter. One lady raised her hand.

'Is everything for sale, tonight?'

'Oh yes. I don't want to take anything home if I can help it! I also take commissions, so if there's something that you can see and you'd like it in a different colour, or size, or you have an idea you'd like me to make, come and have a chat with me. There's plenty of time to order that extra special Christmas gift. There are photographs here of things I've made for people. And I can match to wedding outfits too.'

There was an excited murmur after the mention of weddings and Rosie made a mental note to speak to Carol about that.

'I love that scarf. Could I have that?' The lady who'd asked got up immediately, handing her glass to a quick-thinking Gareth. 'I've had my eye on that since I came in and I'm not letting anyone else have it.' There was laughter.

'Of course,' Rosie said, thrilled inside, but smiling easily and putting it aside to be wrapped. 'I was going to demonstrate how I make these pieces first. Shall I do that while you enjoy your drinks and some more of these delicious nibbles?' Encouraged by their nods, Rosie showed them how she designed and created her felted pieces, and what inspired them.

'I had no idea they took that long,' were the shared reactions. 'I love the colours. It's so soft,' were others.

The evening flew by. Rosie and Carol took sales and wrapped them. Rosie's order book for commissioned pieces began to fill up nicely. Matching for wedding outfits was definitely popular.

'What's the commission if I host a party for you?' one lady asked. Rosie blinked. She'd only thought of this as a one-off for Carol.

Quick as a flash, Carol answered, 'The piece of your choice up to twenty per cent of the evening's sales. And if you're lucky, she'll bring her fire engine too!'

'Oh, she's a beauty. One of these days, if I can ever

afford it, I'll have her converted into a camper van.' Rosie's memory flashed back to the day they'd all collected Bedelia. The fire engine would always be connected in her mind with Gareth. She'd discovered she owned it on the day she joined his course and he'd rebuilt her confidence in her driving. She'd felt empowered that day. And that confidence had lasted, even if their relationship hadn't. She had a lot to be thankful for. Her eyes flicked towards Gareth and her stomach jolted as she saw his gaze was already on her. She'd have to make a decision about the fire engine. It was still in Gareth's yard. She'd kind of ignored its presence. But doing it up would cost a fortune, and wouldn't that money be better spent on the house?

Tuning in to Carol's interrogative stare, she agreed hastily and then wondered if twenty percent was a bit mean. Until she added up her sales in her head … nearly a thousand pounds! A host selecting goods of two hundred pounds would be more than happy – and she would have to work every hour of the day to keep up with the stock if they sold as well as this one had. She wasn't going to complain about that!

Of course, she realised that Carol had done a fabulous job of wooing these ladies with wine and canapés, and the handsome and obliging waiter hadn't been a hindrance either …

Chapter Thirty-Seven

The boxes were a whole lot lighter on the way back to Rosie's car, and with the rear seats folded down, everything stacked neatly. She was exuberant at her success and couldn't stop thanking Carol for her help. She wished she'd thought of the idea of giving Carol a commission on sales. She would make something beautiful for her as a thank you for her considerable and very much appreciated help.

There were hugs all round and Carol and Cled excused themselves, leaving Gareth still hovering, looking awkward.

'Will you be able to manage these by yourself?'

'Yes, thank you. Leanne and Tom will be around to give me a hand.'

'Well, it was lovely to see you tonight.'

'You too. Thank you very much for helping. Please thank your parents again from me.'

'Oh, they enjoyed it. It's been a while since we did anything like this. They should be thanking you.' He cleared his throat. 'Um – would you like to go for dinner with me, one evening, when you're free?'

Rosie, clutching the car key, stepped backwards, fumbling for the car door.

'You're asking me on a date? Like, a proper date, not picking mushrooms at six in the morning, or listening to foxes scream in the middle of the night? Or showing me how to drive my fire engine or jumping waves in the sunshine with your children?'

'Erm ...'

'Because *those* are the things that made me fall in love with you. You helped me to build up my self-confidence and then you dropped me like a hot brick. But you did me a favour because that self-belief has helped me cope through the worst year I can ever remember and I'm finally learning to love myself. I'm starting to find out what *I* want, after years of doing what other people want.

'I don't need candle-lit, fancy dinners – unless they're cooked by you. I *do* need to know we will have adventures. Together. That I can always count on you, as you will always be able to count on me. That you will always be on my side, even if you're not *by* my side. And I don't want to hear you telling me that you love me, because words are easy. I want to *see* that you do.'

Gareth listened. She was wonderful, her eyes flashing, her chin held high. He was so proud of her. She really had come a long way since the scared woman on her way to that first rock-climb.

'I hear you, Rosie.' He held her gaze, wanting more than anything to kiss her fierce, pink mouth. 'But you won't stop me telling you how sorry I am that I hurt you.'

'It was nice to see you tonight, Gareth. Give my love to Lily and Jack.' She climbed into the car, turned the ignition and prayed to the God of driving that she wouldn't kangaroo hop off the drive. He was still in her rear-view mirror as she turned onto the main road. She turned the radio on and wound up the volume, singing lustily.

She didn't want to hear any more of his apologies. She couldn't help loving him but her battered heart couldn't take much more. She couldn't remember a year when she had cried more. She craved for a time without drama. Without the fear and worry of losing the house she'd worked on for so long and grown to love. Had she fooled herself that Gareth was her rock? Was he a dreamer without the courage to pursue his own dreams?

As her throat closed and her face crumpled she mimed instead, scrubbing angrily at her wet face. It wasn't a long enough drive for her to regain composure and Tom, sweet, lovely young man that he was, spotted immediately that something was wrong.

'Uh-oh. What's up, Mam? No sales?'

She shook her head. 'I made a grand.'

'Wow! That's amazing!'

'We bought you some bubbly,' said Leanne, heading for the fridge.

Keira waddled out of the newly decorated room that she and Peck mostly lived in full time now. 'Yo! How'd it go, Mum?'

'She made a grand!'

'Awesome! That's really cool, Mum. Well done.'

'And I've taken a stack of commissions and more people want to host parties.' Leanne popped the cork on the Prosecco and poured her a glass. 'Thank you, my sweet. How lovely of you all. Cheers!'

She took a sip. It was lovely. Dry and refreshing. Leanne handed sparkling elderflower to Keira, then poured two more glasses of Prosecco for Tom and herself.

'Congratulations, Rosie!' Leanne lifted her glass in a toast. 'Your first solo selling party! Here's to many more.'

Taking a long swallow, Rosie smiled round at her lovely family, her cheeks tight with dried tears.

'So – you made a thousand quid? And, that's a brilliant result, right?' Tom eyed her. 'So—?'

'Gareth was there.'

'With Hannah?' Leanne asked.

'No, they've split up.'

'So ... that's good though, right?' Keira settled herself awkwardly on the sofa and everyone scattered to find her the right cushions to prop her up. She raised her glass. 'Cheers, Mum. I always knew you were brilliant.' Tom laughed. 'What? I did! I was just too busy being a shitbag to say it. So, Mum,' she prompted. 'Gareth.'

'Well. He was lovely ... And he charmed the ladies and brought them pink Prosecco, and offered to drive me home if I wanted one ...'

'I was *going* to get pink!' Leanne groaned. 'It's very sweet though, isn't it.'

'And then …?' prompted Tom, stroking Leanne's arm with a smile.

'He said that he'd missed me every single day.' Three pairs of eyes stared back at her. 'And that he was an idiot. But he was an idiot who loved me.'

There was a long pause.

Then, '*Awwwww*. That's so sweet!' from Leanne.

'Who are you, and what have you done with my friend?' Rosie said to her, straight-faced, earning a grin.

Keira sniffed and reached for the tissue box, which Tom handed her. She blew her nose. 'Damn these hormones. I cry at everything these days. So he said that? And you've come home with a face like a slapped arse?'

'I don't always agree with my darling sister, but on this occasion …' Tom leaned forward, elbows on his knees.

'Well, I said that he shouldn't expect everything to just go back to where it was before.'

'And …?'

'And he spent the entire night helping.'

'*Okaaay* …' Tom sat back, twirling his empty glass. Rosie looked down to see that hers had somehow emptied too. Leanne got up to open another bottle, and looked enquiringly at Keira before topping Rosie, Tom and herself up.

'No thanks. This baby thinks my bladder is a trampoline tonight.' Keira smoothed her hands over the bulge. 'So, Mum, how did you leave it?'

'Um, I can't honestly remember. Words just fell out of my mouth.' She took a long sip.

'But – he wants to see you again, right?' Keira said. 'And – I'm going to assume that you want to see him? Or you wouldn't be this upset about it.'

Rosie groaned. 'Yes. Oh, I don't know! I don't want to be

dumped the next time Hannah crooks her little finger at him.'

'He's learned his lesson! Get on that phone, invite him over for a glass of bubbly with all of us, and you two can celebrate with some rumpy pumpy!' Keira adjusted her position, wincing. 'You won't disturb me. Peck's out on the razz with his mates tonight and staying over there. I wear headphones to bed, and these two make their own noise in Leanne's room!'

Tom and Leanne's faces flamed red and they glanced guiltily at Rosie.

'What? Did you think I hadn't noticed?' Rosie smiled. 'I saw it right from the beginning. You two are a perfect pair.' She looked sadly into her empty glass. 'This wine keeps evaporating.' Tom refilled their glasses with a grin. 'Thank you, darling. This is a lovely drop of fizz. Thank you all.' She sipped and looked over her glass. 'The only person in this house who's not getting any rumpy pumpy, is me.'

'Mother!' Keira pretended to look shocked. 'Not in front of the baby!' They all laughed, and she stroked her bump happily. 'I wonder who he'll look like?'

'Hopefully, not me. I was the ugliest baby ever!' Rosie twirled the stem of her glass. 'I looked like a bum with eyes on.'

Into the laughter, Keira said, 'Aw no Mum, surely not. Aren't all babies beautiful?'

'That's what mothers think.' Rosie levered herself to her feet. 'Gosh, my feet have gone a bit numb.' She giggled. 'The photo albums are upstairs. I'll show you.'

'I can't believe I've never seen you as a baby, Mum.' Keira looked up at her.

'Well, this is why.' Rosie clumped up the stairs, her head a little swimmy. She'd knocked back that wine far too quickly. The boxes of her mother's paperwork were still stacked in her bedroom, and she rummaged for the albums. Finding the one she needed, she hugged it to her chest and carefully negotiated the stairs.

'Here you go.' She hefted the book over the back of the sofa to her children and returned to her chair. The bubbly had relaxed her and she felt warm and a bit sleepy. Leanne leaned over Tom to see, as he turned the pages with the book resting on his lap.

'Oh dear, Mum.' Keira shook her head in mock sorrow. 'You really were a bouncing baby, weren't you? How on earth did Granny give birth to you? She looks the same size as you!'

'Your granny was far too posh to push, my darling,' Rosie said, eyeing her daughter through the wine glass. 'She had a caesarean booked from the off. I came out through the sun roof. And you'll notice that she regained her figure almost immediately.'

'Aw look, there's a little note from the hospital saying how big you were and what time you were born. How cute.' Keira peered more closely. 'Blimey. Nine pounds three? I hope my baby doesn't have your genes, Mum.'

Rosie, slumped into the sofa, felt her eyelids dropping, the combined effects of the wine, the emotion of seeing Gareth and lack of sleep taking their toll. Only Keira's strange tone pulled her back from the brink of drifting off.

'Mum, this was taped in. It fell out, I didn't do it! It's addressed to you. I *think* it's from Granny? Look.' Rosie reached out to take the sealed envelope. Despite the loops and flourishes, the shaky handwriting characterised her mother's final years. She stared at it, her throat constricted. A pulse hammered at her temple. What could it possibly say that she didn't already know?

'It's probably full of receipts, in date order,' she said, with a little laugh, seeing her finger tremble as it broke the seal. There were two sheets of paper inside, and she drew them out.

My darling Rosabeth,
Please forgive me. This is a terrible cliché. A confession. Yet another selfish act in a long line of them, I know. I've kept this from you for so long but soon I won't be able to write for myself. And if you've found this letter, it's because you were, in some way, looking for me. Please believe that I did it with your happiness in my mind, but not a day has passed that I haven't worried about what I did.

I wanted you to myself, my dear Rosie. I haven't been a good mother, and I know I don't deserve you. I was so wrapped up in myself and my success that I left no room for anyone else, and now it's too late.

I paid Chester a hundred thousand pounds to leave. I'm not sorry I did it – I'm sad that he confirmed everything I'd ever thought about him – but I am truly sorry that I didn't think it through properly. I didn't have a solicitor present. I knew he'd talk me out of it. I signed it over as a banker's draft. Chester signed a piece of paper I'd written to say he wouldn't come after you for the house, which I enclose. He took the money and ran, and I suppose that was the plan. I could have had him bumped off. Perhaps that would have been better.

If you haven't found out already, this will come as a shock and no doubt you will be angry that I've been so stupid, arrogant and controlling. I beg your forgiveness.

I loved every minute of our time together. You have raised a wonderful family and my darling, you work so hard. I am so proud of you, and what you have achieved. I wish I could have been half the mother you are to your children, and despite my selfish behaviour, you took me under your beautiful wing and cared for me and I couldn't be more grateful.

With all my love,

Mum X

Rosie read the words once, tears blurring her vision. Then in disbelief, again, seeing the firm signature of her mother, and Chester on the second sheet of paper. The ground fell away and her ears roared.

'Mum?' Tom sprang from the sofa and knelt before her. 'What is it?'

She handed him the letter with numb fingers.

Staggering to the bathroom, she splashed her face with cold water and sat on the loo seat, stupefied.

Tom and Keira, white-faced, fixed her with wide eyes when she tottered back into the sitting room. Leanne was still staring at the letter, her brows meeting.

'So, your mother paid Chester a hundred thousand pounds to leave you,' she said. She blew her cheeks out. 'No wonder he thought there was more where that came from.'

'I don't understand,' whispered Keira, tears tracking down her pale cheeks. 'I don't understand any of it.' Tom put his arm around her.

'I understand why Dad took the money, even if that makes him lower than a snake's belly in my opinion. I just don't get why Gran ...?' He ended on a long shrug, shaking his head. Keira moaned and winced and shuffled to the front of the sofa. 'You okay, Kee?'

'Yeah. Wind I guess. Rub my back for me?'

'Course.'

'He went. Just like that. I don't know what that says about me.' Rosie kneaded her tight chest. 'I must be the world's best doormat.' She picked up her empty glass and eyed it. 'Haven't we got anything stronger than this? A hundred thousand would have finished this house and some. She could have paid for the divorce! But she gave it to *him*! And here we are, in an unfinished house, while he's spent the last five years living it up on her money!' Adrenaline seethed through her limbs and she marched to the kitchen. 'I'm sure I had some brandy somewhere.' Fireflies danced across her vision and she held onto the worktop as the world swam around her. Legs sagging, she dropped her head onto her hands.

'Rosie, take some deep breaths. It's not your fault!' Leanne stood beside her, tentatively patting her back. 'It's really not. Chester didn't have to go along with your mother's plan. He didn't have to take the money.'

'Mum. I think Keira's waters have broken ...' Tom's voice broke urgently through Rosie's fog of anguish.

'Or I've wet myself ...' Keira said, her voice small and wobbly. 'But I don't think so.' Rosie looked up and the world continued to whirl around her. She lowered her head again and breathed slowly.

'Call an ambulance,' she said. Leanne hurried to her phone.

'I'll ring Peck.' Keira groaned. Massaging her belly, she reached for her mobile and pressed the shortcut. Holding the phone to her ear, her anxious voice pierced Rosie's heart. 'Mum, it's too early! Four more weeks!'

'Okay.' Rosie's head cleared at last, and she stood up. 'Don't panic. You could be hours yet. Have you packed a hospital bag? The ambulance will be here before you know it.'

'No, it won't,' Leanne said, holding the phone. 'There's been a big accident on the motorway and they're all held up there. Ambulance control says to take her in the car. The hospital isn't far.'

'I'll drive you.' Rosie reached out for her keys.

'You will not.' Keira grimaced. 'Your driving is bad enough when you're sober!' She winced. 'Sorry Mum. I didn't mean it. Stress.'

'No worries, we'll ring a taxi.' Tom carried on rubbing Keira's back as her face screwed up in pain.

'I'm not having my baby in some manky taxi!' wailed Keira.

Chapter Thirty-Eight

Gareth fumbled for his phone. 'Leanne! Are you okay?'

'I'm fine. Are you running?'

'Yes.' Unable to settle since Rosie's departure, he'd pulled on his running shoes and gone.

'Cool. How far do you go?' Gareth heard an anguished cry in the background. 'Oh, sorry! Can you come over right now, Gareth?'

'What's going on?'

'Keira is having her baby. There are no ambulances because of the accident. And we're all pissed.'

'What accident?'

'On the motorway.'

'How far along?'

'Waters have broken and she's dilated, Rosie says.'

'I'll be there as soon as I can.' It could happen that quickly, Gareth knew from experience. He hung up and sprinted the shortcut home. Picking up his keys, wallet and a jacket he quickly relayed the information to his parents.

'Send them all our love, and tell them good luck!'

'I will!' Running to his car, he traced the route that Rosie had taken earlier. He was knocking on the door in twenty minutes. Minutes later, he was back in the driver's seat. A groaning Keira sat alongside him on a pile of bath towels, and three faces stared back at him from the packed rear seat.

'God, it smells like a brewery in here,' he said.

'*Aaaerugh!*' wailed Keira.

'Have you got something to squeeze?' he asked her. She shook her head and he dashed out and retrieved a tub of Lily's Silly Putty from the boot. 'Here you go. Squeeze that.' She did, and it made the familiar farting noise that made his children squeal with laughter. Nobody laughed this time.

'I'm so glad you're here,' Keira told him. 'I am so scared.' He put his hand out to her and she held it tightly for a moment as another contraction gripped her. When they reached the hospital, she directed him to the maternity unit and he parked directly outside.

'Do you think you can walk?' Her howl of pain as she swivelled awkwardly off the seat told him everything, and he picked her up as gently as he could and carried her through the automatic doors. With Rosie, Leanne and Tom just behind, he deposited her in a wheelchair and turned to leave.

'Don't leave me!' she wailed.

'I'm just going to park. Your mum's here, look. With your bag.'

'Do you want me to come with you, darling?' Rosie asked.

'Yes. No. *Wurraaagh!* I don't know! Yes. Until Peck gets here. He won't be long. I hope.'

'Thank you so much, Gareth.' Rosie turned to him as she followed the wheelchair. 'Please stay, if you can. I really, really need to talk to you.' He saw how red her eyes were, her make-up smeary and his heart jumped in apprehension. The car park was quiet and he was back in the waiting room in no time at all. He slid onto the seat alongside Leanne.

'Any news?'

'Tom has gone for coffees.'

'Good call.'

'Rosie's mother paid Chester to leave.'

He jerked upwards. 'What?'

'A hundred grand.'

'*What?*'

'Yeah. Keira is broken.'

'How did *that* come out?'

'She wrote a deathbed confession. We found it tonight, looking through Rosie's baby photos.'

'Oh, no,' Gareth murmured, as the implications of this news sank in. 'Poor Rosie.' They sat in silence. There was a television on but he ignored it, his brain whirring. He sent a text to his mum as Leanne's thumbs were also flying across the screen of her mobile phone.

'I'm making it up with my sister,' she told him. 'I've got to know Keira lately, and seeing her going through this made me think about her. And your kids are pretty cute, actually. So I'm thinking that I've been a bit of a bitch.'

Gareth nodded, solemnly. 'We all seem to be learning a lot lately.'

'I was sorry to hear about you and Hannah breaking up again.'

'Were you?'

'No.'

He snorted a laugh. You always got the truth from Leanne.

'Only because I want Rosie to be happy and she's happy with *you*.'

Tom arrived with a stack of coffees and assorted muffins and chocolate, as a white-faced Peck dashed through the entrance door and straight to reception.

'Good luck!' they chorused. He lifted a hand in acknowledgement before he was swallowed up by the electronic doors. Rosie reappeared through the same doors a moment later. She accepted the coffee gratefully, sitting beside Gareth.

'She's doing okay. That baby wants to meet us, sooner rather than later, I should say. It's so hot in there. I'm shrivelling from the inside out.'

Gareth fetched her a beaker of water from the water cooler and she drained it in one.

'Thanks, Gareth for saving the day. And for coming back. You didn't have to. But I'm very glad to see you. Again.'

'Rosie, I should have been there all along. I'm so sorry.

About, about everything.' He hesitated and then plunged on. 'Leanne has filled me in re Chester. Of course, that hundred grand is also part of your marital assets.' Rosie's eyes widened, and he carried on. 'I apologise if I've jumped the gun, but I've asked Mum to put a private investigator onto him. He's not disclosed any of his finances which clearly means he has something to hide.'

'Genius. Thank you. Won't that be horribly expensive though?'

'Rosie, I owe you much more than money. This one is on us.' Her hands drummed nervously on her knees and he reached to clasp one, to offer comfort. She laced his fingers through hers and his heart soared.

In the middle of the night, a nurse came out to see them. 'One healthy baby boy,' she reported, with a smile. 'Mother and baby doing fine. Keira is asking for Mum and Dad.'

Rosie clutched his hand, tears in her eyes. 'Come on then, "Dad".'

Gareth stood. 'Congratulations. I'm so pleased for you all. But I don't deserve to be called Dad. I'll wait outside.'

Rosie considered him, head tilted. 'How about working on the Grandad role, then?'

Gareth nodded, his throat constricted. He picked up the hand he still held and kissed it. 'I'll give it my very best shot.'

Tom and Leanne smiled blearily, rubbing their eyes. 'Give her our love and we'll see her in a minute.'

Keira lay propped on the pillows, exhausted but serene, smiling down at her tiny new baby boy.

'Hello,' she said. 'Meet your grandson. All five pounds three ounces of him.' She studied them over his sleeping head, her eyes taking in their entwined hands with a smile. 'He needs you both. And so do I.'

Chapter Thirty-Nine

Rosie curled contentedly into Gareth's arms some time later. His solid, warm body had been exactly as she'd dreamed it would be since she'd met him. They fitted together like spoons now, their skins fused together. He snuggled her closer and she felt his need for her again.

'Go 'sleep,' she commanded him, settling herself against him with a happy sigh. 'Oh, that's it. You've asked for it now.' She rolled to face him, reaching for him, his face alight with love.

The new baby was called Charlie Peck. His low glucose levels kept him in hospital for a week, but Keira took well to breastfeeding, and Charlie fed greedily.

'He's growing already. He'll be walking out of here!' Keira joked.

Lana's old bedroom now bore blue bunting with Charlie's name on, a cot, bedding, and a nursing chair. A soft throw knitted by Leanne completed the look.

Gareth and Rosie bought a baby monitor and a lifetime supply of nappies, muslin cloths and wipes. They shopped for tiny, prem outfits and bibs in the softest fabrics along with a cute, fluffy all in one car outfit for travelling home in and delivered them to the hospital for any excuse to see him.

Carol and Cled sent a smart designer changing backpack which Keira instantly fell in love with.

'I could use this to put my felts in …' Rosie mused before Keira put a possessive hand on it.

'Here's a thing,' Gareth remarked to Rosie on the way home from the hospital towards the end of the week. 'I've stopped angsting so much about hospitals since visiting Charlie so often.'

'Aw, sweetheart.' Rosie squeezed his thigh.

'If I dared to use a cliché'—he side-eyed her—'I'd say that I have closure at last.'

'I think I can allow that one.' She smiled up at him.

Some weeks later, with Charlie settled into a routine of sorts, Keira messaged her father, asking him to come over and see his grandson. To everyone's surprise, after several messages assuring him that Rosie would not be present, he agreed. Seeing Tom was apparently also a draw, although Tom was less enamoured of his father, compared to Keira.

'So, let's run over the plan again,' Rosie said. 'Is everyone happy with it? Keira, I don't want you to feel under pressure with this. You can pull out at any time and nobody will think any less of you.'

Keira nodded firmly. 'This is Charlie's future.'

'It's like *Mission Impossible*!' Leanne said, rubbing her hands in glee.

Chester showed up at the expected time, and Tom took him into Keira's sitting room as arranged. Hidden in the cluttered utility room off the kitchen, Gareth and Rosie hunched over the receiver of the baby monitor, their mobile phones fully charged and ready to record. They'd practised this over and over. Nobody would hear them unless they pressed the button to talk.

Rosie steeled herself to listen to Chester's inane, evasive chit-chat about how he'd been and what he was up to. He was genuinely emotional with baby Charlie though, and she remembered with a catch in her heart, what a good dad he'd been when Tom and Keira were little. When they'd been an unconditional audience.

After a while, Keira said, 'It's been lovely to see you, Dad. Might there be a chance that you move back to the UK again, so that we see you more often?' Rosie's heart raced. Sensing the change of conversational direction, she pressed the record button, and Gareth did the same.

'Ah, well, see, I'd like to, but your mum now, she's sticking out for her pound of flesh. I'll end up with nothing if she has her way. It's not fair.'

'Well, I don't know if that's quite right, Dad. She just wants what's hers. What she's entitled to.'

Rosie heard rustling in the room and imagined Chester getting up and roaming round the room. She hoped he didn't wake Charlie, and was very glad Tom was there. She had a sudden sense that this was all wrong.

'I can't do this,' she whispered. 'I can't force our children to take sides in what is our business. I'm going in.'

'I'm coming with you.'

She shook her head. 'This is my battle. Let me do this.' She kissed him and stood up, stretching her cramped back, then she marched into the hallway and tapped gently on Keira's door before going straight in.

'I can't let you do this, my darlings,' she said. 'Chester, it's lovely that you have made the effort to see your family. However, you know perfectly well, that you've had your share of the marital assets.' She spotted the giant teddy in the corner. Very Chester.

'How'd you work that out?' Chester glared, his shoulders hunched. 'Seeing as you're still here, and I'm not?'

'Well, mainly because of this.' Rosie stepped towards Keira and twitched the document out of her hands, holding it to face Chester. 'I know it's been a few years now, but you will recognise your own signature, and my mother's.' He lunged for it but she held it out of reach. 'This is a copy. We have the original in a safe box, lodged with my solicitor.'

'That holds no water whatsoever. It's meaningless. A contract between me and your mother.'

'I realise that. However, it's part of our marital assets. And all the things that you did with that money are *not* meaningless. Let's have a look, shall we?' Tom handed her the thick sheaf of papers and Chester's eyes narrowed to slits. 'Now then, investments dating back five and a half years. Are you sitting comfortably?' She began to read them out. Even after reading them several times, she was still shocked. 'Pity you didn't have this much business acumen when we were together. I might not have had to barter months of ironing and catering for flooring and roof repairs. Did you know, I still don't have drywall in my bedroom?' Her voice was icy cold. She was in battle mode now.

'This isn't fair! You're all in on it!'

'You've mentioned already how things aren't fair, Chester. Tell me what's fair about you taking my mother's money and disappearing with it. Then coming back sniffing about for more when she's dead.' He was silent. Sullen. But he didn't deny it. He couldn't really. The PI's report had been conclusive and evidence backed.

'I suppose you want to get your greedy mitts on it all now,' he grouched.

'All I want, is to keep this house. It provides a home for me, your children, and your grandchild. All I ask for in return, is a clean break, signed at the solicitors, and your name removed from the deeds of the house. That's it.'

Chester grunted, frowning. Caught out. He talked to Charlie. 'Looks like your granny thinks she's got me bang to rights, mate.'

Rosie said, in her reasonable voice, 'You don't have to do this. You can go to court and let the judge decide. I don't mind.'

'I only needed fifty grand. That was all.' His head hung low.

'What did you need all that for, when you already have all this?' She tapped the PI's report. He was silent.

'Dad?' Tom said. 'Have you got involved in something?'

Spreading his fingers, Chester stared at the backs of his hands. Rosie recognised it as one of his stress tics.

Keira said, 'Dad – what was the money for? Can we help?'

'Not really, sweetheart.' He rubbed at the back of his neck. 'My money is all tied up in investments. A golf course. Part of a hotel. A house. That sort of thing.' Acid billowed up from Rosie's stomach. A bloody golf course? Chester's voice got lower and smaller until they were all leaning forward to hear. 'I got into a bit of gambling.' He scratched his goatee. 'And then a bit more.' He sat up, throwing his hands out. 'You know how it is!'

Rosie's eyes met her children's. No. None of them did. None of them had the money to throw away like that, and they didn't have the inclination to either. Into the telling silence that followed, Chester said, 'I got into a bit of debt. And I borrowed it from – some people. And now they want it back.' He looked around at them all. 'Or else.'

'And you thought ...' Rosie's voice was a sibilant hiss. 'Oh, Rosie has always been a soft touch. I'll get it from her.'

Chester ran his fingers through his hair and refused to meet her eye.

Tom said, 'So, what happens if you don't pay these people back? No lies, Dad. We're too far along for that.'

'They'll find a way of making me pay. Or I'll have to do something for them that wipes the debt. I've been living in my van to avoid them. Doing a few pub gigs. Cash only. Enough to get by, nothing that gets me noticed.'

The door opened quietly and Gareth's head appeared around it. 'Sorry to barge in, but I might be able to help.' He brought the other half of the baby monitor with him, switched it off and put it beside its pair.

Chester stared at it, blinking and then threw his hands in the air. 'Is there anyone else in this house, listening in?'

'Yeah. Me.' Leanne came in from the corridor and stood by Tom.

'Bloody hell.' Chester put his head in his hands. 'It's *The Waltons*.'

Rosie saw all the youngsters in the room frown in a

perplexed way, and despite herself, she exhaled a short laugh. There were six of them crowded into this room, seven if you counted Charlie, who seemed to take up more space than anyone else.

Gareth continued, 'You've taken the first step by admitting that it's a problem. Some of our drivers have got themselves into debts, and we've been able to arrange debt counsellors. Would you be interested in something like that?'

Rosie gazed up at Gareth in wonderment. He was like a walking Citizens Advice Bureau. She flicked her eyes towards Chester, who was rubbing his thumbnails together obsessively. Everyone's eyes were on him. She realised that once again, he had an audience.

'Well, I'll leave you with that idea, Chester.' She turned deliberately and made for the door.

'What would it cost me?'

'A lot of it is freely accessible. Your GP can help. I can find out about private counselling.' Gareth perched on the arm of the sofa.

'My GP is in Spain. And I can't go back there, for obvious reasons.'

'Come back here then.' It was all obvious to Keira.

'Ye-ah ... *Noooo.*' Chester fidgeted, playing with his goatee. 'I've got, someone – there.'

'You've got a girlfriend. In Spain,' Keira said. 'And you've left her over there, to fight off these loan sharks you've got yourself mixed up with? *Dad.*' Her voice ended on a reproachful note, and Chester looked mutinous.

'I wasn't expecting to be here this long! If your mother had just given me what I needed, I'd be back there!'

'If she'd given you what you needed, we'd be homeless!' Keira's voice rose, and Charlie stirred, his tiny, smooth brow puckering. She rocked him, lowering her voice. 'Dad, for your own sake, get some help. Sell something, even if it means you lose some of the interest or something. Clear the debt. Start again with a clean slate. We'll all help you. I promise.'

Rosie struggled with the urge to bash him with something heavy and put him out of everyone's misery, but she nodded and said through gritted teeth, 'Yes. Keira's right. I'll help. As long as you help yourself.'

At last, Chester nodded. 'Okay. I'll do it.' He eyed Gareth. 'You're a lucky guy. A man needs his family around him. I've missed this.' He nodded at Rosie, who tried not to roll her eyes at Chester's woeful pronouncements. 'I'll sign whatever it takes to have a clean break. You can keep the house. I'll shake on it.' He held out his hand and Rosie shook it firmly. She felt nothing from his touch. Not a spark of attraction, nothing other than a sense of pity that he'd fallen into this trap, perhaps by her mother's doing.

Back in the kitchen diner, with Chester gone, she flopped onto a chair and faced Gareth. 'My mother has a lot to answer for.'

'Nobody's perfect.'

'You are.'

'I know. You're lucky to have me.' His teeth showed white, and his chocolate brown eyes crinkled at the edges.

Rosie contemplated him, his dark thoughtful gaze, his strengths, his flaws. She reached out to ruffle the beard that was still a little too long. He caught her fingers in his and kissed them.

'I,' he said, 'am the luckiest man alive.'

Chapter Forty

To everyone's surprise, Chester was as good as his word. He signed with good grace at the solicitor, and shook Rosie's hand again after releasing himself from the deeds.

'I'm having counselling. And I've sold off some shares to pay my debts.'

Some, thought Rosie, feeling her lips purse. He went on, 'You always were good for me, Rosie. I don't know why I left, really.'

'Onwards and upwards now, though, eh,' Rosie said, blandly, battling the now familiar urge to kick him. 'Please keep in touch with the kids, they do love you, you know.' Even if you've been an utter shit and don't deserve them.

'Yes, I'm inviting them over to stay with me and the missus, next year. We'll be getting married now this is all sorted.'

'Well. All the best,' Rosie said, brightly. It was finally over. They were finally divorced. Finished with. Rubber stamped and done. She could afford to be magnanimous. She'd got what she wanted. 'Goodbye. And good luck.'

Christmas Day dawned without a hint of a snowflake, but nothing could dampen Rosie's mood. Waking up beside the most handsome man on the planet was the best gift she could want. As Gareth manhandled the most enormous turkey into the oven first thing, Rosie couldn't help reflecting on the differences between this Christmas and the last.

At least her mother had thought she was divorced last year. She'd died believing that her daughter had cut herself loose from her feckless husband at last. Rosie had thought The Circle's usefulness with her grief was over but since the discovery of that letter, with their kind and thoughtful input, she had arrived finally at the conclusion that no matter how awful a decision it had been to pay Chester to leave, Lana had just wanted Rosie close to her at the end. She had come to terms with that. Mostly. Life could never be tied up in a perfect pink bow, could it?

Their mother and daughter relationship had been flawed, but it had made Rosie much more determined to learn from it with regard to her own children. Perhaps she had been a bit too judgemental in the past. After all, it was clear that Peck doted on his baby son, and since the night of his birth, had supported Keira in every way possible. Maybe Lana had seen that in him, who knows, because Rosie hadn't. And now, she and Keira were so much more honest with each other, their relationship steering a very different course than it had been at Lana's funeral.

Smiling, she popped croissants into the top oven to warm and set the table with a selection of jam, fruit and yoghurt. Gareth placed a bottle of chilled Prosecco and fresh orange juice onto the table with glasses.

'Start as you mean to go on. Merry Christmas.' He kissed her as she grinned up at him. Tom and Leanne arrived sleepily at the breakfast table in Christmas pyjamas, and Keira and Peck trumped them all in matching festive outfits that included Charlie.

Carol and Cled arrived shortly afterwards with a pile of beautifully wrapped presents and hugs all round. As they were staying over, Rosie showed them into the "carer's room", vacated by Leanne, who preferred the comforts of Tom's bed. A million photos were taken as they all exchanged gifts, in front of the biggest fir tree Gareth and Tom had been able to find.

Rosie had bought Gareth a soft grey merino wool sweater and he'd bought her another pair of eye-watering leggings as 'one pair isn't enough'.

They video called a very over-excited Jack and Lily, who would be spending the rest of the week with Gareth and Rosie, while Ian whisked Hannah away on a luxurious spa break.

'It's bedlam, isn't it?' Rosie said to Gareth at lunchtime, pulling out trays of crispy roast potatoes and parsnips and raising her voice over baby Charlie wailing to be fed and the Christmas music in the background. He looked up from carving the turkey and smiled.

'It's going to be worse tomorrow when Lily and Jack are here.'

'Bring it on.' Rosie's mouth curved into a smile. 'It's what Christmas is all about.'

The many hands made light work of arranging food on the long table, and Cled stood to raise a toast.

'To loved ones no longer with us. And to new lives, new loves and new friends, a very Merry Christmas.' Glasses were raised and there was a moment of quiet while everyone considered those words. And then the crackers were pulled and the house was filled with happy noise again.

The following morning, Rosie stumbled downstairs in her Christmas pyjamas, topped with the fluffy pink jumper she'd worn on his course. Gareth made her a mug of tea before leaving to fetch Lily and Jack.

'Will your mum and dad be up early for breakfast, do you think?'

'Not if the snoring is anything to go by.' He pushed the cloud of curly hair from her face and kissed her. 'Back soon. Love you, gorgeous.'

'Love you too,' she replied, staring around the kitchen and trying to remember where everything was after they'd drunkenly cleared up the previous day. 'I am never drinking again. Ever.' She squinted up at him. 'Go! I'll get in the shower now in a minute.'

He laughed at the Welsh expression and left as she trudged back upstairs. By the time she returned downstairs, everyone was up. On the long dining table was an array of toast, jams, cereals, croissants and more.

'Oh, goodness, I'm so sorry, I was going to do breakfast for you all!'

'We're all adults,' Leanne told her. 'And it's not like it's hard to find the kitchen. Let us look after you for a change. Tea or coffee?'

'Oh. Fair enough. Tea please.' Rosie sank into a chair at the table, and Peck dumped the warm, fed bundle that was Charlie into her lap. 'Hello, my precious lambkin,' she murmured, nuzzling his sweet smelling head. 'Your granny is being spoilt!'

'And about time too,' Keira said, bending to kiss Rosie's cheek. Rosie, surprised by this sudden show of affection, was about to make a joke and stopped herself.

'Thank you, darling,' she said, smiling at her daughter over Charlie's head. Gareth arrived as they were still sat at their leisurely breakfast and was greeted with a chorus of good mornings.

'Rosie, could you just pop outside a minute? Lily and Jack have something to show you.'

'Erm, yes, of course! What is it?'

'It's a surprise.' Gareth's expression gave nothing away.

'Shall I take Charlie?' Leanne reached out and swept the sleeping baby away with practised ease. Rosie smiled and shook her head slightly. How things had changed. She and everyone else, followed Gareth out of the front door. Rosie scanned the empty space.

'Where are they?'

Gareth guided her by the elbow to just around the corner ... 'There.' He stood back and watched her.

'Oh!' Her hands flew to her mouth. Her fire engine stood, resplendent on the drive. She blinked. 'It's Bedelia! What, why is she ...? She looks beautiful. Different, somehow ...' Jack and Lily, wide-eyed, stood with expectant faces at each end of a long, twisted banner. Gareth hadn't taken his eyes off her. She gulped, peering at the scene before her. What was she missing here?

'It's a lovely banner, thank you, children! Um ...' She

started to read aloud. 'Er ... ease *something something* Dad ... ?' She was squinting and definitely struggling.

Horror crossed Gareth's face. He whipped around and shouted, 'Argh! Guys!' The children's faces fell as they looked from him to the banner.

Lily dropped it and stepped on it and Jack said, in his exasperated voice, '*Lil-leeeeee!* I *told* you not to play with it!' Gareth rushed over and picked up Lily's end, turning it the right way up and handing the end to her with a grin and a kiss. He sprinted to the other end and picked Jack up, turning him over with the banner still in his hands and making him giggle.

'What's that saying about never working with children and animals?' Gareth put his hands over his face.

Rosie laughed, and finally read the letters on the slightly crumpled banner:

"*PLEASE WILL YOU MARRY OUR DADDY?*"

Her hands flew to her mouth, as her eyes read the words over and over. Gareth held out a small box, and opened the lid. 'I was going to buy you an engagement ring. But I thought you might like this better.' Rosie leaned forward to look. Inside lay a tiny red enamelled vintage fire engine, a silver B on a ring with the original ignition key, and several newer keys. She looked up at him, a question in her eyes. 'Have a look.' His eyes crinkled as he tipped his head towards the fire engine. 'Try the passenger door.' He pointed. 'It's this key, here.'

Rosie opened the door and was immediately struck by the scent of newness. Gone was the musty smell of before. Gone too were the ugly and uncomfortable crew seats, to be replaced with properly upholstered seats with seat belts. Her gaze travelled past them to the back of the van, to the sleek lines of a hob, oven, sink, fridge and was that an actual shower? Her gaze swivelled back, caught by something bright. A shiny, lime green whistling kettle stood on the hob and her jaw dropped. Light flooded in from the sun roof. The transformation inside was extraordinary. It resembled a posh apartment. On wheels. She stepped back out and looked at the fire engine. It looked just as it had before. 'Is this the same vehicle?' Everyone laughed, and she looked around at them. 'Did you all know about this?' There were nods and smiles.

'Only bits. Not the finished version,' Keira said. 'Gareth wanted to make sure he'd got the right colours and everything. He's worked his butt off on it. I can't wait to see inside!'

'What do you think, Rosie?' Gareth chewed his bottom lip. 'Is it okay? Or would you have preferred a ring? I will get you a ring anyway, but I thought, erm, you know you said about it being easy to say the words and you wanted to *see* that I loved you? Well, I *do* love you. I hope you can see it now.'

Rosie nodded slowly. 'Did you just propose to me?'

'I did, yes,' Gareth said, swallowing.

'With a fire engine camper van, and a lime green kettle?'

'Um, yes.'

'Oh, Gareth!' Rosie threw herself into his arms. Lily and Jack cheered and hopped about destroying what was left of the banner.

'That's a yes, right?' Gareth said, his mouth against her lips.

'That is most definitely a yes.' She smiled up at him. 'Oh, yes. Yes!'

'Yay!' shouted Lily and Jack as everyone clapped and cheered. 'Can we open our pressies now?'

It was a long and jolly celebratory lunch, and once they'd more or less tidied up, Tom and Leanne suggested a walk to the beach and back. Jack and Lily were quick to agree, and before long, the ten of them, plus a well wrapped up Charlie, were on their way.

Smiling as he watched Jack and Lily running back and forth with his parents, Gareth told Rosie, 'I've had some good news. Mum and Dad have sold the haulage company, and in a few months, I'll be out of a job.'

'What?' Rosie stared up at him. 'How is that good news?'

'Because Mum and Dad are investing in my new outdoor pursuits business. And I've sold some of my shares in the haulage business, so that I can, in turn, invest in us. Also, I don't know what you think of this, but we've been talking about residential courses for ages. Now I have the money we could plan them properly and finish renovating the house to suit? I'd get a solicitor and everything, make sure you're properly protected. Or maybe we could buy something else, if you prefer. I'm still thinking it through and I don't want to seem as if I'm steamrollering you, after all, you've already—'

'Oh my *gosh!*' Rosie interrupted him. She could hardly believe her ears. 'That would be so exciting! We can sort the paperwork out later.' She smiled up at him, hugging his arm with her free hand. 'And Tom wants to be an instructor.'

Gareth nodded. 'And I think Leanne might also be interested.'

'What about her wool?' Rosie asked.

'Maybe I could help with that,' Keira called over, in a way which made Rosie think that this wasn't the first time this had been discussed. 'It would mean staying home with Charlie for longer, and I can help you guys with the residential weekends.'

'Well, looks like I've got the beginnings of a team already!' Gareth grinned. 'You can all help me with a name next.'

'What's that?' Leanne whirled around. 'A team name? Team Storm! *Raah*!'

'*Noooo!*' chorused Gareth and Rosie, bursting into laughter.

Chapter Forty-One

Gareth and Rosie's first trip in Bedelia in the New Year, remained on Gower. Just to check that everything worked properly. The pure chill of the sea welcomed them without wetsuits. Exhilarated after their dip, they'd warm up on the beach, watching the surf with hot chocolate, before returning to snuggle and make love in their cosy, fire engine camper van.

They walked, talked, planned, made fires amongst the pebbles on the beaches, cooked their foraged food and made love, eventually returning home inspired and happy.

A year almost to the day since her mother's funeral, Rosie went to The Circle bearing a big tin of home-made cakes to share.

'My relationship with my mum wasn't perfect, and I will always be sad that she's gone before we properly had a chance to put some of that right,' she told them, looking around at their kind faces. 'But I've learned from it, and I'm coming to terms with it. Thank you all for helping me through this year.'

'You know where we are if you ever need us,' Meryl, the lady who ran the group told her over a tight hug as they left the meeting. 'Take care.' Rosie had hugged her back, her eyes glistening and walked into the warm air feeling her spirit lift. *Bye Mum*, she said, in her head. *Love you.*

The Art Café had risen from its symbolic ashes, and was now part of a completely new venture. The Art Hotel. Previously the Hotel Y Ddraig, and set opposite the same beach as the Art Café had been situated, the wonderful floor to ceiling glass windows that had characterised the original Art Café had been incorporated into the new design. It cleverly retained its charming and friendly décor, welcoming beach goers, hikers and motorcyclists alike with easy-clean floors and tables, but there was now a more formal dining area off the main café, and a smart display and sales area. Gareth and Rosie had thoroughly enjoyed their visits to deliver Rosie's felts and Gareth's photographs, seeing how the hotel and café were growing and fusing together.

At the end of July, Gareth and Rosie attended the very first wedding to be held at the Art Hotel. Rosie had been thrilled when Lucy asked her to make something for her wedding outfit.

Now she watched proudly as the bride walked down the aisle with her father. Wearing a beautiful dress in champagne gold which skimmed her neat, six month bump, her shoulder cape had been made by Rosie, using shimmery pale gold silk, threaded with felted flowers in delicate shades of purples and amethysts, as a homage to the bride's motorbike, which had brought them together. She looked utterly stunning beside Ash, her handsome groom, who clearly adored her.

Gripping Gareth's hand, Rosie dashed away tears of happiness, and gazed in professional satisfaction at the bridesmaids. In complete contrast to the previous year, July was proving cold and wet, and the bridal party were all grateful for the warmth the little capes provided.

Daisy, Lucy's beautiful stepdaughter, along with Nicola and Jo, Lucy's closest friends, all wore shades of plums and purples that they'd chosen themselves, plus colour-matched versions of Lucy's cape.

Bedelia, burnished and resplendent in white ribbons, was parked at the front of the hotel, ready for photographs, and Rosie had promised to drive the happy couple to the beach for more pictures.

'So,' Lucy said, holding Ash's hand as if she was never going to let it go but still managing to scan with eager eyes, the fire engine's plush interior. 'I see your man *was* worth his salt in the end.'

'Oh yes,' Rosie said with a smile, switching on the ignition. 'You're riding in my engagement ring. And we're off to France in it tomorrow, with Jack and Lily. For more family adventures. I don't think anyone will ever say my life is boring again!'

Thank You

Dear Reader,

Thank you for reading this novel, the fourth in the Art café series. I hope you've enjoyed meeting my characters and following their story. As ever, many of the incidents were plucked from my own life, and yes, many years ago, I did turn up at an outdoor pursuits weekend without a sleeping bag, and had to sleep in a pair of curtains!

Written during the Covid lockdown, the novel has allowed me to travel in my head when regulations prevented me doing so in real life. It has made me laugh and cry, and it made me pick up where I'd left off with wet felting, which in turn showed me another way of looking at the diminished world I occupied.

The idea for the title came to me towards the end, and I was delighted that Choc Lit agreed to use it.

Hold on to your hopes and dreams.

With much love,

Sue x

About the Author

Sue McDonagh's career as a policewoman for Essex Police was cut short when she was diagnosed at the age of twenty-four with ovarian cancer. After a successful recovery and a stint working as a Press Officer she moved to Wales.

In Wales her love of art evolved into a full-time occupation and she made a living teaching and sketching portraits at shows. In 2014 she was a regional finalist for the Sky Arts Portrait Artist of the Year. She now works exclusively to commissions from her art gallery.

In 2009 she learned to ride a motorbike, and now helps run Curvy Riders, a national, women only, motorbike club. Her joy of motorbikes and her love of writing inspired her to write the Art Café series.

Sue is a proud mum and granny in the gloriously blended family she is honoured to be part of. She lives a mile from the sea in Wales, and can often be found sketching it or swimming in it.

When she's not painting, she's writing or on her motorbike. She belongs to a local writing group and the Cariad Chapter.

For more information on Sue visit:

www.twitter.com/SueMcDonaghLit

www.facebook.com/SueMcDonaghWriter/

More Choc Lit

From Sue McDonagh

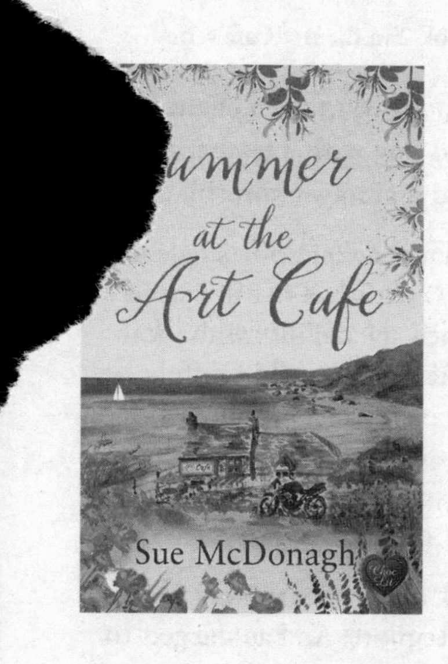

Summer at the Art Café

Book 1 in the Art Café series

From watercolours and cupcakes to leather jackets and freedom ...

If you won a gorgeous purple motorbike, and your domineering husband said you were too fat for leathers and should sell it, would you do as you were told – or learn to ride it in secret?

Artist and café owner Lucy Daumier intends to do just that – but learning to ride is far from easy, especially under the critical eye of prickly motorcycle instructor, Ash Connor.

But gradually she gets the hang of it, and in the process re-discovers the girl she used to be. So starts an exciting summer of new friendship and fun – as well as a realisation that there is more to Ash than meets the eye when she is introduced to his seven-year-old daughter, Daisy.

But can Lucy's new-found happiness last when a spiteful family member wants to see her fail?